LOVE Y♥U
Right

NEW YORK TIMES BESTSELLING AUTHOR

JULIA KENT

by Julia Kent

Love You, Maine Book 1

A missed opportunity five years ago makes for an unexpected encounter now between two people meant for each other—but who square off in a very public battle of wills in the small town of Love You, Maine, where every day is Valentine's Day. Can love conquer all in a town steeped in it?

Kell Luview refuses to be a sucker at love again. Five years ago, he left D.C. with his pride severely wounded and his heart broken. Fiercely protective of his small town in rural Maine, he's determined to save the family tree business and avoid his feelings at all costs, no matter how much he longs to solve the mystery of what happened in D.C.

L.A. native Rachel Hart hates being underestimated almost as much as she hates this small town. She has two goals on this trip: get out of the cheesy tourist trap of Love You, Maine, with a successful business deal, and avoid running into Kell, her old friend from D.C. who never became an old flame because of a huge misunderstanding.

One that still aches.

When her rental car breaks down on a logging road and Kell

comes to her rescue, it's clear he's a changed man—and not for the good. Grumpy and reserved, he pushes all her buttons, still stubbornly convinced she betrayed him all those years ago. He's never forgiven her, and she's never forgiven herself for carrying a torch for him.

A very publicly embarrassing incident gets the town gossip mill going when residents wrongly assume Kell and Rachel are the latest couple to find love in the most romantic place on Earth. But the townsfolk aren't wrong for long...

As Rachel breaks through his defenses and charms the town, he faces his biggest fear: all those pesky feelings he's been avoiding.

Because they're all about Rachel now.

And maybe they always were.

Can Kell and Rachel fight their growing attraction in the one place in the world where you can't avoid love?

If you're looking for a fun read about enemies to lovers, forced proximity, heroines who get their comeuppance and sworn bachelors felled by unexpected true love, featuring a hot bearded lumberjack who's impervious to poison ivy and a jaded urban career woman with a penchant for great coffee, set in a small town in New England—then this is your book.

Grab a cup of (properly good) coffee, a can of hot cocoa mix, a jar of Fluff, and maybe some calamine lotion (just in case), and get your happy meter ready as you read the very first book in New York Times- *bestselling romantic comedy author Julia Kent's Love You, Maine series—where love isn't just a feeling, it's a way of life.*

Standalone
  Slow burn
  Enemies to Lovers
  Small town romance
  Lumberjack and city slicker outsider
  ... and a cat named Calamine

To the man who tells me "Love you" every day of my life. It never gets old.

Chapter One

RACHEL

First week of February

The death rattle under the car's hood was the sound of her career dying.

Rachel Hart was driving up an impossible incline on a dirt road that forked off State Route 33 on the outskirts of Luview, Maine, a dinky backwater town she had never, ever wanted to set foot in.

But here she was, brought from Los Angeles by a work project.

And her own sheer stupidity.

"No!" she ordered the car, as if it were her assistant. "You are not allowed to break down. You are not allowed to make that sound."

She pressed down on the accelerator and the car began to lurch, as if it begged to differ.

"I'm eleven miles from town. Come on. You just have to make it eleven more miles," she encouraged as the car began to cough.

Cough. Like her Grandma Hart, sucking on Virginia Slims back in the 1990s.

The speedometer dropped from thirty to twenty-seven to twenty-three, gravity and a faulty piece of metal or plastic or some sensor–whatever those were–making the car slow down.

And ruining her life.

"You cannot do this. You have to work. Have to! I did not fly from L.A. to Boston and rent this dumpy car to drive three hours into the backwoods of Maine only to have *this* happen. THIS! IS! NOT! HAPPENING!"

The car halted. Bam. Just like that.

Like it decided to go on strike.

Rachel's gaze cut to the backseat, filled with her luggage. There was more in the trunk. Her boss had dangled this assignment in front of her three weeks ago, the memory now painful.

She put the car in park and began gently banging her forehead against the steering wheel.

Luview, Maine–"Love You, Maine"–was the silliest place on Earth. Known as the town where "Every Day is Valentine's Day," it was a cheesy tourist trap, the worst parts of the Poconos, Niagara Falls, and Vegas all put in a Vitamix, pureed, and poured out into heart-shaped molds.

Much like the chocolate her entire career now relied on.

Yes, *chocolate*.

The very same chocolate that was to blame for why she was here.

Even worse, Luview, Maine, was the hometown of the most enigmatic, elusive, and frustratingly maddening man in her life:

Kell Luview, a former co-worker.

A former friend.

A former... well, a *former*.

As in the past.

Good thing he'd taken to big-city life when they'd worked together in Washington, D.C. Plus, she knew through back channels that he didn't live there.

Kell Luview was living his best life right now, Rachel assumed, somewhere in L.A. or Chicago, or maybe still in D.C.

Possibly even London, or Toronto.

Anywhere but *here*.

Whew.

Why was she thinking about the guy she almost kissed five years ago? The guy who rescued her from near death in a lemur costume? The guy who didn't believe her when she decided to warn him that his girlfriend at the time–half a decade ago–was just using him for access to his powerful uncle in Maine government?

Maybe she was thinking about Kell Luview because her rental car had just died eleven miles from the town named after his great-great-great-grandfather.

"Okay, okay, *okay*," she whispered to herself. "Think. You have gotten yourself out of worse messes than this. Remember the time that sewer rat got into the building and nearly destroyed the Kardashian yoga shoot? You caught it with nothing but your own bare hands and an Armani jacket. Have confidence. *Confidence*, Rachel. You can fix this."

Pressing the ignition button, she willed it to start.

Nothing.

Closing her eyes, she took a deep breath and tried to remember the calming ritual she'd been taught.

"I trust the universe," she said aloud, lying through gritted teeth. "I breathe in panic, and I breathe out calm."

Inhale through the nose, imagining the cloud of fear emanating from her being sucked in like a kitchen fan absorbing a burnt dinner.

Exhale a fine, warm mist of love, wrapping her in safety and goodness.

Inhale failure and frustration.

Exhale success and achievement.

Inhale all that is broken with the world, including the car's engine.

Exhale a connectedness with the eternal peace of the wise mind.

She did the cycle three times, following her business coach's instructions.

And then she tried the ignition again.

Nothing.

"YOU STUPID, USELESS BUCKET OF BOLTS!" she screamed, clutching the steering wheel and shaking it.

That felt so much better than all that trusting the universe crap. Sometimes, anger was the appropriate response.

More than appropriate now.

Although it was futile, she reached for her phone.

No *Service*.

The car was broken.

Her phone had no signal.

She was eleven miles from this state's version of "civilization."

The truth asserted itself, like it or not.

Rachel Hart was stuck on a dirt road in the middle of nowhere.

And her bladder chose that moment to announce that it needed a wee bit of attention.

"OH, COME ON!" she screamed.

The rental car's interior was cooling quickly, her ski jacket bulky and uncomfortable. An L.A. girl like her only wore it for weekends in Tahoe.

Not for *survival*.

All the land around her was blanketed in a solid foot of beautiful, pristine snow as she stepped out of the car, stuffed her purse under the front seat out of habit, keys clutched in her hand, and slammed the door, needing to pace.

She never wanted this assignment in the first place. Her boss, Orla, offered it to her after a charity event where she'd met Rachel's mom, fading '80s television actress Portia Starman.

Portia had done some festivals and then a short-lived reality TV series here in Love You, Maine, and still gushed about the town, even when Rachel begged her not to. The memory of how Portia came to Love You was bitter and spiked with nothing but pain.

Her mother didn't care. Not in a cruel way; she just literally didn't remember that Rachel got her the festival gig because she was good friends with Kell Luview and had "met" his mom, Deanna, on FaceTime.

While Deanna was wearing a red lips costume inspired by *The Rocky Horror Picture Show*, but never mind that.

"Why am I thinking about this?" she moaned, shoving the ridiculous memory out of her head as she paced, her suede UGG booties sinking into the snow as she walked, the chunky high heels forcing her calves to work twice as hard.

Fashionable, warm, and reasonably functional, the boots were a fine choice when she bought them in L.A. At the time, she thought this trip would be a breeze, a three-day pop-in while she convinced the owners of Love You Chocolate to sell to Markstone's, the international chocolatier she worked for, who was looking to grab market share in the U.S. by leveraging the small-town, feel-good image of Love You, Maine.

Breaking down on an icy logging road was not part of the plan.

Her new boots, cute in the store, pinched the tips of her toes, which now doubled as frozen grapes. Could body parts get this cold and not fall off? She tried to remember what you did for frostbite.

Crisp, impossibly fresh air assaulted her nostrils, like icicles had formed in there.

Snotcicles were not part of the plan, either.

Still aching from the long red-eye plane ride, waiting in lines, a luggage delay, and driving three hours north of Boston, she lifted her hands over her head and stretched. Her adorable ski jacket pulled up and her exposed midsection instantly froze, so she yanked her arms down hard. A twinge in her shoulder signaled a muscle spasm that rippled down her back.

No part of her body was okay.

No part of her mind was, either.

An image of Kell Luview standing on a city street, angry and righteous as he yelled at her the last time they were together, washed over her. They'd been fellows at a D.C. think tank, and everything had ended badly, but Rachel still couldn't help but want him.

His chiseled jaw. The closely cropped dark hair. Those beautiful slate-gray eyes.

And when he wasn't angry, that wicked, wicked smile.

How they watched Nordic noir television shows together. The night he'd covered them with the same blanket while they munched on snacks and drank beers, having fun, just starting to hint at maybe, just maybe...

Except that last part wasn't how everything had actually ended with him.

Instead, he'd stormed away from her, quitting his fellowship on the spot, leaving her life with a big misunderstanding she'd never been able to fix. Hardening her heart had been the answer and, so far, it had served her.

Screaming a curse word into the woods only led to the flutter of bird wings as a bunch of blue jays scattered.

Halting in place, the realization slammed into her: *I'm really trapped*.

Mental inventories ran through her simultaneously, a symphony of panic in her brain.

Food? She had two protein bars and the bag of mini pretzels they gave her on the plane. If calories ended up mattering, she had a box of cough drops. Flavored lip gloss? That must be edible, right?

Water? She looked around at the snow. Okay, not a problem.

A snowflake, lazy and erratic as it fell, landed on her nose. She looked up, searching for more. Where there was one, there were always others.

Heat? The car would provide insulation, and she had two bags full of clothes she could cover herself with in a pinch.

Bathroom?

She surveyed the area and groaned. No powder room here. Crouching by a tree wasn't exactly her style, and in these boots, she'd be more likely to fall over and end up with her warm butt in the cold snow. Cryotherapy was a trendy spa thing back in L.A., but this was not how she imagined trying it out.

And suddenly, she *really* regretted that full waxing session she'd had three days ago.

Eerie quiet settled in as she began to pace again, the crunch of snow underfoot only emphasizing the silence. The cold was starting to chill her hands. A city girl her entire life, the only time she ever spent in the woods was on dates, when she pretended to be more outdoorsy than she really was.

This was unprecedented.

This was horrifying.

This was *not* her fault.

"Why did I do this to myself? No work project is worth *this*." A flash of her family hit her, her brother Tim's announcement that after graduating from the Air Force Academy a year ago and going into pilot training, his newest achievement was finishing his master's degree in math in one year.

He was on the road to becoming an astronaut, and that was a requirement. At twenty-two, he was on his way. Early graduation from high school? Check. Admission to one of the military academies? Check. Master's degree in STEM? Check.

Tim's life was a checklist to be conquered, moving him higher and higher toward actual outer space.

Their successful entertainment lawyer father had praised him on the Zoom call Tim had scheduled to deliver his news, the four quadrants of faces making Rachel hold her smile even as it killed her.

That call made her go back to her boss and ask for this project after all.

So, technically, this was all *Tim's* fault, right?

In a family of powerhouse achievers, Rachel was the slacker. Her mom was impressed by the Kardashian project she worked on, but only because it got Rachel invited to an exclusive party and she brought Portia as her plus one.

Because Rachel had no plus one in her life.

Rustling sounds behind her made her turn, eyes scanning to pinpoint the location of the noise. A group of three deer in the distance looked right at her, big, black eyes staring back.

Deer weren't carnivores, were they? Her pathetic memory of middle school biology made her think *no*.

No. Right? She wasn't about to be attacked and eaten alive by a group of grown-up Bambis?

"You are losing it, Rach," she muttered, her hushed voice enough to spook the beautiful creatures, who ran off and up a steep hill to her right. Down below, where the road forked and her GPS had taken her up this barely plowed road, she saw a squirrel skitter across the dark asphalt of the numbered state route.

She would have better luck finding help there. Basic survival instinct told her to walk down the icy road and go where there was likely to be more traffic.

Until she began her descent and her high heels betrayed her.

The crack of her tailbone on a patch of ice underneath light snow made stars burst behind her eyes, and not the kind you get from a great night of sex.

Not that any of that was happening lately. Sex was a distant memory, her last relationship a friends-with-benefits deal that ended a year ago when her "friend" decided that stealing her emergency earthquake and wildfire money out of her nightstand was one of the benefits.

"Why?" she sniffled, not caring that she sounded like a whiny little princess. Who was going to judge her? A chipmunk?

One leg splayed to the left, the other was bent at the hip. She was lucky she could still walk. But the fall hurt, even if it didn't break anything.

Except maybe a tiny piece of her will.

As she sat on the ice, a wet, cold feeling began to prickle where her jeans met the ground. She shifted her weight, trying to find a more comfortable position, but the ice was too cold for that.

Down below, the rumble of a car's engine caught her ear.

"HERE!" she screamed, still on the ground and definitely out of sight. Scrambling to stand up fast, she grabbed the wheel well, but there was nothing she could lodge her fingers in to gain a little leverage.

By the time she was up to a shaky crouch, the car was gone.

Each limb ached and cracked, her heart throbbing. She leaned against a tree for a moment, hands on her knees.

"There will be more," she assured herself, one eye on the fading light of day. Her red-eye flight left L.A. last night at midnight. She arrived at 8:30 this morning and went to the Markstone's Boston office to say hello and do a little work. Then she got on the road, and it was now three thirty p.m. Eastern Time, which meant she had been awake for...

Ever. She'd been awake for freaking *ever*.

On her feet but bent over, her slightly damp butt poking out as she clutched the car door handle, she gingerly took one step forward.

And began to slip down the hill.

"NOOOOOOOOOOOOO!"

Clawing at the tiny little pine trees that poked out from the piles of white snow, she finally grabbed one with deep enough roots that it held her weight, her boot heels sliding down as her body elongated, knees hitting the pressed-down snow, her body going belly-flat on the ground.

Just then, the rumble of a car engine cut through her consciousness. If the tiny branch she was clinging to didn't hold, she would slide right under the car as it approached.

This was how Rachel was going to die. Stupidly, too young, and with really bad hair.

Head turned and cheek flat against the road, her arms were up above her head, both hands ice-cold now, gloveless and white knuckled. Her ski jacket pulled up, exposing her bare belly under her sweater, and she began to shiver as the front of her jeans pressed into the snow.

"HELP!" she yelled, relieved that a car had appeared, terrified that it might flatten her like a pancake.

The engine cut. A door opened, then slammed. Footsteps became louder.

"Hey, there. You need some assistance?" The gruff voice didn't sound friendly at all but at this point, beggars couldn't be choosers. Rachel was on her belly and couldn't see him.

"Nope! I'm just fine!" she shouted back. "I like to hang onto tiny little pine trees and single-handedly melt the road with my stomach. It's a hobby."

"Oh. Okay." The footsteps faded, then a car door opened and closed.

The engine roared to life.

Sarcasm. Rachel wasn't going to die because of stupidity. She was going to die at the hands of her own *sarcasm*.

"HEY!" she screamed as loud as possible, rolling over onto one shoulder, trying to sit up. Losing her grasp on the lifeline pine, she felt gravity begin to do its job. Slowly, inch by inch, she slid downhill, one hip and shoulder pressed into the road. What she wouldn't give right now for Spiderman hands, because her fingertips were useless at stopping her descent.

The guy cut the engine again and opened his door just as Rachel slid under it. She grabbed the corner, but it began to shut with her movement.

And then it didn't.

A bear looked down at her.

A bear in human form.

His beard was very thick, the dude wearing sunglasses and a hunter's cap with flaps over his ears.

And he was *enormous*.

Super-broad shoulders covered in classic red-and-black checkerboard flannel, a black down vest, faded jeans and very abused tan leather boots made him look like an actual lumberjack.

The guy had the equanimity of someone who knew he belonged wherever he went.

The dude was a red-flannel bear.

"Come here often?" he cracked, shaking his head slowly. "The view is underrated."

"This is a joke to you?" she shrieked. "I'm hanging onto the bottom of a car door to avoid sliding into a main road!"

He moved his feet so he was standing between her legs.

"There. That'll stop you."

Rachel felt the explosion build inside her, embarrassment mingling with something more. Something warmer. Something intriguing.

And something infuriating, too.

"Look, Mr. Dueling Banjos, I don't know what you think you're doing, but your boots are the only thing keeping me from certain death. Would you do the decent thing and help me to my feet?"

"Preventing you from standing on ice in those stilts you call boots *is* doing the decent thing, lady."

But he bent down and offered her a hand, his scent slamming through her, a mix of woodsmoke, spice, lime, and–

A very familiar feeling.

On her feet at last, she grabbed his truck's hood, the metal still warm. As she pulled off her hat and smoothed her hair away from her face, she realized he was staring.

Hard.

"You're not from around here." Did his voice go lower? Weird.

"What gave me away?"

"Those." He pointed at her designer boots. "And your condescension."

"Oh, please. Don't tell me small towns in Maine don't have condescension. Especially fakey-fake places like Love You, Maine, where everything's heart-shaped and love is a commodity." She sniffed, glaring at him. "And I'm not condescending. If I were, I'd call you a maple redneck."

He stiffened. "That's a strange insult. Where are you from?"

"L.A."

"And you call *my* town fake?"

"You're from Luview?"

"I *am* a Luview."

"Isn't everyone around here?"

"No. We've got the Bilbees. The Chens. The Kendrills. The-"

"Got it." Biting her lips and tucking her ungloved hands into her armpits, she stared at the guy, fighting a weird attraction. "Look, Mr..."

"Deke."

"Mr. Deke, I-"

"Just Deke."

"Deke Luview?"

"No. Deke Bilbee."

"I thought you said you were part of the Luview family?"

"I am. Bilbees are Luviews. A Bilbee married a Luview a few generations back and-"

"That's cute," she said, cutting him off with a flat palm, "but I flew in on a red eye out of LAX, drove up from Boston, and had my car break down. I am freezing cold and I just want a nice hot shower at the inn my assistant booked for me, the one with heart-shaped hot tubs and honeymoon Champagne packages. It's been a very long day."

"You're here on your honeymoon?" He craned his neck around her, peering into the rental car, as if she were hiding a groom.

"What? No! I just had her book a honeymoon suite for me. Figured it would be the least offensive option for me here."

"Mints on the pillow and all that?"

"Can you help me fix my car?" Rachel reached into her coat pocket and found her wallet, pulling out five twenties. "Here. Maybe this will expedite things."

"Put that away." He stared at the bills in her hand like she'd offered to pay him for something that could only be done at a motel that rented rooms by the hour.

"You want more? I have more." Nervous shock hit her. What was she doing? All alone, broken down on a deserted road, and she was telling this huge dude who could snap her in two that she had *more* cash on her?

Every city-girl instinct had melted away when she fell on the ice and was single-handedly heating it with her butt.

Deke turned away and strode over to her car, opening the driver's door to pop the hood. As he bent down, she got a nice view of his back.

And nicely muscular backside.

Something about his body made her think again of Kell, back when they'd worked together at the Earth Endangered Coalition, one of the biggest non-governmental organizations in the world. He'd looked nothing like this guy, but something about him pinged her radar.

Pinged a few unmentionable body parts, too.

"Are you a mechanic?" She checked out his white truck. A logo of three big, shiny, green leaves was on the side, with the words Pulling for You.

In smaller letters underneath was a tag line: *We touch it so you don't have to.*

What the heck was that supposed to mean?

"No." He pointed to his truck. "Read the door."

"I just did. You're a landscaper?"

"I pull poison ivy." Opening the driver's side door, he popped the hood, walked around and lifted it, securing the metal prop.

"That's a thing?"

"That's a thing."

"You have an actual business doing that?"

"Yep."

"Wow. Who knew?"

"L.A. knows."

"Excuse me?"

"L.A. A lot of my clients are from Hollywood."

"Here? You have clients from L.A. in... Maine?"

"Yep."

"You're joking."

"Believe what you want to believe."

"I want the truth."

He just snorted, the sound followed by inaudible muttering as he rooted around under the hood.

Something about the sound rankled her, as if he were being hyper-judgmental.

Of *her*.

It was the kind of sound you make as an indictment. How dare he? He didn't even know her.

"You've got a cracked radiator hose," he announced from under the hood.

"In English, please."

"The doohickey in your whatchamacallit is broken."

Rachel let out an aggrieved sigh. "You would never say that to a man."

"Sure I would. Plenty of men are as ignorant about cars as you."

"I am not ignorant!"

Crossing his arms over his broad chest, he stared at her, sunglasses mirroring Rachel's reflection back at her.

"Then you fix it."

"I have no idea how to fix it!"

"Then quit trying to control everything. And work on your attitude."

"I don't have an attitude! But even if I did, it would be justified. I'm stuck on a dirt road in the middle of nowhere, on my way to work on a project I don't even like, and now I've got some Paul Bunyan wannabee insulting my intelligence."

"Thank you."

"Excuse me?"

"The Paul Bunyan comment. I'll take it as a compliment."

"You know," she said slowly, looking at him closely, his tone ringing bells in her head, "you really do remind me of your cousin Kell."

"My cousin?"

"You said you're related to the Luviews. I assumed."

"Smart. Because you're right. I'm closely related to Kell. I remind you of him?"

"Yes."

"Really? I'm surprised."

"Why?"

"Because he's such an asshole."

Laughter poured out of her, unexpected and raw, the giggles lifting her heart.

"I don't know about that. He sure was stubborn when I knew him, but not an asshole. Just very, very sure he was right, even when he was so, so wrong." The sigh she let out at the end made him jolt a little, cutting a look her way.

"You know him well?"

"I—well, um—no."

Eyebrows raised over the frames of his sunglasses. "That's quite an answer."

"I don't know him now. I did."

"You one of his ex-girlfriends? Heard he's a player. Sleeps around. Public health nightmare. Let me guess—you had his baby a few years ago and now you're here to make him pay." He clucked his tongue three times.

"*Kell?*" Rachel frowned. "That doesn't sound like the guy I knew. And no, I'm not here to surprise Kell with a secret baby."

"Good. A town can only handle that happening so many times."

"You're kidding."

"No, actually, that did happen a few years ago with Brian Mulroy. But not Kell, no. He must wrap it so he's not producing progeny."

"Let's change the subject."

"You brought up Kell. Just telling you what he's like."

"I suppose people change."

"Naw," Deke said in a low, gravelly tone. "They don't."

"You think we're immutable? We should just throw our hands up and say, that's just how it is, oh, well?"

"Sure. Life's a hell of a lot easier if you accept reality."

"That's really depressing."

"So is the broken part on your car. The reality is that you need a new radiator hose." Tipping his chin up, he looked at the sky. "We've got about an hour to get you to town before dark. This car isn't going anywhere but the repair shop. You need a hotel?"

"I have one already, thanks. Remember? My inn. One bedroom. I'm staying in Luview for a few nights."

He let out a low whistle. "That must've been hard. You book it a long time ago?"

"I don't know. My assistant booked it," she answered, but now she was starting to wonder. Dani had sent her a flurry of emails about her hotel arrangements a few weeks ago, when Orla put her on the project, but Rachel had only skimmed them, just reading the itinerary and making a note of the address in her phone for GPS.

"On business, you say?"

"Yes."

"What kind?"

He reached into his truck and rummaged around in a small canvas bag between the seats. The only hint he was frowning came from his glasses shifting on the bridge of his nose.

"Allen," he sighed, the sound closer to a growl. "Took all the duct tape again."

"Who is Allen?"

"My assistant."

"You have an assistant, too?"

"Not the same kind you have."

"What does duct tape have to do with–oh! You're fixing the hose! Well, it's a good thing you can, because–"

He held up his hand and stared at her, the sunglasses reflecting her image. "Duct tape's good for lots of other things."

A creepy sensation started in her tailbone and snaked up her spine, tingling with dread.

Then he pulled out a plastic container of what looked like glue.

"Business trip?" he said again, continuing to pry.

"None of yours."

"Lady, Luview is so small, the American flag at the police station waves a little harder if a dog across town farts."

"Thanks for that ringing endorsement of The Most Romantic Place on Earth."

"We know each other's business, like it or not. Strangers are part of the gossip mill, too, so I'll know what you're doing in town ten minutes after you start doing it."

Deke leaned under the hood, a small gray tube the thickness of a banana in his left hand and a rag in his right. As he began applying the glue, she could see he was going to drip some on the engine.

"Watch out."

"I know what I'm doing."

"You said you're not a mechanic, so how do you know?"

He just sighed.

"You're doing it wrong," she insisted. Stretching, she tried to take it away.

"Stop!"

Who did this guy think he was? It was her rental car, after all. Her responsibility. Her stupid predicament. The glue tip was angled the wrong way, and if he didn't turn it around, he'd get glue everywhere.

Then she realized it wasn't the angle of the tip. There must have been a small puncture in the tube, because as he squeezed, it was coming out the wrong end.

"Look, Deke," she said, trying to show him. He grinned when she said his name, and his smile sent a *zing!* through her core that made her heat up, hormones salsa dancing inside her.

Wait a minute.

Wait.

A.

Minute.

The tips of his fingers maneuvered the tube in exactly the worst way over the hose. Instinct made her jump forward; her boots didn't help, but she began trying to brush the spilled glue off the hose with her hand.

"Damn it, Rachel, cut it out!"

Rachel.

He called her by her name.

A flood of emotion coursed through her, growing with every beat of her heart. Her nerves were already on edge, but this wasn't fear. This was something warmer.

Something she had to fight.

"How do you know my name?" she demanded. She had a good grip on the hose, but so did he, and he wasn't letting go.

Stubborn guy.

"Let go," he insisted, pulling on the hose.

"You let go!"

Already standing next to him, she moved closer, filled with a sense of the familiar, the exciting, and the strange, all at once. It left her dizzy and aching. Thick, wavy hair that curled at the edge of his collar gave the man a rakish look, wild and free, and mixed with that lush, dark beard, he was a true mountain man.

One who smelled like woodsmoke, lime, spices, pine -

And... superglue.

"This is ridiculous. Let. Go. Now!" he grunted.

She tried pulling her hand away, but her four fingers were stuck to the hose. His were attached just above hers.

Shaking her hand hard, she tried to unstick herself, but all she did was cause pain, the cold skin on her fingers stinging as she moved. Using her free hand, she stabilized the hose and tried prying the tip of her index finger away, but the only result was resistance and a surreal sense of panic.

He stopped her by pressing his free hand down hard over the hose, careful to avoid anyplace where their fingers were attached, and he worked the tips of his fingers as well.

No luck.

"I never told you my name," she persisted, wondering how she could seriously have been so stupid as to have missed that this was Kell.

This was *Kell?*

"Must have read it on something in your car."

"It's a rental. And my purse with all my ID is under the seat."

"Huh."

Then his hat fell off his head as he bent over, trying to pry her hand off the hose. The sunglasses slid down his nose. Their eyes met, and she knew.

Knew.

His dark gray eyes were so familiar.

"Are you kidding me? Kell Luview? It's really you? Why would you lie to me and tell me your name is Deke? What is this? What are you up to?"

She tried to get away, tried to pull away.

His hand came with her.

A sigh that sounded murderous turned into a low chuckle of disgust.

"Yeah, Rachel, it's me. And look what you've done, again. Ruined my life."

"What?"

Those beautiful gray eyes narrowed.

"Then again, that's your superpower, isn't it?"

Chapter Two

KELL

In the five years since Kell Luview left D.C., he'd done a lot of thinking.

More than a lot.

That thinking–and a heaping dose of emotion–came roaring back when he found himself stuck with Rachel Hart.

Literally.

The sound of her voice made him want to kiss her. Or turn on his heel and walk away. He wasn't sure which. Given that he literally could not escape from Rachel now, that left only one option.

Kissing her was off the table, though, no matter how tempting.

He stared at their glued-together hands as she tugged lightly, the skin pulling but not releasing. Manicured nails, with tiny white tips and perfect skin, made it clear Rachel hadn't spent the last five years climbing trees or pulling invasive plants like he had.

"That hurts," he said, tearing his eyes away from that soft, beautiful hand.

"No kidding! I cannot believe this!" Tugging a little, she continued her effort to extract herself.

Superglue had its own reality.

"What did you think would happen when you touched it after I told you not to?" he growled.

"I thought you were handling the repair all wrong!"

"Because you've fixed exactly how many engines, Rachel?"

"I don't have to know how to fix an engine to see when someone's doing it wrong. All that glue you were glopping was about to–"

"That's *exactly* how you know someone's doing something wrong: by knowing how to do it right. Or... at all."

"Hmph." The corner of her right eye began to twitch, her mouth twisting with a furious disgust he absolutely did not deserve.

And it gutted him.

"You just took a bad situation and made it worse," he informed her, regretting the words instantly because he was talking too much. Pretending to be Deke had been easier.

"Gee, Kell. Thanks for telling me. I never would have figured that out on my own." Fake eyelash batting commenced, forcing him to look her over.

How the hell did Rachel Hart end up, with no warning, in his hometown?

After she'd screwed him over, five years ago, he'd come home with his tail between his legs. Buried his bruised ego and dented pride nice and deep under his promise to help his dad with the family tree business and eventually take it over.

Dean Luview had been elated, and his mom was like a box of fireworks in the hands of teenagers on the Fourth of July: colorful, explosive, and full of more than a little awe that one of the kids she thought had left for good was back home.

For good.

Took a while before he spilled his guts about Alissa and Rachel to his mom and his big sister, Colleen, but he'd gotten the whole sordid story off his chest, then locked it all up inside his heart, part of a past that was dead to him.

Unfortunately, ghosts knew how to break locks.

Or, at least, how to drive crappy rental cars into town.

Back when they were still friends, Rachel had connected her mother, the TV star Portia Starman, with his mom, who ran some of the town festivals, and a new reality TV show had been born: *Love You Springs Eternal.*

Cheesy title, but there wasn't much about the town that wasn't cheesy.

Kell had managed to avoid Portia almost entirely while she was in town, keeping himself busy pulling poison ivy for the film crew and evading his mother's many requests that he come home for dinner with the star. He had zero desire to be grilled about the past by Rachel's mom.

If he just thought of her as an emotion, it was easy. Kell was an expert at hiding from those.

Love You Springs Eternal had only lasted six episodes. It ran on some channel so obscure that even the local satellite TV company had to go out of its way to add it. But Rachel's mom had lived in "Love You" for two months, filming and basking in the adoration of her Gen X and boomer fans.

Each episode had a theme, starting with the town's history.

One hundred and fifty-two years ago, legend had it, hot springs were discovered in Luview by his great-great-great grandfather, Abram Luview. Abram was unmarried, owned a large tract of land, and worked as a logger.

A chance dip in the hot springs at the same time as a young woman from the next town over, and *bam!* Instalove. Adelaide, too, had been unable to find the right match until that dip, and when two lonely hearts went for a swim in the waters, they fell in love.

Awwwww, right?

Except Abram Luview, who found his bride that day, didn't just see stars in his beloved's eyes.

He saw dollar signs.

The hot springs were on his land.

Abram was an early marketer. Over the years, he and his descendants helped to turn Luview, Maine, into Love You, Maine: Where Every Day Is Valentine's Day.

Back in the late 1800s, he spun the town's image into a place where a lonely man could find a suitable bride by just going for a swim. Trainloads of single ladies from Boston came every summer, searching for husbands, and soon, the town was known as a lovers' paradise. Nice and easy, in a time when rural Maine was filled with loggers who needed a mate.

Pastors set up churches in town to offer weddings, and it all went from there.

In the 1920s, it was a place to escape Prohibition and have a cool drink at Bilbee's Tavern.

In the late 1940s, inns and B&Bs opened to meet the post-war demand for relaxing mountain vacations. As time went on, more and more people owned cars, and motor courts popped up along the roads.

By the 1970s, the ski resorts were being developed, sprawling affairs that brought new tourists to the area.

As baby boomers were born, then went on to have their own kids, the town began catering to families as well as singles. There was something for everyone in Love You, Maine, because love is universal.

We all deserve it, and we all need it.

Many of the residents of Luview earned their living from love. Love You Bakery sold heart-shaped cupcakes. Love You Coffee served your beverage in a heart-shaped mug. Love You Flowers specialized in pink and red roses.

Want a quickie wedding? The Love You Forever Inn and Drive-Thru Chapel was at your service.

As for Valentine's Day? It was February 14th, of course. But it was nothing unusual in Kell's small town because... that's right.

Every day was Valentine's Day in Love You, Maine.

The police cruisers were pink, the library was red, and the fire engines fit right in.

You know what didn't fit in, though? Kell seethed, staring at his hand, which was forced to touch hers, their fingers adhered to a rubber tube that looked phallic enough that he would never, ever hear the end of it from the folks at the ER.

Including his sister, a nurse, who was working a shift there right now.

Rachel. That's who didn't fit in.

Rachel.

All of this flashed through him in seconds as he looked away, mentally calculating.

"Are you going to say something, or just play the brooding, grumpy mountain man?" Rachel snapped.

"Weighing out the pros and cons of the skin on my fingers."

"What does that mean?"

"Stay stuck to you for hours and expose myself to permanent humiliation in my hometown, or let 'er rip and lose a few inches of skin."

She gasped. "You're not serious!"

"Oh, trust me. I am."

"You'd put yourself through that kind of pain just to get away from me?"

His answer was a hard stare.

"This is not my fault, Kell! It just happened."

"Just happened because you can't leave well enough alone and let someone else live their life."

"Now you're personalizing it? You think I *like* being stuck to you?"

Another hard stare. This time, she didn't flinch, giving it all right back.

Huh. She'd changed in the last five years, too. The Rachel he knew would have nervously looked away.

"Why are you here, Rachel?"

"Because I'm retracing my mother's steps and had a craving for a heart-shaped morning glory muffin, Kell."

He stared her down some more.

She gave no quarter.

That's how it was going to be? Fine. Forgetting, he started to cross his arms over his chest and yanked her, Rachel's balance in those silly little boots sending her crashing into him, his hands on her hips, her hair brushing against his cheek.

Hoo boy.

Stepping out of his arms, she clung to the car and blasted him. "And if anyone's asking questions, it's me. What... happened to you?" she asked, eyes roving all over him, from the top of his head to the tips of his work boots.

Her cheeks were pink, and not from the chill.

"What's that supposed to mean?"

"You're huge. And... furry."

"Furry?"

"Yes. Look at you. Did you stop cutting your hair five years ago? It goes down past your collarbone!"

"Nothing wrong with long hair."

"And that beard! At least it's neatly trimmed."

"Are you a hair and makeup expert now, Rachel? You here to work on a movie set? That's the only reason I can think of for you to comment on my looks."

Her cheeks went from pink to a furious red.

"I'm just saying you lied to me and called yourself Deke, and you've changed so much, it fooled me."

"Good. Then it worked."

"Why wouldn't you want me to recognize you?"

His patented hard stare came out again.

"You keep trying to intimidate me with that glare, but it won't work. I've faced down far scarier people than you, Kell."

"I'm not trying to intimidate you. I'm trying to get you to shut up."

"How about you get me out of this mess you created?"

"Me?" He shook their connected hands. "I didn't cause this. You did!"

Waving her unstuck left hand, she rolled her eyes.

"Whatever. Just fix this."

"Have to go into town to the ER."

"Seriously? You don't have some kind of solution to remove this?"

He looked at her nails.

"Got any nail polish remover?" Craning his neck, he looked in her car. The backseat was full of luggage. "Looks like you brought your entire closet. Your trunk's full, too? You moving here?"

He fought the *zing!* that ran through him at the thought.

No.

Oh, no. No way. He was not cracking open the lid to that tightly-sealed box. The worst thing that could happen to him was to have any piece of his D.C. past come into his current life. Especially Rachel.

Because she was the one part of it he missed desperately. He'd been left confused and looping for nearly a year, trying to reconcile how he'd let her in as a friend—and developed complicated feelings for her—all while she double-teamed with his ex to screw him over.

At least his ex, Alissa, had been fairly overt about using him. It was easier to get over her, his girlfriend for five months, than to get over the woman who'd been just a friend for nearly a year.

Emotions were nothing but trouble.

"No. Too hard to travel with it. TSA and all that."

"Great. Just great. Most women with nails like yours have some on them."

"Nails like mine?"

"Perfect nails." He said it with an extra heaping dose of scorn thrown in.

She looked pointedly at his hands, grease around the cuticles, a few small cuts in various stages of healing dotting his fingers. His time in D.C. had been an aberration, his hands used only for office work.

These days, his calluses had calluses.

"You're criticizing me for not having nail polish remover, but you didn't have duct tape, and that's what got us into this mess."

"No. You touched the superglue when I told you not to, Rachel! *That's* what got us into this mess!"

"Quit yelling at me!" Instead of moving away in fear, she took a step closer to him, stretching up to her full height, which, even in her heeled boots, was still shorter than he was. There was a fire in her eyes that was new.

That *zing!* shot through him again.

"I have every damn right to yell at you, Rachel. Look what you did!" Holding his hand–both their hands–up above them, he forced her to stand on tiptoes, her balance off on the snow. People from warmer climates weren't good at driving in snow, much less walking on it.

She wobbled a bit, but held her ground.

"You can hiss at me all you want, Kell, but it's not going to get us out of this mess. We need to go into town and get someone to unstick us."

"Oh, now you're reasonable?" he barked back.

"I'm always reasonable!"

He looked down at her boots and snorted.

"Give me your keys," she ordered.

"What? Why?"

"Because we need to drive into town and get this over with. And you're not ripping half the skin off your hand. We'll be civilized adults and drive to the ER."

Kell sighed, making a cloud in the air between them that was filled with much more than evaporated breath.

"Fine, but I'm driving."

"I have to drive. That's the only way it will work," she said in that officious tone that drove him nuts. The old Rachel wasn't like this. She sounded more like...

Alissa.

He'd left D.C. after they'd betrayed him, Alissa using him to get access to his uncle, Rachel helping her behind the scenes, and the two of them laughing about it in emails. He had no idea what Alissa was up to these days. Sure, social media meant you could stay in touch with anyone you wanted to, 24/7, but Kell hadn't wanted to know.

Yes, he'd checked here and there right after coming home, but he just felt stupid when he cracked open that closed chapter of his life.

Maybe Rachel had gone to work in Big Oil, like Alissa. He knew they'd talked about it.

A chill ran through him, and he took a half-step toward her, anger spiking his blood.

"You're here on business? What kind of business?"

She recoiled, but held her ground. "I'm here to help a local company sell to a larger company."

Damn it.

"Who?"

"Who, what?"

"Whose land are you trying to buy?"

"Land?"

"You work for MonDex with Alissa, don't you? You're here to do a land grab for some pipeline project."

Laughter poured out of her, but her eyes shifted everywhere, confused.

"Geez, Kell. It's been five years and you still can't let go, can you? You think I'm working for Big Oil?"

"I don't know what you did with your life after EEC and I don't care, but I do care what you're trying to do to my town."

"Trying to *do to it?* You make it sound like I'm here to steal all the children and salt the earth!"

He just stared her down.

"Look," she said, shivering. "It's getting dark, and I really, really need to pee." She looked at their conjoined hands. "Given how much you obviously hate me, I'm pretty sure neither of us wants to deal with *that* while we're stuck to each other. So how about we get to that ER, get unstuck, and then I can pee. And you can spend the car ride there telling me all about how awful I am."

Her words were a combination of sarcastic and light, but the tone revealed a pain he wasn't expecting. He turned and they walked awkwardly to his truck. Without asking, she grabbed the driver's side door handle with her free left hand, opened it, and began climbing in. Yanked toward her, he forced his thighs and core to tighten, holding his space, her left foot inside the car as she balanced herself.

"You can't do that, Rachel. You'll have to climb in through the passenger's side."

"Ugh!" Her left hand clutched the steering wheel, knee flexed, giving Kell a fine view of her... assets.

Logistics were his strong suit; his sense of balance and spatial relationships were intuitive skills that came easily to him. They had to. When you're two hundred feet up in a pine tree, harnesses and ropes your only protection, you'd better know exactly where your body, your saw, and your protective equipment were every nanosecond as you moved.

In a flash, his mind made a mental map of their situation, turning into a blueprint with 3D elements... and he almost groaned.

Letting Rachel drive made sense.

Instantly.

He shouldn't fight it, because the alternative made him groan.

Literally.

Her right hand was glued to his left hand. She was right—letting her drive was the only option.

She reacted to the low, deep sound from the back of his throat with offense.

"Look, I know you're frustrated, but so am I. I'm on the edge of losing it, so keep your nonverbal commentary to yourself!"

Smothering a smile was impossible, and as she got angrier and angrier, he found the whole situation funnier and funnier.

"Why are you smiling like that?"

"Because this is so ridiculous. And if you need to pee, go ahead. I won't look."

"I will pee in a hospital rest room like a civilized person, Kell." She looked at their hands. "Besides, I'll fall over if I try here."

"In those boots, sure."

"In general! Guys have no idea how easy they have it."

"Because we can pee standing up? It's not like that's our fault. We didn't design the plumbing."

She shivered again, marching around the truck with him in tow, and angrily opened the passenger door.

"Let's get going." This time, she used her free hand to haul herself up, her butt in the air as she bent over. Her fancy ski jacket obviously wasn't intended for the slopes because it hauled up over the small of her back, revealing a thin stretch of uncovered skin that must have been cold.

No tattoo at her sacrum. He half expected to see a butterfly or a tiny rose.

"I'll just crawl over to the driver's side," she called back, her voice slightly muffled as her right hand stretched behind her, shoulder twisted at a rough angle.

Kell tried very hard not to stare at her backside, but it was inches from his face.

Besides, it wasn't a bad view.

Tucking her right leg into the car, she moved sideways, contorting around the gearshift.

And then paused suddenly with a gasp.

"Oh!"

"What?"

"Your truck."

"What about it? Sorry it's not a Mercedes."

"That's not it!" Her voice went high with something close to hysteria. "It's a stick shift!"

"Yeah?"

"I–"

Their simultaneous groan scared off a few birds in the trees.

"You can't drive a stick?" he asked, incredulous.

"Who drives a stick anymore? Other than my dad, but that's because he loves his Ferrari."

"You grew up with a stick-shift car in the family and never learned?" Now he wasn't just surprised. He was stunned.

"I hate the Ferrari!"

"You poor, oppressed child."

Her butt backed up, nearly smacking him in the face.

"Shut up! Just shut up, Kell! It's not my fault Dad taught Tim how to drive his stupid beloved car and never let me. It's not my fault I have to pee and I am stuck in your truck and would you *move*?"

"I am stuck to you, Rachel. There's only so far I can move."

"Are you staring at my ass?"

"It's impossible not to."

"Are you seriously hitting on me in the middle of this mess?"

"No. It's a physical impossibility not to stare at your butt when you're in this position and our hands are glued together. Physics can't be changed just because you don't like it. Get out of the truck."

Scrambling backward, she nearly kicked him in the face, and he wasn't sure whether it was a close shave or a missed intentional hit, but he dodged it.

Red faced and squirming, she got herself arranged so she was sitting on the edge of the passenger seat, legs dangling. He was tall enough that they were nearly eye to eye.

"I guess you'll have to drive," she sighed.

Now he was the one who turned red, the heated blood racing through him as he realized she didn't understand what was about to happen.

Her right hand and his left hand were glued together. There was only one way to get to town with him driving.

She had to straddle him.

Facing him.

In his lap.

Chapter Three

RACHEL

"Why are you suddenly so red?" she asked, peering down at him. "Whatever it is, it must be bad, because you have so much hair and such a thick beard, it's hard to see around it, but you just turned the same color as your red flannel."

"I'm fine. Just, you know, exertion."

Kell's eyes shifted away from direct contact.

Instantly alert, pride being stripped away with each degree the air dropped, she felt every layer of restraint and control being stolen away, all under the watchful eye of a man who still didn't believe her.

Plus, her bladder was screaming.

His comment about her working for Big Oil with Alissa stung like hell.

And made her need to put as much distance between herself and Kell Luview as she possibly could, as fast as she could.

"You can drive," she conceded, gesturing toward the truck.

He averted his eyes again.

"Yep." He sighed and lifted their joined hands. "You think this through?"

"Think what through? I want to get to the ER. Let's do it."

"You think for a minute about how we have to do it. Do the mental geometry."

"Geometry? What does *geometry* have to do with this? It's a truck. You climb in, turn the key, and drive." Throwing a bit of his own sarcasm right back felt good.

Sort of.

"I mean the logistics of how to drive when our hands are stuck to this." He pointed to the hose.

"What?"

"I see I have to paint a picture for you." Kell pulled his left hand, the one attached to her right hand, and gently tugged her until they were standing behind the truck. Positioning their bodies, he aligned her behind the driver's seat, and himself behind the passenger's seat. Their arms stretched between them.

"I told you I can't drive a stick!"

"Right. So, Rachel, how do we need to move our bodies to get in the truck and make it into town?"

"You just–" She moved to change places with him and instantly saw what he was alluding to. If they turned around, he was facing away from the dashboard, and you can't drive a car that way.

If he was in the driver's seat, she could be in one of two places:

In the road, with the driver's door or window open, or...

In his lap, facing him.

"Oh, no!" she groaned. "This just went from bad to way worse."

"Hmph."

"I cannot believe this. I didn't want to work on this project. At all. Not one little bit. But my boss said the connections I had to Luview via my mother and her stupid little reality show were going to help me. And *you*!"

"What about me?"

"You weren't supposed to be here!"

"I'm *from* here, Rachel. If anyone's out of place, it's you."

"But you loved living in D.C.! You said you never wanted to move back. You were a city guy, converted to urban life. My mom said she never saw you when she worked on her show here! I assumed you were in L.A. or Chicago or some other big city!"

"Assumed, or hoped?"

"Does it matter?"

"People change."

A plume of pure rage warmed her, making her bladder ache even more.

"You know," Rachel said, struggling to control her voice, looking down at the state route below them, "we could flag down a car. I'm sure plenty will drive by. Or you could call a friend to come get us and we can ride in the back seat!"

She didn't mean to sound so cheery at the end, but the idea suddenly came to her and it was a relief, compared to the alternative.

He huffed. "I don't have magic cell service any more than you do, Rachel."

"Don't you have a CB?"

"A what?"

"You know." She waved toward his truck dashboard with her free hand. "The kind truckers use. From before cell phones."

"You think I have some super-secret lumberjack forest radio I can use to call for a rescue when some city girl glues herself to me?"

"That's not what I said, and you know it."

"Do you purse your lips and whistle to get the woodland creatures to clean your apartment for you in L.A.?"

"Stop it."

A buzz shot through her, one she detested, her bladder ready to secede, but it wasn't just the tension between them or his cutting, sarcastic remarks that made her feel bad.

It was that Kell really had changed.

One of the most refreshing parts of their friendship in D.C. had been his nonjudgmental kindness. Never a pushover, Kell had a way of being a strong man without needing to use negativity to reinforce it. And unlike at home, she never felt like she had to prove herself around him. Never felt cut down, sized up, or on edge.

Five years had changed her, for sure, especially after what happened at EEC, but it appeared to have fundamentally altered Kell's personality. The man standing before her was an entirely different human being, and that filled her with a sick, bitter feeling that was quickly turning into tears, because she really, *really* missed the old Kell.

No.

No.

She was not going to let Kell make her cry.

Rachel wasn't twenty-three anymore, duped by Alissa and in way over her head in a cutthroat environment she only saw clearly in hindsight. When she moved on to her MBA program at Stanford, the dynamics she'd experienced at EEC gave her a thick skin and a low tolerance for being a sucker.

After graduation, she'd left environmental concerns behind and taken the most prestigious, ambitious job she could get, with a large international chocolate company.

And now she'd landed here.

In Luview, Maine, staring at a Luview who most definitely didn't love *her*.

The silence that stretched between them felt like an eternity, a hollow pull inside that tunneled deep down. Her warm coat wasn't warm enough. A shiver started again, beginning with her heart.

"There is no way I'm straddling you so we can get into town. We'll just have to wait it out until a car drives by down there."

"Best way to do that is to actually go down and wait on Route 33." He eyed her boots like they were rattlesnakes.

"I tried that and you saw how it turned out."

"I could carry you down the hill."

"What if you slipped? We'd slide into traffic like marbles on this ice."

He peered down the hill. "Might go under the guardrail, too, and hit that gully. It's a good sixty-foot drop, with rocks."

"I have sneakers in my luggage. Let me change my shoes and we can go down there."

"It's not a well-traveled road, Rachel. I've been here with you for the last half hour, and no one's driven by. There's a weather advisory, too."

"Like, snow?"

Booming laughter, coupled with a denigrating headshake, made him seriously feel like a grumpy Paul Bunyan to her.

"'Like, snow?'" he mimicked. "More like a Nor'easter."

"I've heard that term, but what does it mean?"

As if on cue, tiny snowflakes began to dot their clothes.

"Means that." He pointed up. "Those tiny snowflakes are going to turn into very big ones, and that means accumulation.

Big storm coming. Predicted to get up to ten inches. Plenty of people are off the road already."

"Then why are you driving? What made you come up here anyhow?"

"This is an old logging road. I was driving by and saw your car. No one drives up here, ever, but some dumb programmers for a GPS company got the roads wrong and every so often, it tells tourists like you take this route. If your car hadn't broken down, you'd have gone a good mile in and gotten stuck. You need a chainsaw and a winch to make it through that road. Even four-wheel drive won't cut it."

"Why on earth would GPS not know that?"

"Because algorithms are smarter than people," he said cynically. "Didn't you know? The smart thing to do would be to send a human to observe the roads and document it, but I don't make the rules." He looked at their glued hands and sighed. "I just fix the messes."

She wasn't touching that comment with a ten-foot pole.

"Look. I like my idea about my sneakers. Let me–"

A howl pierced the air and she lost her grip on the truck, sliding down and colliding with Kell. He caught her, their faces inches from each other.

"What's that?" she whispered.

"Coyote. Likely not a wolf, but who knows."

"You're kidding." She leaned back and Kell dropped his arms from her.

"Bears, fisher cats, coyotes, bobcats–you name it. All of them could come out if we stay here long enough."

"You're trying to scare me."

"No. I'm stating reality. You're in backwoods Maine."

"You mean back*water* Maine. This place is unbelievably, painfully backward."

"Back*woods* doesn't mean back*ward*."

A huff was all she could muster, hating how her body responded to his suggestion, but the mechanics of their predicament meant he was right. The only way he could drive his truck was if he sat in the driver's seat and she straddled him. Then his right hand would be free to use the stick shift.

And then she realized there was another way.

"What if you sit in the driver's seat, and we hold our hands through the window? You just drive three miles per hour and I walk the trip back to town."

One bushy eyebrow went up. "We're eleven miles from town, and you'd be walking down the middle of the road, as a snowstorm starts. And how are you going to get your arm through the window when our hands are glued together? Climb through it first?" His chuckle made her fury ratchet up a notch. "Don't think I'm going to enjoy having you in my lap, Rachel, but it's the only way out of this."

"I can't believe you did this to me!"

"*Did* this to you? *I* didn't do this. *You* did!"

"I'm not the one who used superglue!"

"You didn't listen when I told you not to touch it!"

"How was I supposed to know you were serious?"

"Because I'm a human being with a brain and you should respect me!"

"As if that's a good reason," she shot back.

"Look. There's no other choice. You have to ride me so we can ride into town." The wolfish smile he gave her was nothing but pure mockery, but the gleam in his eye and the red blush were something else.

"That's puerile!"

"That's the truth."

"You don't have to say it that way!"

"I'll be a gentleman. Promise." He frowned. "You sure you don't want to pee before we do this? Because..."

"That's disgusting! I am completely in control of my body!"

"Good. Because you're doing a piss-poor job of controlling your emotions."

"*Hey!*"

"Oh. Sorry. Shouldn't have said piss."

"You think *that* was the offensive part?"

"Come on, Rachel. I've got places to be and things to do, and we're not going to change our outcome by arguing. Get in the truck and let's go."

"I–"

Another howl, followed by what sounded like screaming women in the far distance, made Rachel instinctively move closer to Kell, who put a protective hand on her shoulder.

"What's that?" she whispered. "It sounds like a bunch of women being attacked!"

"That's the other serial killer, doing his work." He gave her a hideously evil grin. "We split up all the women whose cars break down by the side of the road and I got stuck with you."

"STOP IT!!"

A frustrated sigh came out of him.

"I don't know. A pack getting into a turkey den? Maybe some foxes eating something? Coyotes? Lots of options out here."

As fear flowed through Rachel's veins, replacing every other emotion, she realized with dismay that their options were limited to one.

One neither of them wanted to face.

Reality *sucked*.

Rachel closed her eyes and moved out of Kell's orbit of warmth, madly searching for an alternative.

"How about I drive, and you just do the gear changing?" she asked, peering into the truck and examining the stick shift. "It's not that hard, right?"

"Do you understand how to drive a stick?"

"Sure. You move up through the gears, then down."

"And the clutch?"

"Nothing about this situation is clutch!"

A pained look made his face tighten. "No, Rachel, the clutch *pedal*. You'd have to push the pedal at the exact right time, with calibrated pressure, whenever I shift gears."

"There's a pedal?"

He let out a low growl of frustration.

"Fine. I can't drive at all, then."

"Not without losing control of the truck. Also, you ever driven on ice?"

"Hah. No."

"There's a hill up ahead that is so bad, sometimes you have to fishtail your way *up* it."

"I don't even know what you just said, but it doesn't sound good."

"It's not."

She thrust her chin up with determination and said, "All right. Let's do this with as much dignity as possible."

"That's... not a lot."

Kell walked around the truck and, having no choice, she followed. He climbed into the driver's side, easing the seat back as far as it could go, using their conjoined hands to reach the mechanism on the left side panel.

As she watched, his body stunned her. The Kell she knew five years ago had been bigger than the other guys she knew in the city, but not like this.

This man was *big*. Strong. Full and muscled, his body made clear that he used it for a living. Thick thighs filled out his jeans, and his flannel shirt and vest strained over a powerful chest and honed arms.

"Welcome to Kell's Amusement Park." With his free hand, he gestured across his lap. "All riders must be at least this tall to ride the Kell Train. Fasten your seatbelt and–"

"Shut up."

His throaty laugh was a cover for his own embarrassment, she knew, but it really didn't make a difference.

This was going to be humiliating, no matter what.

Might as well get it over with.

"My purse!" she suddenly exclaimed, coming to her senses. "And my luggage."

Kell looked in the back seat of his truck, her gaze following his. It was stuffed with greasy-smelling boxes.

"I'm moving some equipment and filing for my dad. You'll have to put it in the back of the pickup."

"I'm not letting my Louis Vuitton luggage ride outside in the snow!"

"Then leave it. We can get into town, call Deke, and he'll come up here and fix the car."

"Deke is a real person?"

"Sure. Runs one of the local auto repair and breakfast diner places."

"*One of*? There's more than one 'auto repair and breakfast diner' establishment? What else do you have? Nail salons in laundromats?"

"No, but that's a great idea."

"I need my purse," she declared, taking a step toward her rental car and nearly going flat on the ice when Kell didn't move a muscle.

"You fall, you're taking half the skin on my hand with you."

"Then get out and help me! It's under the seat!"

Kell climbed out and tromped over to the car with Rachel right behind him. He opened the door and fished under the driver's seat. "This it?" he asked, holding it up.

"Yes."

"Your purse is the size of a small child." A long shoulder strap, thick like a man's belt, made it easy to sling over his shoulder and keep his free hand free. That he didn't balk at wearing a woman's purse for the sake of practicality made her start to smile, but she smothered it fast.

"Now you're a fashion critic? The tree guy reviews purses, too–like the auto repair and breakfast diner?" she teased as they went back to his truck.

He tossed her bag in the back seat, on top of a box, and said no more as he climbed back in, eyes hooded with a curmudgeonly stare straight ahead.

She gripped the steering wheel with her left hand and pulled herself up awkwardly, her core tightening as she focused on balancing herself. Thank goodness for Pilates.

Her instructor probably didn't have this maneuver in mind when she taught classes, though.

"What if I sit over there," she said, jutting her chin toward the passenger seat, "and we stretch our hands? I'll sit backward."

"Try it."

She moved over hopefully, but then looked at Kell, who was bent so far with his left arm that his right shoulder rested on the console. He mimicked steering and shifting gears with his free hand.

"As long as I don't have to see, and have the reflexes of a hummingbird to shift, I'm good," he said dryly.

"Fine." She looked in the back seat. "How about I ride behind you?"

"You have monkey arms? Because you'd have to have abnormally elongated limbs, Rachel, and last I knew, you weren't an elastic superhero."

"Cut it out with the cracks!"

"It's a king cab with an enormous console. Nothing about this truck was designed to be compact, and they sure as hell didn't have this scenario in mind. Get on my damn lap so we can get out of this damn mess and go our separate ways."

His cursing surprised her. Yes, it was mild, but it was rougher than she expected.

"You don't have to be mean about it."

"Mean? That's me being very patient, given how much you've tested me."

Screams from the woods made her jump in her seat, the sound closer.

"Will they try to eat us?"

"If they do, your boots will make it easy for me to escape."

"See? Mean."

He sighed. "Just get in my lap and let's get it over with."

"That's what she said," she muttered out of the corner of her mouth as she lifted her right leg and went for it, planting it on the driver's side, knee sliding between the door and Kell's thigh.

A loud laugh from Kell, revealing unexpected humor, was what she faced when she settled in, her butt raised up so she wasn't literally straddling him.

"There," she said to his fading chuckle. "Let's go."

"Can't." His single word blew hot breath on her nose, a hint of coffee attached to it. Ripples of arousal turned her skin to one big erogenous zone, her pulse picking up between her legs, her thighs aching.

Biology, Rachel, she lied to herself. *It's basic biology. This means nothing.*

"What do you mean, *can't*?"

Grateful for having popped a breath mint in her mouth when she crossed the New Hampshire-Maine line three hours ago, she now wondered how to avoid having her face collide with his for the entire ride.

"Your ass is on the steering wheel."

"No, it's not." Moving a bit to prove him wrong, she set off the horn, the blare scaring her into a small scream.

"The horn begs to differ."

Was his palm on her butt? Did he just *pat* her?

Being inches from his mouth, their eyes filled with doubts and tension, made this harder. Her right arm bent painfully behind her as Kell moved their conjoined hands to the steering wheel.

Balance was impossible now.

Slumping forward, forehead resting on his shoulder, she accepted reality.

"There you go," he murmured against her ear. "Now we're getting somewhere."

Her whole body went ablaze at those words.

Chapter Four

KELL

Wrong thing to say, Kell! he shouted at himself in his head.

Every time he let his guard down, a part of him moved *up*.

A part he did not want Rachel to notice.

Because that part had no right to insert itself into the situation right now.

Pun not intended.

"Just drive," she muttered, the soft curve of her body against his making it impossible to focus. How did he drive a truck again?

Insert key. *Insert*. No. Stop it. Don't think about inserting things. It's not symbolic. Sometimes a key is just a key.

Foot on brake.

Depress clutch.

Turn key. No thinking!

Put in gear.

Foot off brake.

How was he supposed to focus with her perfume in his nose? A deep inhale reminded him of a tropical, fruity drink. There was so much nuance to her scent, though, something soft and sweet, a more relaxed, feminine air to her than he had a right to notice.

Or care about.

Her body was so soft and warm against his, the curve of her

upper arm brushing against his, her thighs toned and tight as she spread them across his lap. This was going to be the death of him.

Holding back his arousal.

He would die of restraint.

"You ready?" he asked, using his free hand to push a stray lock of her hair off his face. It fell back again, brushing his lips. No choice. He had to tuck it behind her ear.

"What are you doing?"

"I'd prefer not to eat your hair while driving."

"I can fix that." Using her free hand, she reached up, but lost her leverage, slumping deeper into him, her inner thighs sliding down across the outsides of his legs, their position so intimate, her body turning him into nothing but one big impulse.

And it felt so good.

Too good.

What if he took his free hand, buried his fingers in her hair at the back of her head, and brought her mouth slowly to his? How would she respond? What would she feel like in his lap, moving against him with passion and not... this.

Whatever *this* was?

"Kell?"

"Got it," he insisted, thinking about anything–*anything*–to stop his body from responding to her.

Imagine that dead raccoon he once found frozen in a lake.

Imagine watching the Red Sox lose to the Yankees in the playoffs.

Think about that time he accidentally walked in on his grandparents having sex in the barn.

As his mind raced to conjure every terrible memory that would drain the blood out of places it shouldn't be, she lifted herself back up, incrementally, from his lap and said, "Hello? Come on. Let's go."

"Right."

"You okay?"

But he'd shifted into reverse already, the vehicle lurching as he played the clutch and gas pedals just so, the giant truck doing what it needed to do. A flick of the windshield wipers and he moved the thin layer of new snow off, and down they went toward Route 33.

Pretty soon, cars would pass them, a nine out of ten chance he knew the drivers. They would wave.

He couldn't wave back.

That alone would make a few of them wonder, and peer a little more intently, seeing the back of a woman instead of the full front of a driver. Pretty damn quickly, word would spread.

And his mom would start calling him.

Then his brother and sister.

Calls he would try to ignore.

One problem with the road they were on was that gully, dangerous in good weather, a yawning ice chasm of no return in winter. Kell headed slowly down the road, the flakes falling at a nice, steady pace. It would take an hour or two before the Nor'easter really kicked in, and hopefully Deke could get up here fast enough to fix the car.

It was pure luck that he found Rachel. If he hadn't come along, she'd have been stranded. And those ridiculous boots wouldn't have done her any favors.

The thought of her huddled in the car overnight, alone in a heavy snowstorm, no food or heat, made him grateful for whatever impulse made him happen to glance up at the logging road and see the car. Helping people meant taking time out from routine to do what was needed, and he'd assumed he'd find a family lost on their way to town.

Instead, he got a lapful of unfinished business.

Like a cat, Rachel arched up, her butt brushing against his left hand on the steering wheel. They hit a pothole and she squealed right in his ear.

He gritted his teeth at the sound, then sympathy flooded him. "Your shoulder okay?"

"No. I feel like I've been trussed."

An image of that poured through him, and damn it, now he had to think about something else... deflating. No way was he going back to the memory of walking in on Grandpa and Grandma in the barn, in that hayloft, both of them naked and giggling.

Grandpa never giggled. Except... then.

Dead racoon. Dead racoon. Dead racoon...

"We just have to make it to the hospital. Nine point four miles to go. About twenty minutes at this slow rate."

"Hah. In L.A., nine miles is an hour of driving."

"This isn't L.A."

"No kidding. In L.A., cell phones work everywhere."

"Once we're unstuck, you can head right back to L.A., Rachel, and never see Luview again." The harsh words were a test.

They also helped neutralize his arousal.

"Trust me," she said, her throat clicking as she swallowed hard. "That's my plan."

"You never said exactly why you're in town. I'm going to find out no matter what, so why don't you spill?"

She groaned. "Please refrain from using words like spill, water, or rushing."

He began making a *psssssssh* sound in her ear, knowing he was being a jerk but unable to stop himself, because this line of conversation was bringing things down, so to speak.

"*Stop it!*" she hissed, hard and raspy, in his ear.

"You're right. I'll stop. I'll be the victim if I keep doing that."

"Victim? *You're* the victim? If anyone's the victim here, it's me!"

"Victim of your own stupidity."

He expected a biting retort. Instead, he got agreement.

"I know. On so many levels, Kell. Oh, how I know."

A quick glance at the odometer told him they had seven point three miles to go.

Every mile was a century.

Her long sigh, sweet breath heating his neck, didn't help. All these lush curves in his lap, her fruity scent mixed with his own, and every breath he took turned into a fight within. Rachel Hart hurt him all those years ago, but damn if he didn't want to kiss her right here, right now, desperately.

Pull over by the side of the road and just --

Suddenly, she screamed so loudly, crawling half up his body, that he damn near drove off the road.

"THERE'S A BOBCAT IN HERE!"

A flash of fluffy ginger and white appeared in the corner of Kell's right eye as he juggled driving, a glued hand, Rachel's flailing form, and now a pierced eardrum.

All while headed up an icy hill in a snowstorm.

"Rachel." He mustered as much calm as humanly possible,

because one of them had to be rational and, given that he was driving, it should probably be him. "Quit screaming."

"YOU HAVE A WILD ANIMAL IN HERE!"

The cat sat back on its haunches in the passenger seat, eyes narrowing with a glittering condescension.

"That's my cat."

"That's not a cat!" Rachel was shaking, moving in his lap. "It looks like a lion mixed with a bobcat! And what's that hard thing? It's really big. I'm hitting the stick shift with my thigh!"

That's not the stick shift, he was going to have to announce if she didn't stop squirming.

"Meet Calamine. She's a Maine Coon cat."

"A what?"

"Maine Coon cat."

"Why do you have an enormous cat slinking around in your truck?"

"Because she's my girl. Goes with me everywhere."

"That thing is the size of a dog!"

"Yep."

"Does it bite?"

"Only when I order her to."

Calamine gave him a glare that said, *What's an order, you inferior human?*

At that moment, the cat decided to claim her rightful place in Kell's very occupied lap, going nose in between him and Rachel.

"What's it doing?"

"Trying to sit in my lap."

"It can't!"

"You ever have a cat, Rachel? Try telling it not to do something." His eyes met hers. "Bet you're part cat, huh?"

"There's no room between us!"

"Cats have bones made of liquid. She'll fit in here."

Rachel huffed. "Good thing I'm not allergic!"

Ignoring the arguing humans, Calamine made her way between them, settling in, her soft warmth and sturdy heft making Kell chuckle.

And grateful. Embarrassing appendages settled down exactly where they should be.

"I cannot believe this."

"Believe what? That I have a pet?"

"How many more miles to go?"

"Five point four."

"Good. Ewww, what's that?"

Calamine was licking their conjoined hands.

"Cally's just figuring us out."

"Does cat saliva neutralize superglue? If so, keep licking, Calamine."

"If it did, I'd have hauled her out from under the passenger seat a long time ago."

"You knew she was in here and didn't warn me?"

"Why would I warn you about a cat?"

"That's not a normal cat!"

The first big heart-shaped sign on Route 33 for Luview, Maine, appeared. It had the proper spelling, LUVIEW, but then underneath, the enormous tag line:

Welcome to Love You, Maine: Where Every Day Is Valentine's Day.

Rachel couldn't see it because she was facing backward, but she groaned anyhow.

Then he remembered there were signs in both directions.

"The sign says *Thank You For Visiting Love You, Maine: Where Every Day Is Valentine's Day,* so I assume we're close?" she ventured. Her voice was sounding more and more exhausted with every mile.

"Just crossed the town line. A few miles left to hit the center. Hospital's on the other side of town."

"Can't get there soon enough."

Suddenly, both of their phones started buzzing like mad as all the suppressed texts came through. Reading texts while driving was always dangerous, but in this case, it was impossible.

Couldn't exactly read them right now. Neither of them had a free hand.

The snow blanketed the ground now, the early part of the storm making the roads more dangerous than they would be later. He knew that the fresh snow covered ice patches that made this even more treacherous, and he wasn't exactly accustomed to driving with his hand attached to a woman whose shoulder was wrenched behind her while she straddled him, plus with good old Cally in his lap.

Distracted driving, indeed.

"You're really pulling on my arm, Kell. Can you ease up?"

"Sorry. Gripping the steering wheel. It's hard to see around you, and I'm worried we'll hit black ice."

"Black ice?"

Good grief. She really was an L.A. girl, wasn't she?

"Black ice looks like a puddle of water, if you can see it at all. People mistakenly think it's no big deal, then they spin out. It's really dangerous–a major reason drivers lose control. And now there's snow falling on it, so it's completely hidden."

"I think I know what you mean. I've heard about it in Tahoe." She swallowed hard, her throat clicking again. "So we have that danger added on top of everything else?"

"Yes."

"Okay." Her sudden silence made a shot of adrenaline spike through him, protective warmth running in his veins as well. The gravity of their situation made it clear they had to put aside their overwhelming embarrassment and work together. He eased his grip on the steering wheel as much as possible, shifting position to give her some relief.

"Wow. The last few houses we've driven past have all been red or pink," she said with a laugh he didn't like. "Must be getting close."

She was right. The first handful of houses leading into the town center were red and pink, with white trim, and soon nearly every building they saw would be as well.

They reached a fork in the road, requiring him to stop at a stop sign. Calamine chose that moment to move off his lap and find another spot on the front seat, then changed her mind. She jumped down to the floor and settled below the heater.

Rachel couldn't see the insurance agency, Mike Murphy's home attached to it, the red shutters and door standing out. Next to him was Cassell Fields' CPA office. One of the suites in his small building was rented out to a local tutoring company, another to a physical therapist.

Lorna Leo, Cassell's longtime admin, was climbing out of her car as he drove by, holding a box of files, her bright red hair covered in a Patriots ski cap, long strands poking out. She waved, then let go of the box, her jaw dropping.

Kell couldn't wave back.

As he gently pressed the gas pedal, continuing slowly into town, the snow eased up abruptly.

"Is the storm over?"

"Nope. Just a lull."

"Oh."

She sounded so tired, and her right shoulder must be screaming by now. Whatever their past, he couldn't help but feel sympathy for Rachel.

Even if this was all her fault.

There was a hairpin turn with a guardrail up ahead, and as he navigated it carefully, the entire town came into view, all at once, spectacular and very, very *red*.

Early February in Love You, Maine, was a study in red and pink against a white background. Sometimes, Kell thought maybe he had a penchant for Nordic noir because the town looked like blood-stained snow.

"This is so much worse than I ever imagined," Rachel muttered right in his ear.

"Imagined? Didn't you watch your mom's reality show?"

"No! Of course not."

"Way to support a family member."

"You really think you know everything, don't you?"

"What does that have to do with you being so haughty you won't even watch your own mother's show?"

This time, *he* was the recipient of a hard stare, and at close range, too.

"For your information, my mother has forbidden us to ever watch any of her shows."

"Forbidden?"

"Yes."

"How can she stop you from watching them without her knowledge?"

"She can't. But I wouldn't do that to her."

"Why on earth would an actress want her own family not to watch her shows?"

"She loves when fans do. She hates when we give input."

"Input?"

Rachel let out a long sigh.

"Actors are a weird breed. Some love watching themselves, others can't stand it. Mom doesn't just hate watching herself on camera, she hates the idea that we would see her, too, so yes. Out of respect for her, we don't watch."

"You've never snuck a look on your own? Her old detective series shows up all over the cable channels in reruns. Can't miss it."

"No."

"Never? Not even in a doctor's office, or while you're waiting for an oil change?"

"Really rarely, and then I try to ignore it."

"That's objectively weird. You're right."

She shrugged. "Told you."

"Your mom won't let you watch her shows, and your dad won't let you drive his Ferrari. Your parents have a lot of rules about how you're expected to behave. What else aren't you allowed to do?"

"Allowed? I'm twenty-eight years old. I'm allowed to do whatever I want."

He snorted. "Sure. Okay. If you say so."

"Everyone's staring!" Rachel hissed.

As cars drove past them, the drivers were nearly getting whiplash gawking at the sight of a woman sitting in Kell's lap, facing him. Driving his work truck made it all worse, because there was no plausible deniability.

Willful ignorance was not going to work as a coping strategy.

"It's a small town. We're today's gossip," he replied.

"This is not how this project was supposed to start. I'm not wearing a suit, or even in full makeup."

"Why would that matter?"

"Only someone who wears flannel to work and uses tick spray as cologne would say that."

He sniffed himself. "Huh. Guess I do smell like geraniums."

"What do geraniums have to do with anything?"

"Powerful tick repellent."

"I need a lumberjack repellent."

"Trust me, Rachel, you've got that down to a science. All you have to do is open your mouth."

Quick taps on horns began, asynchronous, making Kell groan. He knew everyone in town.

Because he was related to half the town.

On the left, Love You Bakery appeared. It was known locally

simply as Greta's, after the woman who opened it in the 1980s. A German immigrant who married a local, Greta had come to Luview, Maine, with a single goal: to feed everyone.

A goal she achieved.

Love You Flowers was next, then Love You Coffee.

"Is everything called Love You *Blank*?"

"Pretty much."

"Love You Post Office?"

"No. Government offices are exempt."

"This is sickening."

"Some people call it quaint."

"The tacky ones, you mean."

Kell came to a stop at the next light, hoping like hell his mom wouldn't see them. It was a Tuesday after four, so she was likely back in the office at their tree company, running invoices or balancing the books.

Suddenly, blue lights began to pulse around them.

"Uh, Kell? You're being pulled over."

"I kinda noticed."

"What for? You weren't speeding. And—is that cop really wearing a *red* uniform?"

"Yes."

"The pink cop car is bad enough, but come on! I knew the town was weird, but to see it in person…"

"It's about to get way worse."

Three taps on the window.

Tap tap tap.

Kell rolled down the window to find his brother, Luke Luview, one of the town police officers, giving him a fake stern look.

He was never, ever hearing the end of this.

"Copulating while driving is a moving violation," Luke said drolly. A heavy silence followed. Kell finally pierced it with a sigh. "Emphasis on the *moving* part."

Luke had short, sandy blond hair, blue eyes, and dimples that came out when he smiled. Just like their mom and older brother, Dennis.

No smile right now, though.

Rachel was frozen in his lap.

"We're not copulating, officer," Kell replied. "Just stuck together."

"Stuck?"

Gently, Kell lifted his hand from the steering wheel, drawing attention to their adhered fingers and the hose. "Yes, sir."

The word *sir* came out like profanity.

"How did you–what did you *do*?" It was clear from his brother's expression that only half of him wanted to know the real answer.

"I was trying to fix her engine and she didn't listen and went and touched something she shouldn't have."

"I really don't need to know about your love life, Kell."

"I didn't touch his stupid hose! I was trying to make him see reason! It was dripping!" Rachel hissed, her face turned toward the window, trying to explain.

Luke's mouth twisted with disgust as he held up a palm. "Really. Stop."

"No! Officer! It's not like that!" Rachel exclaimed in horror. "We're talking about the radiator hose! On my rental car!"

"Why would a radiator hose *drip?*"

"Because I was using superglue," Kell explained.

"Duct tape works better."

"I know that. Allen used all mine up and didn't replace it."

"Who's Allen?" Rachel asked, looking flustered. The hand attached to his was shaking, and her voice was going higher, anxiety clearly kicking in.

Kell softened a bit. "Guy who works for me. Remember? My assistant."

"Oh, right."

"I take it you two just met?" But as the words came out of Luke's mouth, he slowed down, peering at Rachel. "Hold on. I know you. Where have I seen you before?"

Given that her butt was the part of her Luke had the best view of, Kell found himself not liking this line of inquiry.

Then again, Luke wasn't looking to meet women right now, so...

"I assure you, Officer, we've never met before. I'm just here on business."

"Business, huh? What line of business are you in? Lap dances?"

Kell couldn't help but snort.

"No! I'm an associate director at Markstone's!"

"What's Markstone's? Like the chocolate company?"

"Not *like* the chocolate company. *The* chocolate company," she said, with a snotty sniff at the end. Might as well have added, *you rube.*

Luke felt it, too.

"Why would someone from the almighty Markstone's be here in little Luview, Maine?"

"I'm facilitating a deal between your local chocolate company and Markstone's Chocolatier."

Both men whistled. Rachel winced—Kell's lips were that close to her ear.

"You didn't tell me that's why you're here. Lucinda's selling out? No way Boyce will ever let her do that." Kell was shocked.

"It's the other way around," she hissed in his ear. "Boyce is eager. It's Lucinda who needs a little convincing."

"What're you trying to get her to do? Hand over the chocolate factory to Markstone's?"

"Markstone's will keep local jobs local," she said in a soothing tone that was too perfectly corporate to be convincing. "Don't worry. I'm just here for a couple of days to babysit the deal, and Love You, Maine, will be all the better for it. Markstone's plans to add thirty to forty new full-time jobs. Jobs I'm sure your mayor will be thrilled to have in this dinky little place. What's the population? A few hundred?"

Luke tipped his hat back an inch or two, exposing eyes that resembled Kell's. Different color.

Same narrowing.

"Two thousand seven hundred and thirty-three, ma'am," Luke said, as tightly as Kell had heard him speak to anyone in a while. Not that he'd heard much from his older brother over the last fifteen months.

Not since everything that happened with his wife.

"That many people live here? I'm surprised."

"It's a big town. No mayor, either. We have a town manager and a town clerk."

"Is the population growing?"

"We lost at least two residents last year," Luke said gruffly, then frowned. Kell winced. "Hold on. I do know you. I never forget a face, and I swear we've met."

Rachel sat back a bit, making Kell's right thigh scream. "Um, Officer? We're sitting like this because we're glued together, and my shoulder is about to separate. Could you kindly let us go to the emergency room and get detached?"

Luke looked at their hands, then at Kell. "You know Colleen's on shift right now."

"Yep. All I need is for Den to make a surprise visit, and my humiliation is complete. Want to invite Mom and Dad to come? Maybe stop by Greta's for some brownies? Grab a bag of popcorn from the cinema?"

A genuine grin stretched across Luke's face, the first Kell had seen in, oh...

Fifteen months.

He smacked the truck's door and called out, "Police escort. You can drive as fast as I do."

As Luke walked back to his cruiser, Kell waited until his brother was in the car. Once Luke passed him, he put the truck in gear and slowly moved forward, ignoring all the catcalls and whistles from gawkers.

"You seem to know each other really well. Friend of yours?"

"You don't recognize him?"

"Am I supposed to? I've never been here."

It shouldn't have pained him that Rachel didn't remember FaceTiming with his brother back in D.C., but it did.

"Never mind."

The drive behind Luke was slightly less torturous, allowing them to move swiftly through town, though he obeyed stoplights.

"Bless him," Rachel whispered.

"Who? My brother?"

"That's your brother?" she gasped. "Oh! Luke and Amber!"

The word *Amber* made Kell's chest tighten.

"Just Luke," he said quietly, but Rachel didn't pick up on his undertone.

"And their baby! Harriet? How is she? She'd be six by now, right?"

"She's great."

The hospital wasn't that far out of town, and as the signs came into view, he felt Rachel's body relax.

"Thank you, universe!" she moaned, the sound clearly intended to be relief, but it only served to set all his nerve endings on fire again.

She felt so good. Smelled glorious. Her softness was killing him, even if her tongue was sharp as a fresh ax blade. Pulling into the parking lot was a blessing.

And a curse.

The truck made a grinding sound as he cut the engine, Calamine picking that exact moment to push her nose into Rachel's belly. With his free hand, he pushed her away, earning a huff.

"How do we do this?" Rachel asked, just as a shadowy figure caught Kell's eye.

Luke.

Dusk was descending, not enough to obscure people, but just enough to make everything a bit dull. Police officers in town wore red, so he didn't exactly fade into the background.

"You're going to need assistance getting out of there. You two are a human pretzel." Luke's voice was non-judgmental, as if supergluing themselves together were no more unusual than helping someone with a flat tire.

"I don't think I can move," Rachel confessed. "My shoulder is frozen."

"You'll have to go first," he said steadily. "Then Kell."

Hands on his hips, he craned his neck, looking at their conjoined bodies.

"I need help," Rachel said.

"No problem. I'm going to place my hands on your shoulder and help you get that right leg out of the truck. Is that okay?" Luke's tone changed to what Kell called his work voice to his face, and what the rest of the family called his cop voice behind his back. It was a neutral, commanding tone that was crystal clear and designed to cut through other people's emotions.

"Yes."

One step closer and Luke had his hand on Rachel's twisted shoulder, which wasn't quite as twisted now that Kell didn't have to grip the steering wheel.

"Kell, you lower your glued hand, very slowly, because–what's your name again?"

"Rachel."

"Rachel here is going to feel some serious blood flow in that hand in a minute. It'll be nothing but pins and needles, but we'll get you standing. Might need to lean against the truck if your feet and knees go weak."

"Okay."

Moving his arm was easy, but poor Rachel's face twisted in pain.

"Hurt that bad?"

"No. I really, really need to pee, and every time I move, it's agony."

A sharp inhale from Luke made them both turn.

"Didn't know that was added to the mix. Got it. Let's get that right foot out carefully, then," Luke said, reaching down to guide her foot as she lifted.

Luke's eyes took in her high-heeled boots, one eyebrow arching, and Kell almost laughed. He knew what his brother was thinking about the utility of those things.

"I can do this," Rachel said. "You don't have to help, Officer Luview."

"If you fall, you'll rip half the skin off my brother's hand, and then who do you think will have to climb trees and help our dad?"

"Oh."

"I may be a public servant, but I'm not *that* altruistic."

With that last word, Rachel slid sideways and got her left leg on the truck's floor, between his, her body pressed hard against his left thigh for just long enough to make her gasp. Friction was a cruel trickster.

Then, in a single jerky step, she was standing on the ground, all her weight off him, their glued-together hands the only parts still touching, his left arm hanging out of the open door.

He felt suddenly cold without her in his lap.

A lap Calamine decided to reclaim.

"Hey there, Cally," Luke said, giving her a nice rub, good enough for the big cat to start a loud purr.

Rachel began shaking her hand, which was still attached to him.

"It really tingles. Ahhhh! I hate this. Don't move!"

"I'm not moving."

"Yes, you are!"

"No," Kell said, staying still, blinking twice for emphasis. "See?"

"You just moved."

He lifted their hands up half a foot. "This is moving, Rachel. I wasn't."

"You jerk! This is killing me!" Her breath inhaled in hitches, and he realized her hand had fallen asleep.

"How're your feet?" Luke asked. "You need to sit down?"

At that moment, Rachel's ankles wobbled, but she squared her jaw and lifted her chin.

"I'm fine, but I need a bathroom desperately. I will not be even more humiliated by peeing in public."

The darkening sky was a beautiful backdrop as Kell climbed out of his truck, Luke at the ready to steady Rachel, and soon, he was standing next to her, Cally in his seat, likely enjoying the residual warmth.

"Let's get you inside and figure that all out," Luke said with an admirably straight face, though Kell knew he was snickering on the inside.

Maybe that's what made him such a good cop. He could hide it.

Kell, however, failed, laughing as they made their way to the hospital's front entrance. They were five steps away when Rachel stopped.

"Could we cover our hands with a jacket or something? This is really embarrassing."

Luke shrugged out of his coat. "Here." He laid it over their hands.

But as the automatic doors slid open, Kell realized:

Walking into the ER glued to a strange woman and a rubber hose was bad enough.

Being escorted in by a cop, with their hands covered by his jacket, made it look like they were handcuffed to each other and in police custody.

Nadine, the admin at the police station and biggest gossip in town, was going to eat this one up. Poor Luke was going to be interrogated like *she* was from the FBI.

"Hey, Kell! What's up? Luke finally arrest you? For what? Pull the wrong poison ivy?" Their cousin, Silver Bilbee, had been an almost-silver towhead all his life, hence the nickname. He cupped his hands over his mouth and whistled. "And who's the hottie?"

Hottie?

Rachel halted and turned to look at Silver.

"Excuse me?"

He whistled again.

"You wish," she called out, stomping with determination toward the front desk, half dragging Kell behind her.

"I *do* wish! That's what the whistle means!" Silver cracked himself up.

A nuclear bomb went off inside Kell, but before he could tell their cousin to cut it out, Rachel snapped back:

"The whistle means you have the social skills of a slug. Good luck dating anyone other than a phone sex operator, one who charges you by the minute, with pickup lines like that!"

Silver slunk away. This conversation would be all over town in minutes, too. Good for Rachel for giving back what was thrown at her, though. The woman he'd known in D.C. would have stammered and blushed, and later come up with the perfect comeback.

Luke gave Kell an arched-eyebrow look that said, *Who the hell is she?*

"That was a lot," Kell said slowly as they waited at the desk.

Rachel nodded. "I know, right? Dude needs to chill. As if catcalling ever got anyone laid."

Luke's composure faltered, a choke turning into an attempted cough as cover.

"I mean, Silver's a jerk, but wow, Rachel. You've got a mouth on you," Kell ventured.

"*I've* got a mouth? What did I say that was inappropriate? *He* was the one being rude!"

"Nothing. That was a compliment. Good for you for standing up for yourself."

"If I don't get to a bathroom *now*, I won't be able to stand up at all, Kell."

"Here." Luke guided them to a single-stall bathroom. "Go ahead."

He lifted the jacket off their hands, all twenty or so people in the waiting room, plus every staff member, watching curiously.

"How?" Rachel hissed. "Kell can't stand outside, it's too far."

"I have to go in there with you."

"This is so gross!"

"Or," Luke said slowly, patiently, like he was talking to a small child, "you can wait until the nurse detaches you, and then you can go."

The distinct splashing of the beautiful floor-to-ceiling waterfall display, part of the hospital's renovation two years ago, came into Kell's consciousness.

Rachel's, too.

She crossed her legs and pulled on their hands. "Fine. You'll just have to turn away."

"I said I'd do this when we were back at the car."

"I didn't think it would come to this, then!"

"And now you've got an audience," he pointed out, unable to suppress a chuckle.

"You said you'd turn away!"

"Not me. Them." He gestured to the waiting room, where literally every pair of eyes was on them.

"Hmph!" she grunted, opening the bathroom door, Kell in tow. As it closed shut, he turned away, then felt his hand graze her belly.

"What are you doing?"

"Unbuttoning my jeans."

This, he hadn't anticipated. His fingers followed hers on the zipper track down, and then:

"Turn around."

"Already am. Don't have to ask twice."

Then... silence.

Might as well check his phone.

Five messages from Allen, three of them asking about a grandfather vine removal job at Oldham's farm.

Two messages from his mom.

And so many notifications from Instagram that he wanted to immediately delete his account. He could only imagine the photos already circulating in town. Hopefully, they got the logo on his truck when they snapped a pic of Rachel riding in his lap.

What was that old phrase? Even bad publicity is good publicity?

He answered Allen, ignored his mom, and got his other texts under control.

More silence.

Awkward silence.

Achingly weird silence.

There were only so many breaths they could take together inside the tiny space before he had to ask.

"I thought you had to go?"

"STOP!!"

"What did I do?"

"I... I can't. It's too embarrassing. It won't–I can't relax enough to pee."

"Then we can wait."

"I can't wait!"

He began making a *pssssssh* sound.

"That isn't helping!"

"I'm closing my eyes and moving to the sink, Rachel." Before he shut his lids, he checked the distance to the faucet. Going on instinct and memory, he found the handle and turned on the water full blast.

Instantly, *he* had to pee.

But he wasn't desperate like her.

"Cover your ears," she demanded.

"What?"

"Cover your ears!"

"I only have one free hand."

"Then cover one ear and start humming."

"Humming?"

"Yes. Then you're less likely to hear."

"I've heard people pee loads of times in my life, Rachel. Your urine isn't special."

"It is to me! This is the first time I've peed in front of someone in ages!"

"That tells me an awful lot about your love life."

"What does *peeing* have to do with sex?" A sharp intake of breath followed that question. "Hold on. You really, *really* don't have to answer that. I do not want to know."

He wasn't taking the bait on that comment.

"When you're in a relationship and you spend the night, sometimes you hear each other pee. Or you share a bathroom."

"Not me!"

"Interesting. High maintenance, huh?"

"I hate that term."

"You hate it because it's true."

"Not wanting to pee in front of other people does not make me high maintenance. And stop talking. You're just stressing me out and I can't pee when I'm tense."

"Then when do you ever pee?"

With that, he covered his ear and began humming, as loudly as possible, the beat to "Uptown Funk."

Complete with a little dancing.

And then he sang the words.

Between the faucet, covering his ear, and singing, he drowned out her nattering, until finally she stopped. He knew it would work, because what Rachel didn't understand about herself was that focusing on her problem was her biggest problem.

Her need for control wouldn't let her let go, even when it was what her body needed.

"Kell? KELL!"

He stopped humming and dropped his hand from his ear.

"Yeah?"

"I'm done."

"Con-grat-u-la-tions!" he said in a sing-songy voice normally reserved for toddlers. "Rachel peed on the potty! Do you want a princess sticker or a pony sticker?"

"You're such a jerk."

"Yeah, but I'm the jerk who helped you."

"You have a funny definition of help." He felt his hand graze her bare flesh again.

"Now what?"

"Pulling up my pants. Have to zip up and button. Sorry."

"No problem."

His hand no longer felt like it was part of him. It was more like a puppet's arm with fingers and flesh. While his mind worked on ignoring the image of what she was doing, the rest of him tried to stay calm and ready to take whatever Luview, Maine's towns-folk were going to throw at him–for a long, long time.

Heaping doses of teasing.

Until the day he died.

"You can turn around now. We have to wash our hands."

"I think that can wait."

"Eww, gross! Now you're the one revealing a lot about yourself. You don't wash your hands after you go to the bathroom?"

"I do. Just not in a situation where you literally can't do it."

"We can put our glued hands under the water, Kell."

"Cleanest radiator hose ever." He ran his free hand through his hair in frustration, sighing through his nose. "Let's get this over with. We'll just go out and—"

Too late. She was already running her left hand under the soap dispenser and covering their connected hands with the white foam.

Fighting it wasn't worth it.

At least his sister wouldn't chide him for being too greasy when she separated them. He knew damn well Colleen would make sure they were her patients. Luke was likely filling her in right now.

Rachel washed with a surgeon's precision. He half expected her to pull out a nail brush and latex gloves. She shook their hands free of droplets and moved to the Dyson hand dryer.

That's when Kell's patience ran out.

Grabbing the door handle, he pulled it hard. Rachel muttered something about her wet hands but she didn't put up more of a fuss. Luke was nowhere to be seen, so Kell walked with Rachel to the intake desk.

Saundra Cooley was there, giving him a wicked grin. Her sister, Melinda, had been his fourth-grade teacher.

"Gotcherself in a sticky situation there, Kell?" she said, clearly pleased with her little joke.

"You know it, Saundra. I'm guessing Colleen's ready for us?"

"Oh, she sure is. Charged her phone and everything."

"Her phone?"

"For pictures."

Kell's Instagram account was about to get tagged to death.

"Who's Colleen?" Rachel asked.

"My sister."

"Your sister's a doctor?"

"She's a nurse."

"Are you related to everyone in town?"

Saundra's brow scrunched a bit.

"We're third cousins, right, Kell? Abram Luview married Adelaide, and they had Alexander, Mortius, Nelson, Helen, and–"

Rachel cut her off.

"That was a rhetorical question. Could you please get us a medical professional to take care of our problem?"

Kell could tell she was seconds away from the officious phrase, "and do your job," which was the fastest way to get anyone in a small town to slow down.

"Insurance card?" she asked Rachel, waving at Kell. "Already got yours on file."

Rachel used her free left hand to reach into her coat pocket and pull out a tiny wallet, awkwardly unsnapping a clasp with her thumb. She slid a card over to Saundra, who inserted it into a card reader and handed it back.

For the next five minutes, Rachel answered a series of standard questions. He learned her birthdate, that she wasn't allergic to any medications or food, her address, and started to wonder if he was eventually going to learn the date of her last menstrual period.

Thankfully, Saundra let them loose before it came to that.

Saundra pointed. "Through those doors, curtain three, left side. Have fun. But I heard you already did. Nice lap dance," she said to Rachel with a big, mocking wink.

Rachel looked like she was about to swallow her own eyeballs.

"I–what–that's–" she sputtered as Kell nudged her to curtain three, left side, where they found his sister waiting.

Phone in hand.

"Wow. Never seen this before," Colleen said, smirking at him.

"I'm sure other people have superglued themselves together."

She pointed at Rachel. "No. I mean her. She's wearing green and blue in early February."

"What's wrong with green and blue?" Rachel looked down at her shirt. "This is Tory Burch."

"It's right before Valentine's Day. In Love You, Maine. If you don't wear red, white, or pink, you get pinched." Colleen's scrubs were pink.

"Like not wearing green on St. Patrick's Day?" Rachel said

with a growl that went straight to Kell's pulse and kicked it like an angry bull.

"Did you do any research about the town, or just fly first class across the country, rent a car, and drive up here with your expense account and your ridiculous shoes so you can swoop in, gentrify us, lie to everyone, and extract whatever value you think you can get before running back to L.A. for lunch?"

Colleen gaped at him.

Rachel's face burned with rage.

They were still attached at the hands, hers warming rapidly, as if fury heated every red blood cell. Her heat surprised him.

And set him vibrating.

Turning to Colleen, she said softly, "Could you please just unstick us while I have a few molecules of dignity intact?"

"I can't promise the dignity part, but absolutely on the glue."

She brought their hands, and of course the radiator hose, to a large wash basin filled with hot soapy water, the heat hitting his skin like a bee sting.

"Ooo!" Rachel gasped, clearly feeling it, too.

"Too hot?" Colleen asked.

"What's in here?" Rachel demanded.

"Water. Soap."

"That's it?"

"Soak in it for a while. It'll soften the glue up. Then we'll use some acetone and that should do the trick."

"See? We didn't need to go to the ER, Rachel. A trip to the drugstore could have covered this." Other than asking if she had a bottle of nail polish remover, he'd never suggested that simpler solution in the first place. He knew better. His nurse sister would have chewed him out.

And here it came...

"No," Colleen corrected him. "You did the right thing. See that cut on her hand?"

Until that moment, he hadn't. Gently, Colleen lifted the radiator hose and it came into view. A long, angry line right where the skin of her pinkie met the hose and wrapped under.

"Ouch," he mumbled.

"Ouch, and in need of some antibiotic cream. Maybe a suture or two. Have to get you two unstuck before I can assess it."

Rachel shot Kell a look that clearly said *I told you so*.

"Sorry," he muttered. "I was wrong."

Colleen gave Rachel a look. "You heard that, right?"

"Yes?"

"Good. I have a witness. Kell Luview finally admitted to being wrong about something."

"Colleen," he said in a low tone of warning.

"Kellan Dean Luview, don't you take that tone with me!"

"Now you just sound like Mom."

"When you do stupid stuff like this, what do you expect? Superglue–really?"

"It was Rachel's fault."

She glanced at Rachel. "That true?"

"Of course not!"

Their hands soaked as the three of them banged this out. A weary tiredness found its way into his bones. If he was this depleted, Rachel must be the walking dead.

The curtain shook suddenly, Luke's red uniform stark in the hospital's fluorescent light. "Hey. How's it going?"

"Peachy keen," Kell informed him, using their dad's phrase. Rachel suddenly looked hollow, Kell's senses going into worried mode. "Can you snag a chair for her?"

"Sure." Luke scooted a chair under her knees and Rachel sagged into place.

"Thank you," she whispered.

"Want a snack? Some water or juice? You don't look good," Colleen said in a compassionate voice, disappearing before Rachel could answer.

"What about me? Am I invisible?" Kell called out to her, seeing her dismissive hand wave back at him. But he knew she'd return with juice and crackers for him, too.

He felt like he was five again.

Living back home did that to him more often than he liked. Joining the family business to help his dad had felt like going backward in time, though he knew that wasn't true. His dad had treated him more like an adult than ever, but Kell had returned from D.C. ready to work hard and avoid conversations. The higher up he was in a tree, the better. Self-preservation there was all about making sure you protected your whole body.

Unlike in D.C., where you were mainly watching out for stabs in the back.

Keenly aware of how raw he was, Kell had thrown himself into all the tough jobs, his dad forcing him to take on young Allen as an apprentice. The kid turned eighteen two days before Kell came home, and now, five years later, he was still green, but at least he didn't puke from vertigo sixty-feet up in a tree.

"Here." Colleen returned with squat little apple juices covered in foil, the kind that felt satisfying to poke through with the thin straw. Kell took them both and did the honors for Rachel, handing it to her with his free hand.

"Dextrous," she muttered, lips curling around the straw.

"Have to be, doing what I do for a living."

"Pulling poison ivy?"

"Doing tree work."

"But your truck..."

Luke and Colleen gave each other looks he didn't like.

"I have my own side business."

"Oh."

"Here." Colleen thrust an opened bag of teddy bear-shaped crackers at him. "Eat. And make sure you brush the crumbs out of your beard this time."

With a grunt, he did as told, surprised by how hungry he was. In under a minute, he'd consumed the juice and the crackers, his hand feeling better from the warm soapy water.

With the snap of a glove, Colleen got to work. He looked at Luke.

"Don't you have kittens to pull out of gutters and old ladies to help across the street?"

He got a gimlet eye in return.

"I broke up a porn network out of the old sugar house on Bondville Road last week. I do way more than you ever imagine, bud."

"If by 'porn network' you mean the three college girls who were running a cam girl operation out of a seasonal cottage, okay, bro. Protect and serve."

"I do need to get home." Luke checked his watch. "Nanny's done in an hour."

"Wait a minute..." Rachel chewed on her last cracker. "Luke! You have a daughter! I remember FaceTiming with you and your wife, back in D.C."

Her eyes cut to Kell. His siblings wore a thousand feelings

across their faces in three seconds, ranging from mourning to intrigue to righteous anger.

That last one was Colleen.

And then Rachel said the worst thing possible.

"How is Amber doing? And Harriet?"

A cold wave of dread washed through him. Luke turned on his heel and left without another word, while Colleen's frown at Rachel was enough to flay skin.

Kell cleared his throat and changed the subject, fast.

"How's it going, Colleen?"

She was using a tiny scalpel to carefully peel Rachel's skin off the plastic hose.

"Pretty close to done. I'll pull out the acetone in a moment. Trying to avoid it because it'll sting on any cuts."

Rachel looked at them both, then toward where Luke had been standing.

"Did I say something offensive?"

"It's fine," Kell said.

"Nope," Colleen said at the same time.

Small towns may be known for gossip, but they're also known for protecting their own, and there was no way he and Colleen were going to talk about what Luke had been going through.

Not with an outsider, and certainly not with the ex-friend who had hurt Kell so badly. Freedom was almost his, and he needed as little entanglement as possible as they finished up.

"Are you sure?" Rachel prodded. "Because that was weird."

Both Luviews went silent.

Mercifully, so did Rachel.

Two minutes later, through the miracle of acetone, Colleen freed them. Kell swore never again to take for granted the ability to make a fist with his left hand.

"Now let's look at that cut on your pinkie," Colleen said to Rachel, her tone a little too professional. Whatever warmth and humor had been there earlier was gone. Rachel wasn't stupid. She noticed, eyes jumping to Kell with questions.

Questions he ignored.

"How bad is it?"

Colleen smiled and let out an odd little laugh. "You're not going to like this."

"It needs stitches? It's broken?"

"Nope." Rummaging through a drawer of medical supplies, Colleen pulled out a small tube.

"What's that?" Rachel asked, suspicious. "Antibiotic cream?"

"No, I already cleaned the wound. This is a cyanoacrylate adhesive."

"Adhesive?"

"Kind of a medical superglue."

Two big groans came from him and Rachel.

"You want to superglue me *again?*"

"I'm going to glue your skin together at the cut, yes. Easier and less painful than sutures."

Rachel stretched, a long one that made her arms go up and wide, her back cracking. "Sorry."

"It's fine. Your muscles are going to ache like crazy tomorrow. The more blood flow the better." Colleen cast him a look. "How about you?"

"I'm fine. I wasn't nearly as twisted as Rachel."

His sister sized them up. "Her right hand, your left. So your right hand could do the gearshift, but her shoulder was twisted back so you could hold the steering wheel. People have been posting pictures of how she straddled you. Now I understand."

"Glad someone does," he muttered.

"Posting pictures?" Rachel gasped.

"Expect to be tagged on Instagram," Colleen said to Kell. "And TikTok."

"Here." Rachel thrust her hand at Colleen. "Do what you must." A long yawn escaped, the kind with a breathy little squeak at the end. "I just want to get to my cottage and sleep for a day. But I have an eleven a.m. meeting."

Colleen got to work, but she looked at Kell. "Meeting?"

"She's here to make a deal with Love You Chocolate."

"Lucinda's selling? No way."

"Apparently Boyce is trying."

"And you work in the chocolate industry?" Colleen asked Rachel.

"Yes. Acquisitions."

"Are you director of acquisitions?"

"Associate director of my division."

"Which is... acquisitions?"

Something about Rachel's face made him groan inside. Here came more condescension.

"It's hard to explain."

"And you get *what* if you convince Lucinda and Boyce to sell out to a bigger company? A promotion?"

"It's not just some bigger company. I work for Markstone's."

Colleen whistled appreciatively. "I love their chocolate Easter eggs!"

"Right?" Rachel showed some actual excitement, for once. "This deal could really elevate your town's stature."

Colleen's eyes narrowed to slits.

"Why would we need to elevate our stature? Something wrong with how we are now?"

Warning bells started dinging in Kell's ears.

Instead of reading the room, Rachel seemed to take Colleen's challenge as a genuine question. "Don't you want more tax revenue? More investment dollars? A facelift? Think about all the potential here!"

A veritable tornado warning siren went off in Kell's head. He was tempted to insert himself physically between his sister and Rachel, because this was about to get ugly.

Rachel brought it on herself, though, even if she was completely oblivious. Someone who claimed to be smart in business should have better soft skills and know when she was offending a townie.

"A facelift." Colleen finished gluing Rachel's hand and stepped back, picking up the wrappings from bandages and stripping off her gloves. "You think my town needs a facelift."

"Hah. Not, you know, a literal facelift."

"Like the kind your mom gets," Kell added, making Rachel smirk.

Something a little unhinged flashed in Colleen's eyes.

"Your mom?"

A big eye roll didn't make matters any better as Rachel said, "I know this sounds weird, but my mom is Portia Starman."

"Your *mom* is Portia?"

"Yes. You know her?" Rachel reared back. "Oh, right. Her reality show. I'll bet lots of you know her, huh? She was here for two months filming that little show she did here." The nervous chatter began, something Kell found remarkably familiar.

Maybe Rachel hadn't changed so much after all.

"Which makes you... Rachel from D.C."

Wow. His sister had a look on her face Kell only saw in those TV news segments about small-town folks who quietly murder their neighbors for leaving the trash bin out for more than eighteen hours.

"Um, no. I'm from L.A."

As fun as it was watching Colleen lose her mind as she dealt with Rachel's unintentional insults and put all the puzzle pieces together, Kell was tired. Calamine was still in his truck and probably close to turning it into a litter box, and Allen was blowing up his phone with questions about the job at Oldham's farm and the storm.

"You're Rachel from Kell's days in D.C., I mean. *That* Rachel."

Contempt dripped from Colleen's words.

"If you mean we were coworkers at EEC, then yes." Rachel's tone started to match Colleen's. Neither of these women was about to back down before the other.

"Right. You're the one who schemed with Kell's girlfriend to screw over our Uncle Ted–"

"Time to go! Thanks, Colleen!" Kell said quickly, knowing he had seconds before his sister erupted.

Inertia meant that an object at rest stayed at rest, but Kell also knew that he could just pick up said object, if need be. Rachel was significantly smaller than he was–especially now versus five years ago. Luckily, another nurse came over to Colleen, mentioning something about an impacted colon, interrupting the brewing argument.

"What was that about?" Rachel groused as she hurried to keep up with him as he spirited them out of the hospital. "What did you tell her about what happened in D.C.?"

"The truth."

They were halfway to his truck, in the parking lot, when she halted.

"Clearly not."

"Look," he said, taking her elbow, which she shrugged off. He tightened his grip enough to make her pay attention. As she looked up at him, Rachel's brown eyes were filled with righteous fury, as if she were somehow the wronged party here.

He was having none of it.

"You do not come marching into my town, treat my people to your sneering little insults, think you're going to gentrify us with some corporate deal, berate me, and grill my poor brother about his private life. You are a transient who is here for a few days to do who knows what, but you're going about it all the wrong way."

She opened her mouth to reply, but yawned instead.

A long sigh stretching back five years poured out of him.

"Get in the damn car, Rachel."

His phone buzzed. More texts from Allen, and one from Luke:

Storm's picking up. Deke can't make it to Rachel's car in time. I'll help you get it in the morning. Deke'll drop a part off at the tavern for you to try yourself in the a.m.

"Luke says he'll help get your car tomorrow. I'll take you to your rental now."

"Thank you," she said shortly. "And please bill me for your time."

"Bill you?"

"You wouldn't take my cash earlier. You're a professional tree guy. Or a poison ivy puller. Whatever you do, you've lost half a day helping me. I have an expense account. Write this up as auto repair or towing or something. Whatever you would charge a client."

"I'm not billing you for helping out another human being."

"Oh, yes, you are. Because there's no way I'm going to owe someone who won't even listen to the truth about who I am. You don't get the moral high ground on this one, Kell."

Her voice shook as she walked around the truck, yanked open the passenger door, and climbed in, shooing Calamine, who just looked at her.

"Don't you dare," Rachel said, pointing a finger in Calamine's face. "I've had it."

The cat, who never listened to anyone but Kell, stood up and leaped onto the console. Rachel settled in and clicked her seatbelt in place. Calamine calmly resumed her spot on the passenger seat, this time in Rachel's lap.

A truce.

Rachel's uninjured hand sank into the soft orange fur as Kell took in the scene, every square inch of his skin buzzing.

"What's the address for your rental?" he barked at her as he gunned the engine and pulled out of the parking lot.

She gave it to him.

He nearly choked.

"Kenny's? You're staying at *Kenny Bilbee's*?"

"Let me guess. Another one of your cousins?"

"Yes."

"Whatever. He must own the inn."

"*Inn?*" If Rachel thought Kenny owned an inn, this was about to get even more interesting.

"Just get me there in one piece, and not attached to anything, and we'll call this day over."

"Deal."

With that, he drove toward his cousin's house, suppressing an evil grin.

Because unlike Rachel, he knew what she was about to face.

And he couldn't wait to watch her as it all unfolded.

Chapter Five

RACHEL

Long driveways were a country thing, Rachel knew. Lots of people had them, so she tempered her excitement as Kell pulled the truck down the already plowed, winding way.

In L.A., anyone with a driveway this long had more money than sense, and a nine-digit blockbuster under their belt.

Here? As Kell pulled up to the modest farmhouse with a slightly crooked porch and wood piles everywhere, she realized how different her life really was from the residents of Luview, Maine.

"This is, um, quaint!" she said, dredging up as much enthusiasm as she could. The snow was making it hard to see anything.

"That's Kenny's house. Your rental's around back."

"Oh! He has a guest cottage at his inn? Or is it a cute little apartment attached to the main house?"

A sharp look greeted her. Was that a smirk? It was hard to tell under the beard. "You have the reservations your assistant gave you, right?"

"Of course." She wiggled her phone. "The information is all here. One bedroom, one bath. She said rentals were tight because of the time of year."

"Yeah. Tight. One bedroom, one bath, huh?"

"Although I did tell her to book me at an inn, with a honeymoon package, so now I'm confused."

The headlights flashed on a small structure, about three hundred feet behind the main house. It looked like a shack. As they drove closer, Rachel frowned.

Hard.

Because Kell was stopping in front of it.

"What is that? A tool shed?"

His shoulders began to shake a little, then a small, strained laugh came out of him. "That's your guest cottage, Rachel. At your *inn*."

"What?" It looked like something people pulled behind a big truck, loaded with motorcycles. "That's not a cottage!"

"No. It's a trailer."

"A trailer! There's been a mistake! Dani booked a suite at an inn, or a cottage!"

"Did she *say* she booked a suite? Or a cottage?"

"She said–she said it was a one bedroom, one bath place."

"Well, it is. That's a nineteen-foot RV trailer you've got there. Kenny rents it out to make extra money during crunch times in town."

"Crunch times?"

An aggravated sigh filled the truck's cab. "It's the beginning of February, Rachel. Luview turns into a circus around Valentine's Day. You were lucky to get this. Your only other option at this point is the bunkhouse above Bilbee's Tavern, and that's mostly filled with drunken frat boys here to hook up. One big, open room with ten bunk beds, doubles on the bottom, singles on top. You have to win at beer pong to get one of the doubles."

"But–I can't stay in that! Where's the bathroom?"

"It's in there."

"And the kitchen?"

"In there, too. Haven't you ever gone camping?"

"No!"

"Wait. That was a rhetorical question. You've never gone camping?"

A yawn was all she could reply with.

"I've been awake for nearly thirty-six hours straight. My car broke down, I got rescued by a guy who lied to me about his identity, I was nearly attacked by wild animals, got superglued to another person, had to ride like a trussed turkey in your lap in front of half the town, dealt with this crazy bobcat pet thing of yours–"

Calamine arched her back and leaped out of Rachel's lap, into the backseat.

"–and now you're telling me I have to spend three nights in *that?*"

"Three nights? You're here for *three nights?*"

"Maybe more if this doesn't wrap up fast."

"Then let's get you settled in. Got your suitcase?"

"You didn't grab it?"

"Why would I grab it? You didn't want your precious Louis Vuitton in the open air of my pickup bed, remember?"

"Because–because..."

No longer able to muster anger, outrage, disgust, or any emotion other than sheer exhaustion, Rachel finally burst into tears.

"I cannot believe that this is ha–ha–happening. I took this stupid assignment because my boss said my connections to the town through my stupid mother's reality show would help persuade the owners to sell. Instead, my stupid rental car breaks down on a stupid logging road and you show up and lie to me about who you are, except maybe you didn't lie, because you're nothing like the Kell Luview I knew back in D.C.!"

"Rachel, please don't cry." Actual caring, real and tender, filled his expression. All it did was make her miss him even more.

And trigger a whole new layer of anger.

"AND THEN! You kept insulting me, over and over, but the pièce de résistance was when you superglued us together–"

"Me? I didn't do that! You did!"

"–and you made me straddle you–"

"Whoa! That was physics! Not me!"

" –and you have a stupid pet bobcat you didn't warn me about –"

"HEY! Now you've gone too far, insulting my cat!"

"–and I'm here to broker a deal in a place where you've already poisoned everyone against me! How can I accomplish this?"

"I poisoned everyone?"

"You poisoned your sister."

"I told my sister the truth about what happened in D.C."

"DID IT EVER OCCUR TO YOU THAT YOUR TRUTH IS WRONG?"

Calamine skedaddled onto the top of the seat back and glared at Kell. Good. She had an ally.

He did a double take. "What, Cally? You're taking her side?"

All he got in response was a good view of the cat's butthole.

"Your cat listens better than you do, Kell. Now," she said, mustering the tiny iron filings of pride she had left. "Bill me for your time. Markstone's will pay you. I'm going into my... *cottage*. I'll figure out how to get my car on my own."

"*My* truth? There isn't a 'my truth', Rachel. There's *the* truth."

Ignoring him, she grabbed her purse and climbed out of the car, holding the door open and leaning back in.

"Then here's *the* truth, Kell: You've become a jerk. But thank you for all your help, in spite of your jerkness."

One enormous slam and she was done.

Crying, she made her way to the trailer's door, which was covered by a small awning. A sign taped next to the door read, "Unlocked! Come right on in."

No way. She definitely wasn't in L.A.

Dinky little metal steps were slippery under her soles, the treads not deep enough to put anything but the ball of her foot on them. A turn of the handle and she felt warmth, then fumbled for a light switch.

As she flicked it on, she saw Kell put the truck in reverse. The snow was starting to fly fast.

A scent of pine air freshener hit her square in the face.

The overhead light was fluorescent, and if she stretched her arms out, she could practically touch both the edge of the bunk bed and the far wall. To her left was a double bed below a single bunk, thick down comforters on both. A tall door was to the right of the bed, then a narrower door. Maybe a closet?

Straight ahead was a small refrigerator, an oven, and a cooktop, with various things set out on the tiny counter. Above the mini range was a microwave. To the right, a little round table and a booth area that couldn't fit more than three people.

"*Cottage?*" she screamed. "COTTAGE??"

A note on the table said, in big, bold capital letters: WELCOME TO LUVIEW! WE 'LOVE YOU' BEING HERE!

She whimpered.

Right next to the note, which explained where to find the key, the Wi-Fi password, and garbage and recycling policies (*What was a trash panda?*), she found an overflowing bowl of red foil-wrapped chocolate hearts.

On the note, Kenny had written with a red Sharpie:

"Some hearts for Rachel HART! Get it? Hope you like the place. Sorry in advance about Randy."

That made her cry even harder.

Who was Randy?

Without thinking, she unwrapped a chocolate heart and popped it in her mouth.

And moaned.

Love You Chocolate tasted so much better than Markstone's. Night and day difference, really. As the milk chocolate melted on her tongue, she was torn. Binge the entire bowl or crawl into bed?

If that thing to her left could be called a bed. It looked more like a sheet of plywood with a piece of foam and a comforter on it.

She'd seen better sleeping arrangements in the homeless shelter she visited with her mom, when her mother was doing a PSA commercial for the organization.

Gingham curtains—white and red, of course—covered every window, but as the wind began to pick up, she noticed a weird crackling sound. It came from the windows. Peeking under the curtains revealed the strangest sight: clear plastic covering each window, taped around the edges.

Why would you ruin the view with plastic? And how did you get fresh air?

Picking up the note and another chocolate, she put her priorities in place.

First, eat about five more of these yummy treats.

Second, hydrate.

In the kitchenette, a pitcher of filtered water rested next to the sink. Within two seconds, she found red plastic tumblers. After she gulped down a glass of water, she returned to her priority list.

Third, call her assistant and scream at her.

Catharsis was important. And get Dani to find a better place.

Fourth, work.

Thankfully, her laptop and charger were in her bag, even if nothing else was. She'd have to sleep in her clothes, then find a way back to her car to get her suit for her eleven o'clock meeting.

The idea of spending one more second with Kell had been too much to bear when he dropped her off here, but now she regretted turning him away. He could have been useful in getting her luggage from her rental car.

She'd just call an Uber in the morning.

Hmm. Maybe she should schedule it now.

Pulling out her phone, she followed Kenny's instructions and to her utter surprise, the wireless network was flawless. Within five minutes, she was fully connected and ready to work on priority number three: screaming at her assistant.

But first things first. That Uber.

The app showed... nothing. No cars.

That couldn't be right.

She checked again, carefully typing in the address of...

Oh. Right. Her car wasn't at an address. What was she going to say? The intersection of State Route 33 and where the screaming women lived in the woods?

Time to move on.

A phone call was better for conveying how angry she was, but a text would get her out of this mess faster. Luckily, it was three hours earlier in California.

Dani, she typed. *You booked me into a trailer! An actual trailer in someone's backyard. I am in the equivalent of a chicken coop. Fix this. I need a new place NOW and an Uber to get there.*

Hitting *Send* wasn't as cathartic as she'd hoped. An email needed to go out as well. Opening her laptop, she found 176 new emails waiting for her.

Of those, 122 were probably passive-aggressive cc's, designed to help other people at Markstone's cover their butts.

Pulling up her original reservation, she read Dani's email chain, where it quickly became evident that...

Shoot.

Dani *had* warned her about the trailer. Rachel just hadn't replied to the emails.

This was her own fault. She had no one to blame but herself.

Backing out of that one, she scanned the subject lines of everything else, categorizing and labeling them. A triage of sorts.

Another chocolate.

Two more yawns.

Then an email from her dad titled, *Tim's in!*

Oh, goody. This meant Tim had done something so note-worthy, Dad had to shove it in everyone's face.

"Not opening that right now," she muttered to herself, because she wasn't a masochist.

What was she supposed to say back? *Yay, Tim! Let me tell you about my success today, Dad. I didn't pee on a guy's lap! Go, me!*

Her phone buzzed with a text.

Dani replied: *Per my last email, I warned you.*

Oh, no.

No, she didn't.

Her assistant did not just *per-my-last-email* Rachel. That was like waving your middle finger in someone's face virtually.

I am in a trailer in backwoods Maine, in a snowstorm! This is unacceptable.

Dani: *It was literally the only place available within a forty-five-minute drive. I offered you a spot at Nordicbeth resorts, complete with hot tubs and a spa, but you said you didn't want to drive that far on snowy roads, so...*

That "so..." did her in.

Did her in because Rachel knew this was really her own fault, damn it.

Did you call around?

Dani: *Of course. It was either the trailer or some weird option above a bar. Want me to call there and get you a bed in something they call a bunkhouse? The dude I spoke with said you got a free continental breakfast, foam earplugs, and as much Advil as you wanted out of the bottle in the communal bathroom shared by up to twenty people.*

Rachel shuddered.

Get me something else for tomorrow.

Dani: *There is nothing else. You want Nordicbeth, in spite of the long drive? They still have rooms. There's a package that includes Champagne, a free couples massage, and an in-room hot tub.*

Kell's description of black ice on the roads floated through her memory.

Rachel stared glumly at the bowl of candy before her.

Walking over to the fridge, she opened it. A bottle of something called Moxie was in there, with a red bow on it. A tiny Post-it note said, *Have some Moxie! Anything in the fridge is for you to enjoy.*

Her eyes drifted down to the next rack. A heart-shaped loaf of what looked like homemade bread, a red ribbon tied around the clasp. A small heart-shaped container of local butter. A quart of milk, in an old-fashioned glass bottle with a red top.

And a heart logo on the glass.

At least she wouldn't starve, but this was nothing but fat and carbs.

On the counter, she saw a tiny maple leaf jar with syrup in it, and a bowl of apples. Mainers sure loved their sweets, huh?

The amenities here are amazing, she texted back. *Maple syrup, some kind of soda called Moxie, and all the chocolate hearts I can stuff in my face.*

Dani: *Sounds like trailer life isn't so bad.*

Then come trade places with me, Rachel double thumbed back.

Anything else? Dani asked. *Because I am late for my manicure. Now you're just rubbing it in.*

All she got back was a smiley face.

Rachel was in the wrong and she knew it. Unlike lots of other bosses at Markstone's, she wasn't a witch with a capital B. If Dani really had screwed this up and hadn't told her, Rachel would be angrier, but there was no one to blame but herself.

And Kell, of course. There had to be a way to make some of this his fault.

A little sick from too much chocolate and not enough real food, she grabbed an apple and washed it in the sink, surprised when the hot water came out actually hot. The trailer was fairly comfortable, as intolerable places went, and as she took a bite of the apple, she looked around. Using her left hand–to preserve her injured right one–made eating a bit awkward, but she managed.

A dial thermostat on the wall didn't show numbers, but was set at the midway point on an arc, with another note taped to the wall that showed how to adjust the heat. She pushed it as far as it went to warm up.

A pacer when she was nervous, Rachel discovered quickly that the journey across the trailer took five steps.

Five.

"This project better be really, really worth it," she hissed to herself, taking another bite of the nice, sweet apple. A satisfying crunch resonated in her head, grounding her.

At least she had a bed. A warm place. Something to eat.

And she wasn't literally stuck to Kell Luview.

Skitt skitt skitt

Jerking her head up, she stared at the ceiling. It sounded like a thousand spiders dancing on the roof of the trailer.

Skitt skitt skitt

Standing stock still, she tilted her head, listening.

Skitt skitt skitt

"What *is* that?" Terrified, she waited, a strange whistling coming from the direction of the door.

Slowly, with bone-chilling dread, it occurred to her that she was alone, with no car, no luggage of any kind, only a laptop, phone, and a purse, and she was in some random dude's back yard, in a trailer any determined bad guy could break into with a single kick.

In other words, she was a prime victim.

Living in major cities her entire life had given her street smarts, a certain kind of knowledge about protecting herself. Following a set of mostly unspoken rules, she avoided trouble by rarely walking anywhere alone, always being aware of her surroundings, and staying hypervigilant.

Rural skills, though? In that area, she had nothing. Zero. Zip. Nada.

She was a sitting duck.

Skitt skitt skitt

Or a sitting... whatever that sound was.

The whistle again caught her attention. Breaking out of her frozen terror, she scanned the room for weapons. What was she going to do? Throw an apple at an attacker?

Pulling out her phone, she texted Dani again.

Text not sent appeared in tiny red letters on the screen.

What?

She tried again.

Text not sent

She checked her signal.

No signal.

The piece of paper with Kenny's instructions had the wireless password on it, so she typed again.

Nothing.

Then she noticed a heading on the information sheet:

WHAT TO DO IF YOU LOSE INTERNET

Okay, there was an answer. She read on:

We live in the boonies and sometimes during storms we lose internet, or even power. If that happens, don't worry! Internet I can't fix fast, but power I can. Wait ten seconds. A generator will kick in, and you'll have electric and heat again. We've got you covered! In the event of a serious emergency, put on your boots and walk up to the house, where we have a nice set of woodstoves and everything you need. Don't want any reason for you to leave less than a 5-star review!

Oh, no.

No no no.

Now she had no internet, and might lose power?

Put on her boots? With *her* boots, she might as well go barefoot.

Skitt skitt skitt

The creepy sound, combined with the note, made her march the two whole steps to her door and peer out. The ground was white, and it was snowing sideways. How could snow fall sideways? Had she tipped over?

Rachel opened the door and looked out, the wind absolutely howling, her face immediately covered in flakes. If she weren't so tired, so cold, her right hand throbbing from being glued, unglued, then glued back together, she'd find it, well...

Beautiful.

Until a little furry face dropped down from above and attacked the edge of the door.

"AAAAIIIIEEEEEEEEE!" Rachel shrieked, leaping out of the trailer, her boots hitting the ground, knees buckling as she pitched forward into what felt like a giant vat of icy-cold cotton. She felt like she was back in gymnastics when she was nine and fell off the balance beam after a flip, crashing into a trash can as the janitor walked by, the contents spilling on her.

"Trashcan Rachel" had been a miserable nickname. Her mother transferred her within a week to a new gym.

Jumping up, she looked around. No one was near, and no

one saw. At least the physical horror wouldn't be compounded by social mortification.

The trailer door slammed shut and she jumped to her feet, batting away at the snow.

What was that thing?

And where did it go?

With the lights on inside, the trailer glowed, quaint and cute in a folksy kind of way.

OOOOOOOWWWWWOOOOOOOO!

Something in the distance howled.

She jumped back up the little stairs, opened the door, and quickly shut it again, breathing hard against the back of the door.

Skitt skitt skitt

Except this time, the sound was louder.

And coming from inside the trailer.

"This is not real. None of this is real. I'm hallucinating. I'm actually at the Nordicbeth spa, getting a lovely Swedish massage with cupping, and I've entered a state of altered consciousness. This is just some limbic system purge, working to rid my body of–"

A furry face watched her from the top bunk as she lurched toward the only human-sized door in the trailer, where she assumed the bathroom was. She flung herself inside.

It was the size of an upright coffin.

Fitting. Because she was about to die there.

On the spot.

What kind of cruel trick was this place? Peeking out, she saw the evil little beast, standing on its hind legs, looking right back at her. Brain working overtime in its overwrought state, she finally pattern matched and realized...

"SQUIRREL!" she shouted.

The thing flew–*flew!*–off the top bunk, onto the little dining table, and stared at her.

"Don't you dare touch my chocolates!" she yelled at it.

The thing put one tiny little paw on the edge of the bowl, as if taunting her.

Per your last email, that little face said, beady eyes going narrow.

Slamming the door shut again, she looked around. Aha! A

toilet brush! Grasping it like a sword, she lifted it high above her head.

And charged.

"I. Cast. Thee. Out. Satan!" she screamed as she ran to the main door, flung it open, and waved the toilet brush at the creature, who grabbed a red foil heart and did exactly as told.

The thing disappeared into the snow, and Rachel shut the door.

"I give up!" she shouted, tossing the toilet brush into the kitchen sink, then throwing her body face first on the double bed. Grabbing the edges of the comforter, she rolled herself up like a burrito and stared at the underside of the top bunk–too stunned to cry, laugh, be angry, or feel anything–until all she knew was darkness.

And *skitt skitt skitt*.

* * *

Steam rose above the heavenly water as she closed her eyes and tipped up, letting snowflakes dot her cheeks and eyelashes, the startling incongruity between the brisk cold and the water's hot pleasure making her smile even more. Floating, floating, at rest and embraced by the buoyant calm, she settled into it, grateful for the balm.

As the water rocked her gently, she turned toward the sound of someone moving through it, her eyes fluttering open to find him smiling at her, bare chested, hair cut short again, beard neat and perfect.

"Kell," she moaned, the water rocking her more, his arms reaching out for her, broad shoulders dripping with steaming heat, gray eyes going dark with smoky promises of seduction and ecstasy.

The rocking intensified and she moaned, her teeth biting the soft cotton of her pillow, the painful push of her injured hand into a hard surface making her sit up.

It was a dream.

All a dream.

Except for the rocking.

And why was she having sex dreams about Kell? Goodness, no. He absolutely wasn't her type. The Kell she knew back in D.C.? Definitely.

This version of him?

Never.

Grumpy lumberjacks with never-wrong complexes were the type of guy she ran screaming *from*.

And lately, there hadn't been *any* guys. Not since Nico ran off with her wildfire and earthquake cash. If she was a success in business, she was a miserable failure at dating, and–

Her train of thought was destroyed by a particularly hard jolt of the trailer. Then it began to rock fast, like it was vibrating.

"EARTHQUAKE!" she screamed, shocked that this was happening here in Maine. Snow? Sure. New England was known for it. Tectonic plates rubbing against each other, though, was supposed to be a once-every-thousand-years thing here.

Or something like that.

Given the last twenty-four hours, maybe her luck really was *that* bad.

Rolled up like a mummy, she carefully turned over, working to free herself as the trailer continued to rock, the latest jolt sending her onto the floor, her unharmed left hand barely able to stop her from crashing her head on the trailer's floor. She realized it was dawn, faint light filtering in through the weird plastic on the windows and the red and white cotton curtains. That pine scent she'd smelled last night hit her hard.

As Rachel struggled to her feet, she grabbed the top bunk edge for support. This really felt like an earthquake back home. Eyes jumping to the closet and cabinet doors, she wondered how tightly latched they were.

"HELLO?" she called out.

The rocking stopped.

Then resumed at a faster pace.

Two steps and she was at the door, not falling for the trick of opening it again. That damn squirrel could be crouched outside, waiting for another chance to steal a chocolate.

Or her soul.

She looked for the bowl, which was slowly edging its way toward the end of the table. Rachel grabbed it just before it tumbled off.

These chocolate hearts were quickly becoming her emotional support objects.

Peering out the tiny glass window in the door, she saw

nothing but white. No sirens were blaring, and no one was coming to check on her. People who rented their places out were normally good hosts.

Who doesn't check on guests in an earthquake?

She was definitely cutting off some stars in her review for this obvious failure.

"WHUUUUUUUUH!"

The low, moaning sound came from the direction of the bathroom, but it was clearly outside. A distinctly loud animal grunt followed, with deep scraping noises on the side of the trailer.

This wasn't an earthquake. The trailer was being attacked by Godzilla.

"HELP!" she screamed.

The rocking began again.

Sliding the little window open, she pressed her face up to the screen and shouted, "SOMEONE? HELP!"

More rocking and grunting.

Her phone was about to fall off the table, so she grabbed it, balancing the bowl of chocolates on her hip. A quick look told her it was five fifty-two a.m.

So much for a good night's sleep.

"WHHHHUUUUUUUUH!"

Bears didn't sound like that, she knew, because she'd watched so many nature shows on the Discovery Channel with her brother when they were kids. Whatever was rocking the trailer was something else.

"Godzilla," she whispered, wishing for cellphone bars or internet, crying out in frustration when she saw none.

With her bladder screaming, she made her way to the toilet, trying to sit on it without sliding off. The rocking did nothing for her shy bladder, but while trying–and failing–to pee, she looked up at the small window facing the source of the rocking.

She stood and pulled up her pants, then reached up and slid the little window open. She was face to face with an enormous eyeball.

"AAAIIIEEEEE!"

"WHHUUUUUUUUH!"

Ever faster, the rocking intensified, until Rachel came up with a plan. Working her way back to the kitchen, she found the toilet brush in the kitchen sink, and returned to the bathroom. The eyeball was still in the window.

Brandishing the brush, she thrust.

A choking sound came out of the creature, but the rocking mercifully stopped, followed by loud whuffing noises.

Breathing heavily, Rachel shut the little window, yanked down her jeans, and promptly peed.

A lot.

Because Godzilla may have attacked her little shack, but she'd triumphed, and to the victor belong the spoils.

She'd take her winnings however she could get them.

The trailer rocked once, then again, very lightly. The whuffing sounds faded slowly, and Rachel assumed the creature had backed off in defeat.

Rachel, 1. Godzilla, 0.

In her mind, Rachel composed an email:

Hey, Dad. Congrats for whatever new achievement Tim made, but let me tell you how I defeated Godzilla with a toilet brush.

Those were the last words her brain could form before she crawled back into bed, covered her head with the comforter, and prayed for another Kell sex dream.

Because it was far less surreal than real life.

And way more appealing.

Chapter Six

KELL

The apartment over Bilbee's tavern, up and around back from the bunkhouse, wasn't fancy, but it was his and his alone. He didn't have to live at home and deal with feeling like he was fifteen again and being smothered by his mother.

Besides, he was twenty-eight years old, worked full-time for his dad, had his own side business, and made a good living. Paying for solitude was worth it.

Freshly showered, he was working on his second cup of coffee and buttoning up a clean flannel shirt over black silk long johns, munching a piece of cheese. Last night's Nor'easter had left about eight inches, a little less than expected, but the wind had been killer. Drifts would be everywhere, and he wondered what the roads were like. There'd be plenty of folks stranded out there, and loads of tree limbs down.

As the clock rolled over to six a.m., he looked outside. Luke was ready for him, the exhaust of the pink police car sending off ribbons of white into the air. Instead of his personal Jeep, he'd brought the cruiser.

Guess this qualified as official business for Luke.

Kell had secured a new radiator hose after leaving the hospital, Deke kind enough to drop one off at the tavern. Rachel hadn't realized she'd left the keys with him. If Luke got him up to the rental car and he fixed it well enough, he could return it to Rachel this morning and be done with her.

For good.

Three nights in town, huh? He could avoid her for three more days. Plenty to do with the big Valentine's Day festival coming up, anyhow. Busier than usual, these two weeks before the big day were an endless stream of jobs and tasks. No such thing as a weekend in this town this time of year. Everyone worked from dawn to dusk and beyond.

Then the big rest began on the fifteenth.

His phone buzzed with a text.

You awake? I'm here.

Luke's text made him chuckle.

How could I miss you? You drive a Pepto-Bismol bottle with lights on it.

He got a crude emoji in response.

Shrugging into his coat, Kell grabbed a freshly washed apple and wedged it between his teeth, giving Calamine a quick look before heading out. She was snuggled up on the big upholstered footstool Kell had long ago given up on as a footrest.

Catrest was more like it.

"Cally?" he asked.

She opened one eye, closed it slowly, and did not move.

A wave of brisk wind hit him full in the face as he pulled the flaps down on his hat, walking carefully down the flight of stairs. His one-bedroom apartment was a funny little place, directly above the tavern's office, and right next to the loft storeroom. No wall came into contact with the bunkhouse or the bar itself, which suited Kell just fine.

Quieter that way.

The strange use of space meant he had an enormous living room and a bedroom just big enough for a king bed, a dresser, and a nightstand. He'd turned one corner of the living room into an office of sorts, if by "office" you meant a battered old desk, a cantankerous swivel chair, and piles of unorganized paperwork.

With a bunch of random pens in a Love You Coffee mug.

The police car was nice and toasty as he climbed in, his brother dressed head to toe in red, including his hat, which rested on the console near the police radio.

"Hey."

"Hey."

Luke backed out of the parking spot, and that's all they said for the next five miles.

But his brother couldn't help himself, finally deciding to use his cop skills to interrogate.

"You gonna tell me what yesterday was all about?"

"Nothing more to tell. You saw enough to get the big picture."

"Pretend I'm Harriet. Tell me a story, Uncle Kell."

"Shut up."

"Rachel, huh? I do remember her. That FaceTime. She talked to... us." He meant Amber, and talking about Amber hurt Luke more than anything in the world.

As you would expect.

"Yep."

"So she's back in your life?"

He bristled at the words. "Not by my choice."

"Lucinda and Boyce are selling out, huh? Does Tom know?"

"I assume so. I don't think he'll be surprised. He's the town manager–he knows lots of businesses change hands."

"No. Lots of businesses close or go out of business, Kell. Not sell out to huge companies."

"Don't know much about how Tom works. Why don't you ask him? You work with him more than I do."

"Now you're just going all grumpy quiet on me."

"I learned it from the best, bro."

"Kell. Man. You *glued* yourself to her."

"*She* glued herself to *me*."

"And you had to go in the bathroom with her."

"I saw nothing!"

"That was weird. Admit it."

"Of course it was weird! Did I say it wasn't?"

"I always thought she was the one you were really interested in. Not Alissa."

And there it was. Luke's whole point.

Kell sighed through his nose, but said nothing, mentally calculating the distance.

About four levels of probing inquiry.

A full-body strip search would be easier than this.

"I don't give you the third degree about your feelings, Luke. Drop it."

"You came home from D.C. like a lovesick puppy who got abandoned by the side of the road. Took you close to a year to seem normal again. We used to point to pictures of Grumpy Cat when Harriet was a toddler and she'd shout, 'Uncle Kell!'. Rachel was part of that."

"Not talking about this."

"Fine. Then let's talk about why she's here. Why *is* she here?"

"To get Lucinda to sell Love You Chocolate to Markstone's."

"And what'll that mean for the town?"

"She says thirty to forty new full-time jobs with benefits."

"So they'll expand the factory?"

"I guess."

"Where? Space is tight downtown."

"No clue."

"That means new development."

"Okay."

"Someone's got to sell them some land if there's going to be a new factory."

"Do I look like the director of development for Luview, Luke?"

"We don't have one, remember? He quit."

"Right. He wasn't here long, was he?"

"Nope. Didn't like all the resistance to his ideas."

"You think Rachel's going to experience resistance?"

"If selling Love You Chocolate means building new structures on the land near town, you bet."

"Then maybe Lucinda won't sell. I don't care, Luke. Why should I care? I just want her gone."

"Why?"

"Because she reminds me of my old life."

"Lots of things remind us of our pasts. We don't want them all to go away."

"I do with this one. She... she reminds me of how naïve I was."

"I thought you guys were friends. You watched that Nordic murder show crap together."

"It's not crap."

"You know what I mean."

"Yeah. We did. It's part of why this is so…" He made a face.

"Hard?"

"Complicated."

"Old feelings coming back?"

"How would you feel if someone you liked a long time ago came back out of nowhere and you couldn't escape her?"

Luke snorted. "Fat chance of that ever happening to me." His face fell. "Besides, Amber and I started dating in high school. The only person who fits that description is…"

"Kylie Hood," Kell said, enjoying turning the tables, bringing back memories of the first girl Luke kissed.

"No way *she's* coming back to Luview."

"How do you know?"

"I don't. You're just bringing this up to deflect."

"Worked, didn't it?"

"Mom's going to hear about this."

Kell patted his phone. "Already been texting like crazy."

"And?"

"And I'm ignoring her."

"Is that why she wouldn't leave me alone last night?"

"Probably."

"You just turned your phone off and didn't answer?"

"Uh huh."

"Must be nice."

"It is."

"Cops can't do that. I have to be available just in case. And parents can't do that, either."

The word *single* wasn't part of Luke's comment, but Kell felt it. Last thing in the world Luke ever expected was to be raising his child on his own. Not that he didn't have help; their mom and dad rose to the occasion, and Colleen and Kell took shifts every week.

Being here to watch Harriet grow had been the one positive about coming back home five years ago.

And it really had meant the world to him.

As they got out of town and onto Route 33, Kell was impressed by how clear the roads were. The sun crept up and gave a dazzling shine to the day, making everything look picture perfect. Half an inch of snow clung to every tree branch, and the piles on the roadside meant the elementary school's sledding hill would be popular after school. Fortunately, the snow had fallen early enough for the plows to clear all the bus routes.

Or unfortunately, if you were a kid who just wanted to sled all day.

"Harriet okay with Nicole?" Luke had recently hired a nanny.

"Yeah."

"How's that working out?"

"Eh. Nicole's good with her. Terrible at doing the 'light housekeeping' part of the job."

"No surprise. She's eighteen. Just out of high school."

"Sure. And I hate asking over and over. Mom's offered to come and train her."

"Train her to what? Pick up toys? Come on, Luke. You're a cop. You enforce boundaries for a living. Make your nanny do what she's supposed to do."

"I know." He let out a long sigh. "It's just one more thing I have to deal with that I shouldn't have to deal with, so I don't. Only so much energy, you know?"

"Yep."

So far, no stranded drivers, which was unusual. When they reached the logging road, Kell braced himself to grab a shovel from the trunk and dig their way up the hill, but he was pleasantly surprised to find it was plowed, right up to the rental car.

"You did this?"

"Got the road crew to do it. Figured it saves us some aching backs."

"Maybe your stupid job is good for something, Luke."

"I'm so glad to have your approval, bro. Been desperate for it my whole life."

Leaving that one out to hang, Kell climbed out and took in a deep breath, loving the scent of fresh snowfall. It never got old.

Unlike his brother's cracks.

Kell unlocked Rachel's car and pointed to the back seat. "If we can't get it started, I'll need to move all that into your car and bring it to her. She has a meeting with Lucinda and Boyce at eleven."

"No problem. I think you can fix this, though."

Under the hood, Kell clamped the new hose in place in under

five minutes, the way it should have gone yesterday. He topped off the antifreeze, just in case.

A glop of superglue on a piece of the frame made him chuckle and flex his left hand. It ached like hell, but his injury was nothing compared to poor Rachel.

A pang of emotion hit his heart, surprising him. In the frenzy of yesterday's fiasco, he had worried about her, but now he wondered how she was, his own pain eliciting a connection to her that wasn't fading with time.

Not one bit.

"Allen's loading my truck up with twelve rolls of duct tape as we speak," he said, lowering the hood. He climbed into the driver's side and started the car right up. It smelled lightly of Rachel's perfume and strongly of pineapple air freshener.

Leaving it running to warm up, he walked back to Luke. The car had squirrel tracks all over the fresh layer of snow, and a few small dead branches littered the top.

Using his arm, Kell cleared the windows and most of the roof.

"I'll follow you back into town," Luke said.

"It's fixed fine."

"Still following you."

"This is the protect part? You already served."

"This is the 'I don't trust Kell to know his way around a hose' part."

"C'mon, Luke. You're never going to let me live down the washing machine incident."

"You 'connected' a hose," Luke said, using finger quotes. "Then it flooded my entire house."

"I'm sorry! Geez! That was four years ago."

"I still step on wet spots on the hallway carpet sometimes."

"That's just Jester marking his territory." Jester was Luke's six-year-old golden retriever.

Luke grunted. Discussion over.

Kell got back in the now-warm car and did a three-point turn, happy to have enough clearance that he didn't have to back down to the main road on such an icy stretch. Soon, he was settled into the drive, Luke's pink car behind him.

Only then could he breathe.

And every breath smelled like Rachel.

The twenty-minute drive back into town was the first real solitude he'd had since the whole mess unraveled yesterday. After dropping her off at her trailer, he'd driven home, eaten a huge piece of lasagna his mother had put in his freezer last week, drank half his weight in water to rehydrate, and fallen asleep binge-watching some documentary about how to build an earthship home.

And dreamed about Rachel.

In the dream, she was swimming with him in the hot springs, smiling with the seductive lure of a mythological siren. That was the entire dream, a few seconds that stretched into eternity.

He'd woken up with a start when his five a.m. alarm went off. Calamine had curled up against him on top of the covers, and he lay there, staring up at the beamed ceiling, wondering what on earth he was doing.

Five years ago, between Rachel and Alissa, he had come home in pain, too stupefied to speak.

Alissa was cunning. She'd lied to him and taken a job with a huge petroleum company, and used him to get a meeting with his uncle, the commissioner of Maine's Department of Agriculture, Forestry, and Conservation.

And Rachel had helped her.

The thing Kell had worked so hard to avoid after moving to the city was the thing that happened:

He'd been played for a rube.

Because he was one.

Dreams don't die easily. For Kell, the idea that he would work in the city and live his life shaping society and nature was so big, it took a lot to kill it off.

Alissa and Rachel dealt the mortal blows, but it took him a long time to bleed out emotionally. Finally, he'd put that dream to rest, buried in an unmarked grave where no one ever visited.

Especially not his pride.

Lost in his thoughts, he found himself revisiting the last five years. Alissa had tried one more time to connect with Uncle Ted, but she'd been rebuffed. Rachel had vanished. He'd searched them out on social media a few times, finding Alissa's incredibly perfect-sounding LinkedIn profile and, once, a mention of Rachel in the Stanford alumni magazine. In disgust, he'd forced himself to stop looking them up.

Turning down the job he'd been offered in the California governor's office, a coveted spot that several of his co-workers were vying for, had been easy in the moment but painful in the long term.

But it had definitely been the right thing to do.

Not one part about the backbiting was appealing to him. Having Rachel here was nothing more than a reminder that he'd made a stellar decision coming home. Working for his dad had gotten boring the last few years, so he'd started pulling poison ivy, of all things.

And it was because of Rachel's mother.

When Portia Starman appeared in town to film the reality television show *Love You Springs Eternal*, there had been a huge problem: poison ivy all over the areas they were using as a set. Crew member after crew member got the horrible rash—one had to be hospitalized—but no one wanted to spray poison anywhere near the town's beloved hot springs.

Kell offered to hand pull it. Fifteen percent of the population isn't allergic to urushiol, the chemical that makes people itch, so Kell had thrown on a Tyvek suit, gloved up, worn a face shield and gone right in, pulling the poison ivy out from the shallow vines, following each one to the end.

After the series was done filming, the next year, there was less poison ivy. The town clerk hired him to pull even more, and word got out.

Pulling For You was born.

Now, he spent a fair amount of time from late April through early November traveling all over New England, organizing a small crew that included Allen, to help pull poison ivy. People who wanted to avoid traditional commercial poisons were willing to pay top dollar, and so far, Kell had escaped ever getting the dreaded rash.

As long as he created a careful protocol and his crew stuck to it, all was well.

Business thrived.

A little too much, according to his dad, who groused about Kell's lack of availability at times. Pulling poison ivy wasn't glamorous, but it kept him busy, and customers were so grateful.

Film crews were his most lucrative clients, though, and his

dad had no idea how much business he was turning away these days.

That was going to have to change soon.

As with any business, as demand grew, he needed more workers. An office manager. More trucks. Kell was the third generation to run Luview's Tree Service, so his father had never had to create a business from scratch. Dean had taken over from his own father, and grown the business, sure.

Yet he'd never taken something from zero to more.

Even now, in the dead of winter, Kell's business kept him busy. Winter was the perfect time to attack what were known as grandfather vines, thick, hairy climbers that wound themselves around trees like boa constrictors. Some of them were twenty, thirty years old, and the concentrated oil in them was so dangerous, one simple touch was enough to cause third-degree burns.

Which was why Kell was so determined to find them anywhere in town and kill them off.

It took a combination of skill, guts, and a little insanity to go after them, a machete often the best tool for the job. Machinery could splatter the oil, and one or two good, satisfying whacks from a big blade was often more efficient.

Mulling over his poison ivy company was a useful way to avoid thinking about Rachel, and soon he was stopped at a red light, caught up in his own thoughts.

Loud honking snapped him out of it. He looked up to find Nadine, the police station admin, pulled up next to him, waving wildly. She rolled down her window and shouted, "NO LAP ORNAMENT TODAY?"

The light turned green.

He drove off without a word.

Luke was behind Nadine, who at some point wove in between them. Kell swore he could hear Luke busting a gut even this far away.

Soon, Kell turned right to cut over to Kenny's, while Luke made a left, headed in the direction of the small ranch he shared with Harriet. Being a small-town cop helped in terms of being able to see her in short little visits here and there.

Honk! Honk!

It was his mother laying on the horn behind him, her beat-up old silver F-150 with the Luview Tree Service logo on it a nearly iconic sight around town.

Oh, boy.

No use fighting it. He pulled over, his mom right behind him, her truck stopped and turned off before he could even get out of gear.

"Kell!" she shouted. "You're ignoring my texts!"

"Yep," he said, rolling the window down.

"This your girlfriend's car?"

"Rachel is not my girlfriend, Mom."

"Hah! I know, honey. I just said that to tease you."

A flat look was all she got in return.

Deanna Luview was one of the most caring people he'd ever known. When it came to her family, she was loyal, generous, loving–and a bit intrusive.

But only because of the loving part.

"Rachel Hart's in town, huh? Did you know she was coming?"

"No. And stop pretending you don't know what happened yesterday. I'm sure Luke and Colleen filled you in."

"On their parts. Now I want to hear yours!"

"I don't have a part, Mom. I fixed Rachel's rental car. I'm driving it to her place. That's the whole story."

Luke appeared behind their mom, pulling over, flashing his police lights exactly once.

Show off.

"Hey!" he called out his open window to Kell. "How're you getting home from Rachel's?"

He shook his head. "Hadn't gotten that far."

"Can't expect her to drive you anywhere, right? She has that meeting with Lucinda at eleven."

Their mom wasn't a huge gossip, but she loved to know more than she told.

"Lucinda? Rachel's working with Lucinda? Is Portia coming back to do a new show? Ooo, something to do with chocolates?"

"No, Mom. Rachel's here to broker some deal where Lucinda and Boyce sell out to Markstone's candy company."

"I love their Easter peanut butter toffee eggs!" she exclaimed. "They want to buy Love You Chocolate?"

"Yep."

"And Rachel's the person in charge of that? How fancy!" She frowned. "I thought she went into environmental policy, like you, Kell. What does chocolate have to do with that?"

"Her career took a turn, Mom. I don't know. I didn't ask."

"Why wouldn't you ask?"

"Because I want to spend as little time around her as possible."

"Kell," she said with compassion. "You're still nursing that wound after all these years? You know, Portia says Rachel lacks killer instinct. I'm sure she didn't do what you think she did."

Every muscle in Kell's body turned to stone. Especially the one in his jaw.

"Mom."

Their eyes met, hers kind and curious, his feeling like two slabs of flint.

"Okay. Message received. Just... don't be a jerk to her."

"I would never be a jerk to anyone."

"You have a stubborn streak and you can come off as gruff."

"That's not a stubborn streak. It's who I am."

"It's who you are now, Kellan. Not who you were before."

"Rachel's a big reason I am the way I am now, Mom."

"Maybe you should listen to her."

"I spent hours stuck to her yesterday. I didn't have a choice."

"You don't carry feelings for as long as you have about what happened in D.C. if you don't feel it deep."

"That's ridiculous."

"If you say so."

"No. It's objectively ridiculous."

"Okay."

"I mean it, Mom."

Luke tapped his horn and shouted, "Give it up, Kell. Mom isn't backing down."

"Neither am I!"

"I have to get back to work. You want to be stranded at Kenny's at 6:30 in the morning? You know how horny that rooster of his can get."

Right. Should he have warned Rachel about Doodle? Too late now.

"Saved by a rooster," Deanna said, bending down to give him a quick kiss on the cheek. "If you have a chance, listen to her."

"Mom."

Rolling the window up, he let the glass protect him from further lobbying.

Then pulled away, her words ringing in his ears.

By the time he drove up Kenny's long driveway, he'd forgotten about Doodle. Kenny had already plowed his driveway and shoveled a path to the trailer door. Like loads of guys in town, Kenny plowed in the winter, running a landscaping company in the other three seasons. He worked for the Luview family tree service sometimes, during surges, to make something extra. His wife, Lisa, cleaned houses during tourism season, which made her wicked busy right now.

Luke parked next to him as Kell got out of the rental car and opened the back door, grabbing two pieces of luggage. He'd tried texting Rachel to give her a heads up that he was coming, but he guessed internet was out here.

A friendly knock on the door would have to do.

He reached the door and was balancing the luggage in his hands, trying to get one free, when he heard a loud scream from inside, a thump, then the creak of the door opening.

And got a full-face whomp as Rachel, wearing only a towel, threw her entire body straight into his.

No arms free to pinwheel, all he could do was pivot so they twisted to land in the softer snow, Kell letting go of the luggage and wrapping his arms around her to cushion her fall.

Legs wet, Rachel was otherwise dry. The large towel wrapped around her was one of the ubiquitous pink, white, and red beach towels sold in every gift shop. It read, LOVE YOU, HOT SPRINGS! TAKE THE PLUNGE!

His shoulder and hip took the brunt of the fall, her face pressing into his earflap.

For someone he hadn't seen in five years, they'd spent a lot of time in each other's faces over the last twenty-four hours. More than he had with anyone in, well...

Five years.

"HELP!" she screeched in Kell's ear, wiggling madly. It was easily below ten degrees outside, and she was naked under that towel. Sweet curves slid against his body, his hands trying hard to find a respectable spot to touch.

And failing.

He had to act fast. An L.A. native might understand what it felt like to be cold, but she clearly didn't grasp what Maine's particular brand of cold could do to her.

"What's wrong?" he asked.

She looked terrified.

"He's in the shower!"

A rush of protectiveness shot through him. Single woman, alone in a trailer, a few hundred feet from Kenny's place. Maybe some guy had decided to have some inappropriate fun. The bunkhouse frat guys could get a little out of hand sometimes.

"Who?"

"SATAN!"

His wiring must have gotten scrambled. They struggled up, her legs tucking under her as she began shivering, the curve of a breast visible for a split second.

"You need to get back in the trailer immediately, Rachel," he ordered. "It's too cold."

Plus, he was getting hard. Delivering her car was about ending involvement in her life.

Not adding to his body's torture.

"But he's in there!"

"Who?"

"SATAN!"

Not a stitch of makeup on her, dark hair wet and resting in flat waves against her face, Rachel was more beautiful *au naturel* than she was yesterday.

Though he could do without the Satan nonsense.

"You didn't sleep nearly enough if you're seeing Satan in the shower."

"SATAN IS A SQUIRREL!"

"You really shouldn't name the wildlife. Don't get attached. They're prey, you know?"

"I AM SATAN'S PREY!"

Kell did not say a word in response to that, because really... there was so much he *could* say. For now, he'd be a gentleman.

"I could lend you Calamine. She'd kill it for you for sport."

"Then I'd have a dead squirrel *and* a blood-thirsty bobcat in my cottage!"

"Cottage." He snorted. "Still milking that delusion?"

"It's easier to tolerate it if I call it a cottage."

"Then I should start calling *you* Mother Teresa."

"Are you going to help me, or tease me?"

Behind him, Kell knew Luke was sitting in the cruiser, laughing his ass off at the sight of whatever this was.

"Anyway," she continued, clinging to her towel, "I'm not going back in there! Satan the Squirrel got inside last night in the middle of the snowstorm, after tap dancing all over the roof of the cottage."

"Trailer."

"Whatever. And then Godzilla came along."

"God... zilla?"

Staying up for so long yesterday had obviously tipped her over into some sort of sleep-deprived psychosis.

"Yes! Some enormous beast kept shaking the trailer over and over all night."

At least he got her to use the word *trailer*.

"Shaking?"

"I thought it was an earthquake! Then I heard the sounds."

"Sounds?"

"WHHHHUUUUUUHHHH," she moaned, her impression of a moose in the middle of mating so distinctly perfect, he burst out laughing.

"It's not funny!"

He was about to tell her he knew exactly what caused the "earthquake" in her trailer, and it wasn't Godzilla, but then, in the background, Doodle the rooster let out his morning battle cry.

"WHAT'S THAT?" she screeched.

"Mothra."

"Stop it!"

"That's Doodle the rooster, Rachel. And you're going to be in bad shape if we don't get some clothes on you."

"I'm not going in there with Satan lurking in every corner."

"We're not talking about your soul. We're talking about the trailer."

"Get the thing out of my place!"

He moved her arms around his shoulders. "Hold on."

"What?"

"When I stand, just hold on." Slowly sliding his arm under her knees, he got his footing and stood in one motion, lifting her.

The towel still around her was enough for modesty, but one glance down and he got a lovely eyeful of cleavage.

"Don't take me in there!"

"Nowhere else that's warm." Carefully balancing, he grabbed the door latch and opened it.

Satan scampered out, carrying a foil-wrapped chocolate heart in his mouth.

"Hey," he said to the little beast. "That's probably toxic for you. Don't eat that, buddy." It ignored Kell and disappeared under the trailer.

"Did you just call Satan your 'buddy'?"

Unceremoniously dumping Rachel on the lower bunk, Kell looked down at her. Considering how flushed and upset she was, the woman was damned attractive.

Maybe he was fighting something he shouldn't. Maybe he should cross the gap between them, make a move, see if they needed to get this out of their systems. Sniping at each other wasn't doing them any favors.

Maybe what they needed was rage sex.

Before he could stop that sequence of thoughts from invading his rational mind, Luke blipped his siren once, just long enough to make the point clear:

He needed to get going.

Closing his eyes and swallowing hard, he lifted his eyebrows.

"I came here to drop off your car. It's fixed." He tossed the keys to her, which she caught in one hand. The action made the towel drop a bit, giving him another nice eyeful he pretended not to see, quickly looking away.

"Fixed?

"Yep. And until you plowed into me just now, I was carrying in two pieces of your luggage. They're out in the snow."

He turned to leave.

"You're just going to leave them out there?"

The huff of laughter felt freeing. She was a piece of work.

"I'm not your bellman, Rachel. You have a working car. A warm place to stay. I cast Satan out of your quarters. My work here is done."

"But–"

"Welcome to Love You, Maine, where even the wildlife likes to watch you naked."

Then he couldn't help himself.

He winked.

Because the look on her face was worth it.

So was the view he got of Rachel Hart wearing only a towel.

And an expression that said she would murder him in his sleep if it were legal.

Chapter Seven

RACHEL

"Hi, Orla."

At least the stupid rental car had Bluetooth.

"Rachel! How's it going in America's Heartland? Get it? *Hart*land! Ha. I slay myself."

"Very funny." Rachel flexed her right hand, careful not to stretch the skin along her pinkie too much. The adhesive needed to stay in place. Her Bluetooth magically worked for the car's speakers, but she'd had to wait until she was closer to town to call her boss to discuss the meeting coming up in an hour.

"Your last name made you perfect for this project."

"I get it, Orla."

"You sound grumpy."

"It was... complicated getting here."

"Travel sucks."

A flash of Satan the Squirrel and the eyeball in the bathroom made Rachel blink. Rachel knew that when Orla traveled on business, she preferred to stay at The Ritz-Carlton.

"No kidding. But let's talk about Love You Chocolate and Markstone's. Any new developments I need to know about?"

"No. You've got this."

"I hope so."

"Well, you'd better." Orla's abrupt change in tone made Rachel remember she was a boss.

Not a friend.

"I know. We have a lot on the line."

"You failed on your last two projects, Rachel. I can't protect you much longer."

A buzz of shame spread across her skin. She knew what that meant. Close this deal or she'd be fired.

Rachel was on a "performance improvement plan" at work, to her utter dismay and horror. The stakes were high here in Love You, Maine, because Rachel Hart's entire career was riding on convincing Lucinda Armistead and her son, Boyce, that selling to Markstone's would be good for them, good for the town, and good for chocolate lovers everywhere.

Most of all, it would save Rachel's butt.

"Thanks, Orla," she said softly, knowing she had to grovel a bit, not liking any of it. "I know how much you've done to help me."

"It's Doug. He's a vice president and you know he's pushing for that executive VP position. Wants all his divisions at peak performance. He's cutthroat."

"You have to be in this business."

"Of course. That's why it's called business and not non-profit."

"Yes," Rachel agreed faintly. The confidence she had been building up in herself on the drive was draining out fast, this mandatory check-in with her boss accomplishing the exact opposite of what Orla was looking for.

The town center came into stark relief, a splash of red and pink against so much white snow. She waited out a red light as Orla mentioned some technicalities, then pulled into a parking spot in front of a bank on Main Street.

At least it wasn't called Love You Bank. Knowing this town, that's what they called the local sperm storage facility.

"Sounds good," Orla said tersely, then changed her tone back to encouragement. "You've got this," she repeated. "I can't wait to hear from you about the signed contract."

"Same!"

"Good luck, Rachel."

The call ended abruptly. Rachel pulled her earpiece out and let herself deflate, all the air she'd been holding in her body whooshing out into the car. The craziness of just getting here, then Kell and the glue, then dealing with the trailer fiascoes, had kept her worry over this deal at bay. She needed it to go through.

She would do it. This would be fine. As she breathed in her fear, she exhaled her certainty. It would all be fine. Everything would turn out for the best.

She deserved good things.

And this deal was a very, very good thing.

Adjusting her hair in the mirror, she sized herself up. Long, dark waves. Red lipstick to fit the motif. Putting makeup on in the trailer had meant terrible light and a bathroom mirror the size of a cell phone, but now, in bright sunshine and a rearview mirror, the job wasn't half bad.

Dark brown eyes fringed with mascara and a hint of eyeliner looked back at her, turning from worried to confident by force of will.

"You will do this," she told herself, then stepped out of the car, walking to the parking meter.

Quarters? The parking meter took actual *quarters*?

Where was the parking app she could use on her phone and pay like a civilized person?

Rachel squinted at the meter.

Hold on. *Hold on.*

It took nickels and dimes?

What was this? 1978? What kind of parking meter took *nickels*?

A shudder ran through her as the wind picked up, her hatless head starting to ache. After her decidedly horrifying encounter with the squirrel and Kell this morning, she wasn't sure which was worse.

Kell.

Definitely Kell.

Being in the snow, rolled up in a thankfully large beach towel, protected from frostbite only by the wrap of his arms around her and his ability to stand up while lifting her was *not* what she thought would happen when they finally were able to separate.

Sure, she was grateful for all his help, but she meant it when she told him to bill her for his time. If he didn't, she'd have Dani create an invoice and run it through Markstone's.

At an obscene hourly rate that would make Kell suffer.

Yeah, *suffer*. She knew how his pride worked. He wouldn't dream of taking a penny from her for being helpful and kind.

At least, the old Kell she knew back in D.C. wouldn't.

"I can't even get actual revenge in my revenge fantasies," she muttered to herself in disgust. "That's right Rachel. Force him take money. That'll teach him."

On the spot, she texted Dani and got the process rolling, though. With so few chances to have the upper hand with Kell, she had to take what she could get.

Carrying her back into the trailer was the second time he'd rescued her from a humiliating moment, and each time, she'd been half dressed. Sure, the incidents were five years apart, but there was a pattern.

What was it about her, public exposure, and Kell being Superman?

All of that was over now. Squaring her shoulders, she lifted her chin and looked around, realizing she had to figure out her parking situation now and stop ruminating about Kell Luview.

Parking in Love You, Maine, was a joke. Right?

One nickel bought you three minutes. A dollar an hour for parking.

She shook her purse and began digging for change. How mortifying. Hopefully, no one from Love You Chocolate was watching.

It took a few minutes, but she found three nickels, two dimes, a Canadian quarter, and a thumb drive that was not useful.

Thirty-seven minutes was not enough.

After shoving all her change in the meter, she took a good look around. Arriving early was a careful business tactic, so that thirty-seven minutes was really only seven minutes once the meeting started.

Spotting a shop called Love You Coffee across the way, she sighed. Kill two birds with one stone.

A caffeinated one.

Get some good coffee, and ask for change. Bingo! Now she could relax.

And rev up at the same time.

All the red, white, and pink made everything a bit surreal. She felt somehow out of place in her charcoal gray Stella McCartney suit and black booties. She'd added a lovely red and teal pair of earrings. Perhaps that flash of red and her white silk shirt would be enough to be plausibly able to claim she dressed in the right colors. The red wool coat, strongly suggested by her mother last year when they went to Vail, turned out to be perfect.

A nauseatingly charming little heart-shaped bell rang as she opened the door to the coffee shop, the heavenly scent of real coffee hitting her senses. While the coffee in the trailer hadn't been horrid, this was what she really needed.

A full-caf latte with skim milk, two shots of espresso, and a generous spoonful of ground vanilla thrown in.

And then a second one for good measure.

"Hi there! Welcome to town." The young woman working the counter looked immediately at Rachel's hands. "Glad to see you're free!"

"Excuse me?"

"You and Kell? Buncha people saw you at the hospital wearing handcuffs, with Luke trying to hide it with his coat." She winked. "Bet it was totally worth it."

Cold confusion ran through Rachel.

"Could you say that again? I'm very perplexed, because nothing you just said makes sense."

"Don't be embarrassed!" She winked again. "We all like to play private games, don't we? And good on you for bagging Kell. Lots of women are going to hate you immediately, though, so watch out." Her fingers formed a claw and she hissed.

"Um. No. I'm not–that's not what happened." Rachel stopped herself from going on the offensive, and shifted into cold urban-woman mode. "I'll have a large latte with skim milk, double shot, and a tablespoon of ground vanilla."

"Ground vanilla? We don't have that. Just vanilla syrup."

Rachel shuddered.

"Then leave it out."

"And we don't have skim."

"How can you not have skim milk?"

"It's not popular here. Kept spoiling. Two percent's the lowest we can go."

"Any chance you have almond milk?"

"Yep!"

"Then half two percent and half almond."

"Want me to go in the back and see if we have any vanilla extract?"

"No. It's not the same as ground vanilla."

"What's so special about the ground stuff?" the girl asked. Her name tag said Skylar.

"It's anti-inflammatory."

"Really?"

"Mmm."

Done with the inquiry, and still taken aback by Skylar's interpretation-via-gossip of what had happened between her and Kell, Rachel looked around the quiet shop, pretending to be interested in the travel mugs and coasters for sale.

The town gossips were spreading a very, very *wrong* rumor. They thought she and Kell had got trapped in handcuffs while they were having *sex? What?* The truth couldn't be more different.

How was she going to face one of the pillars of the community in thirty minutes knowing she thought *that?*

"I love your earrings!" Skylar called out over the frothing machine's hiss.

"Thanks." Rachel touched the chunky gold chains hanging from her ears.

"Where'd you get them?"

"In Los Angeles."

"That where you're from?"

"Mmmm."

"Don't see much snow there."

"We never see snow there," she corrected.

"Why are you in town?"

"Business."

"Everyone's business is our business here," Skylar said cheerfully, as if it were perfectly normal for a total stranger to know everything about Rachel.

No wonder Kell had loved living in the city so much. There was zero privacy here.

Turning the inquiry on its head, she looked Skylar in the eye, gave her a tight smile, and said, "If you don't know why I'm here, then maybe the resident I'm here to see has kept it private for their own reasons."

Skylar nodded slowly. "Never thought of it that way."

A woman in her fifties walked in, her dark hair framing a red-cheeked face under a thick wool cap. She stamped her boots hard on the textured black mat at the door, and called out, "Hi, Skylar!"

"Hi, Deanna!"

Deanna? Deanna Luview?

Friendly eyes the color of Kell's met hers. "Hello, there!"

"Um, hi."

"Enjoying the coffee?"

"This is the lady who was attached to Kell at the ER yesterday!" Skylar called out, ruining any hopes Rachel had of escape.

"Oh, my gosh! You're Rachel!" Deanna gasped, coming in for a huge hug that shocked Rachel to the core. The woman's embrace was so motherly, she even smelled like freshly baked bread, mixed with a cologne Rachel's mother had done ads for in the late 1980s. Who knew Elizabeth Arden was still a thing?

"Hi," Rachel peeped, trying to come up with something to say, her mind suddenly blank.

"How's your hand? Poor thing. Kell told me all about what happened."

"He *did*?" Skylar was scandalized. "Wow, Deanna! Kell sure shares a lot with you! I'd *never* talk about my sex life with my mom!"

"Sex life? Skylar, what in the world are you talking about?"

"Nadine said Jeffy Stewart was volunteering in the baby wing at the hospital and saw Luke bring Kell and Rachel in, with his police jacket covering their hands, and they were handcuffed! Everyone assumed it was a sex thing."

"You mean Jeffy decided in her petty little mind to start a rumor that it was a sex thing," Deanna reframed for her.

"Right. That's what I just said."

"No. That's not what you said, honey. Jeffy made it up. The truth is, Kell and Rachel touched superglue at the same time on a radiator hose and their hands got stuck to it."

Skylar's face fell. "That's way less interesting."

"Sorry to disappoint," Rachel said in an acid tone, arching her eyebrows. "How's my coffee coming along?"

"Oh! Hold on. Just need to pour the shots."

"It's so good to see you, *Friend Rachel*," Deanna said, removing her hat and fluffing her hair.

JULIA KENT

Ouch. A memory from five years ago flashed through her, the
FaceTime call Kell had with his mom when she was dressed up as
a pair of lips for a town festival, all sequins and red, reminiscent
of the Rocky Horror Picture Show lips. At the time, Rachel and
Kell had stressed that they were just friends, and Deanna had
jokingly called her Friend Rachel.

All these years, and she remembered?

Deanna was warm and motherly, the type to keep tabs on
everyone's emotional state to make sure they were okay.

"Great to see you, too, Deanna. Nice to meet in person."

"It is! How's your mom?" Deanna asked.

"You probably talk to her more than I do," Rachel said with a
genuine smile.

"Oh, honey. We email or text maybe once a week. I'm sure
that can't be true."

A quick mental calculation revealed that Rachel was right.
She hadn't talked to her mom in nearly three weeks.

Deanna's smile deepened. "I hear you're in town to convince
Lucinda and Boyce to sell the chocolate company to
Markstone's."

Skylar dropped a small metal pitcher on the ground and
made a squeak of surprise, looking at Rachel with huge eyes.

"They're selling?"

So much for being discreet.

"For the record, I didn't say a word," Rachel pointed out.

Deanna reached across the counter and came to her caffeine
aid, plucking her finished latte from next to the espresso
machine and putting it in her grateful hands. The first sip was
heaven.

Pure heaven.

Bright notes, but not too citrusy, caressed her tongue like
she'd been transported to her favorite cozy spot in front of a
roaring fire, curled up on a couch. The caffeine lifted her as the
coffee's warmth spread through her, an infusion of comfort.

Coffee this good should be everywhere.

"Mmmm," she said as Skylar beamed. "This is amazing. What
kind is this?"

"A special blend we call Love You Awake. Light roast, but
with hints of cherry and butterscotch, darkened a bit by an
undercurrent of oak."

"It's extraordinary. And you really know how to speak coffee!"

"Come back and enjoy it all you want."

"Do you have other stores?"

"No. Just this one. But you can have our coffee shipped anywhere." Skylar pointed to a business card holder. Rachel took one and slipped it in her bag.

"You have a new fan. Is everything made in Love You so good? Because the chocolate company makes the best chocolate I've ever had, too."

"The chocolate factory's been in the Armistead family since the 1950s," Skylar mused, wiping the espresso machine with a white bar towel. "What would a big company like Markstone's do to it?"

"Make it better," Rachel said with confidence. She knew that while Lucinda and Boyce were the decision makers, getting townsfolk on board mattered, too. "Add jobs. Turn the factory into a tourist destination."

"It already is! Lucinda uses water from the hot springs. You know their motto: *A little taste of love in every bite!*"

"None of that has to change. Selling to Markstone's will help her family realize the value of all their hard work, and it'll bring new jobs to Luview."

Skylar perked up. "New jobs?"

"Yes." Rachel knew she shouldn't talk about it, but couldn't help herself. "Thirty to forty full-time jobs with benefits, and maybe more if it all works out."

Deanna's phone buzzed.

"Excuse me." Deanna held up a finger. "I have to get this, but Skylar, can you make my regular order?"

"Already working on it."

"And Rachel–hold on."

Rachel felt a twinge of worry worming its way in. Was she tipping her hand too much? Reasonably confident the family would, in fact, sell to Markstone's, she'd come prepared with the offer, and knew it was a good one.

The Armisteads had a strong local brand and a solid online order system, but they'd faltered in the kind of widespread market penetration they could have had with better coordinated branding and marketing.

That's where Markstone's came in. If the Armisteads sold out, their products would still be called Love You Chocolate, but the family would lose control to the new owners, who intended to find a new angle for a stale niche brand.

Their own.

That's the part Rachel didn't mention: why Markstone's, of all companies, wanted to buy a dinky little chocolate company in rural Maine. Part of the challenge when you were the world's best-known luxury candy company was finding new ways to stay fresh in the consumer's mind.

Love You Chocolate was unique, and Markstone's wanted unique.

If this pilot project went well, Rachel knew it could lead to many other acquisitions of small artisanal chocolate and confectionery companies. The factories would remain individual distribution centers for now, but eventually, the companies would be rebranded as Markstone's, creating a massive chain network of small shops.

For now, though, this was about one small deal in one small town, with big implications for Rachel.

Because this wasn't her first small-town candy shop rodeo.

Blow this and she'd be fired. It would severely affect her career. Closing the deal would save and possibly launch it. And she wanted to be launched before her brother launched, literally, into space.

For once, she wanted to be the one their father bragged about. The one her mother turned to for media connections and opportunities.

The one who got the spotlight, even for a short time.

No one would lose in this situation if the deal went through. The Armisteads would have more money than they'd ever imagined, the town would gain jobs, and Rachel would leave Kell Luview far, far behind, with a secure job and a new project.

All that was left was signatures on a contract.

Deanna looked up from her texting, shaking her head. "Poor Dean."

"What's wrong?"

"Another lovesick guy doing a practice run for Valentine's Day."

"Valentine's Day?"

Skylar and Deanna barked out laughter. "You say that like you're surprised. It's the biggest day of the year here."

"What does that have to do with your husband?"

"We run a tree service. Every year, we get skydivers who try to make a grand gesture, but the wind doesn't cooperate, or they're too green to know how to handle the steering, and they end up stuck in trees."

"And you have to cut them down."

"Yup. Dean and Kell are on it. Finishing up now."

Rachel's heart fluttered at the mention of Kell's name.

"I didn't know tree service workers did that. Isn't that more the fire department's job?"

"We've got better equipment for it, especially if they get caught too high up."

"Wow. So this is a thing?"

"It is, indeed, a thing."

"This town is full of surprises."

Deanna squeezed her arm. "Always, dear. Always. That's what makes it such a wonderful place to live."

An alarm went off on Rachel's phone.

Ten minutes to go.

"Oh, goodness. You must need to get ready for your meeting."

"I do." Rachel pulled a ten out of her wallet and handed it to Skylar, who gave her back a five, two ones, and a quarter. Cheap coffee compared to L.A.

Rachel gave her back the singles and asked, "Could I get four quarters for one of those? The other's for you."

Skylar nodded, handed her the quarters, and tucked the other dollar in the tip jar.

"Parking?" Deanna said with a knowing look.

"Yes. Why doesn't the town use a parking app?"

"Good question. Probably because no one's in charge of anything like that right now."

"What do you mean? Your business development director doesn't handle that?"

"We don't have one right now."

"I thought someone named Harry Cassir was the director." Rachel had done her homework, knowing she'd need to speak with him on this trip. Dani had it all scheduled for her.

"He quit two weeks ago."

"What?"

"Yes. Got tired of people refusing to make changes."

Rachel's heart sank.

"It's that intransigent?"

"Can be." Deanna gave her a reassuring smile. "I'm sure you'll be fine. Lucinda may be unreasonable, but Boyce has his father's genes to balance her out."

Dry humor or the cold, hard truth? Rachel wasn't sure until Deanna started laughing.

"That was a joke, Rachel. You're that nervous, huh? Sorry."

"I'm not nervous. No," she objected. "Just caffeine deprived."

Burying her nose in her drink helped. Rich and creamy, the mix of two-percent milk and almond silkiness was more like a luxury than a practical source of energy, each sip warming her emotionally as much as physically.

If only she could relax and just enjoy that luxury.

But duty called.

"You're going to be fine. I'm sure whatever Markstone's has planned to offer Lucinda and Boyce is going to be exciting."

"I hope they say yes."

Deanna gave her a noncommittal but encouraging look.

"Good luck!" Skylar handed Deanna her coffee and punched something into the iPad that functioned as a cash register.

"Got it?" Deanna asked.

"Yep. In the system." She looked at Rachel. "You want an auto-account?"

"A what?"

"Store your card on file and it auto-pays whenever you order. Lots of people have it. Makes everything easier. And you get a free coffee for every twelve you buy!"

"Oh. No, thank you. I'm only here for two more nights."

"Sure about that?" Deanna winked as she left.

Was that comment about whether Lucinda would sell quickly, or... about Kell?

Either way, Rachel had no plans to be in town long enough to buy twelve coffees, here or elsewhere. Two a day was enough, and if she were still here in five days, it meant something was very wrong with her deal.

"I can take your card and do it in thirty seconds," Skylar said, trying to be helpful. Rachel was saved by the door's bell dinging as a big group of excited men came in. They were about five years younger than her, covered in ski parkas and hats.

"No, thanks. Bye!"

The heat from the large coffee warmed her hand, her coat's pocket perfect for the other. Cursing herself for leaving her gloves in the car, she decided to kill time before the call, jingling her six quarters.

First stop: the parking meter.

As she approached, she saw a sign she hadn't noticed when she took the spot: One-Hour Parking Only.

"Well, shoot," she muttered, finding her keys and climbing in the car. A large blue Parking Lot sign caught her eye, with an arrow pointing to a municipal lot that was quite full, but as she squinted, she saw it said four-hour limit. Four hours was a lot better than one.

Hold on.

She hesitated. Was it worth all this hassle to avoid a parking ticket? How much could they cost here, in a place where meters took nickels and dimes? The fine would certainly be less than a day's parking back in L.A., and she could expense it.

A pink police cruiser caught her eye, moving slowly down Main Street. Better not chance it. Might have another run-in with Officer Luview.

Moving the car was easy, until she pulled into the lot and tried to find a space. Huge piles of snow blocked quite a few of the spots. You would think there would be a protocol for snow removal–this was Maine, after all.

They should be used to it.

How hard was it to move big piles like the ones dominating the corners of the lot, taking up three spaces in a row?

Finally, she saw an opening between two cars and began to pull in.

Until she braked hard and shrieked.

"RANDY!" a man's booming voice called from behind her.

A moose stood in the parking spot, staring her down.

Just like Godzilla.

When she hit the brakes, her coffee had tipped, spilling hot, creamy goodness down her right leg. The wet heat was a sickening reminder of how any day can be ruined by a single error.

And all to avoid paying a possible parking ticket.

"Don't hit him!" Luke yelled, waving his hands behind her. "Back up and give him space."

So much for avoiding Officer Luview.

She rolled down her window. "WHY is a MOOSE in the parking lot?"

"Because he's old and wanders."

"That doesn't explain the MOOSE IN A PARKING LOT part!"

"It's Randy. He got hit by a truck on Route 33 a few years ago, and the vet fixed him up, but his mind's never been the same."

The moose looked at Rachel, eyes narrowing.

She knew those eyes.

One of them, anyhow.

"I'm calling Mel," Luke announced.

"Who's Mel?"

"Mel Chassi. Runs an animal sanctuary."

"She'll come and take him away?"

"No one's making Randy do anything he doesn't want to do, but she's an animal whisperer. If anyone can get him out of here safely, it's Mel."

"Why not call animal control and tranquilize him?"

"You want a half-ton moose taking up a parking spot here in February?"

"You're worried about the parking spot? When you have those huge piles of snow taking up three spots each?"

"Bulldozers on their way to clear that. Can't use one on a moose."

Thunk! Thunk!

Rachel and Luke both turned to look at the moose, whose hooves were now placed squarely on the hood of her car. His head was lowered, nose edging toward the middle of the windshield.

"THIS IS A RENTAL CAR! DO YOU HAVE ANY IDEA HOW MUCH PAPERWORK THOSE DENTS WILL CREATE?" she screamed at the beast.

"Rachel, get out of the car," Luke said in a low voice of warning.

The car began to rock.

Randy the Moose pitched forward, sending Rachel back with some force. Not enough to cause whiplash, but enough to shoot adrenaline through her blood.

And splash more coffee on her leg.

The rocking began in earnest, a remarkably familiar feeling.

"GODZILLA?" she screamed.

Luke gave her a sharp look.

"Randy. Not Godzilla. Godzilla isn't real."

"This is what was rocking my trailer this morning!"

"WHHHUUUUUUUUHH."

As Randy made love to her rental car, Rachel froze; she knew how this would end. A few images flashed through her mind, each grosser than the next, and she realized she did not want a moose gumming up her rental car engine.

So to speak.

Desperate, she laid on the horn, a long, loud honk.

All that accomplished was making Randy pump harder.

"He thinks it's a mating call!" a woman shouted from behind Luke. "Stop honking! Turn off the car!"

Rachel did as ordered, the woman's voice extremely commanding.

Randy stopped abruptly, tilting his head as he looked at Rachel. As if nothing whatsoever had happened, he stepped down from the hood and turned away, walking sedately toward a thick patch of woods at the edge of the lot.

A car headed toward her turned on its signal, about to claim the spot.

"Oh, no, you don't. I didn't fight this hard just to lose it," she muttered, quickly restarting her engine and pulling in. Once she turned the car off, she took a deep breath. Shaken but determined, her pants leg soaked with spilled coffee, Rachel got out, waving.

"LUKE!"

"Yeah?"

"Can you help me as a witness? My assistant is going to have to file a claim with the car rental place, and no one will believe me when I report the hood was damaged by an amorous moose."

Luke gave the trunk a double tap and laughed, walking toward his car.

"Sure!" he called out. "Gotta go on another call, but no problem. You can reach me at the station." He opened his pink car door and called out, "Thanks, Mel!" to the woman who'd hollered. Then he drove away, leaving Rachel alone.

Mel? Rachel turned to the stranger who'd helped with the moose.

"Thank you!" she said to her.

"I didn't do anything special. Just don't honk again. Randy'll think you're coming on to him."

"What's wrong with that moose?"

"He got hit by a truck a few years ago. Never been the same in the head since. Thinks it's rutting season all the time."

"Rutting season?"

"Mating time. Generally September for moose, but Randy's, well... *randy*."

"You're serious?"

The woman shrugged. "Either that, or he's just plain horny nonstop. We're going with the biologic explanation. I'm Mel Chassi."

"Hi. Rachel Hart."

"Perfect last name for our town!"

A small smile was all she could muster.

"Good luck with Lucinda and Boyce!" Mel said.

"How did you know?"

"Word's out." She wiggled a smartphone. "Everyone knows, and the betting grid's already starting."

"Betting grid?"

Mel laughed. "Come to Greta's after your presentation and see."

"Greta's?"

"Love You Bakery." She looked at her phone. "It's 10:57. Better hurry! Lucinda can't stand people who are late!"

"I'm sure if I explain why, she'll..."

"You're going to explain to a woman who was a Shaker until she fell in love with Donald Armistead that you're late because a moose had sex with your car? Good luck. Here's a tip: Never mention sex around her."

"Never mention sex..?"

"Ever. "

"What's a Shaker?" Rachel asked, earning a double take.

"Do your homework, honey. Google Sabbathday Lake. Good luck! Get going!"

Quickly, Rachel pumped her quarters into the meter and hurried off to Love You Chocolate, walking through the door promptly at 11:00, a bit winded but fine. Hopefully, the coffee stain wouldn't show too much on her gray pants. The walk to Love You Chocolate was cold, the arctic air nearly freezing the wet cloth on her leg, but by the time she reached the store's main door, she was determined not to let this minor fiasco ruin her pitch.

The store was packed. *Packed.*

And every person in there was smiling or moaning.

Infectious joy filled the air in the tiny little shop, and even Rachel's tumultuous inner state wasn't immune to it. The rich aroma of chocolate pervaded every molecule of air, and people stood shoulder to shoulder around displays, trying samples and chatting with store clerks dressed in red aprons and heart-shaped hats. There were bags of red foil hearts all over the place. A small sign in front of a tray of samples read, *Try our new espresso toffee hearts,* and Rachel almost snagged one.

It was like falling into the Willy Wonka factory, minus the creep factor.

"Rachel?" Someone called out her name from where three cashiers were ringing up sales. Ignoring a couple of barely disguised glares, she made her way to the front of the line, where she saw Boyce Armistead. They'd Zoomed a few times, so she was certain it was him.

"Hello!"

He motioned for her to lean in.

"I heard you met Randy," he said softly, his voice deep and infused with mirth. He sat behind the counter, working on a laptop identical to Rachel's.

"I–"

"It's okay. My mother is in the conference room. I'm sorry that's how you had to be introduced to our town. Sometimes love goes a little too far in 'Love You, Maine, where every day is Valentine's Day'–especially for old Randy."

Suppressing a snicker, she winced. "It's really ridiculous, isn't it? But I guess it's part of the charm," she added, trying to be smooth as more customers crowded into the already full shop.

"If you say so." He sounded skeptical. "Anyway, nice to finally meet you in person, Rachel," he said, holding out his hand for a shake. "Zoom just isn't the same."

"No, it isn't. A pleasure to meet you."

"Listen," he said quietly. Rachel had to strain to hear him above all the chatter around them. "Before you meet my mother, I want to make sure you understand that a hard sell would be the worst possible way to approach this. She's eighty-eight years old, and this company was her and Dad's baby. It means so much to her. The chocolates are first-class and she's a stickler for consistency. Some might call her old-fashioned."

"Do you?" Looking around pointedly, she made her meaning clear: If Lucinda was old-fashioned, it was working for her.

"Sure. But there's something to be said for that."

"Sounds like quality is important to her."

"It is."

"That's part of what drew Markstone's to your company, Boyce. Quality. Consistency. Customer service. But also, caring. Small town values like you see here in Love You, Maine, should be more common. They aren't. They're special, and Markstone's wants to be able to offer more of your brand of special to the world."

He sized her up. "You're good." The way he drew out the last word made it impossible to tell whether that was a compliment or an insult.

"I'm not good or bad, Boyce. I'm here to make sure you feel heard, and we make our case. No one's going to push or pressure. No cajoling or flattery. Just good old-fashioned information so you can make the best decision possible."

"I want to make the best *deal* possible. Love You Chocolate has given our family a decent living, but not a luxurious one. As Mom gets older, we want to make sure she's well cared for in her final years."

He turned to say something to the cashier on his right, who made quick eye contact and nodded.

"Boyce? Is she here? It's 11:02," a woman's strong voice called out from somewhere down a hallway behind the checkout counter.

"Yes, Mom! It's my fault. Rachel walked in at eleven on the dot." He winked at her.

"Is she alone? I heard she glued herself to the Luview boy."

Two cashiers burst into suppressed giggles.

"Which Luview boy, Mom? There are about twenty of them."

"The poison ivy boy."

"That would be Kell."

Lucinda Armistead appeared suddenly, and when she turned the corner, recoiled slightly at Rachel's presence. In spite of her age, her shoulders were square; her long white hair was rolled into a bun, with not a single strand out of place. Bright blue eyes surrounded by deep wrinkles added to an imperious air. She was, of course, dressed entirely in red, with small pearls in her ears.

Lucinda glanced around the shop, and the look on her face was one Rachel recognized instantly: pride. The Armisteads were deeply proud of their success, and they should be.

"Rachel, I presume? Pardon my manners. Gossip is currency in a small town like this, and I am not immune to it." The hand she offered was dry as a sun-bleached bone, but the grip was strong.

Rachel returned it.

"If it hadn't happened to me, I'd be joking about it, too," Rachel said, using one of her father's business tips: When in doubt, self-deprecate.

She pushed aside the rest of his comment, which was always: *Then again, I never have to, because I'm never in doubt.*

Doubt was certainly in the air after what Boyce had just said. Numbers weren't going to cut it. Rachel would have to use a rusty asset from her toolbox:

Charm.

"Let's talk in a room a bit more suited for conversation," Lucinda said in a voice that indicated Rachel was meant to acknowledge the bustling store.

"Of course. I'm sorry my timing is right in the middle of your busiest time."

"That wasn't coincidental, though, was it, dear? I'm sure Markstone's wants eyes on how well we're doing."

Rachel let a wink slip, eliciting laughter from the old woman.

Smiles were exchanged all around, and Boyce led them down the hall to a small conference room. It was no bigger than most dorm rooms, but with a picture window looking over a beautiful hazy lake, steam rising from the waters.

"Ah. The famous Love You Springs."

"Your mother called it *Love You Springs Eternal*," Lucinda said with a twitchy smile.

"You've done your homework on me."

"No, dear. I ran into Deanna at the stationery store. We exchanged a few words."

"I see there's no need for the internet in Love You, Maine," Rachel joked. "You're all faster than any fiber optic or 5G network."

Lucinda sniffed. "I don't know what that means, but I do know there's no one who runs faster than Nadine with hot gossip to dish about, and Deanna is a close second."

Resisting the urge to pull out her laptop, hook up to the projector in the middle of the table, and get her deck going for the presentation, she knew the chit-chat was as much a part of the deal as the actual signed contracts would be.

Every negotiation had its own pace, one that had to be handled second by second. Emotional tone mattered.

People mattered.

That's one part of acquisitions that her boss's boss, Doug, never understood. He only cared about the bottom line. People selling small businesses cared about their communities. Their blood, sweat, and tears.

Their legacies.

Sure, they wanted profits. No one built a small business from the ground up with the eventual goal of wanting it to fall into ruin and become nothing financially.

More than that, though, people in small towns were connected to each other by tight networks. Upsetting those networks meant changing everyone's life, from a ripple to an earthquake. Jobs could be lost, retail space could go unrented, and entire ways of life could change for the better–or for the worse.

This was part of the reason her last two negotiations had gone poorly. Deep in her heart, she knew that the outcome for the preservative-free keto chocolate company in Billings, Montana, would be a dismantling.

And the teeny female-veteran-owned salt caramel company

outside of Creighton, Pennsylvania, was going to become just a fulfillment center for Markstone's.

Her heart hadn't been in those deals, and both had turned the offers down, deciding instead to focus on online sales.

Orla had been disappointed, but Doug had been furious.

And blunt. Close the Armistead deal in Maine or be fired.

Fortunately, this deal was a good one. Markstone's really did plan to keep all the employees, and add thirty to forty new ones. They wanted to expand the factory, and Rachel had quietly looked into land nearby that could work.

The Armisteads didn't know about that part, but over time, it would be fine. Markstone's planned to invest in Love You, Maine.

Not strip the profits and run.

"I assume you need a dongle for your deck?" Boyce asked, sliding one across the conference table. So much for pacing.

Time for business.

"I have one, actually, but thank you," she said with a smile. Lucinda took a seat at the head of the table, Boyce to her right. Both were more relaxed than she expected, which really helped.

In under a minute, she had her deck on screen, Dani's design flawless.

All the prep work, all the travel, the car breaking down, the superglue incident with Kell, Randy the lovesick moose, Satan the squirrel, and the now-dry coffee on her pants–it all faded away as Rachel went into her earnest selling mode.

She focused on the family's history with Love You Chocolate. How Donald Armistead had decided to try using some of the spring water to improve the product and prop up his flagging chocolate company.

Water ruins chocolate, so it was just a drop. Enough to make for perfect marketing.

How Lucinda had the idea for the red foil, and heart-shaped molds. How they started from their family kitchen, then rented the firehouse's commercial kitchen, finally moving to a small storefront in 1969. The expansion since then, how nearly every high school student in town had passed through Love You Chocolate as a seasonal employee, and their community roots and support.

As Rachel recounted it all, a nostalgic smile floated across

Lucinda's lips, but Boyce became more and more somber. Perhaps it was a kind of death, selling a business you built from scratch.

And perhaps watching your eighty-eight-year-old mother do so was like acknowledging mortality.

Not just in business, either.

In a sense, Rachel was showing them their life, flashing before their eyes, but they weren't dying. Selling a deeply-rooted, long-standing small business in a beloved community might feel like it, though.

If nothing else, there was a sense of grief at the closure, the change, the transition.

And Rachel honored that.

As Rachel pivoted to numbers, the deck moved faster, because the numbers were the easy part. Black and white. Binary.

Either they added up or they didn't.

"And so," she said, affection in her tone, "Markstone's would love to bring Love You Chocolate into its family of small businesses. We'll absolutely maintain all of your current jobs, add more, and retain the local—uh, the local character that—uh..."

Spacesuit.

There was a man in a spacesuit outside the window, walking toward them outside, right at the edge of the springs. The distraction was too much for Rachel's sleep-deprived, already jangled nervous system.

A man in a spacesuit was too much.

He took off his helmet and Rachel gasped.

"Kell?"

Both the Armisteads turned, Boyce snorting.

Kell walked along the perimeter of the hot springs, steam weaving in and out of view. His white spacesuit half blended into the snow, but half stood out against the waters.

"What is—why is—oh! I'm so sorry. I shouldn't be distracted," Rachel said, hating her stuttering.

"That's the poison ivy Luview boy," Lucinda said. "He wears that contraption at least once a week in town. Don't mind him."

Rachel couldn't help it. Couldn't stop if she tried.

"Is he—is that a *machete* in his hand?"

Sure enough, Kell's right arm came into view as he lifted it, the curved steel blade glinting in the sunlight, thick and dangerous.

"Ayup," Boyce said, as if it were the most natural thing in the world.

"Why is he wearing a spacesuit and carrying a machete?"

"He always was an odd little boy," Lucinda muttered.

"Mom, Kell's not odd. He's doing his job."

"His job?" Rachel echoed.

Pausing mid-step, Kell held his helmet in one arm, the machete in the other, and turned toward them, as if he knew they were talking about him.

Then he waved.

Rage, red like the foil that covered the hearts here in the store, poured into Rachel like melted chocolate into a mold. Until he appeared–*in a spacesuit!*–the presentation had been perfect.

Perfect.

And now...

"He cuts poison ivy."

"I knew he had a business doing that. But does poison ivy grow in the winter?"

"That boy finds it year round. Like it's his personal mission to rid Luview of anything that doesn't belong here and might hurt us," Lucinda said steadily, maintaining eye contact with Rachel the entire time.

Oh, no. Her heart seized.

In that second, she knew.

Knew that the deal wasn't going through.

"I admire that," Rachel said slowly, buying time. "Years ago, I learned the hard way that you never know what's going to hurt you in life, so be careful."

Lucinda's eyelids fluttered, as if she weren't expecting the response.

"You're so young," she said slowly. "You have plenty of hurt ahead of you. But you also have joy. Don't let the hurt crowd out the joy."

Rachel looked through the window at Kell, who had put his helmet on and moved out of view, though she could see the bulk of his white costume through the trees in the distance.

"Well, let's get back to our discussion," Rachel said, hoping to recover and redirect.

Boyce's phone buzzed. He looked at the screen.

"Janice had to go home. Her little boy threw up at school."

"Oh, no!" Lucinda said with a cluck of the tongue. "Poor dears."

He stood and gave Rachel an apologetic look. "That means, unfortunately, that I need to help at the counter."

"You don't have people you can call in?" Rachel asked.

"Not enough. It's a small town, and everyone is stretched thin at peak times."

"I'm surprised more people don't move here, if the jobs are that plentiful."

"People don't know that."

"No business development office?" she inquired, then corrected herself. "Oh. Right. The director quit recently, right?"

Lucinda looked impressed. "You did your research."

"No," she admitted, laughing. "Deanna had to tell me."

"As I said, that woman is a one-person town information desk." Lucinda folded her hands and gave Boyce a meaningful look.

He sat down.

"Rachel," she began in a voice that meant she really didn't need to say another word.

Because *Rachel* might as well have been *no*.

"Markstone's' offer is good. I might even say very good. And the money would be nice. I'm not getting any younger, and Boyce needs security. My other son, Brandon, lives in western Massachusetts and runs a farm. I have six grandchildren, and they've all worked at the store at some point. It's not just a business with a balance sheet. It's who we are."

"I can see that, Lucinda."

"Thank you. You're more... personable than I expected. Most companies send corporate drones who breeze into town, try to get what they want, and leave the second they hear *no*. Or push hard and try to browbeat me into a deal."

"I cannot imagine anyone successfully putting a hard sell on *you*."

Lucinda gave her a hard-to-read smile. "You do realize this is a no?"

Rachel smiled back. "I would prefer to think of it as a pause. Neither a no nor a yes. How about we all take a few days to think about it? Let me stay and get a feel for the town, so I can go back to Markstone's and make sure that they understand how rich in love the community really is. Aligning our offer with your values is important to us."

"You want to *stay?*" Boyce interrupted. "I thought you could only be here for three nights."

"I can extend." Rachel frowned. "May I ask what's holding you back?"

"We were warned that Markstone's might not be as trustworthy as we initially thought."

"Trustworthy?"

Boyce's phone buzzed again. He stood, this time for good. "I really have to help. They're swamped now."

Lucinda waved him toward the door, and stood as well. "If it's that bad, let me go out and help."

"Mom, you've never learned the iPad cash register system."

"Then I'll hand out samples and work the room." She winked at him.

Rachel could feel the love in here, but the *trustworthy* comment stung.

"Before you both go, first of all, thank you so much. Could we schedule another meeting?"

"It would have to be after Valentine's Day."

Nine days. Valentine's Day was in nine days.

"That would be fine. February 15?"

"You'll still be here then?" Boyce asked head tilted in surprise.

"I can work from anywhere." She tapped her laptop.

Boyce and Lucinda shared a look. An imperceptible nod from Lucinda made it clear Rachel had a reprieve.

Both came around the table to shake her hand. As she clasped Boyce's, she asked, "You said you were warned that Markstone's might be untrustworthy. May I ask who it was?"

He leaned in and said quietly, "Kell Luview. He said not to trust a word out of your mouth. Mom was going to say no all along, but I was ready to convince her until he said that. Now that I've met you, I'm wondering *why* he said it."

She inhaled so sharply, her lungs hurt, even though it was warm in the room.

"You're wondering?"

"You strike me as a nice woman. Not a corporate killer."

"Glad you see my humanity through this hard exterior," she joked, but her nerves began to fray as the reality of her situation sank in:

She didn't have a deal, she just offered to stay in town for nine more days, and Kell had sabotaged her.

"It's humanity that makes Mom want to hang onto the store," he replied. They turned to Lucinda, who shook Rachel's hand.

"Let's talk on the fifteenth," she said, those piercing eyes reading Rachel. "I'm pleased you want to stay that long. My *no* is now an official *maybe*." She pointed to the right. "There's a back door you can use if you want to avoid the crowds. It's a lovely path along the hot springs, and it's plowed, so you can walk it."

They left her in the room, staggered by what had just happened.

Gobsmacked, Rachel listened to the shaky intake of breath through her nose, filling her lungs, echoing in the hollow of her head. Each inhale took her further away from the meeting that just happened, each exhale clearing her mind.

But not enough.

Rote muscle memory made her hand reach for the laptop, unplugging the dongle, carefully putting everything in cases before stashing it all in her oversized bag. A rush of emotion threatened to make her cry, but she wasn't going to allow that to happen.

A maybe was a maybe. She'd turned a no into a maybe, and that was no small feat.

Boyce's words began pinging through her head, distilling down to four syllables: untrustworthy.

Kell had told Boyce she was *untrustworthy*.

How dare he?

How *dare* he!

Outside, in the distance, a dull thwack caught her attention. Kell was striking something with his blade, his stupid spaceman suit looking extra ridiculous against the pastoral background. He looked like he was starring in a surreal film, destined to become a quirky classic in thirty years.

Quirk was the last thing she cared about, though, as reality sank in, the empty conference room taunting her.

A *maybe* still wasn't a *yes*.

And *untrustworthy* was an outrageous insult, beyond the pale.

Fury nearly made her launch herself at him through the picture window. As she shoved her laptop into her bag and put on her coat, she became nothing but emotion.

Emotion that needed a target.

A target in a spacesuit.

Chapter Eight

KELL

Machetes were cathartic.

Especially when you used them on grandfather vines.

Rare was the opportunity to take something toxic and eliminate it at the root; people just didn't have that ability. Not in society, not in government, and certainly not in corporate environments.

Out here, hunting for grandfather vines and systematically debriding trees of them, one at a time, gave Kell a sense of purpose. Vine removal was an arduous affair, one that could lead to third degree burns if he wasn't careful. Under his Tyvek suit, he wore silk long johns, jeans, and protective windbreaker pants. Triple gloves to his elbows, he had multiple layers for maximum effect.

The trick to killing a grandfather vine was to cut it low, at the base of the tree, then paint only the exposed ends from the cut with poison ivy herbicide. While Kell was no fan of commercial plant poisons, in this case, he could use as little as a few milliliters to do the trick.

Now finished hacking the vine, he pulled out a tiny paintbrush and a little glass container of herbicide. After carefully layering the herbicide on the open vine, he placed the brush and the jar in three layers of ziplock bags, to be thrown away. As much as he hated the waste, this wasn't a job you could do without getting urushiol everywhere, so some trade-offs had to be made.

Done. Not a drop of poison on him, and he hadn't touched the vine at all. Win-win.

After a few weeks, the herbicide would soak in fully, weakening the vine. Kell had cut and painted these vines in flights over the last few years, but this sucker had evaded him. In a few weeks, he'd return, just as carefully protected but with even stronger gloves.

Because the next step involved peeling the vines off the tree from the top down, using a ladder. He'd put them into a bag to be taken deep into the woods and tossed out onto the ground, the bag returned home to the trash.

This was rewarding work. He knew that the hair-like tentacles on the vines represented thousands of future vines that he was killing off, saving people from miserable rashes, reclaiming public space for his town.

Work didn't get any better than this.

Concrete and clear cut, he was doing *good*.

And doing good was in his blood.

"YOU!" someone screamed from off to his left, forcing him to look up and see Rachel storming toward him in a show of red.

Red coat, red face.

Red *rage*.

"What the *hell* do you think you're doing, marching around in a spacesuit in front of my presentation?"

Steam from the water rose between them, making the moment surreal.

"What?" Her words were a bit muffled by the helmet he wore, but he wasn't about to touch it to take it off, unless he removed one of his layers of gloves. While he'd been careful, poison ivy oil was like a virus.

Designed to go everywhere and make life miserable.

"You heard me! Sashaying around in front of that window at the exact moment I was trying to close a deal. And you *sabotaged* me! What are you telling Boyce about me? And who else, Mr. Poison Ivy? Because you might be removing poison from the ground, but you're spreading it all over this town when it comes to me!"

She dropped her bag with a thud on a bench close to the

water, then came back to him, standing right next to the tree he'd just been working on.

"And LOOK AT YOU," she shouted, continuing her rant but glancing toward Love You Chocolate, making certain they were out of view. That's when it hit him.

He'd done exactly what she was upset about. All of it.

Including the comment to Boyce.

"I'm surprised you're not wearing a pink suit during your precious peak season! I've never been in a place so sickly sweet and fakey fake. All that time in D.C., when we'd make fun of Love You, you'd get grumpy about it, but it turns out we were right! The people here are so close-minded. All about community," she said, her voice dripping contempt, "but never thinking about how change could make this an even better community."

"Change." He huffed. "You mean change that benefits you. Not us."

"This is NOT about ME! This is about a business deal, one you had *no* business sticking your nose in!"

"I warned Boyce," he said, stripping off his outer layer of gloves. He set them carefully in an open brown paper bag he'd brought for storing anything with urushiol on it. Then he lifted his helmet off and set it on the bench next to–but not touching–her bag.

"*Why?*"

"Because I want what's best for him and Lucinda, and you're not trustworthy."

"You *personalized* this? You sabotaged me because you still can't let yourself be wrong about what happened five years ago? You're literally destroying my career because your pride got hurt in D.C.? I had no idea you were such a weak man, Kell. Good grief."

Weak man.

Weak man?

Those words out of her mouth were intolerable. Unacceptable.

Damnable.

And they dove straight into the source of his fear.

His chest expanded as he breathed harder. "It's not weak to protect my town and the people I care about."

It killed him to admit it to himself, but she was smoking hot right now, fierce and angry, in his face. Passion like that was never limited to one part of a person. She had every right to be pissed at him, but he had every right to warn Boyce.

The Rachel who was screaming at him wasn't just upset that he'd sandbagged her.

She was upset that he'd hurt her feelings, too.

"Your motives aren't pure! You're poisoning them against me because you have a personal vendetta. You're doing to me exactly what Alissa and John did to you in D.C., Kell! Backstabbing–can't you see it?"

His skin tingled, hands and feet turning to lightning.

"You are so full of it, Rachel. The situations are nothing alike. Don't you dare accuse me of that."

"How is it different? It's *not*. You're just trying to protect your ego by denying it, and that's weak. You're intervening where you don't belong, to ruin my career!"

"Where I *don't belong?* Where I don't... You're literally standing on land that belonged to my great-great-great grandfather! This is *exactly* where I belong, more than anywhere else in the world! And you're here as a corporate drone for Markstone's, looking for a hot business to turn into a profit center for a huge conglomerate. Get in, get out, and get what you want. You just want to use the company Lucinda built for your own benefit."

Just like Alissa used him in D.C., with Rachel's help.

"That's not true!"

"You're not here to benefit your boss? Or your boss's boss's boss? To improve some quarterly report so Markstone's can continue on with its world domination via chocolate?"

"I am here to do my job, but that doesn't make me a less valuable human than you."

He snorted. "Human. Hah. You're nothing like the woman you used to be. The woman you *were*, before you schemed with Alissa."

"I'm the way I am because of *you!*"

Kell stopped cold.

"Excuse me?" he said, struggling to keep the growl out of his voice.

"You heard me. And thank you, by the way. Sincerely. The way I used to be made me a target for people like Alissa."

He almost interrupted her, but stopped because of something in her voice. Cold as steel, sharp enough to make a piece of him from the past bleed a little.

"I was so hurt that you didn't trust me," she said in a voice intended to make it sound like she didn't care now. She added a little huffy laugh at the end, like that was a childish thing from a childish past, but he caught the truth in there.

He really had hurt her.

Deeply.

"I didn't trust you because *you* hurt *me*."

"See?" A harsh laugh poured out of her, and he wanted to unhear it, destroy it, to yeet it as far into the woods as possible, never to be heard again.

Because he had caused that harshness, and he hated the way that made him feel.

Every aspect of Rachel's presence in his hometown was shredding him on the inside, too many warring factions pulling his heart in different directions. Could a heart be drawn and quartered? If so, she was doing it to him.

And it had to stop.

One way or another.

"You're never, ever going to get out of this emotional prison you've created for yourself, Kell, and now you're letting the poison inside you spill over into the town," she tossed out, her voice going low and quiet, hitting him with more emphasis than her screaming.

"You're turning this into *my* fault?"

"You never listened to me! Ever! At some point, you have to let go of the hurt you're carrying around inside you, buddy, and let people tell you *their* experience. Otherwise, you're just living in a cocoon, a miserable existence where you're always right but you never get to really learn and love."

Love. Did the word *love* just come out of her mouth?

"You're preaching to me about love? Here?"

"For a guy whose name literally has the word *love* in it, you're a pretty miserable person. And a jerk. And a backstabber. You turned half the town against me!"

"I did not!"

"If you told Boyce I'm not trustworthy, how fast will that get around in this gossip mill you call a town?"

She had a point.

"I did it for the town's own good."

"You did it because you hate me."

Hate.

How had the words *love* and *hate* come out of her mouth so close together, and both directed at him?

And both so damned right?

"I don't hate anyone, Rachel. You give yourself too much credit. You have to have strong feelings for someone to hate them. I feel nothing but apathy toward you."

"Okay. If you say so."

She leaned against the tree, her action too quick for him to stop her, the palm of her hand leaning flat against the open vine, her pants falling directly along the length of it.

"Rachel, stop!"

"No! I won't stop, damn you! Quit telling me what to do! I have every right to say what I want to say, when I want to say it, and just because you hate me doesn't mean–"

As she ranted at him, her hand rubbed against the vine again.

"STOP MOVING!"

"Now you think you can dictate what I do with my body?" The thin skin of her wrist rolled along it, causing physical pain inside him as he watched it all.

"Stop moving, because you're touching urushiol!"

She hesitated for a second.

"What is oo-roo-she-all?"

"Poison ivy."

"It's winter. Nothing's green. There's no ivy anywhere."

"That." He pointed to the long vine, calculating. Her bare skin had grazed the open machete cut, and she'd directly pressed against about two feet of the winding, hairy vine. She was coated in highly concentrated oil, and third degree burns could result if she didn't get it off her skin and get out of those clothes, *now*.

Moving to his kit bag, he found a bottle of dish soap.

"Take off your clothes."

"WHAT?"

"Take off your clothes, now, Rachel."

"*Seriously?* You're making a *pass* at me? For a guy who feels nothing but apathy, you're sending me some pretty mixed signals. And no. Of course I won't take my clothes off! What's wrong with you?"

"You need to get in the hot springs and soap up."

"What kind of sick fantasy is this?"

"Trust me, this was never part of any fantasy I had about you. This is about preventing you from having third degree burns." He stripped off his second layer of gloves and began unbelting her red wool coat. She batted at him, but he pivoted.

The last thing he needed was urushiol on him, too.

This was tricky. His suit might have some on it, and her hands and the right side of her definitely did. As steam wafted up between them, he formed a plan.

Fast.

"I'm giving you three seconds to start taking your clothes off, Rachel. The urushiol you touched on that grandfather vine is strong enough to cause third degree burns on bare skin."

"Is this some kind of stunt? Am I being punked?"

"It's not a stunt, and I'm completely serious. You have three seconds to get out of that coat and those pants."

"What?"

"Every part of you that touched the vine is putting you in danger!" he shouted, unzipping his suit, peeling off his protective pants and jeans and nearly falling over as he hopped on one foot, suddenly standing there only in silk long johns, earning a gasp from her as he shed his clothes.

"*What* are you *doing?*"

"Rescuing you," he said in a weary tone. "Again."

It only took one good push to get her in the hot springs, his body remembering high school football, the instinct to shove forward and tackle kicking in. He hadn't been on a field in a decade, but the move came back to him quickly. He was clutching the small bottle of soap in his hand.

Then a faceful of hot water hit him as he jumped in.

"ARE YOU CRAZY?" she sputtered, coming up for air, arms flapping. The thick wool coat was open in the front, but it weighed her down. He swam to her and began tugging at her cuffs.

"Get this off. It's pulling you down."

"BECAUSE YOU THREW ME IN THE WATER!"

"I DID IT TO SAVE YOUR SKIN!"

One yank and he freed her right arm, and then he had enough of the coat in his hands to pull it off her. Rachel bobbed underwater for a second, his legs kicking hard in the hot water to keep him afloat.

The wet, heavy coat was hard to chuck, but he did it, the splat as it landed on the edge of shore satisfying.

But this was just the start.

"Get your shoes off," he ordered as he searched for the soap bottle, which he'd let go of. It was only half full and should be floating, but it was nowhere in sight.

If he couldn't get that soap on her skin where the oily residue clung, she'd still get burned, and possibly even worse. Hot water was the worst thing to put on skin that had touched poison ivy, because it opened up the pores, but the soap with the water would do the trick.

Nothing about this situation was perfect. He'd have to do his best.

"I am swimming to shore!"

"Not before I soap you." He grabbed her shoulder and tried very hard to convey the gravity of the situation. "I'm not doing this to be a jerk. I'm doing this because you touched a very concentrated amount of poison ivy oil and I'm not kidding, not pranking, not punking you. The sooner you're out of the clothes that touched the oil, and soap up the parts of you that were exposed to it, the sooner we'll avert disaster. You're especially vulnerable if you touched it with an open wound."

Finally, *finally*, the woman seemed to hear him.

"Oh, no," she said, beginning to thrash in the water, awkwardly bending to unzip her ankle boot. She hauled the waterlogged thing up and threw it toward her coat. It hit shore. "This is definitely the worst day of my life!"

"Yesterday's up there, too," he muttered.

"I'm counting at twenty-four hours," she yelled as she tossed her other boot, then began fumbling under water. "Pants, too?" she asked, eyes filled with fear.

"Anything that touched that vine."

"I was wearing the coat, so my arm is fine."

"Then pants."

"But I'll be half naked in public!"

"Won't be the first time."

"You are not helping!"

As she struggled in the water, he saw the soap bottle behind her. He swam to it and popped open the top, pouring some out.

"Shouldn't we get to shore?"

"We'll do two rounds of soap. One in the water, one out of it." Holding out the bottle, he waited for her outstretched hand, but she was moving toward shore.

"Where are you going?"

"Where I can stand!"

Following her, he reached a point where he could just barely stand, the water to his chin. They were only five feet from shore, but the dropoff was steep.

"Stop here," he ordered, pouring some soap out.

"I still can't stand."

"It's a steep dropoff, you won't be able to. Give me your arm."

To his surprise, she complied, her other hand on his shoulder to stabilize. Once again, they were face to face, trapped by circumstance, but this time, he had to rub every inch of her body that might be at risk from the poison ivy.

A different kind of rescue.

Steam filled the air between them, Rachel's face wet and flushed as he took her arm and rubbed the viscous liquid on her, foaming in the air, her skin soft and slick as he caressed her, moving slow. The job had to be thorough.

"It's cold outside of the water."

"I know," he said. "But you have to lift your arm so I can get the soap on you."

Again, she did as told, his motions slowing down as she thrashed less, now dependent on his steady stance to be able to do what needed to be done.

"Rise up and float on your back," he said as he popped the top back on the soap bottle and slid one hand down to the small of her back, fingers trailing the cord of muscle, finding the swell of a hip.

His pulse picked up.

"On my back?"

"I can get the side of your leg that way."

"Oh."

As she let go of his shoulder, she moved next to him, her legs rising up as she formed her body into a T on the water's surface.

Squeezing more soap into his hand, he grasped her ankle, her toenails perfectly manicured like her fingernails, pink with white tips.

When he touched her, she gasped, the sound sensual and alluring, going straight to parts of him he did not want on display in wet silk long johns.

No siree.

Focusing on her injured hand from yesterday, he coated the glued cut. Urushiol was particularly dangerous if it got in the bloodstream via a cut, and Rachel's hand was a crucial point of entry.

Moving his hand up the side of her calf, he worked with precision to coat her with the soap. They were both silent until he reached her upper leg, then her hip, mentally mapping where she'd leaned against the vine, her breath quickening as he reached the back of her knee, the outer curve of her thigh.

Keeping his own breath steady wasn't easy, either. For all her faults, Rachel was an exceptionally attractive woman, and having her before him half-clothed was maddening.

"Okay," he said softly, soaping his hands as he let her float. "Done."

Dropping her feet immediately, she sighed as the warm water enveloped her again. "How are we going to get out of this? We'll freeze instantly."

"I'll go first and get a blanket from my truck. This is my fault."

"No kidding." Her hand went back on his shoulder, mouth twitching with a smile, eyes focused on him but soft.

Water lapped against them in the small space between their chests, the steam adding a magical quality that made him reach for her, his hands finding her waist, her sudden sharp inhale one of desire, not protest. Years of yearning pumped through his blood, and any fight he had against what he was about to do resolved when she leaned forward, her eyes closing, the kiss inevitable.

As their lips touched, red fireworks flashed behind his eyes.

It was a dream come true.

Until he heard his brother shout, "KELL, WHAT THE HELL ARE YOU DOING?"

Rachel's feet came up and kicked off his knees, pushing

back so fast, she splashed him in the face. They turned to see Luke standing next to his pink cruiser, the door still open, lights flashing. He had pulled up in a clearing between the trees.

"Two calls came in about a couple skinny dipping in the springs. You know the best place for that is down near Greek's Rock! Not here in town where people can see!"

"We're not skinny dipping!" Rachel shouted. "I touched Kell's vine and he had to rub me down."

Luke shook his head, hands on his hips as he turned off the lights and walked closer, staring down at Rachel.

"Do I have to arrest you for public indecency, too? Touching his *vine?* Rubbing you down?"

"You know she's talking about poison ivy, Luke." Kell hauled himself out of the water, the chill welcome as it shrank him. "Be a good public servant and get us some insulated blankets from the trunk of your car." The shock of cold brought him down to earth.

Kissing Rachel was a mistake.

Then why was it a mistake he really, really wanted to make again?

"What are you two really doing?"

"Fighting," Kell said.

"With your lips?"

"Excuse me? I could use some help here. I'm not tall enough to stand, I'm half naked, and according to Kell, hot water makes the oil get in my pores even more. Can you please get me out of here so Kell can put more soap on me?"

"She touched a grandfather vine with bare skin."

Luke's alarmed look validated Kell.

"Why would you do that?"

"Just get the blankets!" Kell snapped as he wiggled carefully into his Tyvek suit, knowing it would insulate him a bit.

Luke was, at heart, a practical man. He jogged to his car, pulled some Mylar blankets out of his trunk, and by the time he was back, Kell had fished Rachel out of the water.

Luke helped her with a blanket, while Kell wrapped the other one around his shoulders.

"I need another one for my legs." Rachel spoke through chattering teeth.

Kell instantly handed his to her, and she took it gratefully. Luke handed Kell a new one.

"A ride to my car would be much appreciated," she said archly to Luke, giving Kell side glances that made him wonder more and more about that kiss.

"Let me soap your arm and leg one more time," Kell said to her.

"I can do it," she protested. "At my trailer."

"Use as much as you can. And shower in lukewarm water."

"I need to get to my car first. That is, unless Randy impregnated it," she muttered, which didn't make a lick of sense to Kell, but maybe the trauma of what just happened fried her brain.

Luke began to laugh, though.

"Get in my car. Both of you. You need to go home, shower, warm up, and rest."

Rachel grabbed her bag and started after Luke, who turned, waiting for Kell.

"I'm fine. Cleaning up here. Get her settled."

A single wave was his brother's reply.

As they disappeared, Kell surveyed the scene in disbelief. He needed more than a little time to process that kiss.

Almost kiss.

Another one.

Rachel's red coat was a partially frozen chunk. Her boots lay at tipsy angles on the bank. Something resembling a pant leg floated close enough to the edge that, once he found a long-enough stick, he was able to retrieve her pants.

And then there was his kit. Fortunately, plastic bags were standard equipment for a poison ivy puller, because containment was job one.

He put all her stuff in a big black trash bag, picked up the kit, and started walking up toward the parking lot, a shortcut to where he was parked on the street. By the time he got there, Luke was pulling in, his passenger seat empty.

"Hey, idiot. Let me give you a warm ride to your truck."

"Nope. Too much exposed equipment."

"Then let me talk some sense into you."

"Good luck."

"Oh, I have zero expectations. Can't help but try, though."

"I don't need a lecture."

"When are you going to make it official and ask that woman out on a date?"

"When hell freezes over."

"Given the weather, not impossible."

"You think I want to *date* her?"

"I think you want to do way more than just date her."

"Are you kidding? She represents everything I hate in the world."

"You cared enough to go caveman on her."

"I'd do that for anyone."

"Really? Like to see you try that with Greta. You'd float together in the steamy hot springs as you took her clothes off and soaped her up?"

"Shut up, Luke. You're the last person who should be talking about anyone else's love life."

Luke went stone faced.

Damn.

Kell took in a shaky breath and pulled the emergency blanket tighter around himself. "Sorry. That was a stupid thing to say. I didn't mean it that way."

"You're not wrong."

Luke's wife, Amber, had died fifteen months ago, in a freak car accident. She'd been walking on the side of one of the winding roads on the outskirts of town when a driver had a heart attack and died at the wheel. He'd slammed into her.

Luke and his rookie partner had found her while driving on backroads, Luke training the new guy.

Nothing could be done.

Now, his older brother was a single dad to the sweetest six-year-old girl on the planet, though Kell knew he was biased about little Harriet.

"Still wasn't fair of me."

"Nothing in life is fair, Kell." Luke looked across the parking lot to where Rachel's car was pulling out, turning right to head back toward Kenny's. "But sometimes, life hands you something you need to explore."

"I'm not getting entangled with that woman."

"It's a little too late for that."

"Absolutely not. I was trying to help her. I warned her not to touch the grandfather vine. If that oil had stayed on her hand, she'd have had burns for sure."

"And the kiss was helping to heal her, huh?"

"Uh." That's all Kell could manage.

"*Uh* is right," Luke said with a laugh. "Get your butt back to your truck, go home, take a cold shower, and help that poor woman with her designer clothes and her useless boots get her head on straight. She might be here to do something you don't like, but you owe her an apology."

"Apology? I just saved her from third degree contact burns!"

"I'm not talking about that."

Luke gave him a look, and Kell realized he was talking about what he'd said to Boyce.

And Silver. And Colleen. And a handful of other people.

Just enough to get people upset about Lucinda selling to Markstone's.

"I did the right thing. You know places like Markstone's are all about coming in and changing everything."

"You maligned Rachel's reputation."

"*Maligned* is a strong word."

"It is. And you did it. You did it because she hurt you, not because she might hurt the town."

"Come on, Luke! That's b.s. and you know it."

"What's b.s. is the long-suffering hurt you've been nursing all these years about her."

"You think I'm overpersonalizing this?"

"Never heard that word before, but it fits."

Rachel's words stung him twice.

"I think you need to go find her tomorrow and have a real talk. The kind adults have when they need to figure something out. The kind Amber and I used to have."

Pain shot through Kell's chest at the mention of his late sister-in-law. For Luke to play that card, Kell really must be screwing up.

"And get her stuff dry cleaned. Least you can do."

With that, Luke rolled up his car window and drove off.

A rustle in the woods made him turn to find Randy the Moose standing there, giant eyeballs on him.

Weak man, those eyeballs said.

Weak man.

Chapter Nine

RACHEL

Fix this, the text from Orla read.

That was it. Two words. Simple, crystal clear, and deadly.

Career deadly, that is. Her career was over if she couldn't get Lucinda and Boyce to sell, and Kell Luview had nearly destroyed her chances for that.

Nearly.

Her shower here at the trailer had been thorough, a quick internet search telling her that everything Kell said was correct. Hot water opened the pores and let the poison ivy oil in. Lukewarm showers with lots of soap were better. Her post-hot-springs dip was followed by a shivering wash-off that left her wondering how bad the rash would become.

Fortunately, Dani made her a little travel kit for emergencies like this, a small bottle of Benadryl at the ready if she needed it, and she could make a hospital visit of it got bad enough.

Shoving her in the waters had been an act of caring, as sputteringly bizarre as it sounded.

And then there was that kiss...

Almost kiss.

Why were they always *almost*? If Rachel's entire life could be summed up in one word, it would be *almost*.

Everything felt like almost. She was *almost* successful. She was *almost* good enough. She had *almost* kissed Kell—twice.

Back at Stanford, she'd almost been included in a high-profile project. Almost been hired by bigger corporations than Markstone's.

Almost got her parents' approval.

Almost had relationships.

Every part of her life felt like it was close... but not quite.

Good... but not great.

Nice try.

Strong effort.

Real potential.

Always a runner up, never the winner.

And now, she'd *almost* clinched the Love You Chocolate deal.

Speaking of which, the bowl in front of her was half full. She popped another candy in her mouth and rolled the red foil into a tiny ball between her thumb and index finger, adding it to the growing pile in the center of the table.

Almost there, she typed back to Orla, hitting Send.

Message failed, the phone replied.

Might as well say *YOU failed*.

Rachel hit Send again and this time, it went through. Already, she was learning a few tricks. Internet in the trailer was fickle.

Like her mother picking a smoothie stand after hot yoga class.

As she logged into her work email, Rachel reached for the sad cup of coffee that tasted nothing like the one from Love You Coffee yesterday.

Yesterday.

Day one in town: glued to Kell.

Day two in town: thrown in the hot springs and soaped up by Kell.

And then there was that kiss.

Okay. Fine. *Almost* kiss.

Every breath she took reminded her of it, the feel of his shoulder under her hand, his chest rising and falling as the danger from what she'd done receded. No one had ever insisted on protecting her so fiercely before. An innocent mistake could have made her life miserable, and he'd seen that. Acted on it.

Made sure she was fine.

Some basic internet searches told her it would be days before her skin would erupt into the rash, so now it was all about waiting.

So much of her life was about waiting.

No way was she venturing anywhere near downtown today. Might as well hide in the trailer and work all day, no matter how dismal it was. Promising the Armisteads that she'd be in town until February 15 had been an impulse, way out of her normal paradigm for how to handle a failing deal.

Now she was stuck for nine more days in Maine, with spotty internet and possible third degree burns. The internet that blew hot and cold like her mother choosing lip filler, and the email from Doug with the subject line *Performance Improvement Plan* didn't start day three off well, either.

Closing the laptop, she stood, three pairs of socks on her feet under her running shoes, a pair of sweatpants pulled over her pajama bottoms, and the down comforter wrapped around her, hair in a messy topknot.

Why did it matter what she looked like? Rachel was going nowhere and seeing no one. If she spent the day hermitting, without a single interaction with another living thing, it would be a glorious day.

Her phone rang.

Jumping out of her skin, she looked at the phone like it was Satan the Squirrel. Was it Orla, calling to chew her out?

Nope. Worse.

Mom.

"Um, hi?"

"Honey!" Portia said, her voice low and smooth. The sound of it evoked lilacs and sandalwood, her mother's scent from Rachel's childhood. "How did the deal go?"

Temporary amnesia struck. Rachel struggled to remember when she'd told her mother she was working on a deal.

"Deal?"

"You're in Maine, right? Where we filmed my adorable little reality show, the one the stupid network didn't appreciate because they lack vision. My wonderful friend Deanna reached out to me and promised she'd take good care of my little girl," her mother gushed.

Rachel's right temple started to pound.

Dani made sure she always had ibuprofen in her work bag, thank goodness.

"It's all good," Rachel lied, searching for her bag.

"You're not eating too many of those chocolates, are you? I cannot fathom why you chose to work for a *chocolate* company, of all places, Rachel! Why couldn't you have been hired somewhere useful, like a Botox company?"

The joke was ancient, but her mother wasn't really joking.

"Ha ha. I'm more likely to drink the coffee here than eat the candy, Mom. You held out on me. Love You Coffee serves some of the best I've ever had!"

"I don't drink coffee anymore, honey. I found caffeine pills. I get the buzz without staining my teeth."

Conversations with her mother tended to suck any tiny bit of remaining fun out of Rachel's life.

"So what's up, Mom? You okay?"

"Of course I am! Why would you ask? I live a charmed life!"

That much was true. Portia met Rachel's father, Stan, when she was eighteen and working in the secretarial pool of his law firm. He was ten years older and fell in love with the aspiring model quickly; the two of them were married within three months.

Her mother's career jumpstarter was a poster that capitalized on the iconic 1980s movie, *Ten*. Posing in a revealing one-piece, long, dark blonde hair in cornrows, Portia's image adorned the walls of every teenage boy's bedroom.

And Stan had swung into action.

Turning Portia Starman into a television star had been her dad's greatest achievement, not because he hadn't succeeded in other ways, but because her mom wasn't exactly a strong businesswoman. Years ago, during one of many lunches with her mom and her mom's agent, Morty, he'd commented that if Portia hadn't married Stan and become an actress, she'd have been a clerk in a flower shop, or a career receptionist.

Her mother had simply said, "I've lived a charmed life."

When Rachel had told her dad the story, he'd laughed and laughed and laughed, then mused aloud whether Morty wasn't past his prime and it was time to switch.

"Mom?"

"Yes?"

"Why didn't you tell me Kell Luview lives in Love You again? When you were here filming a few years ago, you must have run into him."

"Deanna's boy? Why would I tell you about that?"

It hit Rachel hard between the eyes, a memory of Deanna's hug and how warm and welcoming it was intruding on her call with her own mother.

Portia Starman hadn't bothered to say a word about Kell to Rachel because Rachel had never told her parents what happened back at EEC between Kell, Alissa, and her.

It had been too embarrassing.

"Oh, no reason."

"He's a hottie, isn't he? Big old lumberjack… "

"I really don't know, Mom."

Portia sighed. "This deal, Rachel–any chance we could revive my old reality series and do an episode on the chocolate company you're trying to buy?"

And there it was.

Her mother was fishing for work.

"Uh, I don't think so, Mom. Dad's the expert on that." Try as he might, Stan hadn't been able to keep the TV show going. Networks knew a loser when they saw it, and no one had wanted *Love You Springs Eternal* beyond those first six episodes.

"Your father," Portia said in an exasperated tone. "He thinks it's time for me to accept reality and take mother roles."

Those two words, *mother roles*, were anathema in their family.

"I might as well audition for grandmother roles," her mom followed up, cackling as if that were absurd.

"Deanna's a grandmother," Rachel said without thinking. "And she's about your age."

Her mom sounded like she was choking on her own tongue.

"I am *not* Deanna's age!"

"I think you are."

"She's at least ten years older."

"Okay. If you say so."

"Hmph." A distracted sound, then a beep, meant her mom was texting. "Well, I was just checking in with my baby girl. Any new boyfriend opportunities? Not that you'd find your type there."

"My type?"

"You always date movers and shakers, Rachel."

Nico sure did move her money and shake her down.

"I do?"

"Like your father."

"I do not pick men like my father!"

"Not lately. When was your last date, honey?"

Ouch.

Rachel wasn't about to admit it was over a year ago. Nico had been an act of desperation. Hot as hell and built like one of those TikTokkers who wears an apron over a bare chest, with muscles bulging out the sides, Nico had been great in bed and not great for anything else.

"When was your last offer for a role that isn't a mother role, Mom?"

An audible, pained gasp told Rachel her question hit the mark, too.

Yay. Now they'd mutually injured each other's feelings, which meant they were family. The Hart-Starman version, at least. Rachel doubted that Deanna Luview traded painful barbs with her kids like this.

"Sorry, Mom."

"It's okay. I deserved it. I shouldn't ask about your love life. I remember how hard it was being on the market."

"You married Dad at eighteen."

"That doesn't mean the years before that were easy."

"When? In high school?"

Portia ignored that. "Finding the love of your life is hard work. Maybe you're in the wrong job, sweetie. Get a job at a law firm and you could meet a nice man who will take care of you. Worked for me!"

"I have an MBA from Stanford, Mom. I can take care of myself."

"I wasn't implying you can't! But–" Shuffling sounds, then, "Rachel? I have to go. Morty's texting me and he says there's a really wonderful multi-generational women's fiction series, like *Virgin River* meets *Steel Magnolias,* that's being cast and they're considering me for a younger version of Angela Lansbury in *Murder She Wrote*. Has to be a *way* younger version, of course, but bye! Kiss kiss!"

Her mom literally said the words. Didn't make the sound.

Then ended the call.

Long, slow, cleansing breaths to get the mixed emotion out and accept and appreciate the connection with her mother were the only tool in her toolbox.

Portia loved her. Dearly, she knew.

But her mom didn't *know* her.

And Rachel sorely, eagerly wanted someone to know her.

Problem was, she wasn't quite sure who she was, and if she didn't know herself, how could she expect someone else to?

"It's too early in the day to have thoughts and feelings this deep," she muttered, standing and pulling out the drawer where the coffee pods were kept. Before she could flip open the machine, though...

Thump.

Ka-thump.

"RANDY!" she screamed. At least she was armed with his name now, the image it conjured so much less threatening than Godzilla. "PLEASE STOP!"

The rocking began, throwing Rachel's pens into spasms on the table, her glass of water about to slosh over.

"WHUUUUUH!"

"The trailer's just not that into you!" she yelled as the rocking intensified. What made a thousand-pound moose think it could copulate with an RV? Did the trailer's fiberglass coating somehow emit moose pheromones?

The sound of a car engine outside, close to the trailer, filled her with a new rush of alarm. Who was here? Moving her water glass to the sink and securing anything that Randy might knock over, she went to the window. Kell Luview was stepping out of his truck, holding a dry cleaner's bag.

Talk about weird sights.

"RANDY!" Kell hollered, looking to the left with disgust. "Cut that out!"

The rocking stopped.

Rachel saw how Kell's verbal warning was given with confidence, but his body language was wary. He halted right outside the truck, leaving the door open.

Last night, Rachel had googled moose. Rutting moose, to be specific. The search engine returned an image of a moose's uh, member... that was now permanently etched in her brain. Surprisingly large, even for a huge animal.

But she learned that a rutting moose could go crazy on a human. The worst were mama moose protecting their babies, but that was just common sense. What Kell was doing wasn't exactly recommended. The "experts" on Reddit all agreed that being quiet was the best approach, but Kell was born and raised in Maine, and her encounters with Randy had resulted in no good outcomes, so who was she to judge?

Kell's careful stance made it clear that while his intent was to drive Randy off and keep Rachel safe, he was also making sure he could jump back in his truck if the moose charged.

"Whuh?" Randy said, stepping back from the trailer hitch, the tip of his antlers in Rachel's line of sight.

A sigh that was closer to a grunt came out of Kell.

To her utter surprise, Randy turned and walked into the woods without a word.

Final score: Kell, 1. Randy, whatever. How many times had he copulated with the trailer? Her car?

"You okay?" Kell called as he approached the trailer. Rachel looked in wonder at the spot where Randy had just been.

"I'm fine. But you're not supposed to yell at a moose."

"Says who? Google?"

"Reddit."

They both chuckled as he held out the dry cleaning bag. "Here."

"What's this?"

"A peace offering. An apology."

Her heart warmed. "For yesterday?"

"For... a lot." His eyes dropped to her mouth.

Ah, yes. The kiss.

The *almost* kiss.

"Thank you." She looked through the clean, freshly pressed clothing. Her coat and pants were in there, and the boots were in plastic bags. "I didn't expect to ever get these back."

"I grabbed the coat and boots, fished the pants out, and took them to Labrecque's."

"Labrecque's?"

"Dry cleaners."

"They don't call it Love You Clean?"

"Of course not. That would be silly."

"Right."

"Anyway, that's the name of Katie Hanscomb's cleaning service."

"This town," she sighed.

"Good thing you're only here for a short time."

Her free hand was on the door jamb, Kell standing two steps lower but close enough that she could smell woodsmoke wafting off him.

"Actually, I'm staying longer. I just texted Kenny about it."

"You are? Why?"

"In spite of your best attempts to undermine me, I convinced Lucinda to change her no to a maybe."

"How did you do that?"

She batted her eyelashes. "Bucketloads of charm."

"You mean bucketloads of *money*."

"I said what I meant, Kell."

"How long are you here?"

"Until February 15th."

Of all the responses she could have expected, full-throated laughter wasn't one of them. The sound of his amusement scared a squirrel off the small grill next to the trailer hitch.

"You're going to be here on Valentine's Day!"

"I'll hide in the trailer."

"Don't you want to experience Love You, Maine, in all its glory? Consider it the cost of doing business."

"I plan to hide here with a good book, or binge watch something dark and dreary on Netflix." She tilted her head and took a chance. "Do you still watch Nordic noir?"

"Of course. Did you watch that crazy series set in Svalbard?"

"I did. We're probably two of the ninety people in the world who saw it."

"Then that makes us extra special."

The dry cleaning was pulling on her forearm, which was still sore from two days ago. Holding up a finger, she turned and hung it in the tiny closet, then came back to the door and waved him in. "Want some coffee?"

"Kenny's stuff? No thanks. That crap has chicory in it."

"Is that why it tastes so weird?"

"Ayup." His exaggerated Maine accent made her laugh, but she was disappointed he didn't come in.

Kell moved to a spot where two wooden Adirondack chairs were turned upside down. The wind had blown the area fairly clear of snow, exposing a circle of stones on the ground. He stood for a moment looking at a small woodpile, then began pulling out small and large pieces, until the pile was neatly restacked inside the circle.

"Kenny gave you newspaper, right?"

"I think there's some in a cupboard."

"Hand it over. Let's build a fire and talk."

Talk.

For five years, all she'd wanted was to go back in time and get Kell Luview to talk to her. And now he was willing?

Now?

So many responses came to her, most of them sarcastic and cutting, but the truth prevailed. So did her haunting need.

Reaching for the newspaper, she pulled it off the table and handed it to him.

"Here."

"Thanks."

She pulled her ski jacket over the multiple layers she was already wearing and stepped outside. For the next two minutes, she watched as he built the fire, the big pieces of wood laid in a criss-cross, bunched up newspaper crammed into nooks and crannies. Smaller chunks and sticks were poked in between. He carried a lighter in the pocket of his flannel shirt.

Smoke appeared, then small flames. As he blew softly, on his knees, pushing air where it was needed to make the fire catch, something in Rachel lessened.

Relaxed.

Maybe even smiled.

"Hey!"

Rachel turned, stunned, to find a man standing there, waving in such a friendly way she felt embarrassed that she didn't recognize him, until Kell called back, "Hey, Kenny."

Ah.

Her landlord.

"Rachel. Kell," he said, giving his cousin a waggling eyebrow look that made him look like old movie clips of Groucho Marx. "Good to meet you in person, Rachel."

"You too, Kenny."

"Whatcha up to?" he asked, peering at Kell's wood stack.

"You drunk, Kenny? I'm building a fire, obviously."

"Don't see you hanging out at my trailer much, Cuz," Kenny said, his implication clear.

"Helping an old friend."

"Aw. Is Rachel *stuck* in a *bind*?" Kenny slapped his own knee, and Rachel's opinion of him lowered one standard deviation.

"Funny," Kell said, stone faced. "You here to bring her more wood? It's out."

"Aw, hell. Of course. Sorry about that, Rachel. I saw your text about staying through February 15th, and wanted to talk about that. It's booked for the thirteenth and fourteenth. Booked a year ago by the Wilsons. They come every year, but they're on a tight budget, so they always stay at the trailer. Real nice people. Sorry. You'll have to check out the morning of the thirteenth."

"I see." Not expecting that news, Rachel had to bury her emotional reaction, especially with so many other emotions swirling in Kell's presence. "I'll take what I can get, and figure out the rest."

"I'm sure Rider has some bunks free," Kenny said, trying to be helpful.

Kell stiffened. "No way Rachel's staying in the bunkhouse."

"I'm fine," she assured them. "Maybe I'll book at Nordic-beth, like my assistant originally recommended."

The men grimaced.

"You can't, unless you plan on driving an hour and a half each way," Kenny said sadly.

"An hour and a half! I thought it was forty-five minutes!"

"That was before the bridge collapsed."

"The bridge?"

"The one on Route 11. Been out for a few months. Looks like another year and a half before it's fully operational. It's really hurting tourism from the ski resort," Kenny said. "Doesn't hurt rentals, though. Thank goodness, because that's how me and Lisa make a living. I rent 'em, she cleans 'em."

"Well," Rachel said, struggling to find something positive to say, "maybe it's good that my assistant didn't book me at Nordic-beth after all. I'd have had a nasty surprise if I'd gone there."

"But you'd have never had that nasty surprise of gluing your-self to Kell here," Kenny helpfully pointed out.

Kell's flat look shut him up.

Today was February 6. Rachel had a week to find something.

"Do me a favor, Kenny," Kell said. "Put the word out. Someone might have a room to rent for those last couple of days."

"You don't have to do that!" she protested.

"I know I don't. But it's how things are done here. Someone might need to make a little extra money and not mind having a guest stay with them for two nights."

"I don't know about staying in someone's house," she demurred, but then reconsidered. Being here through February 15 was crucial to the deal. "But," she added, "let's see. Maybe something will work out. I'm all ears."

"I would think you'd want to stay somewhere without a lovesick moose humping your dwelling," Kell said, giving Kenny a meaningful look.

"Awww, Randy? He been poking you?"

"He's destroyed my ability to sleep and damaged my car."

"Your car?"

"He tried to, you know..." Rachel thrust her hips forward twice.

Kenny blushed. "Oh, I know. And I'm real sorry. I thought we got him to stop."

"You didn't put that in your notes about how to use the place."

"Please don't leave a bad review! Randy hasn't done it for a while. We've been working on cleaning the pheromones off."

"Pheromones?" Kell and Rachel said together.

"Yeah. The moose juice," Kenny said with a chuckle. "Me and the guys were out here with a fire, having some beers, and Jerry Butalli spilled a bunch on the hitch. Didn't think much about it until poor Randy came along and nearly broke a nut on the bar."

"Thanks for that mental image," Kell said dryly.

"You *knew* you had moose pheromones all over the trailer and didn't tell me? I thought Maine was having an unprecedented earthquake the first time Randy attacked the trailer!" Rachel hissed.

"*Attack* is such a harsh word," Kenny said softly, giving her a hangdog look. "Randy's just looking for love."

"In all the wrong places," Kell muttered.

"This isn't funny! He just did it again! Kell had to make him go away. If I'm stuck in this trailer for another week, you need to promise me you'll do everything possible to make him stop!"

"We tried peeing on it," Kenny said sheepishly.

"*Why?*" Rachel asked, aghast.

"Because male urine can keep animals away."

"That's bullshit," Kell said. "Human male urine perimeters won't keep moose away."

"Maybe a bear, sure," Kenny mused. "What does keep a moose away, though?" Kenny asked. "'Cause Jerry said if we all took a piss on the hitch, it'd be fine."

"Jerry's a blowhard and he's always wrong. What you need is cougar urine."

"Huh. My sister Darlene is in her fifties and she just got divorced. I'll give her a case of beer and she can come over here and trickle out a nice perimeter."

"Not that kind of cougar," Kell rumbled.

Kenny's phone buzzed. He looked at it.

"Yikes. My other rental's got an ice dam and water leaking in through the kitchen window. Gotta go."

Without another word, he stomped off, then shouted, "I'll get you more wood before noon!"

"What's an ice dam?" Rachel asked Kell.

"It's when a gutter fills with snow, then the sun melts it, and dripping water off the roof creates a big, long row of ice. It all refreezes, and the ice can make its way into the house wall, between any seam in the siding, the drywall, the window frames, you name it."

"There are so many ways snow and ice can hurt people. I had no idea."

He shrugged. "Every part of the country has its weather problems. California has plenty."

"Sure. I know what to do in an earthquake. When Randy started attacking the trailer, my mind immediately went to latched cabinets and any shelves that might have valuables that could fall off and shatter."

"Huh."

"At home, I have a fireproof zip pouch for important papers. And plenty of air purifiers for wildfire season," she continued, thinking it through.

He made a face. "I don't know how I'd function living somewhere with so much forest burning constantly."

"You work around the smoke."

"I don't mean that. I mean it would hurt to see so many beautiful trees destroyed in huge numbers like that."

She nodded. "I've driven around some areas in Sonoma County after the fires. Nothing but charred ground and half-burnt trees. The worst is all the dead wildlife. You don't see them, but you know they died. And the sound is creepy. No birds. No rustling. Just... silence."

He shuddered. "No place is perfect. You have to adapt to whatever you're dealt."

"That sounds very philosophical."

"I think it's more practical." He smiled at her. "But I can see how it's both." He turned the two Adirondack chairs right side up and brushed off some clinging snow. "Come have a sit," he said, patting a red camp chair.

"Are we doing this? Actually talking and hanging out? Not glued together, not fighting and going for an impromptu swim," she joked, eyeing the fire with a longing that didn't have words to match.

"Sure. Welcome to Maine. Our favorite pastime is burning wood while gossiping."

"Let's add some coffee to that," she said with a laugh, going back in the trailer.

"His coffee sucks. Remember?"

Rachel found two little pods that were different, and inserted one in the coffee maker.

She went to the door and called out, "I found some without chicory!"

"I'll take it, then. Thanks!"

"You still drink it black?"

"You remember?"

"I'll take that as a yes."

While the coffee dripped, she pulled on a knitted hat, then picked up the mugs. The coffee's heat tickled her nose and she smiled, the domestic comfort of this simple task filling her with a contentment that caught her off guard. As she walked to the fire pit, Kell stood halfway, taking the mug out of her ungloved hands, his own encased in ski gloves.

"You need to cover your hands. Cold out here."

"The mug is keeping me warm."

"It won't in about one minute."

She sat, feeling the intense heat from the new fire. Her back was cold, but her front was warming quickly. A gulp of coffee went straight down her sternum and she pulled the jacket's zipper up higher.

"How do you live with this kind of cold all the time?"

"We just do. It's all I've ever known."

"D.C. must have been tropical to you."

His smile was nostalgic and contemplative. "D.C. was foreign in a lot of ways. The weather was only one of them."

They were headed into prickly emotional territory. Rachel chose to go quiet, wanting to stretch out the sense of grounded peace that was seeping into her pores. If she could have more moments like this, her life would make more sense.

If she could have more moments like this with Kell, her life would be so much happier.

Sitting in silence with another person was an art form.

And Kell had perfected it.

The steady hum of the woods surprised her, a white noise made by nature that she didn't notice in regular life. Then again, in L.A., when would the city ever be quiet enough to hear the backdrop?

As time passed, she watched Kell look up at the sky, a large hawk circling high, wings wide and looping in circles. Each breath brought a sharp, crisp feeling to her forehead, the coffee tickling her nose with decreasing heat as each sip brought her closer to done. Pausing, she listened to the woods and heard distinct sounds.

Squirrels chattered.

Leaves rustled.

And Kell's steady breath continued through it all, his hand

bringing the mug to his mouth, his ability to be at ease filling her with a rush of something pleasant and settled.

As the coffee grew cold, he was right–her hands were turning to ice. Shoving her free hand into her coat pocket helped. Inching closer to the fire helped, too.

Two minutes passed. Then five. At roughly ten minutes, a deer stepped into the clearing behind Kell's truck, big and graceful.

"Look," she whispered, breaking the stillness. Kell leaned toward her to follow her gaze. Woodsmoke filled her nose and the fire's warmth made her knees tingle, her muscles shifting down to a state of quiet relaxation she'd never felt before, as if her whole body were encased in a calm joy.

"Doe," he whispered back. It moved slowly, hooves popping through crunchy snow, sniffing around. Then it noticed the two of them, looked up and froze.

"Hi, deer," she said softly.

It sprinted away, leaving a few bare branches swaying as it disappeared into the woods.

"So beautiful," she murmured.

"Yes," he said.

He was looking right at Rachel.

Phone messages, emails, documentation, meetings–all of it piled up in the sector of Rachel's brain where expectations and responsibilities lived rent-free, taking up space that wasn't real but felt more real than reality itself.

It was oppressive. The constant need to do better was an inner pain she lived with, something that was just there.

Only... right now it was less.

Until this moment, it hadn't occurred to her that she could live without it. That was an option?

"You said you watched the show about Svalbard, huh?" he asked, poking the fire with a stick. A piece of wood propped up on another burning log dropped suddenly, the resulting *poof* of embers making an artistic display.

"Yes. Super weird. It felt almost like watching a reality show, only in fiction form. The American was a bizarre twist. I'm not used to Americans on these shows."

"Yeah. Everyone in the show was an immigrant. Did you cheer when they killed the Finnish dude?"

"Of course. He was the killer."

"I just found him annoying."

"Justice was served, then. He deserved to die because he was the killer *and* because he was annoying."

"Yeah, but Sigrid didn't need to do it by taking his gun away and letting a polar bear eat him."

Both shivered at the memory.

Rachel shut her eyes tight, giggling suddenly.

"What?" he asked.

"You're the only person in the world I can talk to about these shows. I've missed this."

"You don't know anyone else who likes murder mysteries set above the Arctic Circle where death by polar bear is a thing? I'm stunned."

"I know, right? You'd think they'd be the newest TikTok sensation, but *noooooooo*," she joked back.

"Made me want to visit Svalbard, though," he added.

"Me, too!"

"I went to Iceland, you know," he ventured, moving one of the logs down a bit as it burned, eyes on the fire the entire time, but his attention was on her. "It's only a five-hour flight out of Boston."

"You're kidding! I went, too!"

"Really? When?"

"Two years ago."

"Three, for me. Did you go to Reykjavik?" he asked with a smile.

"I was only there on a layover on the way to London. Spent about sixteen hours there. I did fit in a trip to the Blue Lagoon, though, and I drank some good coffee, and got lectured at a yarn shop for knitting wrong."

"Knitting wrong? How do you knit *wrong*?"

"American style."

"You knit? I didn't know that."

"I knit about as well as I fix radiator hoses."

A loud chuckle came out of him, followed by a mirth-filled look that made his eyes shine like the old Kell.

"Please tell me you didn't superglue yourself to some old Icelandic lady's needles."

"Ha! No. What did you see there?"

"As much as I could. I stayed for a month."

"A month!"

"Yeah. I rented a car. Camped as much as I could. The natural beauty there is so extraordinary. And Iceland and Maine have a unique direct trade relationship–Icelandic companies use the Portland port. University of Southern Maine does exchange programs there, too. There's a lot going on between their country and our state."

"I had no idea. You went on business?"

"No. Pure pleasure."

"Did you go with a girlfriend?" The words were out of her mouth before she could stop herself.

He gave her a sharp look.

"No. I went alone."

"Oh."

"How about you?"

"I was alone, too."

"Did you go to Herdísarvík?"

"Of course I did. I don't know how a film crew managed there, but the bleakness is so beautiful on screen."

"Did you ever finish the show we started together?"

Rachel froze. She'd taken a small risk when she said she missed talking to him about Nordic noir. Now he was directly bringing up the past.

Specifically, that night at his apartment, when they were watching *The Valhalla Stalker*. His ex-girlfriend, Alissa, had barged in on them to return Kell's belongings, and also to throw printed emails in Kell's face that made it look like Rachel had joined her in betraying him.

"I did. Took me a while, but I did."

"Good. It's my favorite series, and I'd hate to think you missed out on it because of…"

She expected him to say *what happened*.

But instead he just said, "Me."

"I would never let anything get in the way of a really good show like that."

He let out a laugh through his nose.

"How could you watch so much Nordic noir and not like cold weather? Snow is practically a character on the shows," Kell asked her in a teasing tone, as if changing the subject were the best approach to easing tension.

"I like cold weather in small doses. Like Tahoe. A weekend of skiing, not cold weather that freezes your toes off for weeks and months. My feet are constantly freezing here. Does it ever get better?"

"Sometime in mid-April, we get to feel all our extremities again."

"You're really selling Maine, Kell."

"You really don't like this town, do you?" he asked suddenly, cutting through Rachel's joking words.

"What?"

"Love You, Maine. You've made fun of it since back in D.C. It's just a joke to you."

"It's... a lot. Reminds me of Niagara Falls. The part with Ripley's Believe It or Not and all the cheesy arcades and sightseeing. It's just... trappings. There's no 'there' there."

"And L.A. has a lot of 'there'?"

"Ha. Not much 'there' in L.A., but it's different."

"How's it different?"

"For one thing, you can feel your toes in L.A."

"Bet they have to be perfect, though. Pedicured, and the exact right proportion, or you see a plastic surgeon to fix them."

A memory of her mother moaning about her hammertoes made Kell's comment hit the mark a little too precisely.

"You might be right."

"If you can handle L.A. fakery, why can't you handle Love You fakery?"

"That is a good question."

"I have an idea. How about you let me show you the real Luview, Maine? Not the one spelled L-O-V-E Y-O-U. The one I'm named for. The real people behind it all."

"I have a lot of work," she said reluctantly, loving that he would offer to spend more time with her, but wondering why.

Was it because of that *almost* kiss? Or was something else going on?

Normally, she'd be direct and ask, but the waters were murky between them. She didn't want to ruin this fragile détente. Plus, she plain old wanted more time with him. It felt greedy.

It *was* greedy.

"Let's go."

"Now?"

"Yeah. Now. Let me show you Love You, Maine, from the perspective of an actual Luview."

"I'm not dressed for it."

"That's the beauty of my town: It accepts people as they are."

"Your town is devoted to the opposite of authenticity, Kell."

"*Ah ah ah.*" He wagged a finger. "You can't say that until you let me do my tour. A private, docent-led tour of the secrets of Love You."

"Please tell me it doesn't involve a blacklight." She shivered. "In retrospect, maybe it's just as well Dani couldn't get me that honeymoon suite. With all those drive-thru weddings I've heard about, they must use disinfectant like water."

"*Shhh.*" His hand covered her mouth, the sudden touch making her jump. "Get dressed. No more talking. We're going into town." He glared at the mug of coffee. "If for no other reason than to get you a good cup of joe."

"Why didn't you lead with that? I'm in." Moving toward the trailer, she called back, "Just need to change and brush my hair."

"I'll put out the fire," she heard him say as she closed the door and pawed through her luggage, wondering what to wear. The temperature was exactly what Dani had printed on her itinerary sheet, but Rachel had never experienced what those numbers on a weather report actually felt like. Her two layers of pants and three layers of socks weren't enough.

How was she supposed to survive walking around town?

As she brushed her hair and pulled it into a low ponytail, she realized that the jeans she'd brought were just fine. This wasn't L.A. She didn't need to be perfect, she just needed to be *warm*. And if she got too cold, she'd just stay in the nice, warm truck.

As she bundled up, pulling her ski jacket on, grabbing a cute red tocque, and slipping her hands into gloves, she ignored the pull of her laptop.

Five years ago, Kell wouldn't talk to her. Wouldn't let her try. Wouldn't believe her.

And now, some piece of the past that weighed her down was lifting.

Work could wait.

She closed the door and went down the steps with a little

bounce. Kell was standing by his truck, looking at his phone. He groaned.

"Another heart in a tree."

"Another what?"

"The sky divers. They practice this time of year, especially on nice days like today with no wind. I'm going to have to offer you a raincheck on taking you around town. Gotta help my dad cut a heart out of a tree."

"A heart?"

"Guys do this all the time. Dress up in a heart costume, sky dive, don't know how to steer, and land in a tree."

"I thought that was a joke when your mom mentioned it."

"My mom mentioned it? When?"

"Yesterday. When I saw her before the presentation."

"Yeah. Today's a repeat. We cut about five a year out of trees."

"All in heart costumes?"

"No. Some in tuxes. Cupid costumes. You name it. Cut down Elvis a few years ago."

"I would pay to see that."

He gave her a grin and a contemplative look. "How about you get to watch it for free." He patted her hand. "Come with me."

"With you?"

"Sure. Change of plans. Come meet my dad and watch some stranger make a fool of himself. Think of it as local flavor."

"Love You Chocolate and Love You Coffee are more my kind of local flavor," she replied, but saw something in his face change. Was he disappointed she didn't immediately say yes?

"Okay."

"That's not a no, Kell. I'd love to come. Any chance we could grab coffees from the shop in town, first?"

"I like how you think. It's on the way, but we have to go right now."

The wall of unfinished business pressed hard on her, suffocating as she imagined her inbox, her texts, her incomplete documentation. It all was there, breathing hard down her neck, chanting *We will not be ignored* over and over.

Until she did.

Ignore it, that is.

She just decided to ignore it.

"I'll grab my bag."

As Rachel ran back into the trailer, her open laptop judged her.

Judged her so bad.

You have a job! You're failing! You need to pay attention to me!

Closing it firmly, she turned her back, picked up her purse, shut the door, and walked toward Kell.

They might not be together. They might not trust each other. They might have a lot of unfinished business between them.

But that didn't mean she couldn't choose joy.

And *waaaaay* better coffee.

Chapter Ten

KELL

"Tell me about your dad," she inquired as he pulled out of Kenny's driveway. He wondered how he'd gone from being screamed at beside the hot springs yesterday to having her treat him like a human being worthy of spending time with today, even if it was in a town she openly despised.

"He's my dad." Kell shrugged. "His name is Dean. He runs a tree service. He tells bad dad jokes. You know. Normal dad."

"Hah! He's nothing like my dad, so don't throw the word 'normal' around like that, dude."

"Tell me about your dad, then. Stan, right?"

"Yes. Stan Hart, the rights shark. Dad owns more Savile Row bespoke suits than he is years old, drives a Ferrari everywhere, and has a thing for exotic animals."

"Like, tigers? Joe Exotic?"

"More like koala bears."

"You grew up with a koala bear as a pet?"

"Oh, *no*. Not a pet. We weren't allowed to play with it. More like, Dad wanted his own personal exotic animal collection."

"You had your own *zoo?*"

"See? 'Normal,'" she said, using finger quotes. "My normal is nothing like yours."

"No kidding. What else is weird about your family?"

"Weird? We're not weird. Just... not normal."

"Your mom is an '80s cop show star, your dad collects marsupials, and your brother is–he's still working towards being an astronaut?"

"Yes. At Thanksgiving, I got to hear a detailed description of how he can drink his own pee in space."

"Drink his own *pee*?"

"It's an astronaut thing. They recycle their urine and filter it. They claim it tastes like bottled water."

"I don't even want to know what else they recycle."

"I'm sure Tim will tell me all about it at Easter dinner, over ham. Dad and Mom sit with looks of rapt admiration on their faces and when they ask me about work, all I can say is I helped a small, family-run dairy sell to an international chocolatier. Tim's... extra."

"Okay." Kell held up one palm. "You win. Nothing normal about your family." He made a face.

"But growing up here in Heartsick Hollow isn't normal either, Kell."

He groaned. "Where do you come up with these insults? *Heartsick Hollow?* Really?"

"Reddit."

"Seriously?"

"Seriously. When Dani did a briefing for me on the town, she found some gems. Heartsick Hollow, Schlocky Springs, Cupid City. And those are the clean ones."

"Clean ones?"

She cleared her throat and tried not to laugh. "The Meatmarket of Maine. Lube You, Maine... and the rest are *waaaay* too dirty to mention."

"Reddit's opinion of our town isn't representative of what it's really like."

"No. But it's entertaining."

Laughing in spite of himself, he had to give her that.

"Dean Luview," she said. "Is he nice like your mom?"

"Of course."

"And they've been together since high school?"

"Yep."

"Dean and Deanna? That's hilarious."

"It is."

"Hah! And your parents have four kids?"

"Mmm hmm."

"You're not making it easy to learn anything, Kell."

"I'm answering!"

"Are you guys the ones who really control Luview?"

"Huh?"

"Old families. Power dynamics in small towns. I've seen it in the course of my work. Obviously, Lucinda has power because her company provides jobs, but I suspect she and her husband didn't have much local power before the business became successful."

Surprised by her insightful analysis, Kell had to clear his throat twice before finding the right words. "We're not what I'd call powerful, but we've been here long enough to have influence. Twenty-seven hundred people live here. Human beings are all about forming alliances, but also picking arguments. We don't dominate, because no one should. Every voice deserves to be heard, even if everyone doesn't always get what they want."

"You sound very consensus-based."

"Not really. More like I think ideas that have an impact on people need to be heard, discussed, considered, and then in the end, the majority prevails." He thought for a second. "Unless the majority will hurt the minority."

"You described true, simple democracy."

"Small towns are oozing with it."

"I'm going to guess there are some longstanding rivalries here, though."

Kell's eyes rolled hard.

"Oh, yes."

"Bilbee versus Luview?"

"Very good."

"It's pretty obvious. Two original families. Lots of marrying entwining them."

"The Bilbees are, well... on the whole, they're not fans of all the love stuff. Most of the younger cousins have embraced it now, but years ago, that wasn't the case."

"Are the Bilbees the ones who fight progress?"

She really was paying attention, her analysis making him admire her more than he wanted to. For all the negative comments she made about the town, she was absolutely paying attention to it.

"Mostly, yes. But over time, democracy generally wins out."

"And your dad feels the same way?"

"My dad is happiest in a tree. Like me. He thinks of the woods as his family, second to us. Stewards of the land tend to look at human squabbling and take the long view. Spend enough time around two-hundred-year-old trees and you quickly feel small and unimportant."

"You're anything but small," she said, giving him a fine little onceover he appreciated. "And people aren't unimportant."

"Our arguments are."

So many thoughts rushed into his mind, but the word that prevailed was simple:

Hypocrite.

If squabbles and conflicts weren't important, why had he let one between him and Rachel dominate so much of his life?

"Anything I need to know before I meet him?"

"He'll probably hug you. Mom and Dad are huggers." He thought for a minute. "Are your parents huggers?"

"Mom does air kisses. Dad will shake your hand off, and before you're done he's asking you what your poison is."

"Poison?"

"Drinks. Dad likes a neat bourbon. Pappy's is his brand."

"Whoo! Power drink."

"My father is all about power."

As they approached the first stoplight on the edge of town, Kell turned to her. "Is that why success is so important to you? Trying to impress your dad?"

"I don't have cool stories about drinking my own pee in space to enthrall him at family gatherings. I do my best, but..."

"Why does it have to be a competition?" Moving forward at the green light, Kell began searching for a parking spot. This time of year, the town center was always jam packed. He might have to park behind Bilbee's, in his tenant spot. But that would involve a longish walk to Love You Coffee, and Kell would prefer a quick stop.

Guys hanging in trees were kind of a priority. He knew his dad would need some time to get the equipment in place, but there was time to grab coffee. The poor schmuck in the tree probably could use a good jolt of hot drink, too.

And if he showed up with a half-caf latte for his father, he'd score some brownie points.

"It just *is* a competition," Rachel said with a sigh. "It's how my family operates. Everyone's trying to be the big dog."

"Lots of room in the world for dogs of all sizes."

"I'm tired of being a chihuahua in a St. Bernard world."

"I like chihuahuas. Plus, you remind me of one. Yippy little thing."

She whacked his arm. He grinned at her.

And wondered what the hell he was doing.

She pointed to a sign. "What is Love You Forever?"

"That's the wedding chapel."

"Why does it have a giant garage door?"

"It's a drive-thru wedding chapel."

"What? Like in Vegas? Does Elvis marry you?"

"No. My cousin Brad does."

"He's a minister?"

"Yep. Unitarian Universalist."

"Is that one of the Hare Krishna-type religions?"

"You don't know what the Unitarian Universalists are?"

"No."

"Funny how Ms. I-Know-Everything doesn't know about one of the major New England religions."

"Okay. Fine. We've established my ignorance there. What is the whole drive-thru wedding thing about?"

"It's where you get wicked hitched."

"Wicked hitched?"

"That's their slogan. Get wicked hitched in Love You, Maine!"

"And in this context, wicked means…"

"Really. Or awesomely."

"Wicked means bad, Kell. Or… naughty."

"Not here."

"And not something dirtier?"

"No."

"So it's just a wedding chapel with a gimmick."

"You really are a funsucker sometimes, Rachel."

"How am I a funsucker for pointing out the truth?"

"It's a cool place to run off to when you're madly in love and cannot wait one more second to be married."

"That's called being impulsively irrational."

"See? Funsucker."

"SPOT!" she called out, pointing as a car's red tail lights lit up, backing out of a space right in front of Love You Coffee.

"I never have this kind of luck," he muttered as Rachel preened.

"One thing I am known for in my family that beats my brother: Dad calls me his parking lot good luck charm. I get great spots." She cleared her throat. "For a funsucker."

Kell caught her frowning at the town lot across the street.

"Except for yesterday, when Randy attacked my car over there."

"Right. Heard about that from my mom." He turned off the car and got out, Rachel staying in the truck.

"You coming in?"

"I'm not fit to be seen in public."

"Why? Do you stink?"

"Excuse me?"

"You look fine. Don't worry so much about appearances. You showered today, right? And even that's not a requirement for going into shops here in town. We have a writer's colony nearby, and let me tell you, they have everyone beat in the not-showering department."

Clearly debating internally, she seemed uncertain. Kell ended that by grabbing her door handle and opening it. As she exited the truck, half the people on the sidewalk turned to watch them.

The half who were full-time residents.

"Is that music from a PA system somewhere?" she asked, looking around for the source. The song "Love Will Keep Us Together" was playing.

"Yes. Nothing but love songs everywhere for the next week or so."

Her groan was still going as they reached the shop door. He held the door for her as they entered the coffee shop because it was polite, but also because if his mother ever learned he'd barreled in first, she'd chew his ear off.

"Hey!" It was Skylar. Back when Kell was playing high school football, Mac Lewiston had been his coach, and Skylar was his daughter. She was stacking heart-shaped red coffee mugs on a shelf next to the espresso machine. "Look at you two. Now you can use both hands to do whatever you want!"

Kell narrowed his eyes. Skylar turned bright red.

"I mean, you know, for, like, not doing sex stuff. I mean, like, the sex. I mean–Skylar, stop talking!" she muttered to herself, turning around and disappearing into the back room, leaving Reef Matthews, the manager, gaping after her, thick eyebrows up, nose ring glimmering under the shop's lights.

"What was that about?" he grunted at Kell. Reef had long locs with braids mixed in, more face piercings than a bad guy in a biker movie, and had broken his nose so many times, it was impossible to figure out where the bone had originally belonged.

He wore a long-sleeved red T-shirt with the words *Caffeinated lovers do it with more energy* and the Love You Coffee logo printed under it.

"Dunno. Can you make us four coffees?"

"Sure."

"Two black. Dark roast. One half-caf latte for my dad."

"I don't drink mine black," Rachel said.

"I'm getting one for the poor guy we're cutting down."

"Another heart caught in a tree?" Reef said, laughing. He looked at Rachel, then did a double take. "Well. Hello. You're new." A not-so-covert look at Kell asked a question he didn't like.

Off-limits, or fair game?

Kell ignored it, but he didn't want to. He wanted to growl at Reef and tell him to leave Rachel alone, but he had no claim here. That near-kiss yesterday was an artifact, a moment best described as foolish.

Although foolish moments like that, and the one on the couch in his D.C. apartment five years ago, had taken up most of the real estate in his mind last night.

"What'll you have?" Reef asked, watching her carefully. Coffee people were their own unique breed. They didn't judge you on appearance, job title, or leisure interests.

They judged you by your drink of choice.

"Double shot latte, half two percent, half almond milk," she said quickly.

"That's... specific," Reef commented.

"If you had skim milk, it would be easier."

"Hmm. You're not new, after all." Reef peered at her. "Oh.

You're *Rachel*." His eyes cut over to Kell, the look instantly readable.

She's taken, that look said. Something in Kell unclenched a little.

Reef considered her Kell's.

She wasn't, and Kell knew it, but he felt better, the rush that ran through him stronger than any caffeine.

"Am I infamous?" she joked. "What do you know about me?"

"You glued yourself to Kell, you're trying to get Lucinda to sell out to Markstone's, and you honked at poor Randy."

"Did someone write up a fact sheet on me that's getting sent around?"

Reef finished making her drink and set it on the counter, grabbing a to-go tray that was alarmingly red, and fit two white cups in it with the Love You Coffee logo on them, and began pouring the black coffees.

"Naw. Nadine was in here," Reef muttered, finishing pouring and pivoting to make what Kell assumed was his dad's half-caf latte.

"Nadine? I think I've heard that name," she inquired politely.

"Nadine Khouri. Biggest gossip in town," Kell said. "Works with my brother at the police station."

"A *cop* is the biggest gossip in town?"

Kell and Reef laughed. "Nadine's not a cop. She's the station admin," Kell explained. "Older woman who knows everyone and everyone's business."

"Why did you say 'poor Randy'? I had to honk to get him to leave my car alone."

Reef gave Kell a look that said, *Who's paying for this*? Kell nodded. His credit card was on file, and he reached into his wallet to throw a couple bucks in the tip jar.

That jolted Rachel out of her questions. Lifting her bag onto the counter, she began pawing through it.

"I'll buy! You've done so much for me, Kell."

Reef winked at him.

"I got it," Kell insisted.

"I have an expense account. Consider it a way to bleed the big, bad multinational company you so thoroughly hate."

"Next time, Rachel. You can get it next time."

The way she lit up at his words set something warm off inside his chest. The sensation felt expansive but dangerous, as if tight quarters had opened up into generous but unexplored space.

"Deal. I'll get it next time," she said softly, smiling at Reef as she took a sip from her cup and moaned like she was in ecstasy.

The bell on the door jingled, and two pairs of lips walked into the coffee shop. Dressed like Deanna had been during her Face-Time call five years ago, the two – er, four – lips were a dazzling display of red sequins.

Rachel paused mid-sip, then slowly lowered her cup. Kell thanked Reef, picked up the tray of coffees, and moved out of the way so the next customer could be served.

"Have fun using your hands however you want, Kell!" Reef said with a two-finger salute and a chuckle.

"Why are people in costume?" Rachel asked, openly nosy.

"Because Valentine's Day is in a week and there are lots of rehearsals and activities going on."

"I knew your mom dressed up that time, but that was in May."

"Yep, the Kiss Festival. This is different. Way bigger. You're going to see loads of hearts, some lips, plenty of roses, and heart-shaped boxes of chocolates. Guys in tuxes pretending to propose, and sometimes really proposing. Women in red ball gowns. Girls in red party dresses and prom gowns. Think of it as cosplay for anything and everything related to love."

"Does it get dirty?"

"Dirty?"

"You know. Naughty? The other kind of wicked?"

"Ah." He laughed as they made their way outside to the truck, his phone buzzing. Probably Dad, wondering where they were. The coordinates Dean had given him were only ten minutes away, and they'd be on the road in a minute. "Hang on. I'll tell you more as we drive. That's not a simple conversation."

Once he got in the driver's seat, Rachel took the coffee tray on her lap. Buckled in and settled, he started toward the site of the stranded skydiver and took a sip of his own coffee. Whatever Love You Coffee did to their brew, it was perfection, and Kell had never tasted anything quite like it elsewhere.

"So, naughty, huh?" he broached, and she giggled. "Sure. There are plenty of businesses around here devoted to sex. Not in town, though. The zoning board and town meeting keep it clean."

"Clean?"

"Let's say it's PG-13 here."

"Got it. But I'd imagine there are plenty of opportunities for something a little racier?"

"Oh, sure. There's an adult bookstore and strip club right over the town line. It's called Love You Harder."

"It is not!"

A cackle came out of him, surprising them both. "It is. Every young guy in town wants to go there, but once you do, it's nothing special."

"What I'm hearing is that town officials work really hard to stay on brand and make it all about Valentine's Day and romantic love, but keep the more erotic elements on the edge."

"That's a very astute, business-like way of seeing it."

"Family friendly."

"Oh, yes. We get a lot of families. Loads of repeat business. People come to swim in the hot springs. They might already be in love, or maybe they fall in love here. Then they get married here, have babies, and come back for vacations. Love You becomes an annual family trip. On the way up, they stop in New Hampshire at Storyland and Santa's Village, and the Mount Washington Cog Railway. Drive on over the state line and come here. Plus there's skiing and all that in the winter."

"I don't know what any of those are."

"If you lived here, you would."

Rachel took a long sip of her drink and said nothing, leaving Kell's words hanging out there. He certainly hadn't meant them as an offer, but the air buzzed with new meaning.

"Such a strange mix of cheesy and genuine," she finally said.

"What's cheesy? You use that word a lot, but I don't see it."

"You don't see how fake this all is?"

"Says the woman from L.A."

"In L.A., *people* are fake. Here, the whole town is fake."

"I don't think of it that way. It's my hometown. My people have been here for generations. There's a pure heart here."

"And you can buy it."

"No. You can buy the merchandise, but you can't buy the

feeling in Luview, Rachel. If you don't see that, I don't know what to say. Love isn't just a feeling here. It's a way of life."

"Then why are *you* still single?"

"What does that mean?"

"You've lived here your whole life, the child of two people who sound like they're in love, from the way you talk about them. You've been steeped in love. Why aren't you?"

"Never met the right woman."

"I find that hard to believe."

"What does that mean?"

"Look at you."

He looked down. "Yeah?"

"You're beyond hot. Lumberjack hot—well, *grumpy* lumberjack hot. You must have women lined up, ready to wear red lace and pink thongs, ready to do your bidding."

His eyes cut to her waist. "You still wear red lace panties?"

She whacked his shoulder. "I was making a point, Kell."

"So was I."

Kell turned the truck onto an unmarked dirt road, going by the GPS but also using memory. The turn was a bit sharp and Calamine yowled from the back, startling Rachel, who nearly pitched her coffee into the windshield.

"EEK!" she squealed, grabbing the coffee with both hands, then pressing one palm over her heart. "Your cat is in here?"

"Yep. Cally."

"She's been here the whole time?"

"Sure."

"Does she go everywhere with you?"

"Mostly."

"You know that's not normal, right? Cats are homebodies."

"Cats are like people. Different in every way. I'm her home. The truck is her home. So wherever I go in the truck, she comes."

"What about her litter box?"

"The world is Cally's litter box. She hops out when she needs to."

"And food? Water?"

"Check the glovebox."

Rachel did. A small pet water dispenser and a cat food bowl were in there.

"Wow. You shape your driving life around a cat."

"No. My cat shapes her life around my driving."

Before she could respond, the skydiver came into stark view, the trees suddenly looking like they were bleeding. Red was everywhere; the parachute was caught in a vertical clump, red strings willy-nilly. A dude in a huge puffy-heart costume that was at least five feet wide dangled about twenty feet off the ground.

He waved sheepishly.

Kell's dad's white truck with the words Luview Tree Service on it was parked directly underneath the guy, the truck bed helping to narrow the guy's gap between dangling body and ground..

"Tree landings, man," Kell muttered. "Poor guy."

"Tree landings?"

"That's what this is called. It happens to loads of parachutists, but it happens a *lot* to amateurs around Valentine's Day."

"How are you going to do this? Don't you need one of those huge bucket things? Like electric companies use to fix power lines?"

"A cherry picker?"

"Is that what it's called?"

"Ayup."

Rachel began giggling. "You just said *ayup* again."

"So?"

"In D.C., you never had a Maine accent."

"In D.C, I wasn't in Maine." With that, he climbed out of the truck, Cally leaping on top of the back of the front seat, then out of the cab, at his heels. Rachel followed, carrying the tray of coffees. Kell was holding his, and took a big swig as they neared the tree.

Dean took the tray out of Rachel's hands and gave her a beaming smile.

"Ah, my boy. Trained you well," Dean said, coffee already to his lips before Kell could say hi.

Kell looked up and shouted to the skydiver, "Brought you a coffee!"

"I'll need a really, really long straw!" the guy called back.

They all laughed. Dean held his non-coffee-holding hand out to Rachel. "Sorry to be so rude, but I needed that caffeine. Nice to finally meet you, Rachel."

177

"You too, Mr. Luview."

"*Gee-awd*, no. I'm Dean," he said. Did his father just suck in his gut? Kell grimaced as his dad went on. "None of this Mr. Luview stuff."

"Okay," Rachel said with a sparkling smile. "Dean." She looked up and waved at the poor guy. "Hi!"

"Hi! I'm Joey. Joey Stupid. Call me Mr. Stupid."

Dean shouted up, "Nothing about love is stupid. You just caught a bad wind."

"If you toss me a knife, I can cut myself down," Joey said.

"Now THAT would be stupid, dude," Kell replied, shaking his head. He looked at Dean. "Ladder?"

"Yeah. He's only twenty feet up."

"Is it in the pickup bed? Or do we need to call the fire department?"

Dean looked up, analyzing the guy's situation, studying each rope, the slope of the parachute material, and the guy's harness. Kell's dad was big like him, but all three of his boys were taller, Dennis and Kell the biggest, but Luke was no slouch. Like Kell, Dean worked with his body for a living, so the man was still mostly muscle, though a small beer gut had formed as Kell did more of the hard work and his dad handled the office responsibilities.

"I think if we can get you up on that branch," he said, pointing for Kell to see, "you can cut that line on the right and he'll drop another five or eight feet. That'd make this a hell of a lot easier."

"Yep." Kell drained the rest of his coffee and walked toward the back of his dad's truck for harnesses. Rachel gave them curious looks.

"You're going to climb that tree? It's HUGE!"

Kell shrugged. "It's not that big. I'll use the ladder to get to the thick limb, then ropes to get up there, crawl over to that far red line that's holding him up, cut it, and he'll drop a few feet. Then he'll be close enough that we can grab him."

"Shouldn't the fire department do this?"

"Nope."

"And you aren't worried about the danger?"

"Worried?"

"It's a lot of responsibility. What if something goes wrong?"

"We're not leaving him here to be picked off by crows, Rachel. Someone's got to cut him down."

"What about something to cushion his fall?"

"Are you offering to lay down on the ground under him and do the honors?"

"I was thinking about one of those trampoline things you see in the movies."

By the time she finished the sentence, Kell was half in his harness. He turned to look at her. "This is an aerial rescue. I'm a tree climber. This is what I do, Rachel. We're not hobbyists."

"You're trained for this?"

"Naw. Dad and I thought we'd just come out here and cut some dude out of a tree because there was nothing good on TV."

"Kell!"

He laughed, looking down her. "I am a working arborist. I have a bachelor's degree in agriculture and forestry. I'm ISA certified."

"ISA?"

"International Society of Arboriculture. OSHA, too. I've got my first aid and CPR certifications, and I stayed at a Holiday Inn Express last night. I know what I'm doing."

"I had no idea you knew all of this. Is this new? Since D.C.?"

"Nope. I went to D.C. with all of this training under my belt."

"You never mentioned it."

"I got the impression people would look down their noses about it. Now, we can talk, or poor Joey can get cut down so he can feel his legs again."

"Go! Sorry!"

Dean walked over to Kell and said, "Coupla ways we can do this. He's too far out from the trunk to just use a ladder. He's just high enough up that I don't want to cut that right line without a secured harness on him. Climb up and drop him a safety line."

"Isn't he wearing a harness?" Rachel asked.

"That's for his parachute. I mean one we put on him to secure him to the tree," Dean patiently explained.

"Oh."

"Hey, Joey!" Kell shouted up. "I'm climbing on that branch above you, and dropping you a rope. Secure the clamp to your harness. It's just to make sure you're safe in case you drop."

Joey gave a thumbs up.

"Is there anything I can do to help?" Rachel asked.

"Drive into town for us if this goes horribly wrong," Dean said in a serious tone.

She looked at Dean's truck. "Is that a stick shift, too?"

Both men laughed.

"Kell, you gotta teach her how to drive a stick."

"No kidding." The look he shared with Rachel was warm and comforting.

Destabilizing, too. Here she was, on a rescue run with him like it was no big deal, fitting into his life like she was meant to be here, talking about her being around long enough to teach her how to drive a stick.

He wanted to teach her. Be with her. Have her here in his life, seamless and easy.

Kell wanted to let go of the grudge he held, even if it wasn't just a grudge. Whatever you called it, he wanted to will it away, re-envision how he saw Rachel, and how they were together.

He missed his friend, and here she was, hanging out, up for adventure, helping out. And more than missing his friend — he missed the chance for something more with her. He wanted all that potential back again. All the what-ifs. All the ripe opportunities.

Was that enough to let go of the past hurt?

For the next ten minutes, Kell focused on checking all the lines and clamps for safety as Dean did the aerial assist, throwing weighted ropes with an enviable precision. His dad might be getting older, and his time climbing trees was narrowing, but he had bullseye perfection when it came to throwing.

And then Kell got to do what he loved most about being an arborist: climb.

Moving up required full attention. No one ever wanted a rescue mission to turn into a double. Kell easily climbed the twenty feet up to the big branch Joey was caught on and unclamped the line Dean meant for the poor guy.

"Joey! I'm dropping this to you slowly," Kell called as he balanced carefully, his own harness supporting him fully if needed.

His dad and Rachel were looking up, faces focused but not scared.

Fortunately, Joey got the weighted clamp in his hand on the first try, securing it easily.

Step one accomplished. Dean could hold the line down below and offer leverage now, in case Joey slipped.

Kell shimmied back a bit, then reached for his knife, cutting the red parachute lines that were keeping Joey up.

"Get ready, Joey. Five-foot drop coming."

"Okay!"

Snip.

With an airy *whuff!*, Joey dropped, a groan coming out of him followed by another thumbs up.

"Kell!" Dean shouted. "I think you can just cut the rest. I've got the line. Let's do this without the ladder."

"Be careful!" Rachel called out, as if he weren't. Deanna did the same thing every time she watched an operation, though, so he understood.

Being helpless at the bottom was worse than being in danger up top. At least here, he could pivot as needed to make himself safer.

Watchers didn't have that luxury.

Going back over the same part of the branch he'd just been on, Kell warned Joey, "Here we go!"

Cut.

Joey dropped a bit.

Cut.

Joey dropped more.

"Dad!" he called out. "You need Rachel to help hold the line behind you?"

"Sure!" Dean said something to Rachel, who put down her coffee and did as told, looking eager to be of help.

And then Kell cut the rest of the parachute lines, leaving Joey hanging, Dean and Rachel holding the other end of the line like a pulley, both moving closer to the tree to lower Joey slowly, slowly...

Just as the company that was handling his skydiving adventure arrived, the familiar red truck that read LOVE YOU SKIES appearing in the nick of time.

Or not.

Love You Skies was known for this, an out-of-town company from New Hampshire that capitalized on the Love You name but didn't bother to make contingency plans for when amateur skydivers blew off course.

"Hey," Dean said, waving as Kell climbed down from the tree, trying not to get mad. He knew how this would work. Love You Skies would offer Dean the least possible amount of money for their help, if any at all, and take all the credit by doing the cleanup.

"Man, thank you," Joey said from the truck bed as Kell walked over to him, shaking his hand. Rachel carried over the now-lukewarm coffee for Joey. Kell watched his dad have a low, serious talk with Jimmy, the owner of Love You Skies.

This issue he was leaving to Dean.

"I got it!" his dad shouted to him, as if reading his mind.

"You sure?"

Dean waved him off. "You two go back to whatever you were doing."

Kell could have done without the wink his dad added.

"That's it?" Rachel asked, wide-eyed and excited. "Don't we need to stay?"

"Dad said he'd wrap up. Jimmy's got to handle any medical issues, but he brought Roy to help, and it's their responsibility anyhow. Dad was just helping them out." Kell cut a glare toward the red truck.

"You look mad."

"Let's get going and I'll tell you all about it."

This time she did as told, and by the time Cally jumped in through Kell's open door and he'd settled in the seat, cranking the engine, he was calmer.

"What's wrong?"

He sighed. "It's hard to explain, but it comes down to people like Love You Skies operating a business that uses the town's name but doesn't serve the town. They won't keep an office here to handle emergencies like this. They're based out in Conway. We end up cleaning up their messes."

"I assume you and your dad get paid for that?"

"Dad'll figure out something, but that's not the point. Poor Joey. When you contract with a company, they should take care of you. Shouldn't rely on the goodness of locals like us to bail them out. Don't get me wrong–I'm always happy to help people.

But it's Jimmy and Roy's responsibility to keep track of their skydivers. We've told them over and over again to figure this out."

"Why not stop helping?"

He turned onto the road back to town.

"Because that would hurt people."

"You and your dad are softies."

"I don't think it's soft to want to help a guy dangling from a tree with a crotch harness turning his junk into hamburger."

"Kell!"

"That hurts. I have a ton of sympathy."

"I think you have a kind heart and hate to see people in a bind."

"I am also acutely aware of what it feels like to dangle like that from a tree branch in a harness, so there's an element of PTSD in there, too."

"That was riveting to watch. You must be really good at physics."

"I don't know about that. I'm good at climbing trees."

"Same thing, from what I saw."

He beamed at her. "Thanks. Look at you, full of compliments."

"You deserve them."

"How do I follow up on that? We got our coffees. You watched us cut a heart out of a tree. What can I show you next?"

"It's your town. You decide. Just… stay away from poison ivy and the hot springs, please."

"No problem. Now, do your magic on me."

"Excuse me?"

"Your parking spot magic. Go for it. Find a good one."

Rachel closed her eyes really hard, bit her lower lip, and groaned.

She opened her eyes and looked around. "No luck."

They laughed, Kell making a last-minute decision to park farther out of town so they could walk along the whole stretch.

As he waited to make a right turn into the larger municipal lot down near the hot springs, Luke's pink cruiser drove by, a friendly double tap on the horn making them both wave.

"You run into people you know all day long, don't you?"

"Yes."

"Isn't it exhausting? Smiling and waving and chatting all the time?"

"You mean, being a person?"

"I mean, everyone needs your attention."

"Just a little. It's how it is."

"Not in L.A. Not in D.C."

"I remember how weird that was. Learning not to make eye contact and not to say hi to everyone." He parked and fished around in the console for quarters. Stuck in a cupholder was a heart-shaped plastic cup full of coins; at the end of the day, most guys dumped their spare change out of their pockets into a dish or jar on their bureau.

Kell threw it all in here.

"Felt like home to me," Rachel said with a smile.

"Guess you'll have to adapt while you're here."

"No one knows me here."

"I beg to differ. Everyone knows you."

He plunked the maximum number of quarters into the meter.

"Shall we?"

"Where are we going first?"

"Center of town to the festival setup. The gazebo's being organized. The big day is February 14th, obviously, but that's on a Wednesday this year, so the 10th and 11th will have big crowds, too–the weekend before."

As they started down the sidewalk, Kell tried to imagine the town through her eyes. Yes, she disparaged it, but she was also new to it. What could he show her to make her fall in love with Love You, Maine, as much as he was?

"That's my phone," she said as it buzzed. "Finally have a signal."

"Internet's out at Kenny's?"

"Yes."

"Don't you need to work?"

"I do," she said, double thumbing it on her phone.

"If you need to stop hanging out with me, it's fine. I can–"

Her hand went to his forearm, interrupting his words. "Kell. I'm here because I want to be. I just needed to send a quick answer. Work can wait."

"Words rarely spoken back at EEC."

"I'm a lot more jaded and way more burned out now than I was then. Plus, this is research."

"Spending time with me is research?"

"*Fun* research," she amended.

Picking up her signals was easy, but interpreting them was hard. Was this flirting? Or was she drawing a professional boundary?

And which was he hoping for?

"There," she said definitively. "Dani has what she needs. Now, show me all the town secrets so I'll magically lose my sour opinion of this place and fall in love with it." She snapped her fingers twice.

"That's a tall order."

"If anyone can do it, you can."

The challenge was delivered in a joking tone, but it was still a call to arms, so to speak.

"You've seen the coffee shop and the chocolate shop. That about it so far?"

"Yes, unless you count the takeout that I had delivered from Love You India."

"Right. Their aloo gobi is awesome."

"I had chicken tandoori."

"What else have you been eating in that trailer?"

"I went to the grocery store–I was shocked it isn't called Love You Food."

"Kendrill's Market. One of the few holdouts."

"Red heart-shaped baskets, though? Really?"

"We're good at sticking to a theme."

Her smile made him smile. "I'll give you that. When the receipt came out of the machine, I half expected it to be on red paper."

"We have a Love Committee that reports to town meeting. Maybe you should join."

"Love Committee?"

"Ideas like yours get submitted. It's why the fireworks in July are only red, white, or pink. Zoning codes require red, white, and pink buildings within a certain area in town. That kind of thing. Kendrill's won't change their name, but they have the heart-shaped baskets."

"Maybe they could get custom-designed heart-shaped carts."

"See? You're a natural."

As they walked, Kell stopped in front of Love You Books. "Let's pop in here."

Smothering a grin, he said nothing as Rachel walked in ahead of him, then stopped and looked around. It usually took visitors a few minutes to figure it all out, an uneasy feeling coming over them as they realized something about the bookstore was different but they couldn't quite put their finger on it.

"I've been meaning to read that new book by Max Seeck," she said, moving to the wall on the right, where hardcovers dominated. Illustrated depictions of couples, flowers, high heels, and wedding cakes reigned.

Rachel moved between displays, going all the way to the back. The store only had three or four other customers, a mother with her twenty-something daughter and a couple, the guy looking very bored.

The single register desk was empty. Mo Ceela, the owner, must be in the back, grabbing more books or merchandise.

"Where's the mystery section?" Rachel asked, heading back toward the front of the store. "Or crime? Maybe it's shelved under crime."

"Keep looking."

Overstuffed chairs in different hues of red sat in a row at the front of the store, facing the picture window, with white side tables between all four. Mo even had folded blankets for patrons who really wanted to cuddle up.

"Oh!" Rachel exclaimed as Tilly, Mo's cat, gave her ankles some love. The tabby was named after Roald Dahl's character, Matilda. "Who's this?"

"That's the house cat!" a cheery voice called out as Mo appeared, holding a heavy box and breathing hard before heaving it up onto the counter next to the cash register. "And you must be Rachel. Hey, Kell."

"Hi," Rachel said, clearly still nonplussed by having everyone know her.

"Hi. I'm Mo. Nice to meet you, even if Kell has no manners and forgot how to introduce people."

"I don't need to introduce her when everyone already knows who she is," he replied, earning twin looks of joking reproach from both of them.

Mo wore a red and white flannel shirt, had half their head shaved, and the remaining hair was dyed red. A heart-shaped tattoo on their wrist followed the theme.

"Nice to meet you, too, Mo."

"What's your favorite trope?" Mo asked.

"Trope?"

"You know. Second chances. Best friend's little sister. The billionaire who needs a fake girlfriend. Or are you more into historical? Romantic suspense?"

"I'm actually looking for Max Seeck's new book."

Mo cringed and looked at Kell, who pretended not to understand that Rachel didn't know that Love You Books only sold romance-related books.

"You didn't tell her?"

"I thought she'd figure it out."

"Figure out what?" Rachel asked. As the words came out of her mouth, she looked around her, a panoramic view that made it all click. "Oh! You only sell books about love?"

"Quick study! Yes. Romance novels, non-fiction related to love, history with a love story involved, and fiction with romance in it that has a happy ending, even if it's not strictly considered romance."

"That's a very narrow niche."

"It works here."

"I'll bet."

"Got any favorites?"

"Favorite romance authors? No. I don't read romance."

"Non-fiction?"

"I don't read non-fiction about love. Business books, some self-improvement, but not love."

"You're a person who is all business?"

"Not *all* business, but..."

"When was the last time you read fiction, Rachel?" Kell asked, leaning against a small but heavy oak display table, careful not to tip the books.

"I don't know. A few months ago?"

Mo let out a low whistle. "That's a deprived life you're living."

"My life is hardly deprived," Rachel said, laughing hard.

"On the inside, though." Mo's tone wasn't one of judgment,

it was one of caring. "Our inner lives need to be fed. Nordic noir is great. So is young adult, fantasy, or romance. Anything that helps you connect with yourself and other people in your imagination. It's easy to fall out of the habit of reading fiction." Mo sized her up. "Bet you're the kind of person who will do anything if science backs it up."

"I'm definitely more interested if there's data to support an idea, sure. Who isn't?"

Mo laughed. "Lots of people aren't. Most of my customers aren't data-driven. They're feeling-driven."

As Mo and Rachel talked, Kell decided to let Mo do some of his work for him. He didn't need to intervene in Rachel's first exposure to someone so committed to the town's mission that they ran a bookstore about nothing but love.

In the non-fiction section, he came across a book called *Mama Loves Her Babies: How Mother Trees Connect Forest Families* and slipped it into the crook of his arm. Mo always carried cool books that he would never have found on his own.

As he walked to the counter, he noticed Rachel had two paperbacks in her own hands.

"Finding good stuff?" he asked her with a wink.

"I still want Max Seeck's new book, but Mo says I should try these."

"You'll have to go to the library for mystery and thriller," Mo said. "Dotty makes sure every genre is covered. That was one heck of a fight."

"Who is Dotty?"

"Dotty Chen. The town librarian. About fifteen years ago, the Love Committee tried to make the library carry only love-themed books. I thought Dotty was about to go to actual war over it. Loads of residents agreed with her," Kell explained.

"A love-only library sounds like a terrible idea!" Rachel exclaimed.

"I'm glad you agree. It's also how this store stays unique," Mo said.

Rachel read the title of Kell's book. He motioned for her to add hers to his pile, but she resolutely held on.

"I'm expensing this," she said. "Research."

"Your boss going to let you expense books called *Lord of Scoundrels* and *Shopping for a Billionaire*?" he asked skeptically.

"Research," Rachel repeated, sending Mo and Kell into laughter.

"You're going to love that one," Mo commented with a chin nod toward Rachel's choices. "It's a classic."

"You really make a profit doing this?" Rachel asked, half in wonder, half with the crisp tone of a businessperson.

"I do. We have an internet presence now, and we ship world-wide. We get a lot of romance authors who do readings, and signed books are a huge deal. Romance fans come from all over and make it a vacation. Tourism is all about ripple effects. The inns make money, the restaurants make money, people buy books... you know?"

Rachel added a small bag of very familiar red foil-covered chocolate hearts to her book purchase.

"I do. Thank you."

Kell let her buy her own books, the corporate card with the Markstone's logo on it making him ponder. Was the town really too silly for her? Too cutesy?

Mo's phone rang and they waved as Kell and Rachel left the store clutching their bags. The cold hit them in the face as they emerged onto the sidewalk.

The very next store was Love You Flowers.

Rachel looked in the window. "It's like a volcano of roses erupted in there."

The line out the door, about ten deep, was nothing but men his father's age, some in suits, most in Carhartts and construction boots. One after another, they went in empty-handed and came out carrying a few dozen roses in their arms.

"That's quaint."

"Aside from weddings, this is the month everyone makes their money. The town half-jokingly calls February 14th our Black Friday."

"I can see why."

"Want to go in?"

"It looks too crowded. What else?"

"Bilbee's Tavern."

"It's early for a drink!"

"Not to drink. Just to tour." Kell thought for a moment. "But let's head to the center of town first. The common. You really need to see the heart and soul of Love You, Maine."

"I thought you said the people were the heart of the town."

"They are. That's my point."

The tune "Silly Love Songs" came on the town's PA system, the light-hearted ditty making Kell grin.

"More love songs," Rachel said with a laugh.

"The Love Committee hand-selects the playlists. They carefully curate to make sure the songs are family friendly, and not too sad."

"It sounds like this Love Committee has a lot of sway in town."

"It does. People rotate in on two-year terms."

"You ever serve on it?"

"No. I've tried to avoid it."

"Why?"

The white gazebo smack in the middle of the town common came into view, the trim covered in red heart decorations. An enormous, glittery red heart was attached to the peak of the roof.

"Don't want to spend my free time arguing about which songs get people to open up their wallets, or whether Christina Perri's 'Jar of Hearts' is appropriate. I've got better things to do with my time."

"Like what?"

"Like cut dudes wearing heart costumes out of trees."

Knowing laughter greeted that comment as he steered her toward the gazebo. Small platforms were everywhere, pulled out for the festival. No one wanted to work on a snow-covered common or set up crafts tents in February so, about twenty years ago, people got together and built small pavilions that could be broken down flat, stored away, then reassembled for the festival.

The Department of Public Works cleared the snow off the sidewalks and the paths that criss-crossed the common and, just like that, a winter festival was possible in Maine.

Most of the vendors weren't set up yet but a few had begun already, especially the locals, who got a jumpstart on making money as the crowds swelled ahead of the actual festival. Out of the thirty or so pavilions, six were occupied, and Kell took Rachel right to the one that said Love You Tattoos.

"Hey, Dutch," he said to a young woman who looked like she couldn't have been more than five feet tall and a hundred pounds on a heavy day. Thick eyeliner stretched catlike at the corners of her eyes. Her mouth spread into a huge grin as she stood staring up at a mildly chagrined Kell.

"Hi!" she gasped. She noticed Rachel with an uncertain defeat. Kell had known Anna "Dutch" Connelly since she was born, and had helped build sets for all the school plays she was in, but the crush she had on him was confounding.

"I need a henna tattoo," he said, then looked at Rachel. "You want one?"

Her *no* was right there. He saw it, hoping she got his undertone. Dutch was one of the poorest kids in town, smart and creative, but with two parents who were barely hanging onto the trailer they lived in with her and her thirteen-year-old sister.

They were more into the bottle than parenting.

Both girls worked any odd job they could find to make money. Dean hired them to stack wood sometimes. Dutch's henna tattoo hobby had turned into a way to generate some extra dough.

"Um, sure," Rachel said, giving him a look that said she expected the full story later.

"What do you want?" Dutch pulled out a thick binder of designs, the gorgeous patterns making Rachel brush them with her fingertips in awe, Kell enjoying Rachel's pleasure as she viewed the art.

"Doesn't everyone get hearts this time of year?" Rachel asked. "By the way, I'm Rachel."

Dutch's face fell. "I know."

Kell pulled out his wallet. "How much for a custom design?"

"For you?" the kid said. "Nothing. I owe you for driving me home from play practice all the time."

"Uh uh. You need to be a better businessperson. Charge for your talent and time," he chided her.

"What kind of custom design?"

"Can you take this and–" he pointed to a pattern and whispered something in her ear, and she began laughing.

"SERIOUSLY?"

He nodded.

"Sure, but..." Cutting her eyes to Rachel, she asked, "Who is it for?"

Rachel gave him a quizzical look. "What kind of design are you asking for?"

"How spontaneous can you be?"

"Huh?"

"Are you willing to close your eyes and let Dutch—Anna—put my custom design on you?"

"Depends on where, I guess," Rachel said with an uncertain smile, eliciting laughs from everyone.

"ARM!" Dutch screeched. "On your arm!"

"It's not going to be anything gross, is it, Kell?" Rachel asked nervously. "I'm not a fan of surprises, but I'm intrigued."

"Trust me," Kell said. Rachel inhaled sharply and he wondered if he was making a mistake.

"You want me to trust you?"

"It's henna. It'll wash off after ten or so showers. Will you trust me with this?"

For a few seconds, he expected her to say no, those seconds exposing five years of pain. Asking her to trust him over something so tiny was a test, and they both knew it. She should really be the one asking for trust, but in a way, she had. She wanted him to trust the deal she was offering Lucinda and Boyce. Rachel was spending an entire day with him, and she didn't have to.

Something deeper was brewing between them.

Rachel sat down on one of the two chairs in front of Dutch, closed her eyes, and thrust out her arm.

"Okay. Deal."

Kell handed Dutch double her normal rate. Her outlined eyes got huge.

"That's too much money!"

"Not for what you're about to invent."

"You're seriously scaring me, Kell."

He sat next to Rachel. "Good that you're trusting me. It'll be fun. You need more fun in your life."

Her eyelids closed and her shoulders dropped. "Fine. But you'd better not have anything lewd tattooed on me. I have to fly in a week and go through TSA security."

"It's not lewd. Promise."

"Let me guess. It's the Svalbard flag?"

Kell leaned and whispered in Dutch's ear again. The snicker came out before she could suppress it.

"You want *that?*"

"I do."

"Right in the middle of the design?"

"Yes."

"That's hilarious."

"And I want a matching one, too."

"Oh! Is that why you gave me so much money? It's still too much, but for two…"

"You undercharge, kid."

The word *kid* made her eyes go dark, but Dutch still smiled, pointing to the chair next to Rachel's. "Sit. Let's get you guys tatted up."

"Not fair! Kell knows what he's getting and I don't," Rachel complained.

"Just go with it, Rachel. Learn to relax."

"As if that's a valuable skill," she joked.

"It is. I saw you do it by the fire this morning. Maybe being stuck here in Maine will teach you something."

Dutch's eyes jumped from Kell to Rachel, eyebrows arching. He just gave her a half smile and motioned to Rachel's arm.

Henna tattooing was an ancient art form, and by the time Dutch was done, his request was stunning. She'd taken the pattern from one of the pages of the binder and added what looked like an anime lemur head in the center. It could have looked cartoonish, but Dutch managed to give it depth and whimsical beauty.

It was a shame it would wear off in ten to twelve washes.

"Done?" Rachel asked.

"No peeking! I have to do Kell's now." Grasping his hand in hers and blushing furiously, Dutch bent her head and got to work. "Your arm's harder."

"Why?"

"Hair." She was searching for a clearer spot.

"He's half bear," Rachel declared.

"Nothing I can do about it," he groused.

"You weren't this hairy in D.C."

Dutch's eyelashes lifted again.

"I shaved and had short hair. Sometimes I wore a suit."

Dutch made a choking sound. "*You?* In a suit?"

"He was stylish," Rachel said with a sigh. "Very metro. Very cut."

Dutch caught his eye and mouthed, *She likes you.*

It was his turn to blush.

Bending back down, Dutch put the finishing touches on his design, blowing lightly on his arm, her face red enough to blend in with any heart costume.

A mom with two little kids, bundled up and exploding with excitement, walked up to the pavilion. Dutch looked conflicted, like she was eager for the new customers and their money but didn't want Kell to leave.

"Okay. Open your eyes, Rachel."

She did as told and burst out laughing.

"Oh, no, Kell! *A lemur?*"

Twisting his forearm, he showed Rachel his matching one. "Of course."

"Poor Leo lives on."

Kell grinned and added:

She was beautiful and kind and smart,
But she got her tail caught in a cart."

"Oh, no," Rachel groaned, Dutch glancing at them with curiosity, but her new customers took precedence.

Kell continued:

I was confused by a schemer
After saving a lemur"

He paused, knowing what he wanted to say next, the move bold. Once he crossed this line, there was no turning back.

Go for it, he told himself. *Take the leap.*

He finished with:

But Rachel Hart has stolen my heart."

Those beautiful eyes flared, Rachel's look of surprise and interest making him wonder if she felt it, too. The day had been so much richer than he'd expected.

He wanted more.

She reached for his hand and smiled. "Stolen? That implies I did it without consent."

"Then I need another word."

Rachel's phone buzzed repeatedly and she reached in her pocket with her untatted hand. "Must have caught internet."

"There's a router so people can use their credit cards," Dutch explained as the mom and kids looked over a sheet of her designs, deciding.

Rachel turned to Dutch. "This is gorgeous. You're such an artist. Thank you!"

The girl beamed, handing Rachel a trifold pamphlet. "This explains how to care for it." She looked up at Kell. "You know what to do. That must be the hundredth tat I've given you."

"Call me the henna guinea pig."

With a wave, Dutch turned to her new customers, and Kell felt a swell of pride. She was a sweet kid, and as the youngest in his family, he'd never had a little sister. Dutch was close enough. They were distant cousins, connected through a maze of genetics, and she needed more help than she got at home.

Putting some cash in her pocket while letting her practice something that built up her self-esteem was a two-fer.

As they walked, Rachel stared at her wrist, grinning. Her other hand brushed his and he took it, threading their fingers together, the zing of attraction growing as she squeezed back.

Warmth emanated up from where they connected.

He couldn't help himself. Hesitation be damned.

Rachel gave him a side-long look, but then glanced down. He moved closer to her, scouting the area for a private spot. After that almost kiss in the hot springs, and the easy way they were together today, he felt hope rising in his chest, his heart feeling a bit lighter.

Maybe.

Maybe the Rachel he'd liked so much five years ago was buried deep inside this one, and coming to the surface? Could this work? Spending time with her had always felt natural. Fun. Fulfilling and grounding. While she'd changed, and he certainly had, too, maybe they hadn't changed so much that they couldn't enjoy each other's company.

Which is what he was doing right now.

Enjoying her.

And a kiss would make it all even better.

Bzzz

"That's me," she sighed, reaching for her phone, but pausing halfway. "No," she admonished herself.

"You're arguing with some part of you, huh?" he asked.

"I am."

"You don't have to be a workaholic."

"Tell that to my boss."

"Gladly. Give me your phone. What's his name?"

"Hers. And no," she said with a laugh as they passed an enormous oak tree, the trunk covered with a beautiful cable-knit yarn treesock in red and white, with thick red heart patterns knitted in.

This was his chance.

Pulling her closer to the tree, he rested her back against it and took a leap, his mouth on hers, friendly and pleasant, feeling her out to see if she felt the same way. When her arms went to his neck and wrapped around, her chest against his, he swelled inside, turning the kiss up a notch.

Thousands of moments flooded his mind, all the times he wondered what she'd taste like lining up inside him, the press of his hands against the textured yard sock, the way she pushed back against him to get closer making him hold her tighter.

She tasted like coffee. Like hope. Like years of questions finally answered.

Longing, years deep, rose up in him as he held her tighter and kissed her intensely, her lips parting, his tongue daring. The swell of need and the thrill of her response made him lose himself in her, and they were lost together, her hands pressing him closer, her mouth divine.

"GET A ROOM!" someone called out from across the common, making Rachel dip under him and put space between them, her cheeks pink with embarrassment.

Then she kissed him again.

Putting to rest any question that she was as interested in him as he was in her, the way Rachel kissed him was a preview of how she would be in bed, her hands wandering over his broad back, hips pressing into him, her tongue matching his inch for inch.

There it was.

Exactly as he'd hoped, the kiss was the right move. Heart pumping hard, he let himself revel in this, because while Rachel Hart wasn't supposed to be in Luview, Maine, maybe she was meant to be here after all.

Bzzz

Rachel pulled back, then looked at her texts and frowned.

"Something wrong?" Kell asked as they stood there, his hand on her shoulder.

The deep frown took over Rachel's face again as she read her messages more carefully.

"What's going on?"

"It's my boss, my assistant, and my boss's boss. Work has exploded on me." She sighed eyes jumping to the phone in her hand, clearly distressed by the new messages. "I have to get back to the trailer and my laptop."

"Okay." Not a word about the kiss? Uncertainty filled him, making him feel awkward, like a middle school boy taking his first chance at a romantic gesture.

He pulled her over to the gazebo, climbing the steps to the empty half; the other part was full of sound equipment and microphones. Sound techs were setting up, getting ready for the welcome speech, the bands that would play happy love songs, and more. The town's public address system wasn't piping the recorded music through any longer.

Sound checks dominated.

Kell leaned against the railing, pulling her in for a hug. "More of this, less of work."

She gave a shallow laugh. "I mean it. I really need to go, Kell. My phone suddenly isn't connecting to the public Wi-Fi." Rachel took a few steps closer to a microphone stand.

"It's interference from all the electrical equipment." He paused. "You sure you don't want to stop somewhere else in town before I take you back?"

"Where? Love You Chocolate?" She waved her tattooed arm in the air and he could see something was agitating her, the tone change alarming. "Where I can get some magic-water-infused chocolate that determines the rest of my career?"

"I'm trying to show you the real Love You, Maine."

Bzzz

Another text, this one making her look a little sick.

"And I keep telling you I need to work," she mumbled.

"You work too much."

"Who are you to tell me how to live my life?"

"You're in my town." His words were meant as a joke, but they fell flat. He knew it the second her cheeks turned pink and she began to pace.

What a change in mood. Something about those texts was upsetting her, and as she paced, he realized he was misjudging the situation.

197

But it was too late.

"Oh, I've seen plenty of it! The real Love You is nothing but a backward town filled with people who are too stuck in their ways to see that they're wasting so much potential! Like the coffee shop, where they don't even have skim milk or ground vanilla, and the menu is circa 2005. Or the parking! Who puts *nickels* in meters anymore? Upgrade the meters to use phone apps, and get an electric trolley system for the town like every other small tourist town! How about the horny moose everyone just tolerates because... because *why?* And then there's you! One minute you're telling Boyce not to trust me, then the next you're trying to kiss me!"

Screeeeeech

A hideous sound of feedback cut through the air, Rachel covering her ears with her hands, Kell suddenly noticing the microphone she was standing *waaaay* too close to.

His gut dropped. Every word of that rant had just gone out on the PA system.

Which was why every human being within view was staring, gape-mouthed, at the two of them.

"I'll take you home," he said softly. The feedback had subsided, and Rachel's face was a mask of horror as she realized what she'd just done.

"You don't have to do that."

"I do, actually. You can't call an Uber here."

"Oh."

"Plus, uh... it's more for your protection than anything else. You're getting a lot of attention, none of it positive."

He took her elbow, mentally figuring the most direct path through town to get back to his truck. They were cutting through alleyways to get there, the stink of dumpsters reminding him of that day in D.C. when he'd rescued her from the pedicab that ran over the tail of her lemur costume. Had he somehow angered the gods with the lemur tattoo?

Hah. No.

He'd just let his guard down. Opened up, been playful.

And so had Rachel.

"I can't believe I just did that," she said, breathing hard as she hurried after Kell, his hand holding hers.

"But you did."

"No, Kell. That was–I had no idea the mic was on! I never would have said all those things if I'd known!"

"Gotcha."

"Everyone is going to hate me!"

"Already do. Can't take it back."

"Take it back? It was all true. I'm not taking back, but I didn't mean to broadcast it all over the entire town!"

Something on her phone had set her off, but he wasn't about to ask. The cold reality of how little he knew about her life hit like a slap. Was she seeing someone in L.A.? Were the texts from work, or more personal? She said she didn't have a boyfriend, but...

He was focused on getting her back to the trailer so he could think in silence.

Once they reached the car, she climbed in, set her bag of books on her lap, and rested her temple against the window, staring out for the ten-minute drive to Kenny's. He pulled in the driveway and parked in front of the trailer, and the fire circle seemed like a memory from a million years ago.

So much changed so fast.

"I'm the town pariah," she moaned, her words full of regret.

"You meant every word of that."

"I did."

"And nothing I showed you had any impact."

"It did. Of course it did." Shifting in her seat, she looked at him. "Mo is wonderful. Dutch is adorable. The theater with the romance movies, the chocolate company, the hot springs–this is a town where people really care about each other, but it's also a town that needs to innovate."

"By selling out to big companies like Markstone's."

"By making sure businesses don't *have* to sell out to companies like Markstone's. Innovation is resilience."

"Corporate jargon," he spat out.

His words made her reach for the door handle, pop it open, and climb out.

"Thanks for a lovely time, Kell. I had fun."

With that, she shut the door and stomped into the trailer, the sound of the thin metal door closing stirring up so much in him.

What the hell had just happened?

And where did they stand?

Chapter Eleven

RACHEL

Three texts yesterday on the town common had set off a nuclear bomb in her.

Orla: *Doug wants to send me in to close, but my daughter is giving birth any day now.*

Doug: *look at email I sent re land markstone's may buy in luview crucial you fix this close the deal*

Doug never used punctuation or capitals when he texted. Said it was a waste of time. If he was driving, he dictated it, so every once in a while his drive-thru orders were included in his texts. The guy drank five Splendas in a large coffee and ate a banana with it for breakfast.

Orla had secretly called him a douchebro when they had drinks one night, but never mentioned it again.

Dani: *I can't find any rentals for February 13 and 14, even at Nordicbeth. Popular weekend. Ideas?*

Between the surprise of the lemur tattoo, which was the sweetest gesture on Kell's part, her inner turmoil as her feelings for him grew, and getting hit 1-2-3 by those texts, something in Rachel had snapped.

On a hot microphone.

Of all the stupid places to be standing when she let loose, that one was the worst. Kenny had knocked on the door when he came out to the trailer to deliver more firewood, an aggrieved expression on his face. "Backward? Really? I have a 4.8-star average on Airbnb, Rachel," he'd sniffed, then walked away with a swagger.

Great. Once you lost guys like Kenny, you lost the whole town.

What was supposed to be an extended stay so she could charm locals, plant seeds about how good the acquisition could be for the community, and counteract Kell's interference was suddenly ruined by... her.

And only her.

None of this was Kell's fault. This was all on her.

A long groan came out of her as she realized the last text she'd sent, confirming her next dental appointment, had not been delivered.

No service, her phone said.

She went to her computer.

Wi-Fi: Looking for networks, her laptop said.

The trailer was cursed.

Kell had explained to her that satellite dish internet service was iffy during winter in the mountains, and Kenny's place was proving him right.

It was February 7. After some back and forth, Orla gave her permission to stay rather than return to L.A., because there'd been a new development in the Love You Chocolate project: Doug had pushed Markstone's to look into expanding the deal and buying a small, abandoned tool and die company in town. The idea was to turn it into a parking lot and distribution center to handle the expected leap in sales that would result from the acquisition.

Rachel remembered seeing the place when Kell had driven her through town. It was right on the edge of the vibrant downtown, and would definitely change the character of the cozy shops, but if Markstone's had done a feasibility study and decided that was part of the deal, then she would work hard to deliver.

She *had* to deliver, or be fired.

The internet going out again was the last straw.

Kenny's little one-sheet for the trailer had a section about restaurants and, funny enough, listed the internet service status of each.

The coffee shop, Bilbee's Tavern, a smoothie store, the town library, and town hall all had Internet.

A plan formed.

A painful one.

Spending the day without internet was impossible. Too much work to be done. Already, she was behind because she didn't do work while wandering around town with Kell yesterday.

She would have to bounce around town and use the shops' access.

That meant being in public places right after embarrassing herself by saying all those horrible things about the town.

And yet... business was business.

Love You Coffee was likely her safest place. Skylar struck her as the forgiving type. Packing up all her stuff, Rachel got in her car and made the surprisingly easy drive into town, the roads reasonably clear after a few days with no new snow.

Parking was as hard as she expected, so she finally gave up on getting anything near town and drove to the far edge, finding a spot on a side street, a good half-mile walk away.

Love You, Maine, had a serious parking problem.

The walk did her some good, though, helping to clear her mind and give her fresh air. Each inhale helped her frenzied mind to calm down a bit and line up in an orderly fashion. When she reached the coffee shop, she pulled her hat down a little more, glad she was wearing her red coat and blended in.

Reef was at the counter, glaring at her, though she suspected he glared at everyone.

"Um, hi, Reef. I'd like a–"

"Half two, half almond double shot latte with a teaspoon of ground Madagascar vanilla," he snapped, turning away to start the coffee.

"How did you know?"

"Because I have brain cells and a memory."

"You don't have the ground vanilla, though."

"We do now. Skylar ordered some."

Rachel was stunned. "She did?"

"Said you said it was healthy and tasted good, so you'll get your coffee exactly the way you want, perfect in every way."

Why did that feel like a slam?

"Listen, I know everyone heard me rant yesterday, and I feel bad about it–"

One of his hands was busy working the espresso machine, the other going up to stop her. "You weren't wrong, but a lot of people are pissed at you."

"Are you one of them?"

"I tried the vanilla in a latte. It's good." His mouth tightened. "Really good."

He glared at her like that was a bad thing.

"You like it?"

"Mmm hmm." The sound came out like a growl. "Didn't want to."

"Why not?"

"Sounded stupid. Over the top. But it's not."

"It's definitely not."

"You're helping us up our game."

"Thank you."

"But lots of people don't want to hear they're getting stuff wrong. Be prepared for the haters."

"I've been dealing with them for years. I'll just keep my head down and hide in a corner here." Moving to an empty table as far away from the activity as possible, she set up her laptop so her back was to the door. By the time she was done, Reef motioned to her drink.

She pulled out her credit card.

"You want an account?" he asked.

"No. I'm not here for that long."

"You've already bought six coffees since you've been here, Rachel. More than halfway to a freebie. Give in and get an account." He gave her a hairy eyeball look, a test of sorts, like he was feeling her out.

"I really don't need one." A few small trays of cheese, crackers, and fruit were in the cooler below her. She grabbed one and added it to her purchase.

"Okay," he said, processing the card. "If you say so."

"I'm only here until February 15th."

Reef just snorted and walked away.

What was that about?

The door opened as Rachel took her first sip and opened her email: seventy-seven unread messages. Clicking on the first one, she began putting earbuds in, hoping no one would recognize her, but she felt self-conscious.

Imposter syndrome, squared. There was no way she belonged here in this little town, and she didn't belong at Markstone's, either.

Where *did* she belong?

Woodsmoke filled her nose, the scent imaginary. The memory of sitting around that fire with Kell yesterday morning sent her pulse into a salsa beat and put a smile on her face. It wasn't caffeine that made her heart jump.

It was a sense of joy.

For the next fifteen minutes, she ate and drank in bliss, slowly unwinding, feeling like maybe, just maybe, this trip was salvageable.

Kell had been taciturn on the drive home yesterday, but not mad. A bit amused, even, after a while. Maybe watching her make a fool of herself had some entertainment value for him.

Their kisses ignited something in her, but her rant had extinguished any spark that was emerging. She blew it.

There wasn't a real chance anyhow, right?

Lost in her thoughts, warm, having a fabulous coffee, and thinking about Kell, she didn't notice someone standing behind her.

"Hmph. Stuck, huh? Backward?"

The woman's voice made Rachel hunch her shoulders. Ouch. Didn't even get through a single email.

Reaching for her drink, she decided to play dumb and hope the angry woman went away.

"Excuse me? Rachel Hart? I don't believe we've met. I'm Nadine. I work at the police department." The woman, who now stood to her side, expecting to be acknowledged, wasn't just angry.

She was *righteous*.

Woe be unto Rachel if she got this wrong. There was still a deal to salvage, and if that meant Rachel had to suck it up and face the consequences of her rant, that's what had to happen.

Last night, she'd had plenty of time to run through the implications of what had happened. Thank goodness she hadn't gotten any nastier than she did. Was she out of line? Yes.

But had she been technically wrong?

No. Love You, Maine, needed an upgrade. Not in the emotional connection part. They had that nailed down here. Small-town heart was everywhere, literally and figuratively.

Policies and attitudes were shutting even more people out, though, which would only hurt the town in the long run.

"Hi Nadine," Rachel said, standing to shake the woman's hand. Nadine gave her a limp fish. Rachel shook it anyhow, pulling away as fast as possible.

"Your stunt yesterday hurt a lot of people."

"I can see you're angry."

"Darn right I am. You don't know anything about this town!"

"I shouldn't have said those things. I agree."

Rachel's response seemed to deflate Nadine. Good. That was the goal. A long time ago, her father had told her, "When someone's angry at you in business, agree with them. It's the fastest way to disarm them and buy yourself time to regroup." And he was right.

It really did work.

"Um. Oh. Good that you see it my way," Nadine stammered.

"Can I ask you a question, Nadine? You seem to be one of the power brokers in the community."

Chin rising, Nadine's effusive grin told Rachel she'd said the right thing. "I don't know about 'power broker', but I like to think I do have a great deal of influence here."

"Can you tell me who to talk to about these parking meters?"

Nadine bristled. "What's wrong with them?"

Ah. Rachel proceeded with caution.

"Nothing's wrong with them. I'm just wondering if there's a way to make them more accessible."

"Accessible?"

"Most younger people don't carry cash. They use their phones for everything, including paying for parking."

Nadine sniffed. "I've heard of these app things. You wave your phone in front of a screen and it pays for parking."

"Something like that, yes."

"I would never have my credit card on the internet."

"Excuse me?"

"I know how that works. You enter your credit card number on a computer and then hackers steal it and drain your bank accounts dry. AARP had a whole series on cyber security, and I'm not some stupid old woman. Good old coin is better than exposing people to having their bank accounts stolen!"

Oh, dear.

"That's a really good point, Nadine. Hmmm."

"That's what I told Harry!"

"Harry?"

"Our former business development director. He wanted those app things and I put a stop to the whole mess."

"You did?"

"I did. Protecting people is what I do, working for the police department. I might not drive a cruiser or wear a badge, but I protect and serve in my own way."

"Your commitment is wonderful. You're helping me to see the town in a whole new light."

"Thank you!" Nadine smiled.

"You're welcome."

"I still haven't forgiven you for trash talking my town, but maybe you're not as bad as Kell made you out to be."

All the air in Rachel's chest rushed out at once.

"Right. Thanks."

With a wave, Nadine walked over to the counter and began talking to Reef about something involving a coffee donation to her church auction.

Suddenly, Rachel's email seemed less engaging. That comment about Kell physically hurt.

Burying herself in work was the best approach.

A video-heavy Zip file made downloading a frustrating experience, the coffee shop's internet too weak to do the job right. After trying for twenty minutes, she packed up, went to the counter and asked, "What's the best wireless network in town I can connect to?"

"That'd be Bilbee's."

"The tavern?"

"Yep. Stronger than the library or the town hall."

"People bring their laptops into the bar and work?"

"Hell, no. Rider would shoot you on the spot."

Rachel laughed.

Reef didn't.

"Okay," she said with a long exhale. "Short of Bilbee's, what's best?"

"Library. And Dotty won't lay into you. She'll likely agree with you and your rant."

"Dotty? Dotty Chen? The librarian?"

"You're learning. Memorizing names."

"Have to. It's for work."

He winked at her and pointed. "Two blocks to the right, then a left at the light. Can't miss the red library."

"Seventy-five percent of the buildings are red."

"Seventy-five percent of the red buildings don't say LIBRARY on them."

She stuck her tongue out at him. He laughed.

As she left, the cold air instantly turned the rim of her nostrils to ice. She belted her red coat tighter, avoided eye contact, kept her head down, and hoped the library had those old-fashioned study carrels where she could truly hide.

"Rachel!" a woman called out as she walked past Love You Chocolate.

Lucinda.

Oh, no.

"Rachel," she said, one eyebrow arching in judgment. "I've meant to call you about our February 15th meeting, but the store has been packed."

Every muscle in her body turned to glue. "Our meeting?"

"Yes. I heard your rant yesterday."

"You heard it?"

"I happened to be outside, on my way to an appointment. You have quite the opinion of Luview, haven't you?"

"I can explain."

"You already did. Don't walk your words back. Own them."

Confidence, Rachel, she heard in her head, her mother's voice taking over. *Always, Confidence.*

"Fine. I own them. But I was less than elegant."

"After the four days you've had here, if rumor is correct, I'd be shocked if you maintained your composure, child."

The word *child* almost made Rachel laugh.

Now was not a good time to do anything *almost*.

So she didn't.

"And yet, your words were disturbing. Backward, stuck? *Stuck?* Were you referring to me?"

"Absolutely not."

"Rachel." Lucinda's tone was frank.

"I was referring to an overall pattern here. If you don't innovate, the town will fall behind the rest of the world. And I get it–I do. You don't care about what other towns do. That's not what I mean. There's a huge difference between choosing to preserve the town's character and making yourself irrelevant."

"You really have studied the town."

"Parts of it."

"The poison ivy boy helped show you, didn't he?"

"He did."

"I heard he showed you the hot springs."

"Please tell me you didn't personally witness that from your window."

"No. Just heard about it from one of the cashiers. You've made quite a splash, my dear."

Rachel chuckled at the pun. "I came here to help you sell to Markstone's and make a difference. Instead, I've made a nuisance of myself."

"You have a keen eye for improving the town. Why don't you write up your ideas and give them to the town manager? Or the development committee?"

"That sounds like a lot of unpaid work."

"And how much unpaid rental space are your critiques of my town taking up in your head?"

Rachel blinked. "I've never thought of it that way before."

Lucinda's face was a study in wrinkles, her bright red lipstick and heart earrings in contrast to her white hair and piercing eyes. "May I say something personal?"

"I thought you just did."

Lucinda's demeanor shifted, turning friendlier. "You strike me as being somewhat at a crossroads, Rachel."

"That is a very astute observation."

"And when you're at a crossroads in life, you should always stop before deciding which direction to choose."

"Okay."

"Take your time. No one dictates how long you stand there, weighing out your options. Gather information. Observe. Let yourself marinate in possibility. Then, when you make a decision, you know it comes from your deepest self."

"That is very philosophical."

"Ah, no. It's the opposite. Exceedingly practical advice from someone who has gotten it wrong sometimes and right at others." Lucinda took in a deep breath through her nose and looked at her store. "I must go. It's the *love*-liest time of the year. I won't have many more of these, you know."

"Because you're going to sell to Markstone's?"

"No, dear. Because I am eighty-eight years old and, sadly, mortal."

With a squeeze of her forearm, Lucinda walked slowly back to her store, leaving Rachel more dazed than before.

Had that been... positive? Or one big critique from Lucinda?

Rachel resumed her walk to the library, blissfully uninterrupted the rest of the way.

The Luview library was a small brick building, red enough naturally, but with two huge picture windows on either side of a large door. The windows had bright red shutters and the door was red as well.

A heart-shaped sign said Luview Library, leaving no question she'd found it.

As she opened the front door, she found herself in a small, warm foyer, the blast of heat making her shake slightly. How did people live like this? It was so different from all her years in southern California's more temperate climate.

Inside, the library smelled like books, and she inhaled reflexively. She loved libraries, though she'd never been the kind of kid who just hung out in them. Always busy with whatever lessons her mother had scheduled for her, she was more likely to be at cheerleading practice than reading the newest Suzanne Collins book.

But in college, she'd discovered her favorite mysteries, and now she was determined to get her hands on one.

As she approached the front desk, she wondered how much time Kell had spent here. A lifelong resident, this would have been his library as a kid. Was Deanna the type to bring her family here with empty bookbags, letting the kids choose books to load up and read throughout the week? Did they walk here on their own as they got older?

Rachel's best friend in elementary and middle school, Madi Taylor, had a mom like that. Portia had called her "very domestic," as if that were quaint.

Maybe that's why Rachel found herself drawn to Kell's mom. She reminded Rachel of Madi's mother, Tigue, who was always ready to give them whatever attention they asked for. Countless afternoons of playing Monopoly flashed through her memory.

"Hello! You must be Rachel!"

Drawn out of her reverie, Rachel looked up at the woman behind the desk. Her salt-and-pepper hair was set off by bright red glasses, each eyepiece in the shape of a rounded heart.

"Um, yes."

"I'm Dotty Chen. Nice to meet you. I've heard all about you."

"Thanks. Is that good or bad?"

"Welcome to our town. You're allowed to have opinions about it."

"Ah. You heard."

"Indirectly. But," Dotty shrugged, "no town is perfect."

Rachel looked around the orderly space. "No, but this library looks great."

"What do you need? How can I help?"

"I'd like to check out a book. The bookstore doesn't sell what I want to read, so..."

Dotty laughed softly. "I get that a lot. You know, they tried to do the same thing to this library. The Love Committee."

"I take it that you're not a member."

"Goodness, no. Any committee that tries to get the library to weed out all books that aren't about love is on my you-know-what list."

Rachel chuckled in solidarity.

"Librarians are nice, agreeable folks until you try to remove freedom of choice from our patrons. Then we become warriors."

"Got it. And I agree."

"I have good news and bad news. You're not a resident, so I can't give you a regular card."

"Oh."

"But! If you can show me a library card from your home library, we have a special visitor's card. It's good for seven days, and we allow you to check out one book."

"Just one?"

"One at a time."

"That's all I need." Rachel reached into her bag, found her wallet, and showed Dotty her library card.

"Excellent!" A small box, when opened, revealed a stack of pink cards. In careful penmanship, Dotty filled it out for Rachel, handing it over. "There you go. And if you become a permanent resident, we can convert the card for you."

"I'm never becoming a permanent resident here, Dotty. I live in L.A."

"So many people who come here say that, but the ones who truly fall in love tend to stay."

"That's not going to be me."

Dotty's eyes twinkled. "If you say so, dear. Now," she said with a soft hand clap. "Let's find you a book. What do you like?"

"Mysteries."

"Any specific kind? Is there a book you're looking for?"

"It's pretty obscure. Max Seeck's newest."

"Oh! We have that. Let me show you."

Suppressing her surprise, Rachel followed Dotty to a themed display table. Between Janet Evanovich's newer books and Jonathan Kellerman's, Rachel saw a group of familiar covers.

"Nordic noir? I can't believe you have this!"

"They're books. This is a library."

"No, I mean, it's really niche."

"It is. You can thank Kell Luview for it."

"Kell. Of course."

"He started by asking for *Smilla's Sense of Snow* when he was barely old enough for an adult card. Went from there. As a teenager, he was very vocal in making requests, and now he donates some of the books."

"Wow."

Seeck's book was in Dotty's hands. She held it up. "Let's get you checked out so you can start reading."

Kell was everywhere. *Everywhere.* Pieces of him were embedded in the town, from the way he helped Dutch with her henna business, to building the Nordic noir book section, to cutting skydivers out of trees, to hand-pulling poison ivy in the town center without pay.

There was nowhere in Luview Rachel could go that wasn't touched by Kell.

And she loved it.

"Here you go." Dotty slid the book and her new card over the counter. "Anything else I can do for you?"

"Help me hide."

"Hide? You want me to put you in a cupboard?"

"Hah. No. I just need a quiet corner where no one will see me so I can work."

"I absolutely can." Dotty pointed to a far corner. "Head on over to the display in non-fiction called Epistemology. No one ever goes over there."

The two shared a laugh, and a very grateful Rachel made her way to a tiny cluster of study carrels, dumped her bag on the table, and got to work.

For three hours, no one verbally attacked her, glared at her, or made her into the devil's handmaiden. It was a productive three hours, too. Dotty was right.

Epistemology refuge for the win.

By the time her stomach growled, demanding attention, it was three in the afternoon and her inbox was eighty percent clear. Hours of video had been watched and cataloged, and a long document full of notes was ready to be revised and sent in as a report.

She even managed to find a restroom and a water fountain, amused that she returned to her grade-school self as she slurped from the spout. With bottled water everywhere, when was the last time she'd done *that*?

Stomach rumbling, she began packing up, wishing she had a simple protein bar to stretch out her time here. Time to grab a salad somewhere, and another coffee.

As she made her way to the front desk, she planned to thank Dotty before leaving, but a young girl was checking out a stack of books, chattering away about some book called *Catfishing on Catnet*. As Rachel waited, she let herself breathe, the pull of work and responsibility relieved a bit.

"RACHEL HART!"

A thin, white-haired woman in an enormously puffy down coat, the kind that went down to her ankles, stormed up to Rachel, furious brown eyes buried under wrinkles and anger.

So much anger.

"Anne, please keep your voice down," Dotty said, coming around the counter quickly.

"HOW DARE YOU!"

"Anne!" Dotty pleaded. "Not here!"

So much for hiding at the library.

"This town has been nothing but wonderful for all my seventy-nine years of living here, and I won't have some cold-hearted businesswoman who even Kell Luview won't trust bad-mouthing it."

Dotty took Anne firmly by the arm and hissed in her ear. "Anne, this is not the place. Go outside and yell. My library is a quiet sanctuary and you cannot do this here."

Startled out of her anger, Anne looked at Dotty and softened.

"Sorry. I'm just so mad at her!"

"Rachel, meet Anne Petrinelli. Her husband was the former town clerk and I believe she'd like a word with you." Dotty looked pointedly at Anne. "Out there!"

Filled with dread, her appetite suddenly gone, Rachel walked outside with Anne, who immediately turned to her and said, "Everything you said about this town is wrong, and if my Stan were alive to hear it, he'd have a second heart attack."

"Stan? Your late husband's name was Stan?"

"What's that got to do with anything?"

"My father's name is Stan, too."

"Oh." She frowned deeper. "How... coincidental." An evil eye struck Rachel. "You're not lying about that, too, are you?"

"Lying?"

"Kell told Boyce you couldn't be trusted." She sniffed. "I see why."

"Anne, I–"

"It's Mrs. Petrinelli to you, thank you very much."

"Okay. I can see you're very upset by my words. May I ask what upset you the most?"

"Backward? Stuck?"

"I see. Yes, those were wrong, and I apologize."

"Apology not accepted. You don't rant like that a few days before Valentine's Day. You ruined the whole feel of the town common!"

"It was an accident. I had no idea that microphone was on."

"Hmph."

"I am very sorry, Mrs. Petrinelli."

"Hmph." This time, the sound was more forgiving. Anne pursed her mouth and said, "You mentioned an electric trolley."

"Yes?"

"What's that all about?"

This was not what Rachel had expected, but she'd go with it if it meant Anne would stop yelling at her.

"In some tourist towns, especially beach towns, they have these adorable electric trolleys that take people up and down the main road. They're free–they're designed to help showcase the town and give families an added reason to visit, but they're really helpful for parking problems. You set up larger parking lots on either end of the route, and then there's less traffic in town."

"You mean like Old Orchard Beach?"

"What's that?"

Anne was disgusted again. "You've never been to Old Orchard Beach? Down the Maine coast? South of Portland?"

"I'm from Los Angeles."

A massive eye roll was the old woman's response, until she added:

"I know what you're talking about. Been on the one there. Never thought of bringing one to our town here. They're expensive, though."

"Sure. But your town finance committee can find ways to pay for it. And the increase in tourism, especially from families and people with mobility issues, could offset the cost."

"Mobility issues? I hadn't thought of that, either."

Rachel smiled, relieved that the tone of the conversation was shifting. "It was just a thought."

"A good one, even if it came out in a soup of vitriol, Rachel." Anne contemplated her. "I don't know what to think about you."

Rachel's stomach growled loudly.

"Other than to think you need to go eat." A smile cracked across Anne's face, the two chuckling nervously.

Or, at least, Rachel was nervous.

Anne just chuckled.

"Go eat. Do yourself a favor and get the falafel plate from Bilbee's."

"Bilbee's has falafel?"

"Sure. Rider adds whatever he likes to the menu. Had some great falafel at a restaurant in Cambridge a few years ago and now it's a special."

"That sounds really, really good."

"His prime rib Friday special is even better."

"Thank you for the tips."

"You're welcome. If you're going to criticize my town, you need to get to know it first."

And with that, Anne pulled her ski cap down on her head, turned around, and stomped off.

Leaving Rachel's stomach to gurgle harder.

Falafel, huh? At Bilbee's.

Which was on the other side of town.

Rachel walked back to her car, trying to shake the sense that she had a giant target on her back. Perfect for this town, since bullseyes were typically red.

As she approached her parking spot, she groaned. A white envelope was tucked under the windshield wiper. Opening it, she found – horror of horrors – the parking ticket was on pink paper, and in the shape of a heart.

No.

Just... no.

Those five hours in the library, hiding in Epistemology, had been a break from the stress of everything. Work had become her only break.

What a commentary on her life.

The ticket was punishment for being able to breathe a little.

So unfair.

Snatching the ticket, she climbed into her car and read it, pulling out her phone to send pictures to Dani, so Dani could take care of it. Pausing, she remembered that Markstone's didn't cover parking tickets under employee reimbursement.

The instructions on the envelope read: *Parking violations must be paid by mail or in person at the Police Department. Cash or personal check only. No out of state checks. Credit cards are accepted but incur a $3 service fee.*

Rachel looked at the fine.

Ten dollars.

She could certainly afford a $3 surcharge on a $10 ticket, but she was agog at the ridiculousness of the situation. Cash or personal check only? A thirty percent fee for using a credit card?

Come on.

On impulse, she turned on the engine and drove to the town hall, which was attached to the tiny police department. Outside was a row of four pink cruisers, all parked neatly, looking like a line of bubble gum. And inside, behind the front counter, stood none other than... Nadine Khouri.

Who gave Rachel quite the smug look.

"How can I help you?" she asked.

"I am here to pay a parking ticket," Rachel said loudly. "Which I would pay with one thousand pennies if I had them."

"It's all cash money, honey. Whatever it takes."

"Why do you charge three dollars for a ten-dollar parking ticket if I pay by credit card?"

"I don't know. You'd have to ask the IT department."

"Where is the IT department?"

"That's Matt. He's at the high school right now."

"High school?"

"He gets out of class at 2:05 and is here around 2:20, but he has drama practice today, so he won't be in until 4."

"Your IT department is a high school teacher?"

"Goodness, no. He's a student. Senior."

Rachel groaned, reaching for her wallet and pulling out a twenty. Nadine took the money as a man Rachel didn't recognize gave her major side eye.

"Hey, Tom," Nadine called out. "You got change? The cash box is all twenties and ones."

A tall, lean man walked over. He was wearing tan chinos with an ancient, cracked, brown leather belt, and a blue button-down shirt with a fraying collar under a pilled, brown V-neck sweater. His face was long, ears and nose outsized, and he looked like the kind of man you turned to when you had a problem and needed nonjudgmental advice.

Tom walked over and reached into his wallet, pulling out a ten. "Here."

"I'll keep track and pay you back when I go to the bank next."

He waved her off. "No problem." A hand was extended to Rachel. "I'm Tom Kohl, the town manager."

She shook his hand. "Rachel Hart. You're the one in charge?"

Did something in his face shift slightly when she told him her name, or was it her imagination?

"Not really. More like the cat herder."

"Do you make decisions like credit card processors? Parking design?"

"You think the ticket was unfairly written?"

"No, I definitely overstayed my four hours. But Luview could do so much to increase revenue, and the way you handle tickets, parking fees, and basic transit in town leaves a lot to be desired."

"Tell me more." Tom folded his arms across his chest. The gesture would look challenging on Kell, but when Tom did it, it felt grounding.

Like he was here to listen for a while.

"Parking apps. An electric trolley for tourism and transit, with parking lots on either end of the line. Trolley stops at all the inns and B&Bs so people can go out and drink without worrying. Upgraded systems so town employees worry less about administrative functions and can focus more on growth."

"Growth isn't the only measure of success," he said slowly.

"No. But annoying your visitors with poor parking solutions is definitely a measure of failure."

Nadine piped up. "You know, Tom, she's not the only one to complain. We're getting a lot of families who want to park in town, use strollers and all that, but the four-hour limit is a problem."

"Some towns don't even charge for parking," Rachel added. "There are feasibility studies showing what happens when visitors get free parking. They spend more in shoppes and at restaurants."

"You work in urban planning? I thought you were here to make a deal for Markstone's with Lucinda and Boyce," he asked.

Aha. He did know who she was.

"I took a class in it as part of my MBA," she explained.

"You have some good ideas. Problem is funding them."

"Your business development director should be able to–oh, right. He quit."

Nadine's expression changed to clear disapproval.

"Harry wanted to change everything," she said with a dismissive sniff. "Called us a bunch of rubes."

"He was only here because his wife got a big job at Nordicbeth and he needed something. Once the fundraising job opened up at the university, he split," Tom said. "The guy used a chainsaw when he needed a scalpel."

Rachel's stomach roared with hunger. The sound made them all laugh.

"You need to head on over to Bilbee's and get some food. Or the smoothie place," Tom said.

"What about Love You India?" Nadine offered, the two of them devolving into an argument over which food Rachel should eat making her smile.

"I'm getting the falafel plate at Bilbee's," she declared, earning twin nods of approval.

"How long are you in town?" Tom asked her.

"Until February 15."

"If you want to write some of these ideas up, I can work on them. You've got good thoughts."

"Thanks. Kell suggested the same thing." *Lucinda, too*, she didn't add.

"Smart guy." Tom tapped his temple. "A well-written proposal is better than a screed over the town's PA system."

Rachel winced. "You heard."

"Oh, I heard, and then I've heard about nothing but what I heard. Everyone in town is talking about you, Rachel," Tom said with a hearty laugh.

"You don't seem offended by what I said."

He shrugged. "You weren't wrong. It's just too bad it had to come out that way."

"I know. Thanks."

Nadine handed her a receipt. "Here."

"Great. That's done. Off to find an early dinner."

They said their goodbyes and as she walked out the door, she crashed into a human wall.

A wall that smelled like woodsmoke, lime, spices, and...

Chocolate?

"Hi!" Kell said, his hands on her shoulders as she looked up, her ankle a bit wobbly.

Well, this was awkward.

"Hi! Sorry! I wasn't looking."

"You okay?" he asked. "Something wrong?"

"Other than the way things left off between us yesterday? No. Just paying a parking ticket."

He seemed to ignore her bait. "Ah. Rusty got you?"

"Rusty?"

"He's the cop who writes most of the parking tickets."

"Then yes. He got me."

Kell frowned. "He didn't talk to you, did he?"

"No. Why?"

"Rusty's very... friendly."

"Why would that be a problem?"

"Friendly in a notch-on-his-belt kind of way."

"Town player?"

"Basically."

"I haven't met him, but thanks for the warning."

"He'll try to charm your pants off."

"Sounds like the local pastime."

"Excuse me?"

She winked, already embarrassed, so why not go for it. "You got me to take mine off in the hot springs. But maybe not with charm."

Kell's low, deep laugh made parts of her body tingle, her breath shaky as she tried to hide her response.

"Just watch out for him. And don't get parking tickets!"

"This was entirely my fault. I was hiding and lost track of time."

"Hiding?"

"In the library."

"Hiding from what?"

"Not what, *who*. People."

"Which people?"

"All of them. They all hate me now."

Brows knitting, he didn't say the socially expected nicety.

"You deserve it."

Blunt and grumpy Kell reappeared.

Except he wasn't wrong.

"I know."

"And now you're paying penance. Who's said something to you?"

"Nadine, Anne Petrinelli, Lucinda, Reef, and now Tom. But

he wants me to write up a white paper on my parking logistics ideas."

"A white paper?"

"So does Lucinda."

"Huh."

"Why are *you* here? Doing jail time for being a grump?"

"No. Paying for my annual business license."

"Doesn't your office manager do that?"

"You're looking at my office manager."

"You handle everything? What about Allen?"

Kell snorted. "Allen's good for tree work and pulling poison ivy, and that's it."

"Why haven't you hired admin help?"

"Why haven't you done a thousand things you should do in your life, Rachel? Because I don't have time."

"You have to make time in order to make time."

"Gee, thanks, Mom."

"Why are you so grouchy?"

"I..." He blew out a long breath. "I'm way behind on everything. I have to pay a late fee on the license, and I have paperwork stacking up like crazy. Invoices. Estimates. GDPR compliance for email newsletters. All of it."

"Too much business is never a bad thing, right?"

"It is when I'm part of two different ones."

"I see. Why not pick one?"

"It's more complicated than that."

"I would think it'd be easy to decide—to turn toward the part of your life that gives you joy and holds promise for a wonderful future."

He blinked once. Then twice. Holding her gaze, he softened visibly, gray eyes turning warm as his mouth twisted up.

"Yeah. It should be easy."

But Rachel's phone ruined the moment.

"I'll let you get that," Kell said, stepping aside. "The clerk's office closes any minute now, and I need to take care of this. See you later, Rachel."

As abruptly as they'd run into each other, Kell was running away.

And not a word about getting together again.

Despair gnawed at the edges of her grumbling stomach. She

really had blown it yesterday. Ranting on that hot mic after kissing him wasn't just a big mistake.

It was the death of any chance with Kell.

The day had just nosedived even further.

Fighting tears, she felt her phone buzz again and looked.

Even worse–the text was a message from her mother: *I've been cast in a small role in a new K-drama series set half in L.A., half in South Korea. It's a mother role, but these K-dramas are over-the-top popular!*

Congrats, Mom, Rachel typed back.

Thank you. How's your deal going?

Ugh. Rachel wanted to bang her head against the building's pillar, but instead she started walking back to her car.

Her plan was to go to Bilbee's.

Order the falafel plate.

Eat.

And stare at the wall in existential torment.

Going fine, she lied. On impulse, she added: *When you were here, did you get along with the locals?*

Instantly, her mom responded with: *Of course!*

Any tips? Rachel asked, knowing it would please her mother to be asked for advice.

Avoid that hair salon in the basement of someone's house on Cedar Drive. The woman there has no idea how to do balayage. I looked like Robin Williams' rainbow suspenders.

?? Rachel typed back.

You know. From Mork & Mindy?

Sometimes, her mother made less sense than usual. This was one of those times.

Is that a law firm? Rachel replied, earning a big frowny face in return.

Never mind, Portia answered. *Just be yourself. I'm sure everyone there will love you!*

"Hah," Rachel muttered, back at her car. She climbed in, drove the two minutes to Bilbee's, and found a parking spot in back.

Then she remembered: Bilbee's had the strongest internet in town.

A new plan formed:

Park at Bilbee's.

Order the falafel plate.

Eat.

Do a bunch of work on her laptop in her car.

Part of the reason she'd needed five hours at the library was the video sequence she had to watch and critique. As she sat in her parking spot, she pulled her laptop out of her bag, entered into her work space, and opened a video.

Bam! Lightning loading. Why on earth was a bar the best place for internet in Love You, Maine?

No way was she going to ask.

Closing the laptop, she stuffed it under the front seat and went into Bilbee's. The ancient building leaned a bit, the porch creaky and in such disrepair she strongly suspected it was last painted in 1788, the year the tavern was established, according to the sign.

Bilbee's Tavern, it read, with the motto: "If we don't have it, you shouldn't be drinking it."

A goat was stomping on a red heart.

Great. If Kell was grumpy, his cousins were downright scary.

The bar smelled like woodsmoke and sour beer. Every floorboard groaned as she stepped on it. Patrons were sitting in booths and at tables, and a group of guys were playing pool in one corner.

"Rachel," said a guy at the bar. He was tatted up and looked like he'd lost an eye in a fight with a bald eagle, huge, long-healed scratches around an eye patch. "What can I get you?"

"How do you know my name?"

"Because I spent the last day listening to people gripe about you."

"You must be a Bilbee."

"Rider."

"Hi, Rider. I'm here to get your falafel plate, to go."

"Cool. You know, you could have ordered ahead with the app."

"You have an app?"

"Yep."

"I had no idea."

"Kenny didn't put it on his little Airbnb suck-up page?"

"Excuse me?"

"Kenny's trying to impress all the trailer tourists. Thought he had it on there."

"I might not have read the whole thing."

"Okay. Get the app. A lot easier."

He began keying her order into a shockingly modern system as Rachel looked around.

"What's the deal with your sign out there?"

"What about it?"

"The goat? Stomping on a heart? What's it mean?"

He shrugged. "I dunno. Some version of that sign's been there since 1788. Started with the goat, and I think old Randall Bilbee added the heart when the Love Committee required everyone to have a heart on their sign. The old version had the goat eating the heart, but my grandpa softened it up. Got some complaints from locals who said it was too harsh and scared visitors." He peered at Rachel with his one eye. "Maybe I should change it back."

"Charming," she said under her breath, handing him her credit card to finish the transaction.

"If you want charm, go to the hot springs. We're not about charm. Be about five minutes. You picked a slow time."

Rider disappeared into the back, leaving Rachel to look around. There was an antique authenticity to the place, with low ceilings and windows crooked in their frames. Two small wood stoves on opposite sides of the bar gave the air a cozy feel, and an array of television screens mounted on the wall showed four different games at once. Eight college guys were in a giant horseshoe booth in the back, cheering each other on through tequila shots.

Her phone buzzed.

It was her mom again: *By the way, Tim's part of a team that designed a new machinery part for spaceships! Isn't that amazing?*

"Does it involve using recycled pee to cure cancer?" she muttered to herself.

Rider appeared with a to-go bag, giving her an evil eye.

"Here." He plunked it on the counter. "Utensils are in there. Need water? Something else?"

"Got any disguises handy?"

"Hah."

He abruptly turned away and that was that. She got the

distinct impression that Rider Bilbee was a man of few words, negative opinions, and suffered fools about as well as Kell did.

The container smelled amazing. Walking back to her car was torture, but once she was settled in the front seat, she opened the top and–

Ahhhhh.

Finely chopped lettuce. Eight pieces of falafel, the smell of cumin greeting her like an old friend. A small plastic container held hummus, another some baba ganoush. Lemon slices made it all perfect, and as Rachel filled a pita and began to eat, she actually moaned.

Every part of her felt the vibration shoot through her, the luxury of being alone in a dented rental car, sitting in a parking spot behind a bar, eating takeout turning into the second best moment of her time here in Love You.

Kissing Kell was the best.

Each bite nourished her, the falafel feeding more than her stomach, giving her a different kind of sustenance. Fortitude was in short supply for her. She'd weathered the day, taking the hits as they came, but now she let the food give her a much-needed break.

Who knew macronutrients could be so loving?

The sun was setting as she sat there, slowly savoring every bite. Double-tapping the starter button, she found a radio station, WLUV, that played the love songs the town piped through the streets.

"You're with us tonight at WLUV. Listen. Let go. Love. And now, an oldie but goodie from Percy Sledge. 1966 was the year, but the sentiment is eternal. Here's 'When a Man Loves a Woman.'"

Soothing notes began, the sound soulful and true, the lyrics washing over her as the familiar melody entered her consciousness without words.

Every bone in her body melted, the memory of Kell's hands on her shoulders earlier turning into a montage of all his touches, from first handshakes, to hugs, to sitting shoulder-to-shoulder on his couch in D.C. five years ago, reading through the scrapbook his mom made for him.

Fast forwarding to being broken down on the road, his feet between her legs, then their hands glued together, the embarrassing–and oh, so arousing–ride into town, in his lap, their position so intimate as the emotional gulf between them was narrowed by physical circumstance.

Running out of the trailer after her shower, clad only in a towel, escaping Satan the squirrel. Being held by his protective arms as he helped her avoid turning into a frostbite victim.

Then there was the hot springs, Kell caring enough to throw her in. She reached down and scratched the raised, red area on her ankle, no bigger than a quarter, that was emerging. A quick internet search had told her it could get bigger, but she'd clearly escaped the dreaded third degree burns that could have happened, all because of Kell's caring–if unorthodox–response.

And then there was that kiss. Oh, that glorious, magical kiss.

So close, but yet so far.

Yesterday had been beyond wonderful, being with him, edging into a casual hanging out that felt like they were meant to be together. No one else in the world could make work disappear from the endless obsessive looping in her mind, the worry that she wasn't doing enough fading when she was with him.

Just... *was*. All she needed to do was *be*.

Kell didn't expect her to achieve. To dominate. To crush the competition, or to break records. Not that she did often, but Rachel had chased accomplishment for so long that she knew every detail on its back, every mole, every fold in its rumpled shirt.

Accomplishment was hard to catch. Life felt like an eternal game of monkey in the middle, with her brother, Tim, and her dad, Stan, on either side of her, lobbing it far over her head, unattainable.

Unreachable.

With Kell, she never felt that way.

Ever.

Not back in D.C. Not here.

And that thought was what made her burst into tears, surrounded by empty food containers, the glow of her laptop pushing her to achieve, sitting in a rental car in a bar parking lot because it had better high-speed internet than anywhere else in the middle of Nowhere, Maine.

"Screw it," she said, using the heels of her hands to wipe away her tears, her mouth opening in a surprise yawn. It was only four fifty-six p.m., yet the sky was dark. Tucked away here with no other cars coming in, she knew no one would see her, so she made a decision: one more hour of work. Just enough to keep the hounds at bay.

And then she was going to indulge.

For that next hour, she answered emails with quick responses, not overthinking anything, taking care of a few text messages from Orla and Dani the same way. Once she reached Inbox 72, she stopped worrying about zero, because who was Markstone's to own so much of her life?

"Screw them," she muttered, closing the tab, opening a new one to Netflix.

The screen beckoned like an old friend.

Come on, it said. *Watch allllll you want.*

The Vampire Tracker was a new Nordic noir mystery set in Finland, about a preschool teacher accused of murdering a group of Roma who settled on the edges of a small northern town.

The only thing that would make watching this better would be Kell.

Watching this with Kell would make her decade.

But he wasn't on the table. This would have to do.

As she clicked Play, she eased the seat back and marveled at the internet, fast, smooth, and with zero problems.

And then Rachel Hart did something she hadn't done in five years.

Smiled and enjoyed herself fully.

* * *

Tap tap tap
"Mmmmm."
Tap tap tap
"Unnnh."
"Rachel."

Her eyes felt like two pieces of extremely dry sandpaper.

Blue sandpaper.

And why did her neck hurt so much? She couldn't move it or a stinging sensation, tingling and horrible, radiated down her left arm.

Tap tap tap.
"Rachel!"

Opening her eyes, her mouth wet with drool but dry in other

places, she startled, her laptop sliding to the right, nearly crashing down at her feet. Twinge in her neck be damned, she lunged to rescue it and gasped in pain.

The world was gray and white.

The door handle rattled, and fear spiked through her. Was she being attacked? Where was she? Had she been kidnapped and her blood sucked dry, like in the show she just watched?

Wait...

Show.

Car.

She was in her car, behind Bilbee's Tavern.

And when she turned to look out her window, a very worried face met hers.

Kell.

"Rachel, what are you doing out here?"

"Whaa?"

"Are you okay? Did something happen? Talk to me."

Snow was falling in large flakes, ethereal and lovely. Rachel wanted to stare at them and lose herself for hours.

The tapping began again.

Condensation had formed on the windows, and she realized she was cold. Very cold.

She rolled the window down an inch.

"What are you doing here?" she asked him.

"What are *you* doing here? I *live* here!"

"I know you live in Luview, Kell."

He pointed to a door on the second floor. "No, I mean, I live *here*. My apartment is right there. Why are you in the tenant parking lot?"

Oops.

"Oh!" She reached for the ignition button. "I had no idea!" Turning the car on, she felt discombobulated, ready to flee, nerves pure electricity but firing without aim.

"Don't do that. We've got about three inches on the roads and another six coming."

"Nine inches?" she squeaked.

He smiled, biting his lips. "Something like that."

"I can't drive in that much snow!" she wailed, fully awake now, all of this hitting her at once.

"What were you doing out here?"

"Working."

"Working? In the parking lot of Bilbee's?"

"Yes."

"Then why is your screen on *The Vampire Tracker*?"

Caught.

"Um... long story."

"Come upstairs and warm up. Tell me about it."

"I was avoiding people."

"After that rant, I can imagine. What happened? Your personality changed suddenly." As he bent toward the window, his breath pushed a white cloud into the car.

"I know. I feel like an idiot."

"But why?"

"Work texts. They kept coming, and I'm under a lot of pressure. I needed to leave, and I got frustrated."

"Work can be stressful."

She wasn't about to tell him that she would be fired if this deal didn't go through.

"Plus, everyone here hates me."

"No one hates you."

"You do."

"I don't hate you, Rachel."

"You don't like me."

"Can we just... talk?"

She'd been wishing to hear him say those words for five years.

"If you stay here, you'll become a Rachelsicle."

"My Peloton experience does not indicate that's true."

"I was making a popsicle joke."

"Oh."

"Come upstairs."

She popped the locks and he opened the door. "Bring your bag and your laptop."

"Why?"

"You want them freezing out here?"

"Good point."

Once she collected everything, she climbed out of the car, her muscles screaming from being in the same position for so long. "What time is it?"

"Ten."

"Ten!" she gasped.

"Yeah."

"Wow."

"How long were you out there?"

"Since before five."

"Geez, Rachel. That's..."

"What?"

"Weird."

A set of stairs, steep but safe, met her as he moved ahead before her, stopping at a thick metal door, which he keyed into easily. Inside, there was a hallway with another metal door in one direction and a simple wood door in the other. He walked toward the wood door.

"You live here?"

"I do."

"I thought you lived with your parents."

Harsh laughter met that statement. "My mother would smother me."

"Deanna's great!"

"She is. She would also smother me."

In all her time here in town, she'd never imagined that Kell had his own place, much less what it might look like. The apartment had an enormous living room with furniture neatly arranged around a soapstone wood stove, a galley kitchen cut into the open space, and three doors.

"It's a one bedroom."

He pointed to the first of three doors. "Closet."

The second door. "Bedroom."

The third. "Bathroom."

"Yes, please!"

Kell laughed. "Make yourself at home."

Inside the bathroom, she found a huge clawfoot tub with a plastic curtain hanging from an oval metal rod. The room smelled of his cologne. This gave her the chance to inhale with abandon, but she wondered how smart it would really be to reach the point of hyperventilation and have him find her passed out on his bathroom floor.

Not a great end to an already awful day.

After she finished up, she came out to find him with a big glass of water in his hand.

"Here. Drink."

"How did you know?"

"Just a guess."

Gulping greedily, she finished it all. "Thank you."

"Have a seat."

A green couch with a folded wool blanket on it, with green, red, and yellow stripes, beckoned. She sat. He sat in a brown leather chair across from her.

"Your place, huh?"

"Nothing like yours, I'm sure. You live in a wall of glass, right? With a concierge and a pool and on-site spa."

Damn.

"Good guess."

"Not really a wild guess."

"You think you know me that well?"

"I think you live a certain kind of life, I live a certain kind of life, and there isn't a lot of overlap."

"You seem to know a lot about me. Considering you've thwarted me every step of the way as I try to get this deal done, I assume this is oppositional research?"

"Nope. Gut instinct."

A distinct sadness permeated the air, weird and out of place, yet... not.

Rachel was in a liminal state, hazy from taking an unexpected nap and being awoken by Kell. Maybe her brain wasn't as rational as normal. Maybe she wasn't firing on all cylinders.

For whatever reason, she jumped right in.

"You never heard me out."

From the look on his face, he instantly knew what she meant.

"What was I going to hear? A bunch of excuses?"

"You were going to hear your friend explain how she never would have hurt you the way you assume she did."

Pieces of him deflated, slowly, painfully, beautifully, right before her eyes. First, his shoulders lowered, a sudden release that made it look like he'd been carrying a boulder on them. Next, his hands dropped between his knees.

Then, his mouth, going from a tightness to a looseness that made his whole face change.

Just like that, he looked more like the old Kell than he had in all the days she'd been here.

A small laugh came out of him, a huff through his nose that she couldn't read.

"This is crazymaking."

"Tell me about it."

Blinking hard, he looked torn, different emotions rippling across his face, switching from guarded to open to fierce and back.

"I don't know how to get over this. D.C. changed me."

"I can tell." A lump in her throat, made half of hope, half of fear, formed instantly.

"But you – you're here now. You're different, too."

"Good different or bad different?"

"Different. Just... different."

"I am. And we have a past, like it or not, Kell. A past I've been trying to tell you wasn't what you thought it was."

Some war inside him began to leak out as his eyes flared, the light gray turning dark, the skin around his eyes infused with pain. Struggle embedded itself in his features, his muscles tensing, his breath picking up, chest expanding.

The poor guy looked so conflicted.

Good.

Conflicted was better than dug in. Conflicted meant he was wavering.

Conflicted was a sign of progress.

"There's no way out, Rachel. It's such a double bind. If I believe you now, I have five years of emotional grooves in me that are etched deep. Beliefs I can't just turn off because I want to."

"Do you want to?"

"Of course I do."

"Really?"

"Yes. This," he said, waving his hand between them, "would be so much easier if I could just snap my fingers and..."

"I know. I have all that, too. Maybe we can start over, though."

"Start over? That would involve a lot of forgetting."

"Forgiving, too," she said softly.

"You want me to forgive you for something you say you never did?"

"No, Kell. I want us to forgive ourselves. Forgive our *past* selves. We've been living with a low-grade emotional torture all these years, letting it get in the way of whatever else we can be. I can't convince you of anything about our past. I've tried. All I know is that I didn't do what you think I did, I am your friend, and I want to be part of your life."

All the words coming out of her came from a wise place, her past self watching, wanting Kell desperately, hoping she could break through to him, get him to stand down, open his heart.

He had such a wonderful, kind heart.

"Do you know how much I wanted to hear that, Rachel? How much I've wished for it?"

"Then why didn't you give me a chance in D.C.?"

"Because I was a stupid twenty-three-year-old who was nothing but a wall of disgusted shame after thinking I knew what I was doing. My year in D.C. was starting my new life. New version of me, right? I thought I was going to stand out, make an impact. That I was the king of my life."

"You were."

"After Alissa and John–and I thought, *you*–screwed me over, I couldn't bear to be vulnerable again. You were my friend–more than any of them, in fact. I'd let you inside my inner world more than even Alissa."

"Oh!"

"You know that moment, right before she barged in on us? When we were watching *The Valhalla Stalker*, and you were on the couch in your leggings and Stanford sweatshirt, and I threw a blanket on us?"

"Love You Warm," she whispered.

He tilted his head, one corner of his mouth going up. "You do remember."

"I can't not remember, Kell. I've run through that night a million times in my mind, wondering how I could have made it all turn out differently."

"I was close to kissing you."

"I know."

"But I felt like a jerk about it. I'd just dumped Alissa by text. What kind of guy kisses another woman right after doing that?"

"A guy who's been hurt, and who has a friend who really, really wanted him to kiss her."

They sat in silence, the emotions their conversation was evoking too big to put into words.

"You wanted me to kiss you?"

"More than anything."

"Then I blew it."

"Maybe not. You kissed me the other day."

"Yes. But it wasn't the same kiss I would have given you five years ago."

"Tell me more about that kiss."

"How about I show it to you?"

She smiled. "You must have a really good memory if you can recall an unfinished kiss from five years ago."

Standing, he tapped his head. "I have a remarkable capacity for detail when it comes to wanting to be closer to you." He closed the gap between them as Rachel stood.

"Does this mean you forgive me for whatever you think I did five years ago?"

The kiss was his answer.

And for now, that would do.

That would do just fine.

Five years of yearning and questions, desires and worries were caught in the kiss he gave her, Kell's beard a soft, tickling addition to the already heated kiss.

His arms wrapped around her, fingers pressing between her shoulder blades, each fingertip distinct, as if trigger points in her muscles were begging for the perfect combination to unlock layers of her.

The kiss was everything. *Everything*. All the broken pieces of her that had done nothing wrong felt pulled together, finally whole again, questions swirling and settling, everything chaotic becoming orderly.

All of her was aligning with all of him.

Then he pulled away, pressing his forehead against hers, breathing softly, slowly, as if barely under control.

"Look. This could go in a lot of different directions right now, Rachel. I could ask you to come to bed with me. You could choose to leave, though I don't advise it with the snowstorm. You could sleep on the couch. I could sleep on the couch. We could make love and have a wonderful memory, after which you leave town and we never see each other again. Or we could make love and you could stay here. Lots of branches, like a young tree, growing and trying to understand where it holds space."

"Yes," she gasped, because she didn't know what to say. Every possibility he just laid out was on the table.

The one that hurt to contemplate was the one where she left.

"I don't want to do anything halfway with you. That's not my style. You didn't come here to talk to me and I didn't go out on purpose to find you. Random happenstance led to your being here in my apartment, in my arms." He smiled gently. "And your lips are just too perfect not to kiss. So here's what I propose."

Her heart soared at the word *propose*.

"Sleep."

"What?"

"Sleep. You take the bed. I'll take the couch. Let's give this a night to sink in, try to absorb it, and in the light of day we'll talk."

"Talk."

"Yes."

Oh, how she wanted to do more than talk. So much more. Every word Kell said was sensible. Decent. Deliberative and sensitive.

A part of her wanted to give in to temptation. Be bold. Go wild. Throw herself at him and hope he caught her, kiss him with the crazy abandon of pent-up desire and pure instinct. As her body thrummed with barely contained impulse, she struggled to keep her voice steady.

"That sounds... good," she said, every part of her body screaming *No, that doesn't sound good at all! The opposite!*

Was she reading his expression wrong?

"You agree?"

Each breath took a century to enter her lungs, and another century to exit. Reading him was impossible. Was he being a gentleman? Taking it slow out of care?

Or trying to read her signals? Should she fling herself at him like she wanted, finally touch him and be touched, connect in a deeper way?

Too many layers of fear and confusion cluttered the space between them, so she pulled back. Played it safe.

Left this at *almost*.

"I do. And I'll take the couch. Not you."

Reaching for a familiar blanket that was across the back of his couch, she smiled as she unfolded it.

LOVE YOU WARM, it said.

"You'll need more than that, though." Kell left the room, walking a bit stiffly, and returned with a fluffy bed pillow and a thick down comforter.

He frowned.

"You're a guest. You should have the more comfortable bed."

"I'll be fine." She took the pillow and blanket from him. Awkwardness was setting in, and she wanted space as fast as possible. She yawned, the deep, involuntary act making him laugh and yawn, too.

"All right then. Goodnight, Rachel." He bent down and kissed her on the forehead, disappearing into his bedroom, the door's click as he left making her heart pound.

And other parts of her too.

They had just said no to sex.

Another *almost*.

But this *almost* didn't feel like she had missed out on something.

Quite the opposite.

It felt like she was on the edge of something more.

Chapter Twelve

KELL

The bedroom ceiling was really, really boring.

And no matter how hard he stared at it, it didn't make his body stand down.

What had he just done? *What had he just done?* Rachel had been in his arms, sweet lips on his, wet tongue dancing as they kissed, and he'd pulled away and...

Stopped.

Why the hell did he stop?

Years of feelings had flooded him the moment he'd found her asleep in her car, the glow of the video she was watching on her laptop illuminating her in repose. At first, he'd been annoyed by seeing someone in the parking lot out there, watching something on her laptop.

Once in a great while people got too much alcohol in them and tried to sleep it off in their cars around the bar, but in this kind of cold in February, that was a recipe for disaster.

It was why Bilbee's Tavern had a bunkhouse in the first place. Ten bucks and you got a bed, a jar of Advil, and a place to shower.

He'd gone downstairs in the snow and tapped on the window, but before his knuckle had graced the glass, he'd been shocked to see it was Rachel.

And the screen showed she was watching *The Vampire*

Tracker. Not a supernatural show, but the hottest new Nordic noir series.

Was she that desperate? That lonely? Sitting in a parking lot watching a show, and so tired she'd fallen asleep? Regret had filled him, his behavior less than stellar when she'd arrived. Maybe he'd underestimated her.

There was so much more to Rachel, just as he'd thought back in D.C.

Of course there was. She was human, right? No one was all good or all bad. Everyone had an inner emotional life that was more complicated than the world could see.

Exhibit A – himself.

A small voice, low and insistent, told him Rachel was the one. The one he wanted, the one he cared for, the one who made him feel special, the one who made him feel real and true and smart and *right*.

Being loved the right way was rare. His parents had it, a certainty that became the backdrop for who they were, how they interacted with the world, how they emotionally mapped life itself. With a soulmate, you could relax. Lean on each other. Talk and laugh and plan and dream.

Drawn to her so strongly, he felt that truth like it was the only truth.

She was meant for him.

When he'd tapped on the window, she'd been terrified, and rightly so. At that moment, he'd also seen that the wrong guy coming along could have put her in danger, and that's when he'd decided to invite her up.

Make her sleep in his apartment.

And then she'd been so... direct.

Finally.

Should have been him. The moment he'd laid eyes on her on that old logging road, her body on the ground, sliding down as she desperately clung to the bottom of his truck door, he'd nearly said her name.

Heart racing, mind going back five years, he'd been stunned out of the present. Rachel Hart represented so many questions about who he was.

Not just questions about what had happened five years ago.

Questions about what kind of human being Kell Luview was, at the core.

Now, stretched out in bed, the press of his obvious arousal against the heavy down comforter driving him nuts, Rachel still stirred up too many emotions, too many questions, too many thoughts. Being with her was an endless quest, with infinite roads they could go down to learn something new about themselves and each other.

And he ached for that.

Ached for *her*.

"So why did you turn her down, dumbass?" he muttered into his pillow, giving it a punch for good measure, as if it were the goosedown's fault.

Yet, he knew.

Knew why.

Sleeping with Rachel would feel good. Damn good. More than good, he knew the connection between them would go beyond skin and sighs, deeper than lips and tongues. Hands could do a lot of talking when you were naked with someone, but so could eyes and hearts.

Taking that intimate leap was a point of no return.

And points of no return required more certainty.

If she were just here until February 15, then back to her life in L.A., making love with her would be nothing more than a blip. An enjoyable experience, to be sure, but he didn't just want enjoyable experiences.

He wanted deep love.

Plenty of women in town offered him sex. If he wanted it, he could find it.

Wanting more meant holding back. Holding off.

Holding *out*.

As sleep eluded him, Kell spent the next few hours playing through all of the possible routes his relationship with Rachel could take, until he came to one conclusion:

Leaving D.C. had been a snap decision. He'd broken his life on a line, taking one part back home and leaving the rest.

The clean break was anything but.

And now he had to reconsider everything he thought about Rachel.

Including the possibility that he'd been very, very wrong.

* * *

Sleep came to him in fits and starts until, at 5:18, he finally gave up. An early riser by trade, he was normally up around this time anyhow.

But now he sat up in surprise, realizing something was missing. It definitely wasn't his morning wood, which was stronger than ever.

No. It was Calamine.

The cat was always curled up at his feet on the bed. Where was she?

Sliding his feet into slippers, he pulled on a sweater over his silk undershirt, legs covered in flannel bottoms, and tiptoed to the bathroom. After taking care of business, he walked into his living room to find Rachel deeply asleep, one arm tucked under her pillow, the rest of her burrowed into the down blanket he'd given her, looking cozy.

An angelic look covered her sleeping face. The normal tension was gone, stripping years off her face.

This was the Rachel he remembered.

A rush of desire to kiss her, hold her, sit in silence and just be with her forced him to turn away, until he heard a rustle.

His traitorous cat was curled up on the comforter on top of her feet.

Kell's jaw dropped.

"Et tu, Calamine?"

The cat's eyelids fluttered, but didn't even bother to look at him.

If Cally liked Rachel, that said a lot. In Kell's experience, she was a good judge of character.

Hmmm.

A yawn caught him and he struggled not to make any noise. His body craved oxygen, the flow of blood into tired muscles warming him up.

Coffee.

Time for coffee.

The living room was big, but everything was open, so as he filled the carafe with water and set the filter and grounds in the cone-shaped portion of the coffeemaker, he did so quietly, the satisfying gurgle of the machine sounding like fireworks.

Rachel didn't move.

The first cup of coffee in the morning was a ritual, sitting in front of the wood stove with Cally in his lap, starting the day off slow and nice. Kell opened the stove's glass door, low embers still in there. He put a fresh quarter piece of wood inside and a couple of smaller chunks of untreated wood from a work project.

As he sat in his chair, he made no sound.

Cally made no effort to come to him.

The embers mesmerized him, giving him a brief reprieve from the overwhelm of his mind. After a few minutes, he heard a small gasp, followed by the light sigh of Rachel stretching.

"Mmmm. Morning."

"Good morning."

She smiled at him, running her fingers through her hair as if embarrassed. "Did I snore?"

"Nope."

"This couch is surprisingly comfortable."

"You could have had my bed."

"If you're offering stuff to me, how about a coffee?"

"Help yourself."

She had slept in her clothes, so when she stood up, she shivered but got over it fast, finding a heart-shaped mug on the small rack next to his coffeemaker.

"You have the Love You Coffee mugs?"

"Everyone does at some point. You get them as a present, you win them in a Yankee swap. You know."

"No, I don't. I've never lived somewhere so small that everyone eventually ends up with the same thing from a local shop."

"Huh."

"They're cute, though." After pouring her coffee, she returned to the couch, sitting at the end, closer to Calamine and Kell. Cally didn't move.

Kell's lap felt cold. And for the first time since he'd moved in here, someone other than Calamine could warm it.

She took a sip. "Mmm. This is way better than Kenny's coffee."

"That's because he buys his in bulk from some warehouse club in Conway. It's cheaper than getting Reef's coffee."

"Reef is the manager of Love You Coffee, right?"

"Yep."

"He liked my ground vanilla idea."

"Ground vanilla?"

"It's really good in coffee."

"You ranted about that on the PA system."

"I did."

"Do you have any idea how many people tracked me down to give me their opinion of your rant?"

"Probably even more than the ones who tracked *me* down to chew me out."

Her instant understanding of that truth made him fall a little bit more for her.

"Not all the commentary was negative."

"Really?"

"Some people agree with you."

"*Really?*"

"Sure. Our old director of business development had a few fans, you know. The town isn't one hundred percent of a mind on anything."

"But the majority is anti-growth, anti-change."

"I wouldn't call it anti." He took a big gulp of his coffee, enjoying just chatting with her, here in his own place, like this was normal.

He wanted it to be normal. Normal was feeling fine.

"Then what?"

"People like what they like. They love this town, and they're afraid of losing whatever it is that makes it special. You have to show them how something new will eventually be something they like."

"Persuading people isn't my strong suit."

"You said Tom asked you for a white paper," he teased. "Why not go for it?"

"Because I'm leaving in a few days."

Thud.

There it was.

The temperature between them instantly cooled by twenty degrees.

"Right."

He stood, Calamine opening her eyes and looking at him as if to say, *Oh. You're here, too?*

"I have a big day. And I have to go to the post office to mail some invoices and quotes." He frowned at the messy desk. "There's a huge pile I need to send, but haven't."

"Why not?"

"Just... time. You know."

"It's money, Kell. Invoices mean money."

"I know."

"You did the work?"

"Yep."

"And you just haven't billed?"

"The bills are there. Just have to put them in envelopes, address them, get stamps. You know."

"You don't have anyone to help with that?"

"Remember? I'm the admin."

"And quotes? People ask for estimates and you don't act on it immediately?"

Defensiveness made his shoulders tighten. "Rachel. I've been busy."

"I'm trying to understand this. Not judge you. Pulling for You is growing. You have more work than you know what to do with. But you're behind on estimates and invoicing. What else are you behind on?"

"Website inquiries. Bookkeeping. Yesterday, I had to pay a fine because I was late renewing my business license."

"Please tell me your financial records are in good shape."

"I have a business bank account and a business credit card. I have a CPA who does my books."

"Whew."

"But I'm behind," he admitted.

"You're getting the big things right."

"I am?"

"If you have more clients than you can handle, then yes. The rest can be managed by hiring good help."

"Have to find time to hire and train, and I don't have that time."

"You're in the same bind as every growing business owner."

"Other business owners aren't expected to help their dad climb trees."

Her smile was soft and sweet.

"That is a really good point. But Kell, congratulations."

"For what?"

"For finding something you like, something you're good at, and something that is intrinsically satisfying. Most people never get to the point you're at with Pulling for You. It's admirable."

"You admire me for having a business where I pull a weed out of the ground."

"Don't do that! Don't minimize your accomplishments. It's not that simple. You're performing a service and making a profit. I'm proud of you."

"Proud?"

"I push paper and work six levels down at a mega-corporation where my entire job is helping a business buy other businesses and create uncertainty for the other people, but certainty for the corporation. What you do is so much closer to people. Real people. And you help the environment, too, by using almost no chemicals."

"Never thought of it that way."

"Maybe you should."

The piles of paperwork on the desk judged him. Rachel didn't.

Proud? She was *proud* of him? He thought of pride as something he felt about himself, or something his parents felt about him.

For Rachel to say she was proud of him stirred up so many feelings, new and breathless, a swirl of contemplation.

His phone buzzed. That was his dad.

"Gotta go. Work here, Rachel. The snow will be cleared by noon, but even after that, feel free to work here. You'll have the strongest internet in town, Randy won't hump my apartment, and Cally has decided you're her new best friend." He walked to the tiny coat closet near the door and found the hook where a pine cone keychain hung.

He handed it to her. "Here."

"What's this?"

"Key to the place. I'll be gone all day at work. Pretend this is one of those fancy co-working centers. You even have coffee. There isn't much in the fridge, but feel free to eat or drink anything you want."

"Kell! I can't do this."

"Why not?"

"It's…"

"It makes sense. Kenny's internet has always sucked. Most people who stay in the trailer don't use it as intensively as you do. They're tourists, not teleworkers. Just use my place."

"Thank you." She stood and kissed him on the cheek.

Reflexively, he reached for her, wrapping his arms around her waist and pulling her close. The cheek kiss was fine and all, but he wanted more.

So did she, if her response was any indication. Their hands in each other's hair, mouths searching eagerly, he was ready to call off work and spend the day in bed with her.

"Oh!" Rachel pulled away as Kell's hip buzzed.

"That's Dad. Big project at Sunday River. Trees we need to move." Of all the days to call in sick, this one could jeopardize the project.

Responsibility won out. It always did.

Her fingers wove into his thick beard, a contemplative smile on her face. "I love the beard, but it's so different. You're like two completely opposite men, all in one body."

"Same body. Same Kell."

"Your body changed, too." Sliding her hand along his chest, she let out a low whistle. "You were not this muscular in D.C."

"I was twenty-three, and I wasn't climbing trees. Came home, filled out, and I work with my body for a living."

"It's hot."

Hey, now. She was going there?

"*You're* hot."

Bzzz

They stared at each other, fired up, ablaze, and he groaned, surprised when she stepped out of his arms and blew out a fast, frustrated breath.

Then his phone rang.

"Look. I'll be back by six. Let's have dinner and talk."

"Talk?"

She walked away, heat practically radiating off her, as he answered his phone.

"KELLAN!" his dad boomed. "Where the hell are you?"

"On my way," he said sadly, shrugging into his coat. He ran back to the counter and grabbed a bag of beef jerky, two bananas, and in the fridge he found some cheese sticks.

Breakfast of champions.

"See you in ten, Dad."

He ended the call.

Rachel was pouring herself a second cup of coffee. As Cally rubbed against her ankles, she batted her eyelashes at Kell and said, "Ready for a day dealing with big wood?"

He closed his eyes, pinched the bridge of his nose, and shoved on his hat.

"You're killing me."

Joyful laughter, full of promises and the future, sent him off to work to deal with big wood.

And big questions.

The drive to the Luview Tree Service office was easy, because it was home. Dean and Deanna had a large three-bay garage behind the house, with their work trucks, a cherry picker, multiple stump grinders and chippers of varying sizes, and more chainsaws than Kell could count. The office was upstairs, about the size of Kell's apartment, and held filing cabinets with records going back sixty years.

"Kellan!" Dean boomed as Kell walked in eating a banana, trying to get the food in him long before he had to climb anything. "How are you?"

"Good."

"Anything new?"

"Rachel spent the night."

His dad dropped the stapler in his hand.

"Well, now, that *is* new."

"Mom around?"

"Not yet."

"Good. I don't want her to know."

"We've never pried into your sex life before, son. Not about to start now."

"We didn't have sex."

"*Okaaaaay.*"

"This is more about my love life than my sex life."

"Rachel's a nice young woman. You'd do well to explore this with her."

"She ripped my heart out five years ago, Dad."

"Did she?"

"You know the story!"

"Oh, I know the story. But are you sure? Deanna's said for years she didn't think Rachel was part of it all. Maybe she was right."

"I'm starting to think that way, too," Kell confessed, the words a relief to say.

"Nothing wrong with changing your mind."

"If I'm wrong, it's wrong to change my mind. What if she's just flirting with me to get me to help her close the deal with Lucinda and Boyce?"

"Do you really think that's the case?"

Deep inside, he did a quick inventory.

"No. My gut says this is all real. She was asleep in her car behind Bilbee's last night, and I invited her up."

"She got that drunk? Maybe there are other issues to worry about with her."

"No. Hah," Kell said with a laugh. "She was using the good internet to watch a Nordic noir show."

Dean's guffaw made Kell smile. "Sounds like she's tailor made for you. Any woman who willingly watches that crap is going to be a rare find."

"DAD!"

Dean grabbed a set of keys. "Let's go. Allen's already on his way, and we have Ray and Jared helping."

Long days like this one were the kind that made Kell feel like all his muscles were detached from his body, wrung like someone was squeezing all the blood out of them, then left out in the sun to dry.

For the next eleven hours, all he did was in service of wood.

Rachel wasn't wrong when she made that crack, just... a different kind of wood.

Sunday River was a ski resort and tree removal was an important skill. Anything that might hurt skiers had to be removed, but the trails couldn't be taken out of operation easily, especially in early February during a season without as much snow as usual. Money had to be made when the weather cooperated, though snow-making machines made a huge difference.

By the time he was done, back at the office, and climbing into his truck, it was too late to hit the post office. Too late to think about anything but going home, showering, and seeing Rachel.

All day, he'd either thought about the physics of trees or

chatted with his dad about trees, so the ten minute drive from his childhood home to his own apartment was the first fertile ground for rekindling what had started this morning. Hopefully, Rachel had spent a lovely day getting her affairs in order and resting a bit, but he wouldn't be surprised if she'd changed her mind and just worked, gone back to her trailer, and he would come home to an empty place.

Even Calamine hadn't come along with him today.

Fickle females.

As he opened his front door, though, the sight before him was truly the very last thing he expected.

Not the smell of falafel, which was tantalizing, nor the sight of Rachel, which made his heart leap as she sat on the couch, engrossed in a library book, Cally at her feet.

It was his desk.

What had she done to his desk?

"Uh," was all he could manage, agog at the sight of, well... the surface.

The desk had an actual surface.

What had been giant, leaning towers of papers and binders was now a series of neatly lined up rectangles. A Love You Coffee mug held pens and highlighters that had been scattered everywhere. On the bulletin board above the desk, she had pinned a calendar she must have found buried deep in the mess, as well as some envelopes at an angle. A roll of stamps hung from a long pushpin, in sight and easy to access.

"Welcome home, and thank you so much! I got all my work done, and I'm four chapters into this awesome new Max Seeck book! I got us two falafel platters from downstairs and I can heat them up whenever you want."

The rest of the apartment was how he'd left it, which was already neat. Only the Pulling for You desk had been messy.

And now it wasn't.

"Kell?" Fear flashed in her eyes as she looked at him, then the desk. "Are you upset about that?"

"Uh..."

"Because it was just so disorganized. Easy to fix, though. I walked to the coffee shop when I needed a stretch, so while I was out, I went to the post office and got you some stamps. Then I walked back when I needed another break and sent all those estimates and invoices. That folder of old invoices was easy to sort out, so don't worry. You had over twenty-nine thousand in unpaid invoices! I had no idea pulling poison ivy paid that much."

"I–"

Rachel stood, Cally giving him a look that said he was dead meat for interrupting her fourteenth nap of the day, and walked over to him. He was still in his coat, sweaty and gross from so much work in the cold, the kind where you roast from the inside out but can't take off too many layers or you'll freeze. He processed the moment in a haze of unreality.

Until she kissed him.

It was unexpected and sweet, and he forgot about his aches, ignored the idea that maybe he shouldn't go there with her, pushed aside the uneasy worry that he was being played for a sucker again, and instead–just felt.

Touched. Kissed.

Enjoyed.

When they came up for air, her chocolate-brown eyes were filled with the same conflict he felt, but they were doing this anyway.

Whatever this was.

"Why would you help me?" he blurted out. "You didn't have to do that."

"I know I didn't. I wanted to."

"Wanted to? You have more than enough work to worry about."

"It took me an hour, Kell."

"An hour! No way. There's at least three days' worth of work there."

"I sent off some invoices, that's all. You also had a lot of hand-scribbled notes on a yellow legal pad–looked like more estimates? So I typed them up and found your letterhead. Printed a sample for you to look at. I can print the other twenty or so and get them out in the mail, or you can email them."

"Most of my customers want both."

"Okay, that's easy enough."

"Rachel."

"Mmm?"

"This is amazing. You really didn't have to do that."

"It's easy for me, Kell."

"It's torture for me."

"It's just organizing and mailing."

"I know!" he groaned. "It should be easy for me, too, but it's not. I have two weeks' worth of voicemails from potential customers I'm ignoring. Who knows how many website inquiries in my business email. Doing the job–that's the easy part. The running-the-business part, though..."

"You're serious. You really are overwhelmed by this."

"Wouldn't you be?"

"No. It's second nature. On the other hand, I'd be overwhelmed by climbing trees while carrying a chainsaw, or pulling poison ivy vines that can cause third degree burns."

He was holding her hands, wondering why he was going on about his company when a gorgeous woman had just kissed him, bought him dinner, and organized his life.

"You surprise me," he admitted.

"Good." She squinted, the skin between her eyes tightening a bit. "Make you a deal. You help me get Lucinda and Boyce to sell, and I'll get Pulling for You in great shape."

"No way."

She shrugged. "Fine."

"That's it? *Fine?* You're not going to push?"

"Sure."

"Your mom's right."

"My mother? What about my mother?"

To his chagrin, he realized instantly he'd made a mistake.

"Nothing."

"You can't just drop something like that on me and back out of it. What about my mother? You talked to her?"

"No. But my mom did."

"And my mother said something to your mother about me?"

"Yes."

"That has to do with this conversation?"

He sighed. Might as well come out with it. "She said you have no killer instinct."

Shock made Rachel blink, the look on her face making him instantly sympathetic.

Until she burst out laughing.

"My–my–*my* mother said that? About *me*?"

"I know. Ouch."

"Ouch? No! Not ouch! I'm impressed that my mother noticed anything about me that isn't on my body or face!"

"Your body and face are very nice to notice," he murmured, coming in for a quick kiss. "Look. I'm speechless, Rachel. Let me get out of these clothes and then we can talk."

He heard what he'd just said.

"I meant, let me get out of these clothes and take a shower. Ten hours in the field working on trees has made me a sweaty beast, and I need a hot shower to unwind."

A part of him wanted to invite her in with him. Imagining the soap all over her curves was making him hard.

But her offer made this all the more confusing. Help with his business in exchange for his influence with Boyce and Lucinda? Talk about ouch. The tit for tat felt too much like being used by Alissa.

No, it wasn't the same, because Alissa straight up used him without offering anything in return, but Rachel's proposal left a bad taste in his mouth.

Old doubt crept back in.

He gave her hand a quick squeeze and went straight to the bathroom, turning on the shower and stripping down as the water warmed up. Maybe a cold shower would be better, he mused, turning the knob back.

Tormenting himself with icy spikes was better than the alternative, which was to waffle between wanting to have sex with her on his kitchen counter or kick her out for possibly just using him again.

"Not *again*," he muttered. "She didn't use you the first time. That was Alissa."

Why was he still fighting with himself? Leaving the past in the past shouldn't be so hard. Rachel had urged him to forgive himself, and he had.

Kind of.

The *what if* drove him nuts, though. Some piece of him couldn't let it go. Logic wasn't part of this feeling. Reason certainly had no role.

When something made no sense, it was because it made no sense, his dad used to tell him. The tautology wasn't helpful.

Kell was *stuck*.

Stuck in a loop he couldn't stop.

Rachel was all he thought about. All he wanted these days. Her presence re-ignited him, his mind, body, and soul eager for more. She was quickly becoming the light of his life, an intriguing and alluring presence, opening doors inside him he'd long-ago shut tight.

When he was with her, he wanted more.

So why the inner battle?

"Do it, dude. Just let go," he muttered, as if it would help.

Nope.

Jumping in the shower spray, he did steady deep-breathing exercises and soaped up fast, the two-minute cold shower something he was used to. After listening to one too many podcasts while driving around in rural Maine, he'd stumbled across a neuroscientist who talked a lot about peak performance and cognition. The occasional cold shower made a difference.

Right now, it just got his body to rev a little lower, so more blood could deliver oxygen to his addled brain.

As he climbed out of the shower, he dried off, then looked for his clean clothes.

Ugh.

In his rush to shower, he'd forgotten to grab some. Wrapping a towel around his waist, he walked out to find Rachel on the couch, nose in a book, until his presence made her look up and catch his eye.

Then do a long, slow inventory down his body.

So much for the cold shower changing blood flow patterns.

Without a word, he went into his bedroom, found some clothes, and got dressed, forced to tuck something into his pants a little more carefully than usual.

Running a comb through his long hair, he looked into the mirror.

Rachel was right.

He really was a different man than he'd been in D.C.

Once in a while, he tortured himself by pulling out old pictures from D.C. Clean shaven, hair closely cropped, he had that young executive look he'd worked so hard to achieve. Here at home, the long hair and beard kept him warm.

Or so he told himself.

Mostly, it kept him hidden.

And when he'd come back from D.C., hiding hadn't just been his objective.

It had been how he survived those first few months.

In a sense, the beard and long hair were partially Rachel's fault, then, he told himself, chuckling at the absurdity of it.

Was she more attracted to the old Kell? Should he shave and get a haircut?

"Shut up, dude," he murmured as he rolled his eyes, shoved his feet in slippers, and went back out to find Rachel setting the table, if by "setting" it, you meant putting the recyclable paper containers on the table, adding two glasses of water and two forks, and motioning for him to come over.

"Hungry?"

"Starving."

"Good. Because I got this, and then I went to Love You Bakery and bought their famous heart-shaped brownies."

"Around here, we say you got a loaded brownie at Greta's."

"Greta?"

"The woman who owns Love You Bakery. Locals just call it Greta's."

"I have a lot to learn about this town."

I have a lot to learn about you, he thought, but instead of opening his mouth and making a fool of himself, he took a bite of falafel.

And groaned.

"So good, right? This is two falafel dinners in a row for me and it's as good tonight as it was last night," Rachel said, digging in.

They ate in silence, Kell finishing his in about five minutes, voracious appetite finally tamed by eating his entire container before Rachel had even eaten a quarter of hers.

"Wow. You must go through a ton of calories a day."

"I use my body nonstop for a living. Eating well is a requirement."

A little pink showed in her cheeks at that comment.

"Thank you," he said, leaning back in his chair. "That was amazing and you did not have to buy me dinner."

"Of course I did. You were so kind to me last night, and work was easy today. I have a big video review project and using any other internet has been a slog."

He glanced at his desk.

"Now that you cleared it, use my desk. Keep the key. Work here while I'm gone."

As Rachel finished chewing, swallowing slowly, he watched her take a drink from her glass of water, the way she moved entrancing him. Saying yes to more was getting easier and easier, all the past pain fading.

It was still there. Just a little less intense.

Would it be gone some day? How would life be if he gave over his heart one hundred percent to her?

"Kell," she started, pushing aside her half-eaten container of food. "What are we doing?"

Here it came.

"I think we're figuring that out second by second."

"Then we're experiencing this on the same wavelength, which is good."

"Okay." He wasn't sure how to reply to that.

"But what are we *doing*? I don't feel like there's a plan here. Or even a path. We're flirting, then we're not. The town hates me, then they don't. You thwart my every move, then you kiss me. It's dizzying. Can we talk? Please?"

Her words took him back five years to the sidewalk outside EEC, a rolling duffel bag at his feet, filled with everything from Kell's desk, his mind exploding from the simultaneous blows of being betrayed by Alissa and John, of news that his dad was injured from a fall out of a tree, and from feeling so much physical pain at the idea that Rachel had betrayed him, too.

Back then, she'd said:

"Kell, can we please go somewhere and talk? Please?"

It hadn't been the words. It had been the tone that got him, the impossible contradiction between her betrayal and her seemingly authentic, earnest affect impossible to reconcile.

Now here she was, in his house, feeding him, taking care of his pain point in his business–and she wanted to talk.

This time, it was different.

Or was it?

"Yes. We need to talk," he began.

And then his phone rang.

It was Luke, followed instantly by a call from his dad.

"What the hell?" The last time this had happened, it had been

Mom and Colleen calling at the same time to tell him about Amber.

Amber being hit by a car.

"Luke? What's wrong?"

"No one in the family is hurt," Luke said, reading Kell's mind.

"Thank God. What's going on, then? Dad's calling me on my other line."

"Big car accident. Downed an electric pole, and the pole hit two dead trees that caused a chain reaction. Route 33 is blocked."

"Got it. Let me talk to Dad. Plan for us to be there."

Rachel's face fell.

He clicked over.

"Kell, we have a situation on Route 33–"

"Luke beat you to it, Dad. On my way."

"Good boy."

The call ended and he gave Rachel an apologetic look.

"Sorry. Big accident on Route 33. We have to clear trees blocking it."

"Doesn't the town have a crew for that?"

"We're part of the crew. We contract with them for bigger jobs. This is a multi-tree incident."

"Oh."

They both stood. Kell took her hands, looking down as she looked up, the glow of coming home and having dinner and good conversation at the ready making him want more.

Two big eyes stared up at him from her forearm, Leo the Lemur laughing at them. His thumb grazed the henna tattoo and she joined him in his chuckle, pushing up his shirt sleeve to find his matching lemur face.

Softly, slowly, he kissed her, their embrace deepening as their kiss lingered, until his phone buzzed and he had to go.

"You do so much for the town," she said. "Is this normal?"

"I guess? For this time of year, especially. It's very busy now for us. Always is in February."

"Should I wait for you?"

The question carried so much meaning.

Hesitating, he weighed out the multi-tree blockage, the time he'd be gone, and the inevitable conversation with her that might lead to sex, might lead to nothing, might lead to a path he hadn't even fathomed yet.

His hesitation seemed to give her clarity.

"I'll pack up and see you tomorrow," she said softly. "And I'll take you up on the offer to use your desk. But remember *my* offer?"

"Uh... which one?" He winked.

"Hah! The offer to help you with your business if you help me with Lucinda and Boyce."

His skin went cold.

"Right. That offer. We'll talk later."

It was easier to throw on his coat and boots and get to the accident site than to think about the implications of her words. Was this all just quid pro quo for her?

"Bye," he said, shutting his front door, leaving her and Calamine to do whatever they wanted. Kell's tired body took him to his truck, and soon he was on his way to clean up yet another mess so that other people could be safe.

He was great at cleaning up other people's messes.

His own? Not so much.

Chapter Thirteen

RACHEL

Waking up in the trailer was so much less cozy than being at Kell's.

And she missed Calamine, too. Who knew a cat could provide so much warmth to cold feet?

Yesterday had been one of the best days she'd had in the last five years, hands down, as insane as that sounded when she thought it.

"You're boring, Rachel. Get a life," she said aloud.

That was just it, though: Here in Love You, Maine, she felt like she *was* getting a life.

A life she was starting to like a little too much.

Kell's mixed signals confused her, but she was absolutely sure he was as attracted to her as she was to him, and that they were headed in only one direction when it came to physical intimacy.

Sex was on the table.

And in the bed. And on the couch. Maybe on the kitchen counter...

Coming so close but holding back was turning her into one big hormone, and she didn't have the bandwidth. Her mind was full enough with worrying about being fired, juggling bad internet and a high-stress job, keeping squirrels out of her trailer, and trying to figure out how much time to spend in Kell's apartment without intruding.

That's why she wanted to help him with his business. To pay him back. To give something of value to him.

To help him.

Why had he turned cold last night when she'd brought it up again? The first time she offered to help him if he helped her he didn't really respond, so she'd assumed he hadn't heard. The request seemed friendly. Mutually beneficial.

An even exchange.

Then why did it feel like she'd offended him somehow?

Shaking it off, she made herself a mediocre cup of coffee in the trailer's machine and covered herself with the comforter from the bottom bunk. Then she opened her computer. Three bars appeared on the Wi-Fi.

Hooray! Enough to read and respond to her morning email, which was last night's email from the West Coast. Working three hours ahead had its positives.

Checking her texts first, she found one from Dani, also from last night: *Filed a claim with the rental car agency. The customer service rep had to find a manager to help with the right code for moose attack.*

A simple LOL was all Rachel could muster.

Another text came in, right on top of hers.

Hope you don't mind, the text read from a number she didn't recognize, though it had a Maine area code. *Got your phone number from Kell Luview. If you have more information about that electronic trolley idea, I'd like to hear it. Tom.*

Tom? Wait–the town manager? He was serious?

Rachel turned to her computer and ran a few internet searches, finding what she needed. Writing her ideas into a short document came naturally, the bullet points formatted quickly, with a few links directing Tom to the basics. Gathering details and creating a big picture was intuitive for her, as easy as organizing Kell's business for him.

Why not do something that took her a very short time in a flow state, when it could be miserable or difficult for another person?

What's your email address, Tom? she asked. *I'll send you an executive summary.*

He replied with the address, and twenty seconds later, it was sent.

Done! she replied.

Thank you!

And that was that.

Except nothing felt settled when she didn't know what was bothering Kell, and her growing confusion only added to the sense that it was time to talk to him.

Really talk.

Lay all the cards on the table and make some decisions. The kisses, the affection, the maybe-sorta-kinda-not-sure moments were thrilling, agonizing, sweet, and emotionally fulfilling, but they were also pinging far more serious pieces of herself.

It was time for clarity.

Using her phone to make an actual call, she dialed Kell's number. To her surprise, he answered.

"Hey, Rachel. What's up?"

"Can we talk?"

"We are talking."

"No, Kell. I mean... talk."

"I'm in a work truck with Dad on my way to a job. Can it wait until later?"

"Oh. Sure. No problem."

"You're working at my apartment?"

"Headed over there now. Need anything from the store?"

"You going to Kendrill's?"

"That's the market near Bilbee's, right? I can."

"There's Kendrill's Market, and there are two gas stations with convenience stores attached. When you say 'need anything from the store,' I assume Kendrill's."

"Then Kendrill's it is."

"There's no milk for coffee if you want any. Ran out."

"Anything else? Bread? Butter? Eggs? Bananas?"

"Why did you just name my typical breakfast?"

"Because that's most people's typical breakfast, Kell."

"I don't need a ton of groceries. Milk and bananas work. There's cash in the top left-hand drawer of my desk."

"It's on me. I've been drinking up all your coffee and milk, anyhow."

Silence greeted her. Had she angered him?

Then she realized the call had been dropped. He must have gone out of service. Or...

She had no bars. She'd been on the wireless network, which meant internet was out again.

"Fine," she said, easing herself up out of the small chair, looking around the trailer she'd now spent four nights in, wondering when she'd adjusted to this. Make no mistake–she didn't want to stay in this little chicken coop any longer than needed, but she'd adapted. There were worse places to sleep.

Like her car.

Rachel packed up her bag, put on what felt like five layers of clothing, and walked to her car, the sky a dark gray that made her wonder if snow was coming.

Again.

Kendrill's market was so close to Bilbee's tavern that it would be easiest to park there, then walk. As she reached the first stoplight for town, her phone suddenly buzzed, playing catchup from not having Internet or cell service.

What now?

It would have to wait until she was done at Kendrill's.

Zipping up her ski jacket, she walked with purpose to the market, a blast of hot air hitting her as she entered. To her right, the stack of heart-shaped plastic shopping baskets looked at her expectantly, as if begging her to shop.

The second she reached for one, a woman shouted, "RACHEL HART!" in a tone that said she was about to get chewed out again.

Turning, she was shocked to find Deanna Luview staring at her like she was angry. Normally kind and loving, Deanna seemed so different when she was, well...

Yelling at her.

"Hi, Deanna."

"What on *earth* do you think you're doing?"

"I, uh–you're upset about what I said over the PA address, aren't you?"

"That? No!" Deanna looked Rachel up and down with disapproval. "How could you leave the house looking like that?"

"Like... uh–I showered. Should I be dressed up for something? Did I miss a meeting?"

Deanna leaned in, her lips going close to Rachel's ear. "You are wearing yellow and gray."

"What?"

"You're wearing yellow and gray five days before Valentine's Day, in a town where you have to wear white, red, or pink."

"Oh, come on," Rachel laughed. "You're kidding."

"Are you ready to be pinched?" Unwinding a long red scarf from her neck, Deanna wrapped it around Rachel, carefully covering her shirt collar. "There. *Whew*. Crisis averted."

"You're serious?"

"Of course I am!"

Rachel just blinked at her. Deanna stared back.

"I didn't think there was an actual dress code."

"Kell didn't tell you?"

"Colleen mentioned it. At the ER. I thought she was joking when she said I'd get pinched for wearing anything that wasn't red, white, or pink."

"Absolutely not joking, and pinching is the least of it. During February, the Love Committee is very strict about it."

"Even tourists? Because I'm not a townie."

"Everyone!"

"You run around verbally chiding tourists? That's a fast way to lose business."

"I don't have to. Look around. You're the only person in the store not following the rules. People come here to immerse themselves in the theme, not to buck it."

As Rachel looked around, she saw that Deanna was right. Every single person was wearing some mixture or accent of red, white, or pink.

"You have that beautiful red coat. Wear that from now on." She sniffed at the gray ski jacket.

"Deanna," she said softly, "this is over the top."

"Love You, Maine, *is* over the top, Rachel. That's the point. People don't come here for reality. They come for a fantasy. And we give it to them–dip in the hot springs and find true love. Walk around a quaint village devoted to love. Your eyes see only hearts, the colors of love, and happy, smiling people. We're love on steroids, and that's why we draw so many tourists every year. They come for a *feeling*."

Deanna's words sank in, triggering too many contradictory thoughts. A dress code was stupid, and she knew Deanna wasn't mad at her, but her reaction was definitely unsettling.

"Are you really mad at me for wearing yellow and gray?"

"Mad? No! But," she said, leaning in, "I'm protecting you."

"Protecting me?"

"After the hot mic incident."

"Half the town hates me."

"Exactly. So," she said, adjusting the scarf over Rachel's collar, "give them less ammunition."

"Oh!" Now Rachel understood. "Got it." It wasn't that Deanna ran around accosting random people wearing the "wrong" colors. She was looking out for Rachel.

She *cared*. She had Rachel's back.

"I want you to fit in here, Rachel. A lot of people are still mad at you, but you're turning others around."

"I am?"

"Anne Petrinelli's husband was the town clerk. She's one of the biggest supporters of the town, and she said she thought you shouldn't have done what you did, but you were nicer than she expected. Even Nadine changed her opinion of you, and that takes quite an effort."

"I didn't do anything special. Just talked to them. Told them my ideas."

"Reef is offering ground vanilla for coffees now and all the teenagers are abuzz about it. Makes them feel sophisticated." She smiled.

"I know. He seemed... disgruntled when I asked about it, though."

Deanna chuckled, sliding her arm in Rachel's, steering them toward the produce. "That's Reef. He's skeptical about everything. Nice enough guy, if you get past that."

A bunch of bananas was within reach, so Rachel put them in her basket.

"Deanna? What are some of Kell's favorite foods?"

"Why do you ask?"

"Just curious."

"Bananas. Apples. Pistachios. Prime rib. Black coffee," Deanna ticked off easily. "Potato chips, especially the ridged kind. Lasagna, but not the kind with only vegetables."

"That's good enough. I'm just getting snacks."

"You're shopping for him now?" With a simple question, Deanna conveyed so much.

"Just helping him out."

"Good. Kell helps so many other people. He deserves to have someone do for him in kind."

Rachel reached for some Jonagold apples.

"I would imagine he has plenty of people who want to help him. Especially women."

Rachel knew she wasn't being subtle with that comment, and Deanna gave her an amused side glance.

"When Kellan left for college, all the girls who swooned after him lost their minds. He was popular in high school, but always hard to pin down. You know the type?"

"A player?"

"No–that was my oldest son, Dennis. He went through girl-friends like they were designed to be monthly accessories," she said with a rueful headshake. "Kell was more the nice guy who flirted but never went much beyond that. Always had a date for school dances. Hung out in groups of friends, but never had a serious girlfriend."

"That sounds like all of our generation."

"You've never had a serious relationship?"

A memory of finding her money stolen by Nico flashed through her.

"Not the kind you would call serious, no. I've dated plenty of guys, though."

"Kell seems to last about six months with any woman he dates. He says they dump him," Deanna said bluntly. "Alissa was the first person he ever dumped. But I think it was more compli-cated than that."

"And is he seeing someone now?"

"Other than you? No."

"Me? We're not seeing each other!"

"You're... *something* with each other, though. Don't fool yourself. Dean said he could tell at the parachute rescue that you were into each other."

Cheeks flaming, Rachel suddenly couldn't make eye contact.

"Dean also said you were helpful and nice. You got the Dean seal of approval." Deanna squeezed her arm, then let go to pick up a head of lettuce and put it in her basket. She waved to someone across the aisle.

"I don't know what Kell and I are. He–he doesn't trust me."

Saying it hurt, but not saying it hurt more.

"No, dear. He doesn't. Kell came back from D.C. a changed man. I think he was more hurt by you than by his actual girlfriend."

Rachel closed her eyes and held onto a bin full of oranges. Her legs began tingling and her chest seemed to fold in. Breathing didn't open it up.

"Honey? I didn't mean to hurt your feelings by saying that," Deanna said softly as Rachel slowly opened her eyes.

"I didn't do what he thinks I did, Deanna. I swear."

"Kell needs to feel that truth, Rachel. Having you pop into town was a bigger shock than you–and probably he–realize. I think he needs you, though. More than he'll own up to."

"How do I convince him? Last night, we started to break through. He let me talk a little about what happened."

"Did it help?"

"I think? But then he–" The words all tangled together, making it hard to describe how they'd parted. Some part of him opened to her and then closed, giving her a taste of how it could be for them, together.

Not being able to access that ached.

"Then he closed off, didn't he?"

"Yes."

"Keep trying."

"What?"

"Keep trying," she said emphatically. "Kell is the forgiving type."

An involuntary snort came out of her.

"I know, I know. And he's spent five years nursing this pain, but I think he can heal." Deanna shook her head. "Listen to me, butting in where I really, really shouldn't."

"You're his mom. You care about him."

"He'd kill me if he knew I had this conversation with you."

"You're really easy to talk to, Deanna."

"I'm just a normal mom."

"Kell says that all the time, how your family is 'just normal.' But you're not."

"Oh, come on. You talk to your mother, I'm sure. Or your best friend?"

Rachel's stomach clenched.

Deanna tilted her head, studying her. "You don't, do you?"

"My mom is great, but not the type to talk about my love life. She's been with Dad since she was eighteen and doesn't understand what I want in life."

"And your best friend?"

"I–I don't have one."

"What? We all have a best friend!"

"Not me. My friends from high school are all very L.A. and into acting and Hollywood. College friends are all getting married and having kids. My MBA friends are all trying to be the next Elon Musk or Kendall Kardashian. And the best friend I ever had, well..."

"Was Kell."

Hanging her head, Rachel tried not to cry.

"Yes."

"Oh, honey," Deanna said. "I think that's what broke Kell's heart the most, too. That he lost your friendship."

Rachel almost told her about the kiss.

Almost.

"You two need to talk. *Really* talk. Clear the air. Kell is a stubborn man, but he's not unreasonable. You'll find your way."

"And if we don't?"

"Then you'll know you tried as hard as you could."

Suddenly, Rachel was in Deanna's embrace, the hug sweet and oh, so needed.

"Thank you," she whispered, feeling disoriented. Had she said too much?

"You're welcome. I want all of my children to be happy and fulfilled. Kell needs more happiness in his life. If you're going to spend time with him, I want to know it's because you care about him, and it sounds like you do."

She pulled back and looked Rachel in the eye, her demeanor intense.

"But my Kell was hurt and sad when he came home from D.C., so be careful with his heart."

As Deanna walked away, Rachel's ears were ringing.

For the next ten minutes, she loaded her basket with apples, almond milk, two percent milk, pistachios, ridged potato chips, and some Love You Coffee she found in bags in the coffee section, but she halted in the frozen aisle when four different kinds of lasagna stumped her. Did Kell have a favorite? If he did, she wasn't sure, and decided not to risk it and buy the wrong thing.

The cashier was fast and efficient, friendly but not taking too long. There was a long line now, the place hopping. Rachel took her bags and walked back to Kell's apartment, musing over the conversation.

When she keyed into his apartment, Calamine instantly got up and gave her an ankle rub.

It was nice to be greeted so happily by a being who didn't judge or demand anything of her.

After putting away the groceries, she made coffee and settled in, weeding through emails, processing expense reports, and watching ever more video clips.

That text from earlier was Tom, the town manager: *Please see my email.*

When she checked her personal email, she found a reply from Tom:

This is a great start. Can we meet to talk about how to go forward with this? I know you're only here until February 15, and this isn't your job. Just wondering if you have time for a friendly visit so we can take your idea to the next step.

Rachel bit her upper lip and stared at the screen.

How invested did she want to become? In L.A., she wouldn't have bothered writing that exec sum and sending it to the mayor's office, because she walled herself off and stayed focused on her career. No time for anything else.

Because everything else hurt.

And what if everything else was why she was always *"almost"*? If she were laser-focused on her career, surely she'd achieve success, right? So she weeded out everything else in her life.

Sure, she wrote back instantly, before she could change her mind. *Mornings are best.*

As she hit Send, she realized she was entangling herself here more and more.

Which would make it so much harder if Kell rejected her.

"I can't think that way," she chided herself, taking a few deep breaths to clear her head.

And then she did what came more naturally.

She focused.

Hours passed as she watched and documented, catching new

emails in batches as they came in, until the sound of a key in the door startled her. Kell walked in with a smile, but his eyes were wary.

The wariness made her tip her head down.

Here we go, Rachel. It's time.

"Hey," he said, looking at her as he took off his hat and coat. "You look busy."

"I am. Watching a bunch of videos on an upcoming project. Documentation. It's so fun," she said in a voice that made it clear the opposite was true.

"Desk jobs," was all he said, stretching and yawning, covering his mouth as his big body got bigger, fingertips brushing the high ceiling.

"Long day?"

"My arms are vibrating from chainsaws and stump grinders."

"Fun."

"No."

The blunt way he said it made her laugh.

"There's fresh coffee if you want some."

"Now you're talking."

As he reached for a mug next to the coffee machine, he paused. "Potato chips? Apples? Bananas? You really shopped."

"No big deal."

"You got my favorite chips? How did you know?"

"Do you want the truth, or a lie?"

"Let's not have any more lies," he said, the words stinging.

"I ran into your mother at the market."

"Is that why her scarf is on the chair?"

"Yes. I committed a felony in this town, and she helped me hide the evidence."

"Let me guess: You wore something in public that wasn't red, white, or pink."

"How did you know?"

"Because you seem to only have clothes that aren't red, white, or pink. Other than that red coat. And people here are really serious about the whole color thing."

"She was being sweet. Protecting me."

"Sounds like Mom. And she told you all my favorite foods."

"Yes."

"Wow."

"It was nice. Your mom is great."

"She's just a mom like anyone else's."

"No. She's not. And she said... she said I needed to be careful with your heart."

Kell froze mid-step, holding a red heart mug filled with hot coffee, the steam rising up.

Intense eyes met hers. "We're *really* going to talk now, aren't we?"

"Yes."

The look he gave her was unguarded, all the walls coming down fast.

"Okay. Who goes first?"

"Shall we flip a coin?"

"No. I'll do it. Here goes: I really, really like you but I really, really don't know how to trust you, Rachel."

"And I really, really like you but I really, really don't know how to get you to trust me."

"The great impasse."

"Exactly. I can't prove a negative, Kell. All those years ago, I wanted to, but Alissa set the perfect trap."

"And I'm still caught in it, all these years later."

He took a sip of his coffee, and Rachel's heart melted a bit. She felt for him, and if this weren't about her, too, she'd have the distance to see he was in agony.

Her own agony was too big, though. It cast a shadow over everything.

Even a big guy like Kell.

"Rachel," he sighed. "If I trust you, then I wasted five years. If I don't, I keep hurting myself even more."

"That is a very, very binary way of looking at this. And also, so what?"

"So what? What do you mean, *so what*?"

"If you trust me now, it doesn't mean you wasted anything. It means you're a human being who is learning and growing, and that's how long it took."

His eyes cut over to her. He blinked, then looked away, reaching for her hand at the same time. Fingers threading, he squeezed, his hand callused, so rough, so warm.

And so connected.

"This is a lot."

"It is."

"And I'd rather do this over dinner."

"Dinner?"

"Yeah. Dinner. I just got home, I need a shower, and now my head is spinning and my heart feels like it's being fed through a chipper at the same time it's paragliding."

"Those are very specific descriptions."

He laughed.

"Dinner tonight? With me?" he asked, then stopped himself and groaned, as someone outside beeped the horn once, a rare occurrence in this quiet and polite town. It made her flinch.

Oh, how quickly she'd adapted from living in L.A.

He smacked his forehead. "Damn! I have to withdraw my own invitation. Dad, Colleen, Luke, and I are helping the decorating committee with the outdoor lighting for the festival. That's tonight. They're serving dinner to volunteers buffet style, at the UCC church." He grinned. "That's not the kind of dinner date I want with you."

"I really can't, anyhow. West Coast job means I should work until at least 8:00 Eastern Time," she said, grateful for the break. What she needed most was to go sit and stare into an abyss, gathering her thoughts. A date? He was asking her out on a date?

Or was this just a friend thing? Was "Friend Rachel" the most she'd ever be with him? Sure, it would be a step up from where she'd been, but she didn't want to climb a rung on the Kell ladder.

She wanted to reach the summit.

Besides, there was too much sexual tension between them. Rachel wasn't misreading his signals. Chemistry was elusive, hard to describe, but she knew it when she felt it.

They had it.

Always had.

And now, as she watched him, heat rose inside her, the air charged as his words sank in. Date?

Finally, yes. A date.

He finished his coffee, then nodded. "We can easily eat at 8:00. No problem. Raincheck then. Tomorrow, instead? Dinner. With me. And not at my place. Let me take you on a date."

"A date?"

"A real one."

"Like, get dressed up and go out to dinner date?"

"Yes."

On impulse, she reached up and ran her fingers through his beard, tugging gently. "I love that idea. How fancy, though? I brought business suits, but nothing nicer."

"Around here? That's beyond fancy. A suit is wedding attire."

At his words, her mind flashed there, imagining their wedding.

Are the bridesmaids required to wear pink or red? she wondered briefly.

Then, *Good grief, stop! What am I doing?*

"Rachel?"

"Okay, then..."

"Wear something nice, but low-key. Make sure you wear some red. I'll pick you up at 8:00."

He kissed her cheek and smiled, grabbing his keys, coat, and hat. Then he paused in his doorway, hand on the knob, his smile obvious even under that thick beard.

"I know we still need to talk, but it's almost like we're the old Kell and the old Rachel, right before Alissa barged in on us."

"Not quite," she said, laughing but nervous. "We hadn't kissed then. We have now."

"We have," he said, nodding. Before she realized what was happening, he was back across the room, kissing her until she was on her tiptoes, fiercely holding on. The kiss was hot and heavy, impulsive yet intense–the kind of kiss you give someone when you're in a rush but need to transmit all your feelings through your lips.

His heart beat hard under her hand, his familiar scent transporting her, the way he held her so steady, so right.

Message received.

Kell was definitely interested.

Breathless, she gasped as he pulled away, jogging toward the door, his ass the last thing she saw before the night ate him up.

This was happening.

She was about to go on a date with Kell.

Maybe, just maybe, there was something to this love thing after all.

Chapter Fourteen

KELL

The checks were pouring in, along with email requests for Kell's website to take credit cards. Twenty percent of the quotes had been accepted, and that was only from the batch Rachel mailed out. The new ones she'd typed up had made it easy for him to email or print and send them. Two of those had turned into contracts as well.

All those appointments were in his phone calendar now, spring and early summer very, very full.

As he finished his second cup of coffee, Kell was staring at a fifty percent increase in job scheduling for spring, and that was without really trying.

Just having someone do the admin work for him.

Rachel was right.

Rachel was a *godsend*.

And she claimed it was no skin off her nose.

He'd come home from helping his father, Colleen, Luke, and about ten other volunteers set up all the red, white, and pink lights around town and the common, every tree now sparkling with the favorite colors of Love You, Maine. It was an annual ritual and he enjoyed it, but this year there had been a tug.

A pull.

A regret that he wasn't spending time with Rachel.

His apartment had been as tidy as he'd left it. Nothing was

different after having Rachel there half the day, except for a new batch of neatly organized documents on his desk. At her request, he'd given her access to his business voicemail and email.

And now he had a printed list of every voicemail.

A printed list of every new invoice she'd created from organizing his emails.

A legend for how she labeled emails and put them into folders.

Another legend for the color coding she used on a new spreadsheet to track incoming leads, with a handwritten Post-it note on top mentioning customer relationship management software he might want to consider.

And then more handwritten notes:

You had 223 unanswered emails in your Inbox. I organized them all, but 22 remain for you to reply to. If it was a request for an estimate, it's documented in the Estimates to Be Made folder. If it's asking about invoicing, it's...

As he read her notes, he couldn't stop grinning.

She was amazing.

And he felt bad.

Bad that he'd turned Boyce against her. Bad that he'd made it so hard for her to do her job. Bad that he'd been gruff that first day, when her car had broken down.

But mostly, bad that he knew how to do everything she was doing for him, but couldn't.

It wasn't that Kell didn't know how to use a computer, a printer, envelopes, stamps—that wasn't the issue. This wasn't willful helplessness.

It was all just hard.

Rachel's neat, orderly lists looked like she'd spent days getting this all structured, but she swore it was only two hours. Everyone had a different set of natural abilities that aligned with certain tasks. For Rachel, this was easy.

And now he'd asked her out on a date, a real one. That had been easy for him, the way it had all come together another sign that she was meant to be in his life.

More and more of those pointed him in only one direction.

This had to be explored.

A neat stack of mail sat to the right of his phone, and he

flipped through it, tossing junk mail. A letter addressed to him, from Markstone's, made him halt.

Once he opened it, he laughed and laughed, slowly tearing up the check for "roadside assistance" provided to one employee named Rachel Hart.

Sure, it was a huge corporation, and it wouldn't hurt to take the money. That argument didn't hold water with the gentleman inside, preparing to take her out for a night of fun.

The check reminded him of the gut-punch in the moment he realized who she was on that logging road, his bewilderment at her sudden appearance in his life after all those years, and the confusing mix of feelings her predicament had generated.

Never, ever would he have guessed that after supergluing themselves to each other, he'd be *dating* her.

Tackling the list she'd made of callers, he grabbed his phone and his coffee and plunged in. He made seventeen calls, securing six new jobs on the spot and leaving messages for the rest. The work had an order to it; if he had an office manager, that person could handle it.

Results were what Kell cared about, the actual work in the field. Everything else could be taken care of by someone who liked that kind of work. Wasn't that how life should be? Everyone doing what aligned best with who they were, and making enough money to be happy?

Email was better with Rachel's system, too, her labeling system so clear and meticulous that Kell followed it easily, tagging the new emails that had come in, sorting out junk, and unsubscribing from old emails he didn't need anymore. Until she'd tidied it, he'd been overwhelmed.

Now he could keep it all going.

Maybe she could help him interview a new office person. The transitional cost—not money, but his time—had always been daunting, the secret shame of being so disorganized a factor, too.

Not that Rachel would understand that. She was the consummate businesswoman, an MBA. There was no professional failure in her life. For the first time since coming home, he felt a twinge of underachievement.

She was so much more put together than he was, especially in business.

Running his fingers through his beard at the chin, he remembered how she'd touched it when they'd kissed. Was that a subconscious sign that she didn't like the beard? Didn't like the long hair? They'd met when he was Urban Kell, clean cut and well dressed.

Now he was Rural Kell, all flannel and furry.

What if she preferred Urban Kell?

In an instant, he made a snap decision, grinning as he did it.

And the next phone call he made clinched the deal.

"Hey, Annabeth," he said, calling the owner of what she now called Love You Hair, but used to be called Annabeth's Answers, back when she ran her salon out of her house. "It's Kell Luview. Any chance you can fit me in for a walk-in today?"

"Hey, Kell! You helping that woman Rachel out? Getting her a hair appointment?" Annabeth was Nadine's daughter, and one of about ten hair stylists in town. She was the only one who also was full barber certified.

If anyone was going to help him get rid of his beard and go back to a stylish hair cut, it was her.

"Actually, it's for me."

"WHAT?" Her squeal made him pull the phone away from his ear in self-preservation.

"Yeah."

"You? You're not going back to D.C., are you?"

"No. Not moving. Just want a change."

"It's because of that Rachel, isn't it? I knew it. I've been telling Maisy not to hold her breath."

"About what?" Maisy Bilbee worked the counter at her dad's auto repair shop outside of town. Her dad was Deke, whose name Kell had borrowed when he first ran into Rachel.

Maisy was something like his fourth cousin twice removed. Literally half the women in Luview were off limits for dating because...

Gross. Cousins.

"Oh, come on. As if you didn't know Maisy had the hots for you. Like half the single women around here."

This wasn't much of a surprise, though he was pretty sure most of those women really wanted his recently widowed brother. Poor Luke had to fend them off with a stick after the one-year anniversary of Amber's death. It was as if a switch

JULIA KENT

flipped and they could all start love-bombing him on the day after Thanksgiving.

And he was having none of it.

"That walk-in appointment, Annabeth. Got one free today?"

"For you? Hell, yes! Can I video this and put it on TikTok? Hairy lumberjack goes billionaire stylish?"

"Absolutely not."

"I was joking!"

"I can go on over to Debbie's Do-house just as easily as get my hair cut by you, and she won't want to post it online."

"Debbie!" Annabeth snorted. "Debbie can't cut her way out of a paper bag! And besides," Annabeth sniffed, "she has a basement salon. Mine is on Main Street now."

The vocational high school three towns over offered a cosmetology program, and as a result, half the basements in town had salons in them. True achievement for these women (and a few men) was the ownership of an actual storefront salon. Rents had shot up in recent years, and smaller spaces were hard to come by.

"Give me a time," he insisted.

"How about in an hour?"

"An hour?"

"Sure!"

"Okay, then. Will do. Thanks."

"No problem. It's an honor, really. This was so much fun when we did it five years ago, but you had *waaaaay* less facial hair then. I'll charge my clippers!" With another *squee!* she ended the call, and Kell stared at the phone.

"All right. Hair taken care of. Suit next."

Hidden in the back of his closet, Kell found the zippered plastic bag holding the four suits he owned. One of them was his ancient black funeral and special occasion suit from high school, the other three from his time in D.C. As he sorted through them, he came to the charcoal gray and smiled.

This was always his favorite.

Memory took over and he conjured the image of himself in a mirror, pink shirt, navy and pink tie with white flecks, and patterned socks to match.

"This is crazy, man," he muttered to himself as he stripped down to underwear and began dressing. The shirt was too snug. It wouldn't button, and not because of an overgrown gut.

"Uh oh," he said, reaching for a white shirt that had always fit a bit large. This one was a perfect fit, as if custom made, the loose spots he recalled gone.

If the loose shirt fit just right, then what about his suit? His date was tonight. He didn't have time to get anything tailored, and he certainly wasn't in the right place to go out and buy a new one, unless it was a work jumpsuit at the farm supply store.

He groaned as he thrust one leg into the pants and then the other, his thighs pressing hard against the seams.

He had thickened.

Rachel was right.

Tall and broad, he'd always been effortlessly muscular and his football years were easy, even if he'd grown to dislike the game. By the end of junior year, he'd bailed on it, to the chagrin of Coach Lewiston. The year in D.C. had been nothing but slug work, his body constantly wanting a run, to climb, to lift, but he'd made do with the gym to stay the course of his new life there.

Coming home meant his body was free again. Free to climb trees, to chop wood and stack it, to use chainsaws until his arms vibrated on their own, to help put up fences and hang drywall, shovel walks and fix cars.

And as his mom said, "Men are done growing at twenty-five, and Kell's proof that some men use up every last minute."

The suit didn't fit.

Nature's way of making him pay for being a maximizer of puberty.

Scratching his beard, he left the pants halfway up his thighs and pulled out the jacket, slipping it on and hunching immediately.

It "fit," but he looked like a character on a children's show.

A character to be mocked.

Not quite the look he wanted for his first romantic date with Rachel.

Another try at the pants and he pulled them all the way up, his butt clenched to get the crotch where it belonged. By holding his breath and pulling his ribs up, he managed to button and zip. He was officially "wearing" the suit.

But blood flow to his nether regions was cut off, and he really, really wanted those regions to be fully functional tonight.

Slipping his feet into his dress shoes, he was relieved to find that they still fit. *Whew*. But when he walked, gingerly, to the full-length mirror in the bathroom, he stared at his reflection in horror.

This would not do.

Mind racing, he ran through all the possibilities. The town had no menswear store, other than a rent-a-tux shop for weddings. A thrift shop called Love You Frocks sold only women's clothing. Another, Love You A Second Time, was great for casual wear but never had suits.

Dad? Could he ask to borrow one of Dad's suits?

His father was too big in the middle, and shorter by three inches.

Luke?

Laughing suddenly, Kell tried to imagine his brother in anything but a red police uniform or jeans. The only time Kell ever saw him in a suit was–

Funerals.

Amber's funeral.

At that sober thought, Kell undressed quickly, grateful for oxygen again. Calamine wandered in and decided that his suit jacket was the perfect cat bed.

"Get off there!" he said, shooing her. She jumped down and showed him her butthole.

A glance at the bedside clock showed he had fifty minutes to get to Annabeth's, which was fine since it was a five-minute walk, but how could he solve the clothing issue? The only man he knew who might have ideas was Moore Mottin, Luke's best friend.

Moore's family ran Love You Jewelry, and he was constantly in Boston and New York, doing gem and metal buys. The guy was easily the best dresser in town. Even by D.C. standards, he was on his fashion game.

Kell grabbed the suit and shirt and picked up his phone, deciding a call was best.

"Hey Kell. What's up?"

"I need help."

"Something wrong?"

"I need help with my suit."

"Your suit?"

"I have this old suit I need to wear tonight, and it doesn't fit. I've outgrown it."

"Outgrown?" Moore began laughing. "Second puberty?"

"Ha ha. You're so funny. I bulked up. You know. I bought it in D.C. years ago, and now it doesn't fit. You're the only person I know who wears a suit all the time, so..."

"Got it. You free for lunch? Bring the suit. I'll talk to Anya."

"Anya?"

"You know Anya. Works in the back at Labrecque's."

"The dry cleaner's?"

"Yep."

"Anya? No. Never met her."

Moore grunted. "She's been there for six years."

"Wait. The old woman who doesn't say a word?"

"Yes. And she has a name."

"I don't exactly go into the dry cleaners on a regular basis, Moore. Had to get Rachel's stuff cleaned this week and saw her for the first time. She didn't say anything."

"Anya's quiet. She's Grady's grandma." Grady ran the store with his mother, Judy.

"Grandma! Grady is my mom's age!"

"Yeah, well, we'd better hurry, then, because we don't want Anya dropping dead before your big date. If anyone can take that suit and make it fit, it's her. Meet me there at 11:00."

Mentally calculating out his day, he said, "No problem. That'll be after my haircut and shave."

"Fancy. I get to see your face again after all these years? Has it improved?"

"I see your sense of humor hasn't."

"My sense of humor isn't trying to impress someone I'm dating."

"That explains why you're still single, Moore."

"I'm only single because your sister's off limits."

The joke about Colleen was an old one, Luke and Moore being best friends since they were born, and Colleen having an obvious crush on Moore since they were teenagers. Living in a small town meant knowing everything about everyone because you were practically in each other's DNA.

"Dating your best friend's sister is the fastest way to end a friendship."

"So is making me see your face today, Kell," Moore said with a laugh.

Kell just hung up on him. Easier that way.

All he needed now was a restaurant reservation.

Calling his cousin Blake got him a voicemail system, so he left a message asking for an 8:30 reservation. Blake Bilbee ran The Food Alchemist, a farm-to-table bistro right on the edge of Luview, near the hot springs but on the other side.

The Bilbees didn't like naming things according to a predetermined Love You theme, and they didn't care who knew it. For the most part, if a business didn't have the words Love You in it, it was run by a Bilbee.

The longstanding rebellion was part of the character of living here. Jedidiah Bilbee didn't much mind his sister, Adelaide, marrying Abram Luview, but boy, did he hate what Abram did with marketing Luview, Maine. A strict Calvinist with a healthy dose of Puritan sexual oppression in him, Jedidiah declared it all a manifestation of sin and refused to participate.

Over the generations, his descendants had agreed, but there was a problem when a Bilbee married a Luview. Family cultures had a way of becoming part of your own identity, and while their rivalry was nothing like the infamous Hatfields vs. the McCoys, there was an undertone of cynicism among the Bilbees, mixed with proprietary pride.

We were here first, the Bilbees would often say. *You Luviews just put the place on the map.*

Bilbee's Tavern had been around since 1788, and the Bilbees were here in what was then unincorporated land for more than a hundred years before young Abram Luview migrated from the old country to Maine and bought his land. He was a sharp, hardworking man with a vision, while the Bilbees shunned anything involving worldly matters.

Which was why the town was named Luview, Maine and not Bilbee, Maine.

Kell's phone buzzed. The text made his heart drop.

Got your voicemail, cuz. Sorry. No reservations. We're booked solid through the 15th.

Even for a relative?

Dude

That single word said it all.

Can you do anything for me? I have a date.

Maisy finally snagged you?

What was with people knowing about Maisy and he didn't?

No. Someone else.

Who? The woman you glued yourself to?

Kell sighed.

Yes.

Tell you what. We can give you a takeout meal. Make it fancy and everything. You can pretend you cooked it and serve it at your apartment.

Not a bad idea. The goal was to end up in bed, eventually. Being twenty feet from his bedroom wasn't a bad idea at all.

And yet... Rachel had been spending her days in his place, working. And he wanted this to be romantic. He lived in the most romantic town on Earth, but he couldn't give her better than his apartment over a tavern?

No. Kell needed something special.

If you want the takeout, let me know. We'll package it up nice. Insulated bag. You just unpack and plate it. We have a surf and turf special. Four courses. I'll make sure the wine pairs nicely.

Rachel would care about the right wine. Kell used to be a little more into it, but now he just thought of wine in terms of red, white, or rosé.

Thanks, cuz, he wrote back. *I'll take you up on that. 7:30?*

Done. See you then.

If you need any poison ivy pulled, let me know.

Kell surveyed his situation.

Haircut and shave? Check.

Suit crisis under control? Check.

Dinner covered? Check.

One last problem: the venue.

How could he find a place that was special, romantic, and had a great view of the hot springs, like The Food Alchemist did?

A look at the clock told him it was time to go to Annabeth's. Worst case, there was his apartment, but he didn't want to settle for that.

Grabbing the suit bag, he shrugged into his coat, Calamine at his heels.

"Sorry, girl. I'm walking."

279

Calamine looked at him like he was dirt, turning away and jumping up on the couch, closing her eyes, waiting for Rachel.

Who would, he hoped, work from here all day.

As he walked toward the salon, no fewer than ten people waved and called out hello, something he took for granted.

Wonder if they'd recognize him in an hour.

"Look at you!" Annabeth squealed, coming in for a hug after he hung the suit bag on her coat rack. Annabeth's fingers went straight for his thick dark beard. "This is going to be so awesome! Mind if I film it for social media?"

"What?"

"It's a thing. Like watching pimple popping videos. People love to watch long hair get cut."

"My hair's not that long."

"This beard is going to be a HUGE change. You, clean-shaven again. Your mom know?"

"Why would I need to tell my mom?"

"That's a no. Kell, your mom loves all of you nice and clean shaven. Dean won't even need to give her a present on Valentine's Day. You're doing it for him!"

"Can we, uh, just get on with this, Annabeth? I have a meeting at 11:00."

"Meeting?" She looked over at the coat rack. "What's that about?"

"Nothing important."

When you were the daughter of the biggest gossip in town, you butted into everything because your mother taught you to. Annabeth strode over to what she called the hair chair and tapped the back of it.

"Sit. This is going to be fun."

Fifteen minutes rolled time back five years.

That's all it took.

Fifteen minutes.

First, she cut the beard off in chunks with scissors, leaving it short and scraggly until the end. Then she began cutting his hair, thick waves falling to the floor.

"Short in back? Quarter inch?"

"Whatever's stylish. A little longer in the front, but not too long."

"Like you had it five years ago?"

"Yeah. Been a long time."

"I remember. My salon was still at my house then. We've both made a lot of changes, Kell."

"Sure have."

"But you're not planning to move back to D.C.?"

"Hell, no. I told you, not moving."

She was cutting the front now. As the hair disappeared, he saw the shape of his temples again, the lines of his face emerging like she was a sculptor turning marble into a person.

"All these years, you've looked like the lumberjack you are. Now you don't fit the part."

"Lots of tree guys have short hair and no beard."

"Lots of tree guys aren't you, Kell."

Time to pull out the grunts and go quiet.

By the time she finished shaving him, brushing off the stray hairs, buzzing with the clippers along his neckline and sideburns, he was antsy from sitting so long and starting to second-guess himself.

What if Rachel didn't like it? What if he was going overboard? What if he was over-assuming?

And what the hell did he think was going to happen on February 15, when she had a meeting with Lucinda and Boyce and... finished her project, left Luview, and went back to L.A.?

Emotionally investing himself like this in tonight's date was out of proportion to reality.

And yet he didn't care, because it felt so good.

"Oh. My. Goodness! Kellan Luview, look at you!" Annabeth gushed as she pulled off the cape and turned the chair to face the mirror, revealing him to himself. She held up a mirror behind him so he could see what he was now feeling, his hand riding up the closely cropped back of his head.

His head felt like a helium balloon.

"That hair weighed a lot."

They looked down at the piles of dark brown hair circling his chair.

"Looks like a couple of ferrets," she said.

"You have fun with that."

Laughing, she began to sweep it all up, the dustpan needing to be emptied twice.

He put cash on the counter under the mirror, including a hefty tip.

"Thank you." Rubbing his clean-shaven face, he marveled at how cold his skin felt. "This is—it's been a while."

"You haven't had a haircut in five years, Kell." She peered at him. "Unless you've been cheating on me with some other stylist?"

"Nope. Just trimmed it myself once in a while."

"If every customer were like you, I'd be out of business. You want to schedule an appointment for six weeks from now, to keep it like this?"

"Let me think about it. Not sure I'm sticking to this look."

"You look good either way, Kell." Annabeth was a few years older than him, single, and had her eye on his brother Luke. One of the many women who decided a single dad with a solid job and no thoughts of ever leaving town was a hot prospect, she was part of the gaggle of women trying to win him over.

Which took the heat off Kell.

"Thanks. Off to my next errand. Talk to you later, Annabeth."

"You, too. And I got the video. It's going on TikTok!"

"Do people seriously like to watch some dude getting a haircut?"

"It's the transformation that matters. People love to watch other people change. It gives them hope."

Grabbing the suit bag, he headed for the dry cleaners, her last words echoing in his mind.

When he entered Labrecque's, Moore was already there. The whistle he let out would have turned heads, but only Grady, the owner, was there to hear.

"Look at you, Kell! You remind me of those videos on YouTube of the stray dogs. Their hair's all long and matted, then they shave the poor things and suddenly, there's a dog underneath."

"Shut up."

"Who's the lucky woman? It's Rachel, isn't it?"

"You met her?"

"No, but Colleen did. And everybody's talking about her rant."

Plunking the suit on the counter, Kell looked at Grady and said, "Can I just work with you and ignore him?"

Grady was about his parents' age. Kell knew him, but since he almost never went into the dry cleaner's, it was more surface level. Grady was single, had no children, and lived with his mother, Judy.

"I'll get Grandma," Grady said, disappearing into the back of the shop. Kell gave Moore a look.

"I thought you said Anya is Grady's grandmother."

"Yep. Grady calls her Grandma, but she's actually Judy's grandma. She's, like, ninetysomething."

"That's not possible! Isn't Grady my mom's age?"

"Grady's around forty-five. Judy had him young."

Kell did some math. "Really young. Must have been in high school."

"Guess so. Judy's mom is in a retirement village in Florida. Anya's up here. Refuses to quit working."

"Wow."

"Yeah. Speaks a little English, enough anyway. Stays to herself."

"Where's she from?"

Moore frowned. "Maybe Poland? Not sure."

"And she knows what she's doing?"

"You don't exactly have a lot of choices, dude."

"True."

An old woman who looked like a raisin with gray hair hobbled to the counter and looked up at Kell with a huge grin.

"Suit?" she said, reaching for the bag.

"Yes," he said, suddenly awkward. "It's too small."

"Too small?" She waved her hand at the bag. "No do."

"No do?"

"Not enough fabric."

He unzipped the bag and showed her. As she looked at the seams, her eyes grew wider.

"So much allowance! This custom?"

"It was made for me, yes."

Stroking the seam like it was a lapdog, she marveled at it, grinning even wider.

"Good work. I do. Come back." She motioned to the rear of the store. "Take off pants."

Moore snickered.

Kell followed her, feeling like Paul Bunyan behind the tiny woman. One gust of wind could blow her away.

She pointed to a small partition. "Put on suit."

"It's tight."

"Okay." She stared at him.

He did as ordered, his poor crotch practically holding its breath. As he hobbled out, she burst into braying laughter.

"You fold in half," she finally gasped. She began touching him like he was a mannequin. "Waist too big. Crotch too small. Thighs very tight. You change!"

"I used to work at a desk. Now I work in the trees. I'm a tree guy."

"Dean son."

"Yes!"

"Dean nice. Deanna very nice. Deanna want wedding. You having wedding?"

"I'm just going on a date."

"Deanna need more grandchild."

Oh, boy. Did his mother arrange this conversation?

"If you can't let out the crotch in these pants, Anya, that's not happening."

It was clear from her giggle that her understanding of English was actually very good.

Using a measuring tape, some pins, and a little piece of chalk, she finished examining everything, and finally said, "I fix. How fast you need?"

"Can you do it today?"

She nodded. "Moore said. Seams easy. Your tailor left enough."

"My date is at 8:00."

"I have done by 6:30."

On impulse, he kissed her. As he pulled away, she laughed.

"Deanna get no grandchild from me. Save kiss for date."

Pressing his palm over his heart, he said, "You're the one who got away."

A wave of dismissal combined with a laugh was all he got. He stepped behind the partition, took off the suit carefully, put on his clothes, and handed the jacket and pants to her.

"I fix fast. 6:30."

"You're an angel."

At those words, she reached up to a necklace she wore and began mouthing what sounded like a prayer. Grady motioned to him to head back to the front of the store.

"See you at 6:30. It's a rush job, so..." Grady rang up the fee, which Kell happily paid as Moore double-thumbed a text on his phone.

Once it was done, he turned to Moore and said, "Bilbee's? Lunch?"

"Hell, yeah. I think Luke's there already."

"You invited him?"

"No one's invited, Kell. People just come."

"Right."

As they walked toward Bilbee's, people who knew him called out, loads of "Hey, pretty boy!" and "Kell!" in surprised tones. Not in the mood to deal with it, he waved and walked faster. He hadn't realized how much his beard and long hair had acted as a shield, a wall to hide behind. Even the air felt like an assault, sharp and stinging. He felt exposed, vulnerable.

Raw.

Because he was.

When they passed Tom, the town manager, and he didn't even wave, Kell realized that he was actually unrecognizable to some people.

Hmm. Maybe that was the upside here.

"WHOA!"

As they walked into Bilbee's, which was very full for lunch, Luke had a table with Allen, Kell's assistant, and–

Oh, no.

Dad and, of all people, Maisy.

She was a perfectly nice woman and, if they weren't related, he'd find her hot, but the Luviews were strict about, you know, marrying outside the bloodlines.

Maisy, however, had different standards. As Kell looked over at the table, her jaw dropped.

"*Kell?*" she screeched, jumping up and winding her way through the crowd to reach him. Moore twisted his neck and grinned, pretending to study a menu that he knew by heart. At lunch, Rider had plenty of servers, but all the locals knew it was easier to order at the counter and let the waitresses deliver.

"Hey, Maisy."

"What did you do to your hair? Your face?" she gasped.

"Oh." He rubbed his chin. "Just wanted a change."

"It's HORRIBLE!" she groaned, making Kell smile.

"It is?"

"YES! You look AWFUL!"

Who knew the way to turn Maisy off was a simple shave and a haircut?

"Sorry."

"Ugh! You just... ugh!" Turning on her heel, she went back to the table, snatched her coat, and left abruptly.

His dad looked at him and put his palms out in a questioning gesture. Kell shrugged back.

Women, Dean mouthed.

Kell gave him a thumbs up.

The line moved fast because Rider just wrote down your order, waited until he had five slips, then ran back to the kitchen. For whatever reason, he didn't use the fancy electronic system today.

Soon, Moore and Kell were seated with Luke, Dean, and Allen. The waitress, Doreen Kelly from Luke's grade, rushed over with a pitcher of water.

"Drink?" she asked Kell.

"Water's good."

Moore nodded and she took off, rushing to the kitchen to pick up orders.

"You look weird," Allen said to Kell. The guy wore a thick black beard, extremely short hair he buzzed with a quarter-inch razor every month, and his bushy eyebrows rested over bright green eyes. "Like you're only half-finished."

"Did I ask your opinion?"

Allen shoved a fry in his mouth and chomped. "No. Giving it anyway."

"February 10th, huh?" his dad said loudly, clearly trying to help Kell end the stupid conversation with Allen. "It'll all be quiet again on the 15th," Dad said, looking around with a big, nostalgic grin. "I love seeing it so busy."

"Me, too," Moore said. "We're selling Valentine's Day inventory like diamonds are in short supply. Have to modify my orders for next year. I'm thinking about making a Boston run for more."

"That's amazing. Business is booming," Dean said, reaching for his bottle of root beer.

Luke stared at Kell. "You look weird."

"Says the man in the red cop's uniform."

Moore laughed through his nose.

"You look great!" his dad said. "Your mom will be thrilled."

"I didn't do this for Mom."

"Got a hot date with Rachel?" Luke asked.

Kell nodded.

"He's getting his suit tailored," Moore told them.

"You gain too much weight?" Luke asked. "You filled out when you came home."

"Too much muscle."

Dean patted the small paunch he'd acquired recently. "I remember when I had more muscle."

"What's your goal with Rachel?" Luke asked.

Doreen appeared, saving Kell from answering. She was carrying a tray with five plates, all burgers and fries, some with cheese. Kell's had cheese, bacon, and pickles, and Moore's had...

Peanut butter.

"How can you eat that?" Luke groaned as Doreen set the abomination down.

"It's good. Cheese, peanut butter, mustard. Yum."

"You're a sick man, Moore," Kell said, making gagging noises as he watched Moore take a bite.

"Not sick enough to change my appearance for a date with a woman who's leaving in a few days."

"Says the man who was divorced twice before thirty," Luke poked.

"You're a confirmed bachelor," Dean said to Moore around a mouthful of fries. "This is all about love."

All the men at the table froze at the mention of the L word. They ate and said no more.

Within ten minutes, they were all done, phones buzzing away. Dean stood first, looking at Kell.

"You ready?"

"I'll drive separately." Kell wasn't looking to be grilled or given advice on the way to their job site.

"You want to make sure you make it back for your date? I can do that."

"I'll drive, Dad."

"You really want to get this right, huh? Is everything set up? Where you taking her to dinner?"

"That's the one problem."

"Blake can't get you in at The Food Alchemist?"

Kell shook his head. "Best he could do was offer me takeout surf and turf."

"Sounds perfect," Moore said matter-of-factly. "Have dinner at your place. Easy transition to the post-dessert festivities."

Dean looked uncomfortable. Luke just laughed. Moore was like that.

Direct.

"I want it to be more romantic."

"Being stared down by a Maine Coon cat isn't?"

"Cally actually likes Rachel."

All the men halted.

"She does?" Luke asked, incredulous.

"Son," Dean said, hand on Kell's shoulder, "marry the woman. That cat hates everyone except you."

"I know."

Everyone tossed cash on the check folder, Dean tucking it neatly under the clip. They all walked to the door, Luke peeling off first, then Moore, then Dean and Allen.

Kell walked around the building to his truck. It was nearly 1:00, and he had to work with his dad all afternoon. The job site wasn't far away, no more than twenty minutes, but his father had a tendency to prolong their work. Always up for a good gab, he would go on and on and *on* with the public works crew or whoever else was around.

For the next four hours, he, Allen, and his dad worked a job taking out a beautiful, two-hundred-year-old beech tree that was threatening a house. By the time 5:30 rolled around, Kell announced he was leaving. Dean and Allen were chatting with the house owner, exactly as Kell had thought.

He'd done the right thing.

As he drove back, he looked around, the town more red than usual. The red, white, and pink holiday lights gave the main drag a cheerful sparkle that he looked forward to seeing every year. The Love Committee liked it so much, they decreed that it had to stay up through Sweetest Day, October 15.

Which basically meant the lights came down, Halloween happened, and then the town was covered in Christmas lights.

He parked at his apartment and started to walk to Labrecque's, the cold air clearing his head.

His phone buzzed. The text was from Rachel.

I'm at the trailer now. I'll drive into town and meet you for dinner. Easier that way.

Park behind Bilbee's, he wrote back.

A thumbs up was all he got in return.

And the thrill of anticipation.

As he entered the shop, an older woman waited in line in front of him, her white hair pulled up in a tight bun.

"Hello, Mrs. Armistead." She turned with a start, then smiled at him with a confused look. Always imposing, she was a fixture in town, the kind of person you have to acknowledge, even if you're a little intimidated. Kell wasn't a kid anymore, but seeing Lucinda reminded him of Rachel's real purpose in town.

She wasn't here for a fancy dinner with Kell. Not here to kiss him or sleep with him. The entire reason Rachel had come to Luview was this woman, standing before him with a piercing, curious look aimed at his head.

Confusion was not a natural state for Lucinda Armistead.

"I'm sorry, do I know you?"

"It's Kell Luview."

"Oh, my goodness, Kell! What did you do to your face?"

"I pruned it."

The old woman reached for his chin, grasping it in smoth, dry fingers, tilting his head slightly.

"I can see that! Who knew such a handsome young man was underneath that bear costume!"

Grady shot him an amused look.

"What made you do that?" she persisted, dropping her hand, giving him an expectant look, as if Kell were supposed to answer her question with a very strong reason impervious to debate.

"I wanted a change." He leaned in. "I have a date tonight."

"With Rachel?"

"How did you guess?"

"Oh, please." She looked smug. "It's obvious. I'm an old woman and my husband died a while ago, but I do understand love, my dear."

"I don't know about love. It's our first date."

"You understand love perfectly well. Whether you under-stand *women* remains to be seen."

Kell couldn't argue with that.

"I assume you're taking her somewhere nice?"

"Every place is booked solid. I even tried the cousin angle, but no luck. Blake's giving me takeout. Filet and lobster tail." He had no idea why he was telling her all this, but something about Lucinda made him flap his lips.

His newly hairless lips.

"You need a nice, romantic place to take her."

"I wish. I'm stuck with my apartment."

"You most certainly cannot do that! It's too much pressure for a first date." She looked horrified.

"Pressure?"

"Your bedroom is there! That's not acceptable!"

Kell tried really, really hard not to laugh.

"When is this date?" she asked.

"Eight o'clock tonight."

"You are in luck, young man. I will offer you the chocolate shop. Our conference room has a view of the hot springs–you can set up your dinner there. Bring candles."

The image began to form in his mind. For as strange as the idea sounded, it had a certain appeal.

Especially that view.

"You're serious?"

"I would never have offered if I weren't."

"Mrs. Armistead?" Grady interrupted them. "You're all set. Here are Boyce's shirts." He handed over two hangers in plastic covering.

Lucinda sniffed. "Thank you, Grady. And for goodness sake, call me Lucinda. I've been telling you that since you were eighteen."

"I can't start now!"

"And you, too, Kell. Boyce will text you the code for the front door. The store closes at seven. Come at seven-thirty."

"You're sure–I mean, thank you again, Lucinda."

"Might as well show Rachel the beauty of the place she wants us to sell. Maybe she'll understand the magnitude of this decision a little better."

As she exited the store, Kell watched her in awe. The woman had presence.

And she just saved his butt.

"Come back!" Anya said, poking her head out from behind Grady. "You fit."

Kell eased behind the counter and followed the old woman to the partition, where his suit was hanging on a hook.

"Try on."

He did as told, nervously sliding one leg in, then the other. The cloth fit snugly, but he could breathe.

Blood could flow.

Lifting his arms, he stripped off his sweater, still wearing his sweaty undershirt.

"You work?"

"Cut down trees."

"Good work." She reached for his biceps and squeezed. "Strong man work."

Having Anya's approval made him feel good.

The jacket fit, too, a very close cut but way better than he expected. He carefully put it back in the bag, leaned down, and kissed her cheek again.

"Thank you, Anya."

"You find girl. Marry. Give Deanna grandbaby."

"Did Deanna pay you to say that?"

Anya winked and walked away.

As it headed toward six, he rushed home, the shower a longer affair than normal as he had to wash his hair twice to get the stray cut pieces out of it. As he stood in front of the mirror, styling the short locks, he paid closer attention to his appearance than he had in...

Forever.

Five years, at least.

Tonight was happening. Yes, it was a first date, but he also knew it was probably going to be their first time having sex, too.

Examining his body in the mirror, he wondered if it was enough. What was Rachel's type? Back in D.C., she'd shown them all pictures of her boyfriend, Logan, a guy she dated her final year of undergrad. He'd looked like a jerk.

And when he dumped her a few months into the fellowship,

never bothering to visit her in D.C., always making her fly back to L.A., he'd proven that to be a fact.

"This is silly," he muttered to himself, going into the bedroom, finding the shirt that fit, and getting dressed. Dark gray suit. White shirt.

And, of course, a red tie and red socks.

It took him three tries to get the knot right, but soon, it was like looking in a mirror from five years ago.

Plus twenty pounds of muscle.

"Not bad, Luview. Not bad at all," he told his reflection.

Revved up and in need of something physical to burn off the spike of adrenaline, he decided to walk to The Food Alchemist to pick up their dinner, then head straight to the chocolate store.

But wait–candles? He wanted candles.

A quick text to Blake: *You have any candles I can borrow?*

An immediate reply: *Sheila already thought of it. Packed you up two glass holders, candles, matches, and some rose petals like we sprinkle on our tables. Also a red tablecloth, white napkins, wine glasses, water glasses, and two sets of utensils. Need anything else?*

You're the bomb.

I am, indeed, Blake wrote back with a bomb emoji.

I owe you, Kell replied.

I've got a nasty pine on the north side of my house. I'll collect later.

Kell replied with a thumbs up emoji.

As he approached The Food Alchemist, regret crept in. The windows were all lined with soft white lights, looking magical against the snow. Candles were set on the steps of the front porch, with red accents wrapping around twin pillars. As he stepped inside, the extraordinary aroma made his mouth water, and the warmth and happiness in the place made him wish he could have brought Rachel here.

How was a chocolate shop conference room supposed to compare?

"Kell!" Sheila called out softly as he walked in. She gave a low, approving whistle. "You look amazing."

Sheila wore a red silk dress that hugged her ample curves. Her updo accentuated her long neck, garland earrings glittering in the restaurant's low lighting.

"You are a vision of beauty," he said as she hugged him, her laugh making him grin. He pulled out his wallet to pay, but Sheila waved him off.

"It's a trade. You're helping with tree work."

"This is worth way more than tree work."

"Wait until you see the pine you're removing."

"You sure?"

She batted at his wallet. That was enough of an answer. She looked him over again.

"Not only do you look like some fancy politician, you sound like one. When have you ever uttered the phrase 'vision of beauty' before?"

"When he's looking at my prime rib," Blake interrupted, walking into the entry with a large black insulated bag and a smaller kraft bag with the restaurant's logo on it.

Sheila considered that, then nodded. "Fair enough."

"Here," Blake said to Kell. "The black bag has all the hot food. Salads and crème brulée are in here," he said, holding up the brown paper bag with handles, "along with the utensils, linens, candles, etc. Put the dessert in the fridge."

"This is amazing."

"It's what we do."

"You don't offer four-course takeout, Blake."

Sheila gave Kell a happy look. "You're our test case. We might offer this in the future, because why not? We have to turn people away because we don't have enough tables. But we could handle more food volume, you know? Thanks for forcing us to try something new!"

"I'm about to try something new, too."

Blake and Sheila shared a raised-eyebrow look. His cousin placed a hand carefully on Kell's shoulder and looked him hard in the eye.

"First time tonight? You need some tips?"

Kell shrugged him off as Blake cackled.

"Shut up," Kell growled, reaching for the bag handles and heading for the door. Sheila opened the door for him, giggling. A wall of cold air hit them.

"No coat?" she called out as he left.

"I'm running hot tonight!" he called back, passing a couple walking toward the door, people he didn't know. The woman murmured something to her partner about takeout.

"Good luck!" Sheila called out as Kell turned to the right to head back toward Love You Chocolate.

Everything was working out perfectly. He had his haircut and shave. The suit now fit. Dinner was in his hands, and he was headed to a romantic location.

And then it hit him.

Rachel had no idea where their date was.

"Geeeez," he groaned as he picked up his pace, reaching the store's front door quickly. As he set the bags down, he dug his phone out of his jacket pocket.

Whew. Boyce had texted him the code.

Once he was in the store, the scent of chocolate invaded every pore, the store itself cool but not too cold. Boyce's text told him how to operate the thermostat in the conference room and gave him the code for the walk-in cooler where they stored delicate ingredients, in case he needed a refrigerator.

It ended with:

Please be discreet.

Kell didn't have to wonder what that meant. Of course he wasn't planning to actually have sex with Rachel in the chocolate shop.

That would happen later.

At his apartment, in his nice, big bed.

Although, as he entered the conference room, he did eye the table. It was nice and wide, with an ethereal view of the hot springs, the steam rising up, shimmering in the moon's glow.

But his own bed was still better.

He got to work setting up the table. A quick text to Rachel telling her to meet him here at Love You Chocolate set off a firestorm of replies, with Rachel asking a ton of questions. That was understandable, of course–she wondered if this was about Lucinda and Boyce.

Guiltily, he realized he should have clarified.

Don't worry, he texted her. *It's all good. I promise.*

He got back a heart in reply.

The clock now showed he had twenty minutes, which he put to good use, the red table cloth and the white napkins a beautiful contrast, the small white votive candles giving off a subtle flicker. He sprinkled the rose petals, just like they did at the restaurant. The food was keeping warm in the insulated bag, with plates next to it, ready to go when she got here. Salads and crème brulée were in the cooler. Blake had sent a nice red wine that didn't need to be chilled.

Kell was ready.

In the bathroom, he washed his hands. The reflection in the mirror startled him. Seeing his jawline, so surprisingly clean now, he felt his nerves start to really kick in.

Was this all too much? Was he reading into her signals too far?

And worse–if this worked, and they slept together, then what? Would they just go their separate ways after her February 15 meeting? Would they try for a long-distance relationship? What would be the end game?

He was never, ever leaving his hometown again. Roots he was born with had grown stronger these last five years.

And yet... love was a mighty force, too.

His phone buzzed.

I'm here, the text said.

Kell took one last look in the mirror. He flattened his palms against his suit jacket, smoothing it across his chest and hips, then he marched to the front of the shop and opened the door.

Rachel's eyes nearly popped out of her head.

"*Kell?*" she gasped as he took her arm and guided her inside, the nighttime chill increasingly sharp.

"That's me."

"You–*wow!* You look like you again!"

"I've always looked like me," he said as he pulled her into his arms. No pretenses tonight. He gave her a kiss on the cheek and went for one on the lips, but she giggled and pulled back, staring at him.

"I–I'm sorry! It's just a shock. You look like twenty-three-year-old you!" Eyes combing over him from crown to toe, she said, "No, you look *better* than you did five years ago! That suit is on point."

"It is?"

"The close fit is so in fashion."

All the trouble he'd gone to today to get the suit tailored... he burst out laughing.

"And you have a face again!"

"It may surprise you to learn it's always been there, Rachel."

She used one finger to stroke his jaw. "I know." Then she frowned. "I'm not sure which look I like more."

"Come inside. Let me take your coat." Rachel's dark hair was a cascade of curls, pulled over one shoulder, her eyes catlike and large. Something was different with her makeup, and she smelled like roses and vanilla, a strange blend he liked.

Doing the whole gentleman thing, he helped her out of her red coat and liked what he saw. Her black suit jacket was cut to nip at her waist, red icicle-shaped earrings shining against her dark hair. Lips that were fire-engine red and a red silk scarf were beautiful and perfect for Love You in February.

"Let's talk about you," he said as he slung her coat over the back of a chair behind the cash registers. "You look stunning."

Her thousand-watt smile made all of this worthwhile.

"It smells like heaven in here."

"The chocolate. It's intoxicating."

"I meant you." She moved close, her lips by his ear, and whispered, "You always smell like woodsmoke and lime, and pine. A few other spices, but there's a signature scent that immediately makes me think of you when I smell it."

"When do you smell it?"

"When I'm close to you."

"Then let's give you as much as possible."

The kiss wasn't planned, but it was definitely what he needed. Her mouth was perfect, and having her in his arms was a welcome feeling. His suit was snug, and he knew his mouth would be bright red from her lipstick, but it all felt so real, so perfect.

So inevitable.

Fate had brought her to his town for a reason.

Time to make sure he didn't lose her again.

"So," she said, pulling away, gazing up at him. "Is dinner nothing but chocolate?"

He jokingly smacked his forehead. "Why didn't I think of that? It would have been so much easier."

"Easier?"

"We're having a four-course dinner."

"Where?"

"Here."

"Here? Are Lucinda and Boyce, uh, joining us?" She frowned. "And by the way, why are we here? Is this business?"

Her voice started to go up, tension filling it. A visceral sense of change made Kell pull her close.

"I'm sorry I didn't explain. No business. Lucinda lent me the place for our date."

"She what?"

"It's weird, I know. I asked you out, but I forgot it's February 10. You can't get a reservation anywhere. Even Bilbee's Tavern is full. So I called my cousin Blake, who owns The Food Alchemist, and he set us up with a takeout dinner, but it was either my apartment or find somewhere nicer."

"Your apartment is nice!"

"Not this nice." Guiding her to the conference room, he paused before the door, looking at her.

The expression on her face was not one of anticipatory joy, as he'd hoped.

"What's wrong?"

"This is where I presented my deck to Lucinda and Boyce. Where you walked in front of the window looking like a deranged Neil Armstrong and distracted me in the middle of my pitch. And where they said no. A *no* I had to convert to a *maybe* by thinking fast on my feet."

"Oh."

He held back saying a curse word.

With a flourish, he opened the door. Rachel gasped.

"I didn't think about any of that, Rachel. I'm sorry if the room has bad memories for you, but maybe we could replace those with some good ones?"

Candlelight gave the room a warm, womblike feel, the big window showing the steaming hot springs as the moonlight bounced off the water's dark surface. The linens, the silver, the wine glasses–it all lent the room a romantic quality that made Kell relax.

"This is so sweet," she whispered, turning to him, taller than usual in high heels. As she tipped her head up to kiss him, his fingers sank into her hair, the lush sense of being exactly where he was supposed to be–suit or no suit, beard or no beard, restaurant or no restaurant–fading into nothing as Rachel kissed him and he kissed her back.

Nothing else mattered.

No one else existed.

He was with her and she was here, in his arms, and that was the meaning of his life.

Lost in the kiss, he felt years of anger and hurt float off him, evaporating like the steam on the other side of the window. Why had he clung to it for so long? Why had it attached to him? As it lifted, he thought back to that fateful moment in his old apartment, about to kiss Rachel, and he saw the last five years as a blip in his life.

A painful time, but a blip.

Letting that betrayal define him was the mistake, not the betrayal itself.

"Kell," she whispered against his mouth. "Thank you."

"For what?"

"For this." She motioned to the romantic space he'd created for the two of them, the wide table in this conference room an ample spread for an...

Ample spread.

"We haven't even had dinner. Thank me after."

Her eyes twinkled. "Is that an offer?"

"Rachel," he said, moving his hand from her waist to cup her ass. "That is more than an offer."

He started to kiss her again, but she put her fingers on his lips.

"If we don't eat dinner first, we'll never eat. And I have a meeting here in this very room, to try to pitch the deal again, in five days. Boundaries, Kell–boundaries. I refuse to have sex on this conference table."

"The thought never, ever occurred to me," he lied.

"Liar."

"Caught."

With a deep laugh he adored, she handed him the bottle. "Why don't you uncork this and we can start with a lovely glass of wine?"

"Fine. The table is off the table."

As Kell got busy with Blake's corkscrew, Rachel wandered over to the window, gazing out. The view of her from behind was exquisite, his brief touch a glimpse of what was to come.

He hadn't had sex in a long time. Not for lack of offers.

More like lack of the right offer.

Pop! The cork came out easily and he poured two glasses, offering one to her.

"A toast," he said smoothly, feeling more and more like the sophisticated man he'd hoped to become in D.C., but also grounded here in Maine. "To new beginnings."

"And to old friends."

As their glasses touched, he caught her eye and said, "Friends?"

"I want to be your friend again. I've wanted that for so long."

"Just friends?"

"Friends and more. But Kell, I missed your friendship so much," she confessed, breaking his heart a little because he felt the same way. Losing their connection five years ago had been about lost potential, that *almost* kiss a glimpse of what could be.

Losing her as a friend, though–that had been the true gut punch.

"Mmm," she said, taking a sip. "The sommelier knew what he was doing."

He sipped. "It's good. It's... red."

"Not a wine connoisseur?"

"Not anymore. More of a beer guy."

"Bearded Kell? I believe that. This Kell? You look more like the kind of guy who can tell me all about micro-distilled gin."

"I'm more conversant in poison ivy identification and removal techniques than I am in gin."

"Which is why your company is growing by leaps and bounds."

Pulling a chair out from the table, he turned one, then a second chair, toward the window, urging her to sit. There, they stared out at the mist and sipped their wine, Kell reaching down to unbutton his jacket, enjoying being able to breathe again.

"My company is a source of confusion," he admitted.

"Why?"

"I love it. Really enjoy going out and providing a service that's hard to find and desperately needed."

"I'm surprised people don't just use herbicides."

"They can. But plenty of people don't want that, or the ivy is resistant. No one wants to use an herbicide too close to a vegetable garden, for instance. Or their well. Or they have kids, or pets."

"You get very excited when you talk about this."

"Because it's exciting!"

"Why not do it full time, then? It's clear you could have a bigger business if you wanted. Hire more people."

"It's hard to find the right people. You have to follow a careful protocol. I pay very well, but it's still hard."

"How hard have you tried?"

"Not very," he admitted.

"I think I know why it's so difficult for you."

"You do?"

"It's psychological. Not operational."

"Okay, Dr. Freud-Hart, do tell."

"If Pulling for You becomes too successful, you'll have to choose between working with your dad and running your own business. You don't want to break your dad's heart."

"You think I'm sabotaging my own success?"

"Not sabotaging. Just that all the work that's required to succeed becomes an obstacle for you. You can limp along and do the actual physical work no problem."

"I enjoy that part."

"The administrative side isn't that hard. Not yet. If you grow, the scope will grow, of course."

"Complexity, too," he added.

She had finished her wine and he almost had, the first glass loosening him up. After Rachel set her glass on the table, he took her hand.

She let him. They sat in silence for a few moments.

"I can see why it's hard. I wouldn't have understood even a few days ago."

"Why not?"

"Because it's not just a straightforward business question. You have your dad, your family, and your town and all the people you know here to consider."

"I do."

"You barter a lot, don't you?"

He kissed the back of her hand and stood. "Speaking of bartering, let's start dinner."

"The wine isn't a course?" Rachel began to stand. He pressed her shoulders down gently, kissing the back of her neck.

"Let me serve you."

"Whoa, buddy. Are you sure you're not designed by artificial intelligence to be perfect?"

"Nothing artificial here," he murmured against her ear, giving it a quick, impish bite. She lifted her shoulder into her ear and giggled as he left the room for the small counter next to the cooler, quickly creating the bread basket, oil dip bowl, and bringing two small salads with him.

As he set everything down on the table in front of them, Rachel gave him a wondering look.

"All this? It's like being in a four-star restaurant without the hassle!"

"The bread is homemade by Sheila, my cousin's wife. Salad is from a hydroponics farm in Bethel. They're a farm-to-table restaurant and they work very hard to source as much as possible from nearby growers and producers."

Rachel took a bite of what smelled like sourdough bread. "Mmm." Kell did the same and his mouth exploded with flavor.

Not that he wanted to replace the taste of her, but...

"I didn't realize how hungry I was!" Rachel said as the two of them worked their way through the bread, the oil, and their salads.

"Same. Blake and Sheila make such good food."

"This is as good as anything I'd have in L.A.," she gushed. "The dressing has something I can't quite name, but it's amazing."

"I think it's ground fennel seed?"

"Mmm."

He loved her appreciation of good food. Loved the little sounds she made as they ate together. Loved that she wasn't nervous or tense, but instead fully present, sharing time and space with him.

"Why," she asked, after setting down her fork on an empty salad plate, "can't your mom and dad just hire someone else to do the tree work?"

"Dad wants to hand it off to one of his kids."

"Okay, I can see that. But he can still run the business for at least another decade, right?"

"Sure. Can't climb that long, but yes."

"Then why don't you build your business and help him part-time? Not the other way around. He can hire people to help now, but when he wants to retire, you take on more of a managerial/owner role, instead of being the one in the field?"

"That's not how Dad does things."

"He wouldn't be the one running it then, Kell. Who says you have to do it his way when you take over?"

The thought made him feel every red blood cell in his body. Rachel's words reached down to another layer in him, tying together years of loose thoughts and feelings that had never quite fit together.

"That's a lot to consider," he said, at a loss for words. Needing to do something, he stood slowly, her face turning from curious and engaged to alarmed.

"What's wrong?"

"I'm just going to get the main course."

"Oh! I thought I'd offended you."

Crouching before her, he looked up into her gorgeous face, took her hand, and said, "You didn't offend me. You *enlightened* me. Never, in all the years I've struggled with this issue, have I considered when you just said. That the tree business would be mine. That I could run it my way. Not Dad's. Not Mom's. *Mine*. If they want me to take on the responsibility, I have to have the autonomy, too."

"Exactly!"

As he stood, he kissed her, hard and intensely, cupping her face in his hands, his fingers tickling the backs of her ears, their tongues finding lazy ways to get to know each other, the rush of electricity pumping through him a welcome sensation.

"This is nice," she said as they broke apart.

"It is," he agreed, standing, their fingers trailing against each other as he moved off to the little kitchen and took a deep breath.

This night was going so much better than he ever dreamed.

Blake had sent strict instructions on plating the food, which Kell appreciated, because the last thing he could claim was to be a chef. Once he'd arranged everything, he carried the two plates to the table, Rachel laughing and clapping her hands with glee.

Their wine glasses were refilled, hers already half consumed.

"Is that filet and lobster?"

"Yes," he said, reaching for his own glass, savoring a mouthful. "With root vegetables in a reduced lion's mane mushroom and currant sauce."

"You sound like a server in a fine restaurant."

"Nope. Blake wrote it all out for me."

"Lob-stah!" Rachel said in an over-exaggerated, and extremely pathetic, attempt at a Maine accent.

"Don't do that in town where other people can hear you. *Ever*."

She nearly choked on her water, she was laughing so hard.

"You really like it?" he asked, worried he'd chosen the wrong thing. "No food allergies, or special diets?"

At the word *diet*, she visibly tensed.

"Did I say something wrong?"

"I hate the word diet. My mother is constantly on me about dieting."

"You? You don't need to diet!"

"I know. And no, I have no allergies. I like real food, though. Raised by farmers. I cook a lot at home. Buying fresh at a farmer's market is one of the few things I do for fun."

"I just realized I've never really asked you about your life in L.A."

"Ask away."

"I assume you don't have a boyfriend."

"Uh, no."

"What's that 'uh' for?"

"I don't have a boyfriend."

"No husband?"

"Nope!"

"Wife?"

"I am completely unattached. My last... whatever you call it... involved the guy stealing my wildfire and earthquake emergency fund out of my nightstand."

"Ugh."

"Yeah. Pathetic, right? I can pick them."

"No, I mean, ugh on that guy! I want to find him and–"

"And what? Beat Nico up? Are you suddenly my bodyguard?"

"I'm your friend who hates to see someone take advantage of you."

"There's that word again. Friend."

He touched her hand, threading their fingers.

"You're more than a friend to me, Rachel. If this... continues."

"Why wouldn't it continue?"

Pure magic. She'd just spoken the magic words.

Rachel dropped his hand and surveyed her plate. "No offense, Kell, but I'm a sure thing tonight. This lobster tail, though–the drawn butter is getting cold, and it needs my attention right now more than you do.."

"Gorgeous, smart, *and* practical. How did I find it all in one woman?"

The look she gave him squeezed his heart as much as it made it soar.

"You mean that?"

"I wouldn't say it if I didn't."

Setting her fork and knife down, she rose up from her chair and leaned in for a kiss. It was easy to pull her right into his lap, one arm around her waist, the other sliding along the line of her ribs, the outside of her breast, making her moan into his mouth.

One of Rachel's hands splayed across his back, roaming the expanse of his shoulders, moving down to the small of his back, then stopping at his waist.

"We really need to eat," she said, panting, "before it's ruined."

"Yes. Also–we really can't do anything here. I promised Boyce, and if Lucinda found out, I think she'd spontaneously combust."

"Join the club," Rachel murmured, moving out of his lap and into her seat. She speared the entire lobster tail, dipped it in butter, and took a bite from the end.

So much for impeccable manners.

"Well," she said, setting the fork down. "That was vulgar." Another moan, this one inspired by the lobster, made him want her even more.

"That was hilarious to watch."

"You're really missing out. Eat! Eat!" she said, moving her fingers in a shooing gesture designed to make him dig in.

Spearing his lobster tail with his fork, he held it aloft.

"LOBSTAH!" he called out, plunging it into his butter, and doing a more brutal, Viking-like imitation as he ate it.

Rachel began hyena-wheezing as her laughter got out of

control. Kell barely got his mouthful of tender, perfect shellfish down before he joined her.

"It's so great to be two adults out on a proper date," she gasped as Kell reached for his wine and took a sip, trying to collect himself.

"Eh. Adulting is overrated."

"Says the man who arranged for all this wonderfulness." She used her knife to daintily slice another bite off her lobster tail, resuming basic table manners.

Kell realized he'd almost forgotten something important. Reaching for his phone, he set the radio app to WLUV. He hoped the special message he'd sent in would be broadcast as requested, within the next fifteen minutes.

WLUV took special requests for songs, heartfelt messages they would read on the air, and pretty much anything that helped keep their listeners thinking about love.

"Only four more days until the best day of the year," crooned Selena Martinez, WLUV's only full-time staffer. The rest of the station's DJs and newscasters were part-timers, volunteers, and the occasional high school or college intern. *"Joe Cocker's 'You Can Leave Your Hat On' is up next."*

As the opening notes began, Kell's mind instantly went to wondering what Rachel would be like doing a striptease.

And whether she'd ever relax enough to try it.

Oblivious to his inner musings, Rachel ate happily, Kell joining in until they had cleaned their plates. Rachel's appetite impressed him; for someone from L.A., she wasn't a picky eater. All her talk about her mother being so diet obsessed had made him assume she would be, too.

He was wrong.

The lights flickered briefly, Rachel looking up as Kell looked outside.

"Weird. No storm. Wind is quiet," he said, the lights going back to normal.

"And no earthquake," Rachel said.

"Between the two of us, we have both coasts covered when it comes to natural disasters," he joked.

"All we're missing is tornado experience," she quipped.

"We were talking about your life in L.A.," he said as she picked up the plates.

"Where do these go?" she asked.

"I'll take them."

"I can."

He walked her into the kitchenette, where the insulated bag and the other supplies were.

"Ah. I found your secret."

"Wasn't a secret. Blake set me up." He opened the cooler.

"There's more in there?"

"Dessert."

"If you tell me that's crème brulée, I'll–"

He snaked his arm around her waist and pulled her close, enjoying the instant heat between them.

"You'll what?"

"I'll sleep with you."

"You already said you're a sure thing."

"I'll sleep with you twice in a row."

"That's the part where *I'm* a sure thing, because I already assumed that."

"Really?" Her eyebrows shot up. "Are we negotiating, Mr. Luview? Because that's my area of expertise."

"Is it, now?"

"Yes, indeed."

As he reached into the cooler and pulled out the covered white ceramic dish, the crème brulée revealed as he removed the top, she chortled.

"Wait a minute," he said. "You knew!"

"I figured it was either crème brulée, tiramisu, or a flourless chocolate raspberry torte."

"Why would you assume those three?"

"They're the classic Valentine's Day desserts."

"I'd prefer a hot fudge sundae, myself," he admitted.

"Then I'll eat your crème brulée for you."

"Hah. No. I like it well enough."

When they were seated again, Rachel reached for a spoon and tapped the back of it against the burnt sugar crust on top of one, then took a bite. "Mmmm! Cinnamon!"

The casual way she broke all the rules of a special dinner endeared her to him more. The suit hadn't been necessary. The shave and haircut weren't, either. Even this elaborate dinner in the chocolate shop, over the top but fun, wasn't required.

Rachel was happy to simply hang out with him. Drink good wine, have good conversation, eat good food.

None of this was about anything more than presence. Connection.

Them. *Together*.

They turned their chairs back around and looked out at the hot springs. This section of the water was secluded from the larger, more touristy area on the other side, closer to Blake and Sheila's restaurant. The spring was partly hidden when his great-great-great-grandfather had discovered it, but as the town gained a reputation based on the "love waters," roads and parking spots were carved out closer to it.

Now most of the exposed one-acre spring was visible from Main Street.

"This is so beautiful," Rachel said, taking another bite of her dessert. "What a perfect night."

"It's not over yet."

"Even if it ended right now, you'd have given me a perfect night."

"Perfect, huh? How can I beat perfect?"

"Ooh, I don't know. What's better than perfect?"

You, he thought but didn't say.

"How about we find out." The kiss he planted on her neck felt more perfect, her shiver an invitation to use his tongue to gently lick her earlobe, her sharp inhale of desire making him rue the tight-fitting suit pants.

Back at his apartment, there would be no clothes.

His new mission: to get them there as fast as possible.

And yet, this was lovely. Fun. Intimate and delightful, a truly perfect first date. There was no rush, because they had all the time in the world.

Almost.

Almost all the time in the world.

A six a.m. job with his dad was the only issue here, but it was barely nine o'clock now and they were almost done with dinner.

Plenty of time to take Rachel back to his place and make love for hours. Hopefully, she would spend the night. Having her in his arms as they slept, waking up to her, making love again –

That was it.

That was what came after perfect.

She reached over, fingers stroking the nape of his neck.

"I think it's time we move this party to a more private location."

"Private? How much more private can it get?"

"Let me be more precise: Let's go back to your apartment."

"Technically, it's less private there, because Calamine is hogging a third of the bed."

"She will not be on the bed when we're on it!"

"Of course not," he said, nuzzling her neck.

His phone buzzed, and Kell groaned.

"Sorry. Forgot to turn this off." It was a text from his dad, but he didn't read it, powering the phone off instead. It was probably just something about tomorrow's job.

"Hey, all you lovebirds out there," Selena crooned. *"This is a message from one lover to another. It's a strange one, but love is strange, right? Here goes: Leo the Lemur asks–"*

Rachel's eyes were suddenly huge as she listened, giving Kell a half-terrified, half-amused look.

"–Do you still wear red lace panties? Let's find out."

The song "Lover," by Taylor Swift, came on the radio.

He groaned. "I did not pick this song!" Selena was playing one big prank on him.

"It's, um, an interesting choice," Rachel said diplomatically as they both burst out laughing, Kell's romantic gesture turned into a farce. "And it is about love, after all."

Their eyes met, his own longing reflected back in her gorgeous, dark eyes. A man could lose himself in there and never once miss the world.

The slow beat made Kell stand and offer Rachel his hand, turned so that the henna tattoo Dutch had given him was exposed.

Laughing hard, but blushing furiously, Rachel showed her tattoo as well. Kell pressed his wrist against hers, then took her hand.

"Dance?"

Her eyes seemed to look into the past, guarded but hopeful, and her smile was strangely sad. They shared a breath, her eyes going soft, the worry fading away as he waited for her hand.

Which she offered.

"You just took perfect and made it better, Kell."

"Only because you make it so easy, Rachel."

As they moved to the music, the words flowing and such a good fit for everything he felt in this moment, with this beat, with this step, with this woman in his arms—it all felt, well...

Perfect.

Her face against his shoulder, they danced, moving slowly, the sway simple, the steps unnecessary. Having her in his arms, their dance candlelit, the mist outside making them feel enveloped, all made them feel timeless.

"I've missed you," he confessed, dipping his head down to say it in her ear.

"I missed you, too. I never – "

"*Shh*. I know."

That was as much as he could say, some piece of him letting go, dropping anchor in his soul as he stopped and gave a piece of himself to her, a chamber of his heart.

It was right. It was enough.

For now. He had three more, after all.

"Kell, remember how earlier today, I said we needed to talk?" As the final lines of "Lover" receded, a new song began.

"Perfect," by Ed Sheeran.

They both gasped, laughing a little at the DJ's uncanny choice.

He looked down at her, Rachel's minky brown eyes on his, their gaze centering the world.

"We're talking," he said softly. "And the song is right."

With that, he kissed her, each stroke of their tongues giving him clarity, each little breathless sound from her a direct shot into his soul.

Suddenly, Selena's voice cut into the music:

"Hey all you lovers in Love You, Maine—where every day is Valentine's Day—this is Selena Martinez at WLUV with an unusual announcement."

Kell froze in place. That text from his dad that he ignored.

No.

No, no, *no*.

Please let everyone be okay, he prayed. Amber's shocking death had made him fear surprises like this.

"Kell? Your hands are ice cold. What is it?"

"Dad's text. The one I ignored. What if something's wrong?"

"*A blown transformer has wiped out electricity along a three-building stretch of Main Street in Luview, Maine,*" Selena read. "*Repair crews won't be able to fix for several days, which puts Love You Flowers in a tough situation. The flower shop is the only business in the three buildings that requires large coolers, and they need the community's help. For tourists and visitors in town, no worries! Your orders are safe and will be delivered on time. Last-minute shoppers will still be able to purchase their roses, but here's where townsfolk come in.*"

Kell's shoulders dropped with relief. Turning his phone back on, he saw all the new texts. Rachel reached for her bag, pulled hers out, and turned it on.

Nothing.

"*Come on over to Love You Flowers and help Marty and Stella. They need your cooler space! Your business space, extra room in your fridge–it doesn't matter! They have over three hundred arrangements and twelve hundred roses, with more arriving in shipments tomorrow, so let's do what the town of Love You does best, and – help them out!*"

Rachel looked at Kell, who felt the pull of two directions.

Help Marty and Stella, or take Rachel back to his apartment and make love.

It was Rachel who chose for him.

And captured more of his heart.

"Where is Love You Flowers?" she asked. "It's across the street, right?" Leaning over the table, she blew out the candles with two quick puffs.

"Yes. Down to the right half a block."

"We have to go help!" she insisted, reaching for her coat.

Before she could even get one arm in a sleeve, he had her in his embrace, bent back for a kiss, the rush of love too great to control. When he pulled back and set her upright, she was dazed.

So was he.

"Raincheck, big guy," she said, patting his ass.

And before he knew it, she was ahead of him, out the door, but coming to a skittering halt at the front door.

Boyce stood there, a sheepish look on his face. "Sorry, folks. You hear about the electrical outage?"

"Yes!" they said in unison.

"We're on our way to help," Rachel explained.

"Great!" Boyce had a line of people behind him, all carrying some kind of flower arrangement. "That cooler I told you about, Kell? The one you could use for cold food? We have to make as much room in there as possible. Figure we can handle fifty or so arrangements."

"That's amazing!" Rachel gasped as a line of people, all carrying some kind of flower arrangement like ants in formation, came in after Boyce.

"Fifty down, two hundred fifty to go. Placing the rest plus twelve hundred roses is going to be hard," he called out.

Kell grabbed her hand and they made their way to the street. At Love You Flowers, where Marty and Stella Cambridge were standing in a swirl of helpers, the phone was ringing off the hook.

"Stella!" Kell called out. "How can we help?"

"Grab that extension cord behind the counter! Run it out through the side door," Marty called out. "Our generator's only good for one of the coolers, so we're borrowing portable generators and running lines outside for other things."

Kell saw the store's phone plugged into a power strip, which was now connected to a bright orange heavy duty cable that snaked out of sight. He grabbed his own phone and texted his dad:

Bring every long extension cord we have.

Dean immediately replied: *Already on it.*

The phone was ringing and ringing as Kell went out the side door and found Joe Kendrill in the alley, filling a generator with fuel. Kell handed him the cord he was carrying and ran back inside.

"That!" Stella was pointing to the phone. "Someone get that!"

Rachel lunged for the phone. "Love You Flowers. How can I help you?" She grabbed a pad of paper and a pen and began scribbling madly. "Room for two? In your fridge? Okay, and your name? Address? Can you come get them or does someone need to deliver?" Rachel caught Kell's gaze, and he gave her a thumbs up. Marty walked between them and stared at Rachel like she had a third eye.

"Who is that?" he asked Kell.

"Rachel Hart. My, uh, friend."

311

"The one who blasted the town on that hot mic the other day?"

"The one and only."

"Huh. Well, she's doing a great job handling the phone." The store had two lines and Rachel was switching back and forth, asking the same questions, writing everything down.

Then she pointed to Kell, covering the receiver. "Can you get my laptop out of my bag? I'm going to create a Google Sheet to organize data, so we can track the logistics."

Hearing that, Marty pressed his palms together and bowed to her.

"Thank you. We can handle getting everything into some kind of cooler or fridge situation, but we can't organize it."

"Leave it to me!" Rachel chirped. "This is my superpower."

Kell handed Rachel the laptop from her bag.

"Even if *some* people think ruining their life is my superpower," she said under her breath. The wink she shot Kell's way took some of the burn out of that, but she was right.

He had said it, after all.

"KELLAN!" Stella boomed. "WHAT HAPPENED TO YOUR FACE?"

Everyone in the store turned and stared. Stella was never known for being subtle.

"I got a transplant," he replied.

"Well, ya look like Dean when we were in high school. No question. Deanna definitely didn't step out on your father."

Rachel, quite surprised, kept her composure.

"You're such a shrinking violet, Stella. Hey, son." Dean had come in and was grabbing an arrangement. He looked at Rachel, who was now perched on the cash register stool, laptop open, phone pressed between her ear and shoulder.

And *way* overdressed.

"You two fancied up for this," Marty said as Stella began explaining to Rachel about the fifty arrangements going to Love You Chocolate. Kell heard her say something about Skylar and a clipboard before Marty cleared his throat, expecting an answer.

"We were on a date."

"And you left that to come here?" Marty nudged Kell. "You really do take your commitment to this town seriously."

"She's the one who insisted we help."

"Hmph," Marty said. "After the nasty stuff she said on that gazebo, I'm surprised to hear it."

"Hey, now." Anne Petrinelli was standing behind them in a Patriots ski cap and a bright red parka. "Rachel isn't so bad. And look at you, Kell! Nice to see your face again!"

Love songs from WLUV played outside, the tinny sound barely audible over the din of the growing crowd.

"I have a garage fridge. Can probably fit six," Anne told Marty.

Skylar appeared, wearing a red glitter hat, red and white pajama bottoms, and pink unicorn boots. The clipboard she carried had notes, simple scribbles like:

St. John #57, 58, 99
    Demorgan #60, 61
    Jones #62
    Petrinelli #63-88

"What's that?" he asked, looking at it.

"We're numbering all the arrangements so we know who has what and we can figure out delivery. This is Marty and Stella's biggest single day, and they won't have electricity back in time for Vday."

"So this isn't an overnight thing."

"Definitely not."

"EXCUSE ME!" Rachel stood on the rung of the stool and clapped her hands twice, ignoring incoming calls for a moment. "Stella is organizing the Love You Chocolate cooler items!" She pointed to Skylar. "Skylar can help with walk-in offers. I am manning the phones and tracking data. Everyone else should be foot soldiers, hauling items to the right locations. IF YOU NEED A JOB, ASK MARTY!"

Everyone immediately began moving in a more efficient manner. Kell checked with Stella, grabbed three large baskets, and made his way outside and over to the chocolate store.

The next three hours were a blur, but by midnight, they were more than half done.

And exhausted.

Reef showed up with gallons of coffee from his shop, and Greta and Wolf brought dozens of pastries from Love You Bakery. Joe Kendrill dragged in case after case of water and soda. Blake and Sheila appeared around eleven thirty with big foil trays of chicken and pasta.

"We cooked up what we could and everyone can sample," they said.

Rachel, meanwhile, stayed on her perch, fielding all the calls and typing on her spreadsheet as fast she could. Kell caught glimpses of her in between trips, able to catch her eye every third time or so. She was in the zone, working hard.

At midnight, Kell nearly crashed into another volunteer.

It was his mom.

"Oh! Excuse me, I'm so–" As Deanna looked up, her mouth formed an O of surprise. She punched his chest. "KELLAN LUVIEW WHAT DID YOU DO TO YOUR FACE?"

"I traded it with Prince Harry, Mom. What do you think I did?"

"OH MY GOODNESS! You look so good! Look at you! I haven't seen you in that suit in years!" Then she spotted Rachel at the desk. Her lipstick was long gone, there were dark smudges under her eyes, and she'd used a pencil to secure her long curls in a bun.

"Rachel's helping, too?" she gushed, clapping lightly.

"Hi, Mom. Kinda busy."

"I know! I just got here. Had to help with Harriet. Poor Luke was on a shift and this is crazy."

"We're more than halfway. Ask Marty for a job."

Marty pointed to Kell, then one of the coolers. "Numbers one sixty through one seventy can go to the coffee shop. Reef says there's room where they store their milk."

"Got it." Kell took 160 and 161, both fruit arrangements, while Deanna grabbed two smaller glass vases, and they headed outside.

"So," she said, making him groan.

"Mom. Do not pump me about my date."

"Was it going well? Before the interruption?"

"Yes."

"How well?"

"Mom," he growled.

"Just asking. Things seem to be going well with you two."

"Not talking about it."

"It's sweet of her to help out."

"She isn't just helping out. She's running logistics on everything."

"What do you mean?"

"She's the one who insisted we stop our date and help. Then she walked right in and started answering phones. Using her laptop, she's created a spreadsheet that tracks every arrangement so Marty and Stella know where everything is and they can figure out delivery arrangements."

"That's amazing! What a sweet girl! Smart, too. She's the whole package, Kellan."

Then his mother winked.

But she wasn't wrong.

On the front steps of the shop, Selena was standing with Marty, interviewing him for a live radio segment about the outage and doing more harm than good as helpers squeezed around her.

"We're live here at Love You Flowers on Main Street in downtown Love You, Maine–where every day is Valentine's Day–at the scene of a power outage. Townspeople have come together to help the beleaguered florists, who–"

"Selena Martinez, either start helping or get out of here!" Anne Petrinelli shouted, walking up to her, wagging a finger in her face.

"We're *live!* This is radio journalism, Anne."

"I don't care what you call it, you're in the way! Help or leave!"

Kell and Deanna picked up more arrangements and left quickly, avoiding whatever argument was brewing. Given those two strong-headed, determined women, it would be a doozy.

Halfway across Main Street, he tripped, nearly pitching an arrangement of chocolate-covered strawberries and red roses onto the double yellow line.

"Kell!" his mom called out.

"Got it! It's fine!"

Slow and steady, he reminded himself.

After they delivered that batch, he chose one at a time. Most of the volunteers were his parents' age, and over time, the biggest beasts were safely stored at Love You Chocolate, the smaller ones sent to people's homes.

The final fruit arrangement smelled like candied apples, with an array of apple slices cut into heart shapes, dipped in caramel and various shades of chocolate, with white roses and babies breath sprinkled throughout. As he delivered it to Love You Chocolate, Boyce eyed the cooler warily.

"That has to be the last one, Kell," he said. "We're full."

"No problem. Plenty of room elsewhere. Rachel says we've had a hundred and twelve people offer their fridges."

"Great. Looks like we can save Valentine's Day for Stella and Marty." He clapped Kell on the shoulder. "You and Rachel have been fantastic. Sorry your date got ruined."

Kell shrugged as they walked outside. "Not ruined. Just different."

Boyce walked with him across the street, the two immediately told where to deliver the next arrangements.

As midnight became one a.m., then two, the crew thinned out, down to Kell and Rachel, Dean and Deanna, Annabeth, Wolf from Greta's, Skylar, and Stella and Marty, plus a few folks Kell didn't even know.

Which meant word had *really* gotten out.

At nearly three a.m., Kell and Deanna finally made their way back, arms aching from carrying so many flowers. Rachel was drinking a bottled water, loose strands of hair around her face, her eyes looking tired, but the blue glow of her screen showed she was still entering data.

"Done?" Deanna asked as his dad came over and pulled her in for a hug.

Kell yawned. "Dunno. Ask Marty."

With a flourish of her right hand, Rachel hit a button, then called out, "It's done! All the data entered, including Skylar's notes. All the phone calls. We have a database of where all 323 arrangements are located, and all 1200 roses, plus 800 carnations, 100 bundles of baby's breath, and ten dozen tulips."

Marty walked over to Rachel and kissed her on both cheeks, then one for the crown of her head. "You are a goddess!"

Stella was in tears, her arm around Skylar's waist. "Thank you so, so much. All that inventory. All that money. We would have lost it. We owe everyone so much."

"No, you don't," Dean said, sounding tired but clear. "You and Marty were so helpful to us when... when, well, you know..." he said, his voice cracking on the last word. "Every person in this town helps everyone else. It's our way. Nothing we've done for you is special. It just is."

A tear rolled down Rachel's cheek as Kell watched her from across the store. Moved by her emotion, he walked over to her and wrapped her in a hug. Rachel's whole body melted into him.

"I am so tired, Kell. *So* tired!"

"I know. Come back to my place."

"I want to, but..."

"To sleep," he whispered in her ear. "I just want to curl up with you and sleep."

"Oh, bless you."

As Marty and Stella hugged them goodbye, and his mom and dad did, too, for good measure, Deanna whispered in his ear, "Blake said he cleaned up everything back at the chocolate shop. You two just go to your place. You must be exhausted, and you and Dean have that job at six."

Rachel's tired eyes grew big at that.

"Oh, Kell," she said in a voice that said everything.

"Yeah. Let's go."

He wanted to pick her up and carry her back to his place, her high heels so small and not optimal for three a.m. walking in the bitter cold, but the walk wasn't terribly long. He keyed into his place and led her straight to his bedroom.

Unwrapping the belt of her coat, he eased her out of it, then bent down to slip off her shoes. She groaned with pleasure.

"I'm so sorry," she said, a huge, jaw-stretching yawn following her words. "That was... a lot." She peeled off her suit jacket, revealing a red silk camisole underneath, and she slipped her dangling earrings out of her ears. Finally she stepped out of her suit pants and sat on the bed.

"Here," he said, plucking the pencil out of her messy bun, hair cascading over her shoulders.

She was delicious.

Maybe they could...

Before he could finish his thought, Rachel slumped to the side and curled up in a ball, her head on the pillow.

No. They couldn't.

317

And that was just fine.

As he took off his suit jacket and tie, toed off his shoes, and pulled the top sheet and comforter back so she would be warm, he heard her steady breathing. He wondered if he should have offered her pajamas, but too late now. With a sigh, he quickly changed into a t-shirt and flannel bottoms, crawled in beside her, and spooned.

His last thought before he faded off to sleep was simple, yet elegant:

Rachel Hart really has stolen my heart.

Chapter Fifteen

RACHEL

Waking up in his arms was so much better than she'd ever imagined.

Waking up to being kissed like this was pure bliss.

If there had been any doubt about Kell's attraction to her, it was put to rest by the way the man was touching her, a hazy morning light shining in through his window, the kiss urgent, the way he stroked her hip so loving, slow and sure.

His phone buzzed.

Kell groaned so loudly, she felt the vibration deep in her bones. It made her feel even more connected to him.

"I have to go."

She touched his thigh. "Are you sure?"

"No," he said, rolling on top of her, giving her a deep kiss as her body nearly exploded on the spot. "But yes. Big project at Nordicbeth. Dad's on his way to pick me up. This is the early morning job." One eye open, he glared at his clock. "I can't believe I got less than three hours sleep."

"You shouldn't be climbing trees in your condition!"

"Fortunately, it's just meetings. Takes an hour and a half to get there because of the stupid bridge closure."

She eyed his bedside clock. "How long do we have?"

"Ten minutes. I can't even shower. I don't want to rush with you, Rachel. I want all the time in the world."

"It generally doesn't take *that* long," she said.

He kissed her again.

Ten minutes, huh? she thought to herself, debating.

Pulling back, he gave her a wicked grin. "You've never slept with *me*."

"Way to set expectations, Kell."

He laughed, but peeled himself out of her arms, making her pout. "Nordicbeth meetings, then I'm meeting Luke for a family thing."

"Oh."

"I feel like an ass. Dad will seriously be here in ten minutes. I'm normally not so busy, but it's–"

"–Valentine's Day," she finished with him. "I know."

"You sound disappointed."

"I am."

"I hate disappointing you!"

A sultry smile on her lips, she patted the spot on the bed he'd just vacated. "Then come here."

Calamine took that as her invitation, jumping up and capitalizing on Kell's warm spot.

"Not you!" Rachel groaned to the cat.

"Stay here. I want you here when I come home."

"I have to go back to the trailer to change. And I should probably, you know, work?"

"I know all about work," he sighed, snuggling up for a kiss. "This is our busiest time. If you'd come in early January, I wouldn't be leaving so much."

The assumption that this was meant to be made her smile.

"If I'd known this would be the outcome of saying yes to this project, trust me, Kell–I would have signed on much sooner."

His phone buzzed again.

"Damn. Dad's outside, waiting." He pulled a sweater over his shirt and leaned down for a kiss. "Promise me you'll be here?"

"Promise."

"Yesterday was wonderful," he said. "I wish we had been able to–"

Pressing her fingers over his lips, she looked at him, so earnest, so full of potential. "We did the right thing yesterday, even if it meant we didn't do what we wanted last night. There's plenty of time for sex. The community needed help last night, and we did what we needed to do."

"Rachel! You sound like a townie."

"Maybe this place is rubbing off on me."

"Tonight," he said with a kiss, "I'll be rubbing *on* you."

With that corny joke, he ran out the door, Dean tapping the horn once before the door shut and Rachel slumped back into bed.

"You," she said to Cally, "are a very poor substitute for Kell."

The cat made it clear the feeling was mutual.

Exhaustion let her fall back to sleep, the cat's warmth on her feet making it easier. When she finally woke up, with a start, it was eleven a.m.

"Better," she murmured, stretching, with an ache between her shoulder blades and a charley horse starting in one calf. As the first hint of pain made its way to her brain, she forced herself to stand and stretch more seriously, Calamine jumping off the bed in surprise, then glaring at her.

"Might as well work," Rachel grumbled. She picked up Kell's t-shirt from the bed and pulled it on. Then she shuffled into the living room, her bare feet cold on the floor.

A cup of coffee did wonders for her spirits, and when she checked in on work, she found a surprising twist in the Love You Chocolate deal.

An email from Orla, with attachments that were maps and took forever to download even with great internet, gave her pause. Rachel had to read it through twice before it all sank in.

Markstone's was now looking seriously at an enormous parcel of land that was about to go on the market, outside of town, toward the Nordicbeth resort.

The perfect place for a theme park that would be bigger and better than their rivals.

Feasibility studies were in their infancy, as the land wasn't even officially being sold.

Hundreds of acres of rich forest land would be razed, the timber sold, and the land reinvented as a love-themed amusement park with a chocolate and candy focus. Throngs of high-rise hotels would be built around the perimeter, also serving the ski resorts in winter. Doug was the one who had found the land, but

Orla didn't elaborate on how he found it. It sounded very cloak-and-daggar.

The message was clear: Get Love You Chocolate to sell on February 15, or Orla would be out there to do it for her, and Rachel would be fired. If she closed the deal, she would stay in Luview a little longer to finalize details.

Life back in L.A. was simple. So simple, she didn't have to worry about a thing while she was away. No plants. No pets. No boyfriend. No... nothing.

There was literally nothing keeping her in L.A., other than her parents, and she spent so little time with them that she'd probably see them more if she lived elsewhere. Then her visits would be an event, and they'd actually clear their schedules.

That was true for major holidays, at least.

Indulging herself, she imagined life here in Luview. What kind of job would she have? Markstone's might let her telecommute, or there was a division in Boston. She certainly wouldn't live in the trailer–there must be nicer apartments to rent. Cost of living would be super cheap.

Getting a mani-pedi might be hard, and her mother had warned her about basement salons, but that sounded like Portia's snobbery.

"I'm being silly," she muttered as she drank half her coffee in large gulps, but the idea pulled at her. Kell hadn't given her any reason to think long term. Staying here without being in a relationship with him would be foolish. As time passed, though, the town had charmed her.

Maybe it was time for a huge change in her life.

If not here, another small town? Someplace away from the enormity of L.A., where people greeted each other by name, where you could serve on committees that made a real difference, and where people came together to support others during crises.

In L.A., kids like Dutch and her sister were less likely to be supported by a community.

In L.A., Rachel never felt welcomed. On the other hand, no one considered her a pariah there, but at least in Luview, she was seen.

Known.

Acknowledged.

In Luview, she wasn't *almost* anything, other than almost done.

The events of the past few days had been so constant, so demanding of all her energy, that she hadn't been caught up in the fear that lurked deep inside. What if Lucinda and Boyce didn't sell?

Sadly, she knew what would happen. The last two failed projects she'd worked on had involved a lot of shame, some angry almost yelling from Doug (the worst kind of *almost*), and an identity crisis that had led her here.

To take the job Orla had mentioned a few months ago.

While she'd been ninety-nine percent certain Kell had gotten some job in a big city, she'd known when she'd made the trip here that there was at least a chance the guy lived in his hometown.

Seeing him immediately, when she was stuck on the side of the road with a broken-down car, was a scenario that had never occurred to her—much less being glued together.

And then there was that ride into town.

If she'd been harboring any small, hopeful fantasies inside her when she'd come here, they hadn't exactly come to fruition, but *parts* of them had been fulfilled.

It was as if a very impish genie had granted her a wish, just... with a few twists.

The email from Orla said that she should go to the tract of land, an old summer camp, and take a look around. Rachel's idea of summer camp meant drama classes, or gymnastics and cheer, hours spent indoors practicing, with a lunch break and a swim class.

Big woodsy camps with cabins were something she only knew from television and the movies.

A quick look outside showed her it was not snowing and miraculously, had not snowed last night. A trip to the old camp was in order.

She took a fast shower and was forced to put last night's suit on again. Earlier, she'd been sorry she didn't have anything dressy to wear for their date, but now she was thankful she hadn't worn a cocktail dress.

Rachel pitched the rest of her coffee when she realized she could get some in town, and grabbed her keys and coat. As she pulled her gloves out of her bag, she remembered that her boots were stowed in the car, so she retrieved her heels from the bedroom.

All the preparation for just going somewhere felt weird. You needed a coat. A hat. Gloves. To think ahead in case you got stranded. Kell had warned her to carry extra protein bars, and had given her a Mylar blanket, folded neatly in a pouch, like a kids' balloon that never got to have fun.

Who wanted to live somewhere like this? It took forever to get out the door, your fingers and toes were always cold, and driving was an act of faith.

Or maybe a skill she hadn't acquired.

This morning, as she took the roads carefully, but with growing confidence, she learned something new, sliding into town and searching for a spot.

Love You Coffee was closed.

In disbelief, she saw the sign that said, "Back at 11!" and gaped.

They were the equivalent of a public utility. How could they close? Or maybe, like her and Kell, they were just too exhausted to function.

Poor Kell, though. He and Dean were powering through.

Sighing, she drove on, following her GPS. She'd taken a screenshot of a map for good measure, just in case.

So barbaric.

The drive up the old, narrow logging road made her nervous. This time, she was wearing gloves, had a back-up battery for her phone, and had texted Dani to tell her that if Rachel didn't text her again in three hours, call the police.

Dani's response?

Are you safe now, Rachel? Because this sounds like the plot of a Lifetime movie.

Once she'd explained it, Dani had understood, and now here Rachel was, climbing up an icy, winding road. A big wooden sign made her sigh with relief.

Camp Wannacanhopa.

Orla's email about the new development had given Rachel pause, this deal suddenly way bigger than she expected. In fact, this potential deal—Markstone's acquisition of land, building a theme park, developing hotels—was so big, she would have expected Orla to be taking her place, expectant daughter or no.

Or even Doug. But Orla had addressed that:

Lucinda says you're the only person she wants to work with and we're honoring that for now. Whatever you're doing, keep doing it. Doug wanted the deal closed sooner, but at least you don't have a flat no from her, like the last acquisitions person did. Keep up the good work, but as this gets bigger, be prepared to be replaced. Please remember your job is on the line. You have to close this deal or I can't protect you. You know how it is.

Oh, Rachel definitely knew how it was.

Having no idea where to go, or exactly what her boss and boss's boss expected her to do, she decided that pictures and a basic written report were in order. Nothing was ever good enough for Doug, anyhow. He was king of the vague demand, so you never knew exactly what he was looking for. You could do your assignment and be ignored, never knowing whether you got it right or wrong and therefore unable to improve and get it right next time. Sometimes, the goalposts were shifted without warning, so the praise you expected turned into a terse dressing down.

As she climbed the road, starting to get nervous that her little rental car wouldn't cut it, the road became a flatter surface. A cluster of buildings came into view, arranged around a central common with a huge flagpole.

And then she saw something she really wasn't expecting: a very familiar truck that said *Pulling for You* on the side.

What was Kell doing here?

Pulling into a parking spot next to the other vehicle, she steeled herself. Seeing Kell was not part of the plan, and just the sight of his truck got her belly fluttering. She'd thought she'd have some time to just think and process without interacting with him for a bit.

Life said otherwise.

"Hey!" he called out from behind her as she got out of the car, walking toward her with a look of frank curiosity on his face, but that turned into a happy smile. Another man was with him, covered in cold weather gear, but when he took off his hat, she saw that it was Luke. "Are you stalking me?" Kell joked.

And then it hit her.

She had to lie.

Lie about why she was here.

No one in town could know why she was here. Even Lucinda

and Boyce couldn't know. Markstone's had a bulldog legal department, and she couldn't tip their hand in this acquisition, because it was no longer just about Love You Chocolate. Now the deal included the old tool and die shop in town *and* this huge camp.

"I, uh, I went for a drive and my GPS failed. Took a wrong turn," she said, scrambling for a plausible excuse, her gut turning to twisting lead as she lied to his face.

He reached for her, the hug natural and warm. Under any other circumstance, she'd be thrilled at the embrace.

Now, she felt like a piece of slime, accepting it. She didn't deserve his warmth. Her job was forcing her to become exactly what he'd said she was five years ago.

A liar.

"You were driving out this far?"

"I was trying to get to Nordicbeth. My boss wanted me to check out how they operate."

"Markstone's wants to buy them, too?"

"Hah. No, but we have contracts with larger hospitality companies. What about you? You left this morning with your dad. How'd you get your truck?"

"I drove separately. He just wanted to make sure I left on time."

"Oh."

He slung his arm around her shoulders like it was the most natural thing ever. "Come look around with me and Luke."

"Hey, Rachel," Luke said, looking a bit sad.

"Hi! What're you guys doing here? Tree work?"

"Nope." A few beats passed, and then Luke said, "Thinking about buying the place."

Every molecule in Rachel's body shattered, exploded, fell into an abyss.

She literally went numb.

"What?" She could barely get the word out.

"It's crazy, right?" Luke said, laughing with a strange bitter sense she couldn't understand. "Four outbuildings. Bunch of cabins. A director's house. Lodge and dining hall. A hundred and fifty-one acres. Three docks, two beaches, and a ton of boats and equipment."

"Not crazy. Your idea is a really good one." Kell insisted,

giving Luke a look that made it clear whatever doubt Luke had, it was misplaced.

"Idea?" she choked out, then coughed to cover her weirdness.

"Luke's got this idea to buy the camp and turn it into a big family home, kind of a compound. Get Mom and Dad, me, Colleen, and maybe Dennis to all live here. The tree service could store all the equipment here, and use the camp office. We'd take cabins and buildings and renovate them to have separate houses. There's way more land than we'd ever need, but there are timber rights we could exploit to help pay it off, and if we pool our resources, it might work."

Luke looked at her. "And we'd preserve all this land. I know some company might come in and just turn it into a big old field of condos. I hate that idea."

"Right," she squeaked out.

"I spent every summer from the age of four to eighteen here," Kell said in a tone of wonder. "Mom started me off in the preschool zone. Dennis was a junior counselor that year, so she was willing to let me go."

"I couldn't start until first grade," Luke said with a sniff. "No sibling old enough for that."

"Poor deprived Lukey."

They laughed, Rachel joining in, hoping her voice didn't sound too hysterical. The Luview family wanted to buy the camp? And create a big family home here?

The day just went from bad to apocalyptic.

"It's commercial property, isn't it?" she asked, realizing her error the second the words were out of her mouth, hoping they didn't become suspicious.

"We don't have a lot of codes around here. Easy to make it mixed use, anyway. Mom and Dad can have the tree service here. Kell can pull weeds. We can all live here, too."

"I do more than pull weeds!" Kell protested, the argument giving Rachel insight into how his older siblings treated him.

"Of course you do. I just sent all those invoices out. You make a lot of money providing a delicate and difficult service to people across the region," Rachel said, defending him against Luke's obvious condescension.

"Huh. And here I thought he just pulled weeds," Luke said dryly, walking toward a building that said OFFICE.

"Are the utilities on?" she asked.

Luke shook his head. "No heat. Pipes were bled for winter. Electric's on, though. Want to look around?"

"I actually have a meeting in a little bit," she said, which wasn't a lie. If she didn't text Dani by two, Dani had been instructed to call the police.

Given that twenty-five percent of Luview, Maine's police force was standing in front of her...

"Ah. Then you have time," Kell said, tilting his head, the sudden appearance of the sun from behind thick clouds lending a brilliant shine to the snow-covered land.

"Sure!"

"Let's give her a tour," he said to Luke.

"On foot, or truck?"

"Foot."

"Okay, but I have to go, too," Luke said. "There's a play at Harriet's school at one thirty."

"Oh! How fun for you guys," Rachel said.

"Oh, I'm not going," Kell said, laughing. "I have to help Dad with a quote."

"I meant Luke and Amber."

All of the fresh air floating between them turned to a cloud of horror as Luke looked at her with so much anger and disgust, then turned to Kell.

"You didn't tell her?"

"I assumed she–oh, damn it, Rachel, you don't know." Kell looked so guilty suddenly.

"Don't know what?"

"I'm so sorry, Luke," he said, but his brother was already stomping off. Rachel had no idea what she'd said wrong, but she knew that whatever Kell was supposed to have told her wasn't going to be pleasant.

"Kell! I didn't mean to say anything horrible. What did I say?"

Gently, he pulled away from her, somber eyes meeting hers with a distinct grief that made her toes tingle with fear.

"I'm sorry. I should have realized you didn't know. Amber is dead."

Gloved hand flying to her mouth, she covered it, throat spasming.

"No!"

"Yes."

"When?"

"About fifteen months ago. On Thanksgiving Day."

"Oh, my God!"

As the news sank in, Kell held onto her, letting out a long sigh filled with grief.

"It's been terrible."

"Of course! And little Harriet!"

"Luke's sole purpose in life now."

"She was so nice! So sweet in that FaceTime call we had! I was hoping I'd run into her." A memory hit her of asking about Amber at the ER when they'd been glued together, and how Luke hadn't answered.

Colleen and Kell had avoided the question, too.

"It's the worst thing that's ever happened to our family."

"May I ask–how?"

"Car accident."

"No! Was Harriet in the car with her?"

"Not that kind of accident. An older man in town, a good guy, had a heart attack at the wheel. Amber liked to go on these long, rambling walks, and sometimes she walked on the road for short stretches, between trails. Wasn't much snow, and the roads were clear. It was just the worst timing ever. He lost control of his car and–"

"Don't. You don't have to say more. I understand." Tears filled her eyes, then her nose, the sorrow too great to be contained. "I didn't really know her, but she was lovely, and your whole family must be– oh, Kell."

Reaching for him, she pulled him into a hug, one he took with a tender touch as they held each other, her sadness at the shock of the news receding slowly.

Imagining the Luviews all handling the news, Luke becoming a young widower, little preschooler Harriet, and Colleen, Deanna and Dean – how did families get over tragedies like that? The Luview family was trying.

Trying *by buying the camp.*

A new wave of self-recrimination turned her skin colder. The whole family was banding together to buy the camp because of what happened to Luke and Harriet, weren't they? This was how their loving extended family had decided, collectively, to move forward.

By becoming tighter.

"Oh, no," she moaned into Kell's shoulder. "It's not fair."

"No. It's not," he said back, having no idea she didn't just mean what had happened to Amber.

She meant all of it.

And her role in this mess was so much more complicated now.

"I can't believe this," she murmured.

"It was hard. Still is. Luke got through that first year like a zombie. He's nothing like the fun-loving guy he used to be."

"People change," she gasped as they pulled apart, Kell taking her hand, their legs doing a lazy walk as he seemed to need to talk.

Rachel could listen. It felt safe to listen. It did not feel very safe to speak right now.

"We do, don't we?" he said. "It's like fate throws us different lives to try on. Some of them we choose, but some of them are chosen for us."

"What do you mean?"

"You ever have this image in your head of who you are? And another image of who you want to be? Once I got to D.C., it was like a whole new Kell got a chance to exist. D.C. Kell wore suits and sat at a nice, clean desk all day. Got fancy coffees and sat in meetings with congressmen and women, met with policy makers, learned the ins and outs of how government intersects with society. D.C. Kell went out for happy hour with his work friends, lived in an apartment where he could walk to everything he needed, and could walk down the street without a single person knowing him. No need to wave or smile, make small talk, absorb petty criticisms, or be asked to take sides in arguments. I was free to reinvent myself. It was nice. Really nice."

"That was a life you chose."

"Right. Luke had this whole life with Amber. High school sweethearts. College sweethearts. He chose to be a small-town cop, she got a bookkeeping job at the hospital, and then it was time to have the four kids they always wanted."

"Four?"

"Right. They got one." Kell opened his mouth to say something more, then closed it.

"And now, Luke has a life he didn't choose."

"He's turned into someone he didn't choose."

"I understand."

"Do you? Because it turned out there was a whole other Kell who emerged in D.C. I call him Sucker Kell."

"Oh, no." Sharp, cold air filled her lungs as she inhaled, bracing her for this conversation.

"Oh, yes. Sucker Kell chased after Alissa, who it turns out just wanted to use him to get access to his high-powered, government-official uncle in Maine. Sucker Kell thought he was living his best urban life, moving up ladders, dating a strong, smart career woman who kept him on his toes. Sucker Kell had his work friends, like John and Jonas, and his Nordic-noir-watching friend Rachel, who tried to warn him about his not-so-great girlfriend."

"You weren't a sucker, Kell."

"The hell I wasn't. Getting gut punched over and over and over like that made it impossible to breathe. You can only absorb so many blows before you stay down, Rachel. I got out before that last one *kept* me down. If I'd stayed in D.C. one day more, I'm not sure who I'd be right now. That scared me more than anything else. All the pieces of who I thought I was were suddenly unrecognizable. I see some of that in Luke these days. He has no idea who he is. He sure as heck didn't choose to be Widower Luke. Single Dad Luke."

"No one chooses pain like that."

"It's not the same–not at all–but if I'd stayed in D.C., it would have been like choosing pain. It's why I had to come home. At least Hometown Kell is someone I know. Someone who isn't ashamed all the time."

"Ashamed? Why would you ever have felt *shame?*"

"I felt shame for being too stupid to see what Alissa was doing." He sighed. "And what I thought you did."

"I *didn't* do it, Kell. I've told you over and over."

"I know."

"But you'll never believe me, will you?"

"I'm starting to."

"*Starting* to? Not all the way?"

"I want to be there."

"You can choose to be there."

"Can I? Because it doesn't feel that way. Something's stuck inside."

"Did it ever occur to you that I have other versions of myself, too? That the Rachel who worked at EEC was one with so much hope about being connected to other people who cared about the same things I cared about? *That* Rachel was doing good, ethical work to save the planet and make life better for people. I wanted to look around and see that I made a tangible difference. I wanted to work with people I considered my friends, to push through projects with purpose, to feel like I was part of something bigger than just me. And I wanted to do it in community."

"Did you?"

"No. Everything fell apart so fast. Alissa turned into a sabotaging witch. John and Jonas were backstabbers. Lila faded out as fast as she could. And Karen acted like this was just how it all worked. That people were awful to each other behind the scenes to get a leg up, but we were all a team doing good for the world, so it was somehow normal."

"EEC was anything but normal."

In truth, the hardest part about EEC for Rachel was what had happened with Kell. How it destroyed a piece of her that she was only barely reclaiming right now, being with him.

Rediscovering something she lost so many years ago was unbelievable, this second chance with Kell a celebration.

But everything she just learned at work set her back. Hard.

"Stanford wasn't much better," she muttered, needing to say something as Kell watched her.

"And now? Your work with Markstone's? I'd imagine it's even worse."

"Oh, it is." If only he really knew. "More backstabbing going on than a butcher shop."

"Why work there, then?"

"At least the stabbing is all out in the open. There's no illusion that we're all in it together, or that we're working collectively to improve things for humanity. We're making deals that earn investors unseemly amounts of money. But at least I know what the real stakes are, and the rules are out in the open."

"That sounds like a harsh place to spend your days."

She thought of her boss's boss, Doug.

"It is."

"Then why stay?"

"I—"

Admitting the truth—that her job was on the line—was so shameful, she couldn't do it. Once she said the words, she could never unsay them, and it felt like a kind of death to admit how badly she'd screwed up.

Add in the truth of what was coming—Markstone's' mercenary interest in this beautiful little camp, the clash between the megacorporation she represented and the needs of the grief-soaked Luview family—and it was too much.

Too much pain.

So she lied some more.

"It's a solid job," she said, shrugging. "And I was on the path to becoming director."

"*Was?*"

Oops.

"Yeah. I'm thinking about a job change after this project."

That was not technically a lie.

"Really? Same path, or something different?"

"I haven't thought that far out."

"*You?* Haven't thought that far out? Rachel, you were always thinking ahead. You were the only one of us who had decided on grad school, long before the rest of us were starting to consider what to do at the end of the year. Your five-year plans had five-year plans."

She shrugged. "Maybe I've become more spontaneous over the years."

Concern flashed in his eyes. "Or maybe you're going through more than you're letting on?"

The crunch of other boots on snow made them turn toward the sound.

"Kell." Luke was back, guarded and avoiding eye contact. "We need to go."

Rachel dropped Kell's hand and walked toward Luke. "I am so sorry."

His eyes met hers. They softened.

"It's okay. You didn't know. I didn't know you didn't know."

"None of it is okay. I am so, *so* sorry for your loss."

"Thanks." He scratched his eyebrow. "Still don't know how

to respond to that. I appreciate the caring. I do. But I still don't know what to say back."

"You don't have to say anything."

Gratitude filled his eyes. "Thanks."

"We doing this?" Kell asked his brother. "Mom and Dad have most of the down payment. If we pool our money, we can swing it."

"You'll give up your apartment over Bilbee's?" she asked.

"That's the plan. Colleen would leave her place. Mom and Dad would sell our childhood home. Luke would sell his house in town. Not sure about Dennis. Consolidate and team up. Best way to live."

"I don't know. It's a huge financial commitment," Luke said.

"You have all those invoices coming in," Rachel said to Kell, who frowned.

"The piddly little amount Kell makes pulling weeds isn't going to help buy this place," Luke said dismissively.

"Twenty-nine thousand dollars for September and October is anything but piddly!" she exclaimed, instantly earning raised eyebrows from Luke and a tense jaw from Kell.

Uh oh. Had she screwed up again?

"You make that kind of money?" Luke asked Kell, astonishment in his voice.

"That's not even all of it," Rachel continued, the truth important to convey. "That's only the delayed invoices."

"Yeah," Kell said slowly. "It's been growing."

"Does Dad know?"

"Not really."

"And he's in demand! More companies want him, plus film crews!"

Luke looked impressed. "I had no idea."

"I'll help out with buying the place," Kell said. "But you know you can do this already, right?"

Luke's face turned to stone.

"I don't want to use the–the–*her*–money," he choked out.

"It's there for a reason, Luke."

"You know I never took that policy out on her."

"I know. No one said you did. It was a standard work policy. Amber just chose to max it out and pay the highest premiums."

"Right after Harriet was born," Luke said sadly.

It took a moment for Rachel to realize what they were talking about.

Life insurance money.

Luke wore an old-fashioned watch, a cheap black plastic thing that was nothing like the flashy designer timepieces guys wore in L.A. He checked it.

"I gotta go. Harriet," he said to Kell. "Nice to see you, Rachel."

"You, too."

Kell walked her to her car and gave her a kiss, the kind that is supposed to be casual and loving, but this one had an edge to it. A promise.

A craving.

"I meant to call you," he said as the kiss ended. "Are you using my place for internet?"

"I was going back there after this."

"Good."

"I'd like to do more to help with your business. Please?" she practically begged, needed to pay penance somehow, to make up for feeling like an evil villainess.

"You really mean it?"

"Yes!"

Those gray eyes took her in, searching her soul. Hiding the lies was hard. So hard.

"If you could keep up with my voicemails and emails, that would be great. Plus, I'll give you access to my website. The Contact Us page has a ton of backlogged inquiries. I don't even want to think about all the unanswered crap in there. And," he said with a smile, "I'm happy to talk to Lucinda and Boyce about your deal."

"NO!" she shouted, surprised by her own vehemence.

Utter confusion covered his face.

"It's just–I mean–this isn't quid pro quo."

Relief was evident in his exhale. "It's not?"

"No. It never was. I don't need you to push for me. I've got it under control."

"A word from me could make a big difference. I know how important this deal is to you." He pulled her closer. "I also know that you're a good person, and now that you're getting to know the town, you wouldn't do anything to jeopardize it."

"Right," she said weakly.

A moment passed.

"I like this version of you, Kell," she whispered. "The one in D.C., too. I like all your versions."

"That's one of the nicest things anyone has ever said to me, Rachel. Your versions are all wonderful, too." His tone changed. "So you'll be at my apartment when I'm done with work?" he asked softly. The implication was clear.

Be there, and we'll make love.

"I have a huge project meeting starting at 7:00," she lied again. "It's crunch time. I have no idea how long it will go on."

"Oh. Sounds intense. What about internet? You can use my place."

"It's confidential stuff. Let me see if internet works at the trailer and go from there. How about we get together tomorrow?"

"Absolutely." He leaned down for a kiss and she accepted it with a racing mind and a limping heart. "I'll text you. How about some Nordic Noir and Chill?"

"Murder and Making Out don't exactly go together," she said with a laugh, but then paused. "Or, maybe they do. Hmm."

As they laughed together, she was dying inside.

With that, he jogged back to his truck, leaving Rachel to climb into her rental car and look in the rearview mirror.

The version she saw was nothing but a liar.

Exactly what Kell feared most.

Chapter Sixteen

RACHEL

Last night, she'd spent a tormented night alone in the trailer, wondering how to get out of this mess, her stomach in her throat and her heart dislodged.

Every possible way out was impossible.

Tell Kell about Markstone's' plans? If she did that, she could be in serious legal trouble with her company. That wouldn't be the worst of it, though.

She would be ruined.

Her name would be on every corporate do-not-hire list. She would be known as someone who threw a deal for personal reasons, and that was the kiss of death in her line of work. Disclosing her company's plan would put her in a deep professional crater she would never, ever climb out of.

And she could be sued into oblivion.

Keep her mouth shut and hope Lucinda wouldn't sell? That was leaving everything to chance–too risky, and she hated uncertainty.

Torpedo the deal and get fired? This seemed the easiest path. Kell had prematurely turned Lucinda and Boyce against signing with Markstone's. All Rachel had to do was be less enthusiastic and subtly point out all the smaller flaws in the existing offer, without mentioning the additional land deals.

Run away? She was seriously considering that one. How hard

was it to join a convent these days? Or she could go on a three-year Buddhist meditation retreat, like the high school home-coming queen from her school recently did.

Living alone for three years in a garden shed and never speaking was starting to look appealing.

And, really, none of those worked. Each option led to someone either having their heart broken or their life destroyed.

Or three years with bad coffee and no wine.

She hated double binds. Triple binds.

Lose-lose situations.

Her father always said that if you find yourself in a lose-lose situation, it's because you're a loser.

Rachel didn't much appreciate her dad's business advice these days.

An entire night had gotten her nowhere in figuring out what to do. She was falling deeper and deeper for Kell at the same time that she was deceiving him.

"Sick, Rachel. This is sick, and it has to stop," she murmured as she answered yet another email from her trailer. Her excuse to get out of seeing Kell had been fabricated, but at least the internet had worked all evening, letting her clear her inbox.

Didn't clear her mind, though.

This was one of those moments when she desperately wanted a best friend. What do you do when the person you're closest to is the one you can't talk to?

Kell was her closest friend, even in this tentative space they inhabited. There was no one else in the world she wanted to be closer to. No one else who understood her.

No one else she lied to like this.

An email alert came in. It was Tom.

I heard about your help the other night with the flower shop. Thank you. Between that and your transportation and parking ideas, any chance you'd consider staying? We are looking to hire a new director of development. I know it isn't L.A., but we have great coffee, beautiful mountains, and the best chocolate in the world. We're starting interviews in a week. Shoot me a resume and cover letter if you want to throw your hat in the ring. A red hat, of course. ;)

"Oh, come on!" she snapped at the email. "Can life *be* any more complicated?"

Now she was being offered a chance at a job she never wanted, when the job she did want was about to be pulled out from under her? And the only way to save it was to throw Kell's family, and the entire town, under a bus?

Tom's email stared at her, as if the software developed human eyes that judged her.

What would it hurt to apply? the email seemed to ask.

A quick internet search pulled up the job listing. Full-time director of planning and business development for Luview, Maine, with a regional component tapping into some of the larger chambers of commerce. Grant writing. Community development. Job creation. Some planning work. Rachel had enough experience between paid employment, internships, and degree work to cobble together a reasonable resume, but then she looked at the pay and laughed.

She looked again and laughed harder.

They'd been paid more at EEC in D.C., and that was a fellowship.

"What am I doing?" She stood and began to pace as best she could in the tiny space. The sound of her own voice was a poor substitute for a friend, but it would have to do. No way was she inviting Satan the Squirrel back in here for a talk, and Randy's idea of conversation involved rhythmic movement.

"If I tell Kell about Markstone's buying the camp, and word gets out, I could be sued. If I don't get Lucinda to sell, I lose my job at Markstone's and I'm a failure. If I keep my mouth shut and Kell finds out later..."

She groaned.

As she hit Reply on Tom's email to say—what? she wasn't sure—the internet went out.

"Damn it!"

Blinking hard, standing still, she ran back over her own words.

"If I do tell Kell, but word doesn't get out, then maybe..."

She needed a change of scenery. And internet.

Packing up her stuff, she walked out to the car, and started the engine. Muscle memory took her to Bilbee's Tavern, the drive that used to be a careful navigation on snowy roads now so much easier. She'd only been here a week, but it felt like months.

Coming to Kell's place after ten seemed safe. It was cozier

than the trailer, had good coffee, and she could help with Kell's business. It was the least she could do, knowing she represented a company that intended to change the town in ways no one here wanted or expected.

And then there was all the lying she'd done for the last day. Atonement eased a bit of her guilt.

Settled in, with Calamine at her feet, she plugged in her laptop, turned it on, and *voilà!* Perfect high-speed internet.

If she were director of development, she'd look into broadband grants.

And electric trolleys.

Parking apps.

Job training programs.

"No. I can't. I have to figure out which path to take," she said to herself as the coffee pot finished gurgling. Calamine was toastier than any slippers.

The doorknob rattled and Rachel leaped to her feet.

Kell was gone on a big job forty-five minutes away, according to his morning text, so either he was back by surprise, or someone was breaking into his apartment.

One look at a relaxed Calamine told her it wasn't the latter.

"Yoo hoo! Anyone home?" Deanna Luview's voice was a welcome intrusion, far better than anyone other than Kell. Arms laden with shopping bags, Kell's mom came to a halt when she saw Rachel.

"Oh! You're... is Kell here?"

The tone asked, *Are you and Kell together?*

"The internet barely works at Kenny's. Kell's letting me use his apartment while he's at work, after he found me asleep in my car in the parking lot the other day."

"Oh, goodness. Is Randy bothering you that much? I heard he calmed down a bit after they washed the pheromones off the trailer."

"You really *do* know everything that's going on here, don't you?"

Deanna winked. "I try."

Nervous and twitchy, Rachel took one of the bags out of Deanna's arms and set it on the counter. "What's going on?"

"I thought I'd surprise Kell after everything that happened at the flower shop. Seeing you shopping for him at Kendrill's made me think about doing something nice. Plus, he mentioned he might make you dinner, so I brought some food."

Deanna opened the fridge and burst out laughing. Rachel hadn't gone to it yet, her coffee just finished brewing.

The fridge was full of red roses.

"He has quite a Valentine's Day planned for you!" she said to Rachel, who frowned, then fingered the tag on the top bouquet and laughed.

"Hah! No. These are from Marty and Stella's place. He's storing five dozen roses for them. I'm surprised they haven't asked for them yet."

"They're working on it. Our garage fridge and regular fridge are finally cleared out. What you did for them was amazing."

"I didn't do more than anyone else."

"Don't be modest. You have a gift for organizing and analyzing."

"Oh, thank you."

"Kell told me what happened. When all those people showed up, they had great intentions, but there wasn't any leadership. Marty and Stella were stressed. You took the bull by the horns and helped it all flow. Logistics and operations are the hidden glue in keeping a business together. You do it intuitively."

"Like with Kell's business," Rachel said softly.

"Oh? You're helping him?"

"I am."

"You two are getting closer."

Deanna's simple comment made Rachel burst into tears.

"Rachel! What did I say?"

"I don't know what to do," Rachel wailed, slumping into a chair at the dining table, burying her face in her hands. "This is so awful."

"Awful? Getting closer to Kell is awful?"

"YES!"

"You're going to have to explain that one, dear. My son is anything but awful."

"Kell isn't awful. I am!"

Deanna went to the coffee maker and poured two cups. She pulled out a carton of two percent milk from between the roses, her fingers grazing the almond milk.

"How do you take yours?"

Rachel stood, wiping her tears. "I can do it."

Once they had their coffees, Rachel began to pace. Deanna sat down, watching her as she moved.

"I have to tell someone but I can't break the contracts I've signed with my company."

"Okay." They stared at each other, Rachel hoping telepathy worked even the tiniest bit. Her hint seemed obvious but maybe Deanna wasn't picking up on it?

"Oh!" Deanna said. "Let's play Twenty Questions!"

Rachel's shoulders dropped in relief. She walked all the way across Kell's big living room, then back.

"Is it a person, place, or thing?" Deanna asked.

"Place."

"Is it Luview?"

"No."

"Is it in Maine?"

"Yes."

"Is it the chocolate company?"

"No."

"Is it Kenny's trailer?"

"No."

"Is it this apartment?"

"No."

"Huh. That's... hmmm. You're not making this easy!"

"Because it's not easy."

"A place. There's place here in Luview that is causing you distress. You can't mention it because of work. Is it part of the deal?"

"I can't say."

"That means it is. Hmm. How would I find out about a place that's being considered for something connected to Markstone's?"

"That's not a valid Twenty Questions question."

"Okay. Is it a place where there's a public record I could see that would give me clues?"

"Ask that question a little differently."

"Is there a public record about this place?"

Before Rachel could answer, Deanna's eyes narrowed.

"Hold on. This is about some kind of land or building other than Lucinda's shop. Your company is buying something else?"

Rachel pressed her lips together.

"Is the place big or small?"

"Big."

"There isn't much available around here, other than–oh!" Alarm filled Deanna's face. "The camp?"

Rachel closed her eyes.

As the daughter of a lawyer, she knew she'd just gone too far, but as a human being who cared about the town, and who loved Kell–yes, loved–she couldn't let this happen.

Once again, Rachel was stuck in *almost* territory.

She was almost breaking her contract with Markstone's.

Almost clinching the deal with Lucinda.

Almost in a relationship with Kell.

And all these *almosts* left her walking too many tightropes.

Eventually, she was going to fall.

She could leave that up to chance, or she could choose which one.

In fact, she just had.

Opening her mouth and closing it twice, all she could do was look down, like a little girl being chided for breaking a rule.

"Oh, dear. No. *No!*"

Rachel inhaled slowly through her nose, Deanna's distress unbearable.

Even more unbearable because she was part of what caused it. No, she hadn't found the camp. Someone at Markstone's had.

But she was a messenger.

She wasn't supposed to be this kind of messenger. Tipping her hand like this could be the death of her career. She could be sued into oblivion.

"No wonder you're so tormented. Oh, Rachel. I am so sorry."

Deanna couldn't have shocked Rachel more if she'd slapped her.

"What?"

"This is an impossible situation for you! I mean... uh, hypothetically. You know something this big, and you also know that we're all rallying around Luke and Harriet to create this shared family haven. It must be agony for you. How long have you known about all this?"

"Hypothetically, since yesterday."

"The rug was pulled out from you! I saw how you jumped right in during your special date with Kell, joining the rest of us to deal with Marty and Stella's emergency. You were one of us in that moment! And Kell–oh, my son was bursting with love for you. The man changed for you! Shaved his beard, got his hair cut, went to all that trouble to get the tailor to redo his suit. Got Blake to do takeout for the very first time ever, and somehow Lucinda lent him the chocolate shop. All for a single date with you! You must be so special to him."

"And now it's all ruined!" Rachel moaned, her mouth shaking as she forced another sip of coffee. "If this deal doesn't go through, I'm fired!"

Clapping her palm over her mouth, she stared at Deanna in horror.

That wasn't a breach of confidentiality, at least. But it was a shameful truth Rachel hadn't planned to reveal.

"Fired?"

Rachel nodded sadly. "Fired. Destroyed in my industry. Put on the 'no hire' list in every HR department. It's a small financial world and people who reveal company secrets are, well–ruined. Professionally, at least."

"You have a lot riding on Lucinda selling to Markstone's."

"Or not selling," Rachel whispered. "I'm damned if she does, damned if she doesn't. I'm a failure either way."

"Failure? What on earth?"

"Yes, *failure*. Either Markstone's buys the chocolate shop and the camp and I keep my job but the town is ruined and your family dream is destroyed, or Lucinda refuses to sell and I'm fired. I could hypothetically tell Kell, but he might not believe me because he doesn't trust me."

"He wouldn't spend all this time with you if he didn't trust you."

"He doesn't, though. Not all the way. He's getting there, but this? This will ruin it. I have to choose between the man I'm falling for and my job. But worse than that–my job will destroy so much of this town and this family I really, really like."

"What do you want to do?"

"I want it to all go away!"

Deanna chuckled, a rueful sound that reflected wizened experience. "Wouldn't it be nice if we could do that."

"Yes!"

"I think you know what you really want, Rachel."

"What's that?"

"You want a feeling. Everyone does. We make a huge mistake fixating on goals. We think meeting our goals will make us happy. But happiness makes us happy. Being accepted. Being loved. Being seen. Being *known*."

"Feelings aren't achievements."

"Sure they are! Most people spend their lives avoiding their feelings. The really lucky ones are able to craft their whole life around the ones they want to feel."

"You think I want to build a life around–what? Love? Like this town?"

"Would that be so bad?"

"That's ridiculous. You can't focus your entire life on love."

"Why not?"

"Because you can't pay the bills with love. You can't buy a house with love. You can't–"

"You can. You just think you can't because no one's ever talked about it with you before. You've heard the language of achievement, not love."

"What's wrong with success?"

"Nothing. In your case, it's all external. What about internal? You have to want to achieve because it feels good from the inside out, not the outside in. Nothing you work hard for is ever going to be enough if it doesn't come from within. And what's the feeling everyone wants most in their life?"

"Love," they said in unison.

"Love," Deanna repeated softly, stroking Rachel's face with a soft, warm hand. "You love my son."

"I do."

"And I think he loves you right back, honey."

"Then what do I do, Deanna? This really is impossible. There's no way out."

"First of all, you never said a word to me other than yes or no. I'm a smart woman. I can figure stuff out on my own, and if anyone gives me flack, I'll point that out! I'm going to reach out to our real estate agent and pump her for information. I am sure I can get the scoop on Markstone's' interest from her directly, and then you have plausible deniability."

For a small-town tree service owner, Deanna was wily. Rachel suddenly had mad respect for her.

"Second of all, isn't your father an attorney?"

"Yes."

"Why not ask him about all this?"

"Me? Call home and tell Dad I'm–I'm doing what I can't say I'm doing?" she said cagily, earning a conspirator's wink from Deanna. "Admit my failure to my father? I'd rather listen to my brother tell me all about how he drinks his own pee again."

Deanna gave her a flat stare.

"And you think our little town is weird?"

Deanna's suggestion, though... would her dad actually be able to help her? Distraught and unsure, she wanted help. *Needed* help to settle this painful dilemma.

Stan Hart had a cunning mind. If he knew what your desired outcome was, he could arrange all the pieces of information, add new ones, and identify possible paths to the goal.

Then help you implement those steps, one by one, to win.

It was how he negotiated well. How he'd married well.

And how he terrified Rachel.

Because asking her dad for help was uncharted territory. Sure, he'd always offered her the world. Private school, private university, her MBA. Anything she needed, he provided.

But Rachel didn't ask. If it was offered, she accepted.

Go to Dad and admit she had a weakness? That she couldn't fix her problem on her own and needed help? In a family of over-achievers, that felt like a kind of death.

Deanna opened her arms and Rachel gratefully stepped in for a hug. The woman should hate her guts, and instead here she was, giving advice, acting like the friend Rachel deeply needed in this moment of crisis.

What kind of person hugged the woman who represented a company intent on destroying her way of life?

Deanna Luview. That's who.

"There is no situation so bad that talking about it and asking for help can't make it better," Deanna said in a soothing tone, stroking Rachel's hair. "And your father is in a unique position to help you. Parents love to help their kids, especially once they are adults. It makes us feel important and needed."

"It does?"

"I'm going to take a fairly educated guess and say that your dad will be thrilled to have you call and need him."

"My father? He needs his Ferrari. He needs his astronaut son."

"He needs his smart, intuitive, kind daughter, too."

Taking in a shaky breath, Rachel nodded. "Okay. I'll call him."

"I'll put these groceries away while you call."

Rachel looked at the clock. Ten fifty-two. That meant it was seven fifty-two a.m. in L.A., so unless her dad was traveling, he was in his office after an hour at the gym, and likely on the phone.

Dialing his number, she waited, knowing his executive assistant would answer. This was her father's personal number, but Beatris still screened for him.

"Hello, Rachel?" Beatris's surprise was evident in her tone. "My goodness. Is everything all right?"

"It's fine, Beatris. Is Dad around?"

"He is. You normally speak on the third Friday of the month at five."

Stan Hart was, if nothing else, incredibly consistent.

"Yes. I know. I need to speak with him now."

"Can I help? If you need something ordered, or overnighted, or–"

"Beatris," she said sharply, going back to her L.A. voice. "My dad. *Now.*"

Deanna started and gave Rachel a raised eyebrow.

"Of course."

Second later, her father's booming, smooth voice came on the line.

"Rachel! Sweetie! What's wrong?"

"Why do you assume something's wrong, Dad?"

"Because it isn't our usual monthly call, and you never, ever call me otherwise."

"I–well, something is wrong."

"Is it about money?"

"No."

"Then why would you call *me?*"

"Dad, when have I ever called you unexpectedly before, about money or anything?" Her heart pounded so hard in her chest. This wasn't going well at all.

"Hold on, hold on. We're starting off on the wrong foot here. Hi, Rachel. Do you need help?"

"Yes."

"What do you need?"

"Legal advice."

His voice changed instantly. "Are you being detained? Don't say a word. I'll send someone. You'll be out in an hour, tops. Your mother said you were in New England. Vermont? Rhode Island?"

"Maine."

"Don't say a word."

"Dad, I'm not detained."

A rush of air filled the phone. "Thank God. Then what?"

"It's a more delicate matter involving Markstone's."

"You embezzled?"

"DAD!" Discreetly, she walked into Kell's bedroom and shut the door.

"How am I supposed to know? You've never asked for help before, sweetie!"

As Rachel explained the mess to him, Deanna finished unloading the groceries, then tapped on the door.

"Hold on, Dad."

"I'll let myself out," Deanna whispered, giving Rachel a thumbs up. Rachel returned the gesture and went back to her story.

Once she was done, her dad sighed.

"I don't see the problem. Push the deal ahead."

"Then I keep my job but lose Kell and his family's plans are crushed."

"You love this guy? Really? Some lumberjack in Maine?"

"I'm not sure I *love* love him, but I'm falling in love with him. And he's not just some lumberjack, Dad."

"Your mom said he was."

"He owns a poison ivy pulling company. He works with the film offices in Montreal, Toronto, Boston, and New York on sets. He did his fellowship with me at EEC."

"Nice." Stan chuckled. "Your life is taking a turn I never saw coming."

And there it was. Judgment.

"I fell in love with your mother hard, too."

Whoa.

"You did?"

"Love at first sight, kiddo. Not what I planned. I was twenty-eight, she was eighteen, and no way was a guy gunning for partner by thirty going to attach himself to some barely legal secretarial pool chick. But... I didn't have a choice. When Portia looked at me that first time, I was a goner. *Poof!*"

"Awwww."

"And then that poster, the television series, her stardom. You two kids. I thought I'd have a wifey-wife supporting me on my way up, and instead we had to learn to juggle two high-powered careers so we could both get what we needed."

Never in her life had Rachel heard her father speak this way. They'd never had a conversation where he talked about his feelings.

Where he talked about anything other than achievement, deals, success.

Where he spoke to her like a complex, layered person.

"You and Mom found a way, though."

"We did. And it sounds like you will, too."

"Not if I have to keep lying to Kell."

"That's the worst, isn't it? I hate lying to your mom."

"You lie to her?"

"All the time! 'Sure, honey, that filler makes your lips look great,'" he said in a fake voice.

"Dad!"

"I love your mom the way she is. I just wish she'd relax and stop worrying about aging. I'm not trading her in for two twenty-eights, you know?"

"I had no idea you're such a softy inside, Dad!"

"Don't let word get out. I'm a shark at work. Always."

"Always."

"Look, kiddo, it sounds like you've done everything right. You tipped Deanna off. She can go do the rest and be the one to expose the land deal to everyone. You maintain plausible deniability. And if Markstone's comes after you, I've got your back."

"What do you mean?"

"If those assholes try to sue my little girl, you will have the full force of every attorney I have ever known who owes me a favor. Plus, I know a few things about some of Markstone's' executives. I'll play dirty if I have to. This is about protecting my little girl."

"Dad!" More tears. Rachel wasn't normally a crier, but today she sure was.

"Rachel, sweetie, you never, *ever* ask for help. Ever. Give me a chance to flex my Dad muscles."

"Only if I need it!"

"You're so different from Tim."

"I know. I'm the family slacker."

"What? No! I meant in the help department. He's constantly asking for help."

"He... he is?"

"Who do you think got him into the Air Force Academy? I had to pull in so many favors. And he did well, sure, but you got into Stanford all on your own. You didn't ask me to help."

"I wanted to prove I could do it."

"That's what I mean. You and Tim are different. He's always asking for money, for me to network for him, for Beatris to act as his personal bookkeeper and pay all his bills and run his life for him while he trains or goes to more astronaut crap. You never ask. You're the easy, quiet kid. It's a relief to know you trust me enough to reach out."

"I–" Rachel was speechless.

Speechless.

Tim asked for help all the time? The perfect brother, the overachiever who made her feel worthless, was actually being constantly aided by Mom and Dad?

And asking her dad for help made him feel good?

"Dad, thank you. Thank you so much. I guess I don't ask for help. I feel like it's a sign of weakness. Or I'm some kind of loser."

"Nope on both counts." He went on mute, then came back shortly. "Kiddo, I have to go. K-pop deal in Seoul. It's an emergency. Love you. Call me whenever."

"Love you too, Dad."

Call ended.

Dazed, Rachel stared at her phone, wondering how her day could already, before noon, have jerked her in so many emotional directions.

Dad told her she'd done everything right.

He thanked her for reaching out.

Most important, he wholeheartedly had her back.

Closing her eyes, she drank the rest of her coffee slowly, heart calming down, mind finding some peace.

Maybe–just maybe–everything was going to be just fine.

Confidence, Rachel, her mother's voice said in her head. *Always, confidence.*

Chapter Seventeen

KELL

"I was wrong," Kell said, earning raised eyebrows from both Boyce and Lucinda, making him instantly see the resemblance between the two. After everything that had happened with Rachel the last few days, he'd come to one conclusion: He needed to own up to his mistakes and make amends.

Withdrawing his entirely unfair "untrustworthy" accusation against Rachel was a start.

Here he was, at Love You Chocolate, righting a wrong. When he walked in the door, he'd texted Rachel, to tell her what he was doing.

No response.

He knew she was planning on working from his place, so he wondered why she wasn't answering his texts. Maybe she was deep into work. Excited to see her, he wanted to do the right thing, then go home to spend time with her.

In bed.

Exactly where they belonged, finally.

"Wrong about what? Rachel?" Lucinda asked with a sly smile Kell did not like one bit. It was one thing to recognize the error of his ways.

It was quite another to have his nose rubbed in it.

"Yes."

"At least you're man enough to admit it," she added as they

stood in the midst of the store's organized busyness. The last couple of days before Valentine's Day were always a madhouse, every register with lines ten customers deep. Temporary workers were walking around holding iPhones, ready to swipe credit cards for simple purchases.

Red foil-covered hearts were selling by the pound, thousands per hour. High school students picked up shifts here in the weeks before Valentine's Day, working hard to earn money while they could. An unofficial agreement reduced extracurricular activities and sports at the local high school to a minimum the first two weeks of February. That meant that the high schoolers all got a chance to work at one of the stores in town and feel like they were part of the Main Street efforts to keep the economy going strong.

The centerpiece of the store was an enormous chocolate sculpture, a work of art made of pink, red, and white chocolate, depicting Cupid with red gummy heart wings and a white chocolate diaper. Lollipops, small, flat versions of the sculpture, stuck up from displays, disappearing faster than staff could replace them.

Flat boxes of chocolate letters that spelled out LOVE YOU, with the centers of the O's shaped like hearts, were flying off the shelves. Everyone had a sweetheart to buy for, and when Kell was done talking to Lucinda and Boyce, he planned to load up a basket and join the lines at the cash register. Tomorrow was the first time as a grown man that he would have his very own reason to celebrate Valentine's Day, and go to the Love Games–with Rachel.

The thought made him grin.

"I know you have some Luview blood in you, Miss Lucinda, because that's exactly the kind of thing my grandmother would have said. 'Always be man enough to admit when you're wrong, Kelly,' she used to say," he remembered. The childhood nickname brought back memories.

"No Luview blood that I know of, but you live in this town long enough, you pick up plenty from the Luview family," she said, laughing. She edged them over to a corner, away from the hullabaloo. "Rachel is a smart, forthright woman with a good heart and a vision for making things better. I don't need anyone's input to know this, Kell. Whatever you used to think about her, her time here has proven her to be quite worthy of trust."

"Which is why I think you should sell to Markstone's," he stated firmly. "Her deal is a good one. She's not a cutthroat city woman coming in to skim profits off the town. Rachel obviously cares about what happens here."

"I saw," Boyce said. "She really helped when the electricity went out at the flower shop."

"And she helped cut down a skydiver."

"She also alienated half the town," Lucinda said with a sniff, a disapproving look on her face that slowly turned to a sly smile. "That takes guts."

"Then sell. You're in good hands with Rachel. Your lawyer can probably help you negotiate an even better deal, but other than details, I think it's best to–"

A loud sound made everyone turn to look, a display of red hearts falling over, hundreds of chocolates spreading on the ground in a reflective wave.

"Mom?" Kell said, surprised to see a very flustered Deanna bending down, scooping the hearts back into the clear plastic bowls of the display. Boyce and Kell dropped to help her, the mess easy to fix, but her nervousness didn't sit well with him.

"What's wrong?"

"You're encouraging them to sell?"

"Yes. I was wrong. I think the deal could be good for the town. Why are you here? You look upset."

Deanna looked at Lucinda and Boyce. "Could we talk in private?"

"Sure."

As Deanna smoothed her brown hair off her face, static electricity impishly making her long hair stand, Kell's gut tightened. Why would his mom show up like this?

And so agitated?

"Mom, this is weird."

"I agree, Kell. But don't worry. It's about to get even weirder."

Images of his date with Rachel rushed through him as Boyce closed the conference room door. His pulse quickened, and he stroked the fading lemur henna tattoo with his thumb, smiling.

Deanna cleared her throat. "There's been a... development in the sale of this business. Lucinda, Boyce, you can't sell."

"What?" they all gasped, Deanna looking at Kell like she really, really wished he weren't there.

"Mom, why are you doing this? What's going on?"

She turned to Lucinda and Boyce. "I just talked to the Louis family. Joanie and Paul had someone contact them. A law firm out of L.A., asking about the property."

"Why would someone contact Joanie and Paul about our chocolate business?" Boyce asked.

"Sorry," Deanna said, shaking her head. "I'm frazzled. I mean they called Joanie and Paul, offering to buy their camp."

"WHAT?" Kell barked out, utterly stunned.

"Joanie got really weird when I asked if anyone else was interested. She said it was supposed to be confidential. But it looks like Markstone's wants to buy Love You Chocolate, the old tool and die land down the street, and the camp."

"All of that?" Lucinda asked, perplexed. "Why?"

"I don't know," Deanna confessed, wringing her hands, eyes darting away. "I just know it's all part of a larger plan."

"Rachel never said anything about this to me," Kell said, wheels turning fast. "And she knows we want to buy the camp—knows how important it is to Luke. We ran into her at the camp!"

"You did?" Lucinda asked, eyebrows high.

"What was she doing there?" Kell muttered, trying to fit all the puzzle pieces in place.

"Scouting it out for her employer?" Boyce asked.

"She told me her GPS went out. That she just got lost." A sick feeling grew deep inside him, stretching back five years and five hundred miles.

All the way to Washington, D.C.

"Awfully funny coincidence," Boyce remarked.

"Damn it. She lied to me. Again!" Kell struck the table with the heel of his hand, hard.

"No, Kell," Deanna said, eyes wild. "She didn't lie."

"She did! Ask Luke! He heard it all, too." Pressing his palms against his face, he felt exposed. Childlike. The beard had given him cover. Wearing his emotions on his face was a lot easier when people couldn't see much of it.

"I meant that she didn't intentionally lie. People in Rachel's position have to balance all kinds of complexities we can't even imagine."

Lucinda shot his mom a very sharp look, but said nothing.

"Markstone's is the kind of corporation that will come in here and slowly take over the town. What're they doing with the tool and die company? We'll get parking lots. Condos. Time-shares. All the things we don't want. Soon, they'll control the town and we'll just be a Markstone's profit center. It's everything we didn't want, and exactly why I warned Lucinda and Boyce about her in the first place!"

"No!" Deanna argued. "You have a personal vendetta with Rachel, and you crossed a very serious line when you did that, Kellan."

"Warning them had nothing to do with my personal feelings about Rachel, Mom!"

"I knew you were stubborn, but I had no idea you were delusional, too," she argued, making Kell feel even worse than he did two seconds ago.

"Rachel fooled me again," he said through gritted teeth.

"I did not!"

Everyone turned to find a red-faced Rachel breathing hard in the doorway, her red coat wide open, the belt hanging at uneven lengths aside her thighs. She looked at Deanna, who shook her head slightly, like they had some kind of nonverbal code Kell wasn't part of.

"Bullshit!" he threw back. "Mom just told us all about how Markstone's wants Camp Wannacanhopa. You *knew!*"

Rachel slowly made eye contact with him, Deanna, Lucinda, and Boyce, before turning her attention back to him.

"I am here because you texted me that you were coming to encourage Lucinda and Boyce to sell."

"I *was*–I'm not now, now that I know you–good grief, Rachel, how could you *do* this?"

"I'm not doing what you think I'm doing, Kell."

"You sound just like Alissa!"

"Would you stop thinking about her and think about *me*, for once?"

"I don't think about her!" he yelled back, thrown by her reply. "Never!"

Deanna and Rachel snorted at the same time.

"You do!" Rachel said. "She got under your skin and hurt you, and you can't let it go. You moved five hundred miles away but you're still stuck back there. You lump me in with her and I'm not her, Kell. I won't be in a relationship with someone who can't trust me fully, and especially with someone who lumps me together with a schemer like her. She hurt you. She hurt me. Don't associate me with her! You just *Will. Not. Let. It. Go.*"

"I have! The last week, all I've done is fall for you all over again, Rachel. All the pieces of you that attracted me when we were in D.C. are still there, better than ever, but this one–the part that lies to me–that's where I draw the line."

"I am between a rock and a hard place with you, exactly like I was at EEC, toward the end. There's a reason I can't talk about what's going on with the camp–or what is not going on with the camp– and a mature adult who can see that would let me explain to the best of my ability what's going on. There's more to this than you know."

"From my position, it's pretty simple. You lied to me. Once someone lies to me, trust is gone. It's black and white because lying is binary. You do it or you don't."

"What about white lies? What about lies of omission to save someone's feelings? What about competing interests, like an NDA you can't break versus a friend who doesn't understand you cannot break it? What about telling your dad you'll help run the business when you really don't want to? You lie, Kell. We all lie. You just draw your lines and act like they're moral when they meet other needs. And for some reason I'll never understand, you have something inside that *needs* to paint me as some kind of bad guy. And at the same time, you're wooing me and taking me out on a beautiful date and promising more."

He started to leave–needing space, needing room to explode, hating her words but knowing some of them were right–but Rachel blocked the door, moving with him as he tried to get through, her face finally settling inches from his as she stood on tiptoes.

"You will listen to me this time, Kell!" She didn't raise her voice, but she spoke with a command and intensity he'd never heard from her before. He felt like the hair on his forehead blew back.

His mom caught his eye and she nodded.

He leaned against the edge of the conference table, folding his arms over his chest.

"Fine. But nothing you say is going to matter."

Because you broke my heart again, he didn't add.

"There's no hometown to run away to now, is there?" Rachel began to pace in the small room. Boyce, Lucinda, and Deanna moved against a wall like they were in a line-up and Rachel was identifying a perpetrator.

"Five years ago, you disappeared," she snapped at Kell, "and I was too afraid to make you let me have my say, but you know what, buddy?" She poked his chest, harder than he expected, the anger behind that finger bigger than he'd ever guessed. "This time you can't run!"

His mom took a seat and leaned forward on the table. Might as well have gotten a big old tub of popcorn and a diet soda. Lucinda's eyes flared, while Boyce looked at Kell with an expression that said, *You're dead meat, man.*

"You are a stubborn jerk! You get these pig-headed ideas and you won't let them go. Five years ago, you were awesome! The D.C. version of Kell was who I fell for. And then I came here and fell for THIS version of you, and you know why?"

Stunned. He had no words. She was yelling at him, but wasn't saying what he expected. He was being yelled at about her... *attraction* to him?

"I–"

"That was a rhetorical question!"

"Uh–"

"BECAUSE I LIKE ALL YOUR VERSIONS! Every part of you, even the grumpy Deke version that day we glued ourselves together. The Kell whose lap I straddled, driving to the ER. The Kell who cut the skydriver out of a tree. The one who built me a fire. The one who said we should wait to have sex, then covered me with a comforter while I slept on your couch."

Lucinda looked scandalized. His mom looked like she'd won Mother of the Year.

"The one who went to all that trouble for our date. Who pitched in to help the flower shop. All those versions make you who you are, and I see them, Kell. I like them. I want to get to know more of you. All of you!"

If this was some kind of trick to get him to stand down from being angry at her, it was working.

"But you don't seem to extend the same respect to me, do

358

you? You think there's some awful, scheming, backstabbing Rachel inside me who is just salivating at the thought of deceiving you. Or proving you're a sucker. Or–I don't know what the hell you think, because you won't TALK ABOUT IT! You won't LISTEN TO ME! I didn't hurt you five years ago. I didn't work with Alissa to turn you into some kind of tool. I never did it, and you'll never, ever believe me, will you?"

Breathing hard, like she'd run a sprint, she poked him again in the chest.

"Rachel, you can't–"

"Can't what? Tell *my* version? Because I have versions of versions, Kell! I'm a whole, full woman who has been nursing five years of hurt about you, too. And I came here to cement a deal but I fell in love instead!"

"With me?" he choked out.

"I fell in love with this stupid, backward town!"

"Hey, now," Deanna and Boyce said in unison.

"IT IS MY TURN TO TALK!" Rachel shouted, holding up a palm at them. "I fell in love with how charming this place really is. People care about each other. The touristy, lovey-dovey stuff is cute and pays the bills. I get it. You think you're selling some kind of over-the-top Valentine's Day fantasy, but people come back over and over because the town makes them feel loved. *I* feel loved here."

"You do?" Kell asked quietly.

She looked at Deanna. "Yes." Then she looked back at Kell. "By everyone but you."

Pain flashed in his chest.

"So why didn't you tell me that Markstone's wants to buy the camp? Why did you lie to me?"

"First of all, I can neither confirm nor deny that Markstone's wants to buy the camp," she said officiously, making his blood boil. "Second–"

"You're doing it again. Business first, people second."

Her eyes narrowed, shoulders dropping, chest expanding with a long, slow, deep breath that was more powerful than any other act. In real time, Rachel was responding to him, listening, working off his cues.

"I want you to think very, very carefully about what you're

359

saying, Kell. Some words can never be taken back once they're out."

An electric line ran from the base of his neck down to the small of his back, connected directly to her words, her heart, her tone. She was calling him out and striking at the core of the conflict between them. If he was wrong, this was irrevocable.

"I've seen you do good, Rachel. Seen you care. Watched you jump in and help for no reason other than kindness. You didn't have to help me out of a business bind, but you did. Didn't have to make amends after that hot mic incident, or email your ideas to Tom. Even Cally–you didn't have to give Cally love, but you have. You certainly took the lead when our date was interrupted by the flower crisis. But Rachel, I can't tell if that's all really you. It's like you're *almost* that woman. Not quite, but almost."

As he said the word *almost*, she flinched, like someone stuck a live wire against her wet skin. The second time he said it, her throat spasmed, a shaky breath fading to nothing.

His mom crossed the room, inserting herself between them. "Kell, no. You need to understand."

"Wow. Just... wow." Rachel shook her head, furious tears rimming her eyes. "You really think that about me? Screw you, Kell. I'm not *almost* anything. I am fully me. And I am sick and tired of not being enough. Not enough for you, not enough for my family, not enough for my job. I *am* enough. I am whole and real and here and you don't believe me. You're so afraid of being vulnerable or a sucker or *whatever*, that you'd rather be alone. Fine. I'm out of here. You get your way. Congratulations."

Grabbing her bag, she looked back at Lucinda and Boyce. "I hope you make the right decision. Listen to Deanna."

And with that, she stormed off, leaving Kell with clenched fists, an aching heart, and *waaaaay* too much adrenaline pumping through him.

"Can you believe that?" Boyce said softly, a low whistle following.

"Right? She's a piece of work, isn't she?" Kell replied. "I came here to tell you she wasn't untrustworthy, and then she proves me wrong. Again."

"That's not what I meant, Kell." Boyce's tone was sharp. "You didn't hear her out. Rachel's right. And you're wrong."

"How am I wrong? Mom came here to tell us about the plans

Rachel's company has to buy the camp! She knew and said nothing."

"Kell," Lucinda said in a withering voice. "How do you think your mother knew to call Joanie and Paul and ask if any other buyers were interested in the camp?"

He frowned. "I–I guess you were just making sure?"

"Why now? And how would Deanna know to ask if the interested buyer could be Markstone's?"

Wincing, he shut his eyes, dawning recognition making him feel even more raw. "Mom?"

"You know the answer, Kell."

"Rachel told you?"

"No," Deanna said pointedly. "Under absolutely no circumstances did Rachel tell me anything. Because if Rachel were to have, oh, *hypothetically* learned this, she could face legal action from her employer if she were to tell anyone. She could also be run out of her industry and find herself unable to be hired, ever, for violating a strict confidentiality contract. Rachel saying a word to me would be an act of self-sabotage. Almost an act of self-sacrifice, even. So," his mom said, standing up and crossing the room, getting in his face the way Rachel just had, "Rachel did not, and would not, ever tip me off about what Markstone's is up to. I freely, on my own, because I had a whim, called up my old friends Joanie and Paul and asked some questions."

"Oh, God," he groaned into his hands, covering his face with them, the light stubble judging him alongside the three folks in the room.

"That young woman has been tormented and pulled in too many directions by complex forces behind the scenes. By *not* saying a word about this whole mess, and doing everything in a *perfectly legal* way, she's risking a relationship with the man she says she is falling in love with. But she was trapped, because if she has said a word, which she did *not*, she would have been sacrificing her career for a town she's only known for a week. A week! She took a huge leap in not saying a word about this whole mess. Add in being haunted by the Ghost of Kellan Past for five years, and–"

"Mom, I–"

"And you! You're throwing away the best kind of love just

361

because your pride walks around crouched in attack mode, carrying a beard-covered spear!"

"That makes no sense."

"NEITHER DOES HOW YOU TREAT RACHEL!"

"I don't even know what to say."

"You were hurt. Everyone gets hurt by people they trust. The mark of maturity is learning from that hurt. Not carrying it around like it's some pain trophy you silently hold up so people stay away."

"I don't–"

"Look me in the eye and tell me you don't do that."

He closed his eyes and sighed. Took another breath. Stood tall and looked up at the ceiling through another breath. Then slowly, he opened his eyes, looked at his mom, and said:

"I didn't know it was that obvious."

Chapter Eighteen

RACHEL

There is no situation so bad that talking about it and asking for help can't make it better.

That was Deanna's Rule.

Rachel's Rule: There is no situation so bad that she couldn't create a spreadsheet to help make it better.

Too bad the front seat of her car made her elbows fold under her breasts as she tried to type. Blurry vision from crying didn't help, either.

Confronting Kell like that and standing up for herself had been gutting, but also surprisingly liberating. Five years ago, she had pleaded with Kell for a chance to explain, but he'd shut her out. For the longest time, she'd felt an uneasy shame, wondering if she had in fact done something wrong. Picking through every detail, she'd almost wanted to find a sliver of responsibility, a morsel of blame she could claim for herself to make sense of a nonsensical situation.

She never had.

Now, as she sniffled and the top of her shirt bloomed with dark spots from tears, she felt a burden lift.

The burden of unspoken words.

She typed:

. . .

Column 1: To Do
    Column 2: Personal
    Column 3: Work
    Column 4: Notes

In the first column, she wrote a long list:

Check email
    Change plane ticket to leave tomorrow
    Freshen up resume
    Reach out to alumni career offices
    Ask to quit and not be fired
    Check lease to see break clause
    Ask Mom and Dad about living in the guest cottage as I relocate
    Find out where to search for small-town jobs
    Get a cat

"No." She deleted that, and wrote:
    Get two cats

"Hmm." She edited *that*, changing it to:
    Get two Maine Coon cats

Second column, Personal:
    Open online account with Love You Coffee and create monthly shipment
    Get a better ski jacket

Third column, Work:
    Reply to Tom

. . .

Her fingers hovered over that last one. No. She couldn't. As much as she reflected on life in L.A. and decided it was time for a change, staying here wasn't going to work. Being business development director in Luview, of all places, would be a daily torment.

It wasn't that she was worried Kell hated her. He didn't. Or that he would obstruct her. No longer burdened with those concerns, she saw the whole situation differently. Kell had a Kell problem. Not a Rachel problem, not an Alissa problem, not a Love-You-Chocolate-being-sold problem.

Rachel couldn't do anything about an issue he – and only he – could deal with.

Just like Kell couldn't help her as she worked on owning her own crap.

If anything, she should thank him, she thought as she cried harder, the spreadsheet blurring. All these years, she'd carried a torch for him, thinking that there must be a way, a bridge, an airing of truth that would set them right again. Not that she had spent five years holding her breath. It was more a fantasy.

Then fantasy became reality for a few poignant, sweet days.

Except that "reality" was fantasy, too. Kell had tried. She knew he really had. But the blockage inside him was too great, too blinding. He couldn't see beyond his own misguided hurt to trust and respect her, and she was actually grateful for that.

Because Kell Luview had just taught her a valuable lesson about her own worth.

No matter how much she still wanted him, how close they'd been, or how much she'd hoped to become closer, no matter how beautiful their relationship could have been, brimming with potential and love–if he kept her in *almost* territory, she would be doomed to live an *almost* life.

No.

No.

And at the very same time, Markstone's, and especially Doug, had taught her a lesson about her values.

Lucinda wasn't going to sell. Rachel had a narrow window to make some big decisions. If she quit, she could preserve her dignity and prevent her HR record from having a firing on it. She wouldn't get severance or unemployment, but frankly, she didn't need them. Her father would give her whatever money she needed until she got on her feet again.

A few days ago, she would never have asked, but now – now it was all different. Her dad had made it clear that the only reason he hadn't offered to help her was that she hadn't asked.

Now, she could ask.

The lump in her throat grew bigger, her chest spasming as she cried.

Logging in to her airline account, she did a search for flights out, calculating what she would need timewise to accomplish it. Without a mouse, her trackpad made it hard to navigate a site that required so much clicking, but soon she was looking at times and seats.

Working out of her car in the back parking lot at Bilbee's, away from Kell's apartment but on the other side of the building, was an act of desperation, but the high-speed internet was gold. Plenty of open seats on flights to L.A. Maybe people didn't travel much on Valentine's Day? For whatever reason, the re-book was simple.

In the morning, she'd check out, drive back to Boston, spend the night near the airport, fly home, and start the search for a new job.

At least she knew the direction she was going in next.

Back in her work email, she saw one from Orla, then her phone buzzed with a text from her. The preview line for both said, *Did you say anything to the Louis fam...*

Laughter bubbled up from under her ribs, like little soldiers marching across erratic terrain, not quite certain where they were going but determined to get to the front lines and meet their fate.

"It's over. It's all over. There goes my career. Flush! Down the toilet. My career is like the emergency cash in my nightstand. A great idea until I made a really bad decision and had to face the consequences of my own stupidity."

Except she knew that wasn't right. Tipping Deanna off wasn't a stupid decision.

Not telling Kell at the camp why she was really there – *that* was the big mistake she'd made.

Frozen and terrified, her mind had gone to the lie so easily, so quickly. It felt awful as she did it, scared and scrambling to buy herself time to sort it all out later. The rush to fix the problem just created a bigger, worse problem downstream.

One that looked completely unsolvable.

Always, since she was a little girl, she'd needed more time to process how she felt than other people seemed to need. When conflict happened, she froze. When a decision had to be made, she needed time and space to assemble all the possibilities, so that the great sorting hat inside her could decide what to do and how to react.

Back in D.C., she'd never hinted at her attraction to Kell because after her college boyfriend, Logan, had dumped her, she'd needed time. And when she was finally ready, Kell was attached to Alissa.

Out of sync with the world, she never seemed to line up with other people, but today–today she had. Being able to react in the moment, stand up for herself, stand up to Kell and make it clear that she was worthy of respect and trust meant, ironically, walking away.

And sobbing uncontrollably in her car in the back lot of a bar while her career and life crumbled.

"At least I finally made him listen," she whispered through a salty mouthful of dignity.

Tap tap tap

The scream came out of her like it was wound up tight inside, a spring inside a kid's pop-up toy, her laptop flying up and hitting the steering wheel then sliding down under the dash as she looked at her steamed-up side window, heart pounding.

"Rachel? It's Luke."

Oh, great. Just what she needed. Was she parked illegally? Or was the Luview family brigade coming to say their piece?

"And Colleen." She heard a woman's voice muffled behind the glass.

Pieces. They'd come to say their pieces, while Rachel's pieces were all jangling around inside her.

Rachel slid her laptop into her lap and closed it, rolling the window down an inch.

"Um, hi."

"Hi. Come inside with us."

"I really don't want to," she said honestly. "The last thing I need is to add alcohol and yelling to my day. More yelling, I mean."

"We won't yell at you," Luke said. Colleen just cleared her throat. Rachel saw Luke nudge his sister with his elbow.

"We won't," Colleen said with an eye roll. "Come inside. We just want to talk."

"I'm kind of in the middle of something."

"Looks to me like you're in the middle of crying and questioning your life choices," Colleen replied. "You can do that over a beer."

"I don't drink beer."

"Come inside," Luke insisted.

"Isn't it packed? It's almost Valentine's Day."

"Moore is saving the table."

"Moore?"

"My buddy," Luke said.

"Hey, he's mine, too," Colleen muttered, kicking a snowbank.

"He was mine first," Luke said emphatically. "If we're going to argue over who gets to claim Moore, can we do it over our beers? I only have the sitter for so long."

Rachel wavered. "Why do you want to talk to me? If it's to tell me what a horrible person I am and how I'm hurting your brother, no thanks."

"It's not," Luke said. "Really." He shot Colleen a look.

"What? It's not," his sister said defensively. "It was my idea to make her come inside! I'm the one who saw her out here. Why would I bring her in to yell at her when I could do that out here?"

"We just want to understand what's going on. Mom texted me and told me to help you if I saw you. And here you are. You look like you need a drink."

Rachel debated with herself.

"I really appreciate it. I do. But I'm going to have to take a pass. I've had too much of Love You, Maine, today to spend any more time here," she said, pressing the starter button as she raised the window over their protests.

Nothing.

The engine didn't turn over.

Nothing again, and again, as she kept pressing it.

Tap tap tap

"Something's wrong with your battery. Or your alternator," Luke said.

Rachel slumped forward and began rhythmically banging her forehead on the steering wheel, not bothering with meditations or mantras, a river of foul language pouring out of her like she was a soda stream.

It looked like she was ending her time in Luview the same way she'd started it.

With a broken car.

"Now you *have* to come in. It's too cold to sit out here. I'll call Deke and ask him to bring jumper cables and take a look at it," Luke said kindly.

"You mean the real Deke?"

"Huh?"

"How much is an Uber to the nearest airport?" she asked as they laughed.

She was utterly, completely serious.

"If it comes to that," Luke said as she gave up and opened the door, grabbing her bag, "I'll personally drive you there. And it's Portland or Manchester. Right now, Rachel, come inside. Have a drink. Eat. Talk."

Resigned to her fate, she got out of the car. Halfway to the main door, she stopped and asked, "Kell's not in there, is he?"

"No," they said together.

"I really don't want to see him. Not after what just happened."

"How about you tell us what happened and we'll interpret our brother for you?" Colleen suggested with a little smile.

"Interpret?"

"Kell is like a foreign language. If you're fluent, you know the quirks. If you're new to it, you feel like an idiot speaking. If you're somewhere in between, there'll be a lot of misunderstanding," she elaborated, making Rachel let out a dark laugh.

"I think I'll have that drink after all. Fifty-fifty chance I can't drive that stupid car tonight, anyway."

"Tell you what, Rachel," Luke said. "I'll make sure you don't have to drive tonight. Someone will drive you to the trailer, even if I need to get a fellow officer."

A guy in a suit, his shirt collar open, was waving at them.

"Anyone but Rusty," Colleen murmured as they sat down.

"Hey, Rachel! I'm Moore." The guy stood and held out his hand, their shake simple and perfunctory over a cluttered table.

"Nice to meet you. Bad circumstances, but that's not your fault."

"Whose fault is it?" he asked with an open expression that made her want to spill her guts.

"Mine. Kell's," she began.

"No one's," Luke cut in. For brothers, they didn't look much alike, Kell's coloring and shape different. Where they were similar was in their demeanor, matter-of-fact and practical. Salt-of-the-earth men. Stable, kind, giving, and...

She began crying again.

"Hey, no! You haven't even had a drink yet. You'll dehydrate yourself at this rate." She wasn't sure if Moore was joking or not.

"I'm a mess."

He pushed a basket of tortilla chips and salsa at her. "Talk." Then he handed her a glass of water.

She took a mouthful, the icy liquid clearing her mind a bit.

"Not much to talk about. Kell thinks I lied to him again."

"Why?" Moore asked.

"Because of you," she said softly to Luke, whose stunned expression made her heart sink.

"Me?"

"Remember that day I ran into you at the old camp?"

"You were scouting it, weren't you? For Markstone's?" Luke asked, a low, disapproving sound in the back of his throat following his words.

"Um, I can't technically answer that."

Anger made Colleen's nostrils flare. "You knew how important it was to Luke and our family, and you still–"

Rachel interrupted her. "And I decided on the spot to, well..."

"Tank the deal," Moore said in a tone that was half admiration, half disgust. She could tell he was a businessman and yet he was a townie, too.

A blank look covered Colleen's face, her mouth still open, but her words stopped.

Rachel looked at Moore. "I can neither confirm nor deny that. My employer–soon to be ex-employer–could sue me easily for it."

"*Ex*-employer?" Moore prodded.

"I'm about to be fired. *That* I can talk about freely. This is my third small-town candy company deal I couldn't close, and my boss's boss is trying to become an executive VP. I'm making his department look bad, so there has to be a scapegoat."

"Why did the other ones fail?"

"Basically, because I liked the owners and knew my company wasn't giving them what they deserved. My heart wasn't in it."

"You almost closed the Love You Chocolate deal."

"*Almost* gets you nothing."

"Intentions aren't nothing," Luke said in a slow, meaningful tone.

"There's no line for them on a balance sheet."

"Human beings aren't balance sheets," he replied.

"Tell that to my boss and her boss."

"Why don't you quit first?" Moore asked, as if reading her mind, their shared smile making Rachel really, really wish she could move here and have friends.

Real friends. The kind who had conversations like this, even if Colleen glared at her a lot.

"I was about to when Luke and Colleen tapped on my car window."

Her phone buzzed.

It was Dani: *I'm so sorry, Rachel. If you need anything, use my personal phone. Not sure how much longer your work phone will still be in operation. Doug is on a rampage because the family with a lot of land up where you are told him there was no way they'd sell. He thinks you blew the deal.*

Rachel read the text aloud to the group. Moore and Luke let out low, sad whistles. Colleen wrinkled her nose.

"That's got to hurt," she said, her voice holding more sympathy than Rachel had a right to expect.

"Not as much as it should." Cradling her chin in her hands, she sighed, then stood. "I am going to have that drink after all." She pulled out her wallet, reached for the corporate card, then slid out her personal credit card instead.

Crowds weren't her thing, but there was no choice on the evening of February 12 in this town. She felt like a piece of Play-Doh being squeezed, but finally made it.

At the bar, she waved to Rider, who walked over, drying off a glass.

"Yeah?"

"I'd like a white cosmo with Meyer lemon and Reyka vodka."

His eyes narrowed. "We've got well vodka and red cranberry juice. What the hell is a Meyer lemon?"

"Okay then, bourbon, neat. Paddy's. Make it a double."

"*Pfft*," he said, followed by a low whistle. "You think we carry *Paddy's*?"

"What's the best you have?"

"Makers."

"I'll have that."

He nodded with approval. "That's a power drink."

"It's what my father drinks."

"You got daddy issues?"

For the first time all day, Rachel barked out a laugh.

"Just give me the damn drink, Rider."

A tight quarter-grin twisted his lips. "No problem, Rachel."

Instead of taking it with her, she threw it back in one big swallow, enjoying the burn. Tangy and hinting at something not quite sweet, it was a sensation that she could fixate on instead of her heartache.

When she made it back to the table, Moore looked up at her and said, "You know, the director of business development job is open here in town." He ignored a glare from Colleen.

"I know. Tom asked me to apply."

Colleen nearly knocked over her beer. "He did?"

"Yes."

Moore peered at her intently. "Would you ever consider staying?"

"You mean moving here? Of course not. Why would I move to Maine?"

"For love."

They all turned to see Deanna and Dean, both holding beers, Deanna grinning wickedly.

"Love?" Rachel repeated stupidly.

"It's a feeling. Remember? Maybe what you're looking for is a feeling, not a goal?" Deanna said it softly, with such kind eyes, Rachel almost started crying again. The fire in her belly seemed to almost restart her tears.

Forget the almost. No more *almost*. Rachel was crying.

"I'm sorry about Kell's temper. He gets an idea in his head and can't listen to reason when he's in that state," Deanna said.

"I know all about it. This wasn't the first time I've seen it," Rachel said forlornly.

Every Luview studied her keenly.

"That's right," Dean muttered. "D.C. We only heard Kell's side of the story."

"I don't really have a side," she said. "He just wouldn't let me explain what happened."

"What *did* happen?" Luke asked.

"His ex-girlfriend really did use him to get access to your uncle."

"We know that. Ted told me," Dean said.

"And she sent me an email that said she was getting a job at MonDex. I jokingly asked if she'd help me get one. I was being sarcastic and kind of trying to score points with her. Be edgy. Funny. Never did I ever imagine she was actually planning to work for them, and using Kell to get access to a government official. When Alissa showed him the email, Kell assumed we were both using him. It did look that way if you didn't know I was joking."

"And it hurt him more that you'd do that than Alissa," Deanna declared.

"What?"

"Honey, he got over Alissa quickly. Wrote her off and never talked about her. But you? He *mourned* you."

"Then why does he think I'm like her?"

"Because he knows, deep down, that when he walked away from D.C., he walked away from you. If he'd stayed, it would have been so messy and tense. He was twenty-three and as green as he feared. Walking away meant leaving all the potential between the two of you behind, too. He had to justify that by thinking you'd hurt him."

"But I didn't!"

"I know that. You know that. But you were both so young. I saw you take him on today in that conference room—hoo, girl! You told my son *off*!"

Colleen and Luke looked at Deanna like she had a second head.

"And he deserved every word of it. Now let me ask–did you do that in D.C.?"

"Tell him off?"

"That, or tell him how you felt?"

"I–uh, I tried."

"*Try* isn't the same as *do*."

"Mom sounds like Yoda," Colleen said to Luke, who clamped his palm over her mouth.

"Deanna, he was so upset," Rachel protested.

"You could have pushed."

"No–I couldn't. He was just–it was–I didn't know what to do."

"Because you were young and it was new and you didn't know how to act."

Deanna's words hit her.

"Just like Kell," she whispered.

"Just like Kell." Deanna left Dean's side and gave Rachel a huge hug. "You two don't just need to talk. You need to forgive yourselves and each other. You are so obviously right for each other, but you'll never know because you're so hard on yourselves. Loosen up. Forgive. Move on–and move *forward*."

"Excuse me!" said a man's deep voice, muffled by the crowd noise, people being jostled. "COMING THROUGH!"

Rachel pulled away from Deanna. She knew that voice. Great.

What else was he going to yell at her about?

As the crowd parted, Kell appeared, locking eyes with her, pain etched in those gray eyes, his arms loose, his face open and worried.

"You're here! I've looked everywhere for you. I checked the trailer, I asked Kenny, I went to the coffee shop. Checked the town hall. Finally, I found your car out back but you weren't there. I was worried something bad had happened to you."

"Oh, it sure did. *You*."

"Oh, burn," Colleen said under her breath.

"Rachel, please. Can we not do this?" Kell begged.

"Why not?" Rachel challenged. "You made it perfectly clear you don't want me in your life."

"BECAUSE I AM AN IDIOT!" Kell blasted back.

"Moore," Colleen said, "go order the big appetizer platter. This is getting good."

With a two-finger salute, Moore did as told. Luke finished his beer, eyes on Kell.

"Keep going," Rachel said, rolling her wrist. "That's a good start."

"Why didn't you tell me you told my mother about–"

Deanna leaped to Kell, slapping her hand over his mouth.

He craned his neck back and peeled her palm away. "About, *you know*. And how your job is in jeopardy. All of it."

"Would you have listened?"

"You didn't give me a chance."

"If I'd said at the camp why I was really there, you're telling me you'd have had an open heart and stayed curious instead of jumping to judgment and getting angry?"

Colleen, Luke, and Dean all snorted at the same time. Deanna whapped Dean, who choked on his beer.

"Yes. Maybe. I don't know," Kell faltered.

"Can we talk about this elsewhere?" she asked.

"No! I'm not delaying it, and I'm not going to take a chance that I'll just screw this up again. Don't leave. Don't stay quiet and don't lie to me. Don't assume I'll judge you, or lock you into some past version of you that I have in my mind. I won't do that. Not anymore. All it does is hurt us both. I can handle my own pain, but I cannot stand to think that I'm hurting you. And that's what I've been doing all along, except I couldn't see it, Rachel. I've been hurting you, and I'm so sorry. I'm so, so sorry."

The din of the crowd made for a very odd backdrop of sound for this conversation. He paused for a second, then went on, the sour scent of beer and liquor, along with humid shared air, making it harder and harder for her to think.

"I can't breathe at the thought of letting you go. For the last two hours, I've been walking, and walking, and *walking*. I walked, wandering the town until the sidewalks ran out, then I walked the trail around the hot springs. I've retraced every moment with you since I found you on the old logging road. I've been trying to figure out why, with all the joy you've brought into my life, I'm just fixated on my fear of something that *isn't real*."

He reached for her hands. His were so warm. Hers were ice cold.

"I am so grateful for you, Rachel."

"Grateful?"

"Yes. You came here like a whirlwind, going toe to toe with me, pushing me to look at my own life through a different lens. You said you see and like all my versions. I think you see versions of me I don't even know about. And some of them are raging assholes."

Colleen and Luke clinked beer bottle necks and drank to that.

"You deserved to be treated so much better than I behaved toward you in D.C. And when your car broke down. And when I threw you in the hot springs. And–"

"Got it," she said softly, conflicted eyes boring into his. "I just don't know if this is going to work."

"Rachel. All I want to do is kiss you and pray that I'm not pushing you away. I hope you want to bridge the gap between us as badly as I do. That you can try to understand that I'm growing, and growth is not linear. Sometimes it's really screwed up and messy–*I'm* screwed up and messy. I should never have treated you the way I did at Lucinda's–"

As their mouths met, she didn't melt into him. That would have been so easy. Instead, she turned into a firestorm in his arms, her kiss hard and insistent, demanding, fully equal.

Abruptly, she pulled back, and he looked at her like he half expected to be slapped, but she kissed him again, this time with a full, whole-body embrace, catcalls and whistles around them making it impossible to concentrate.

Someone poked Kell in the ribs, and he broke the kiss.

"Son," his dad said. "You live upstairs. Do this without an audience."

"DAD!" Colleen called out. "Moore's getting appetizers so we can watch."

"He's your brother, not the Red Sox."

"But it's the ninth inning with two outs and the bases loaded."

"I think *you're* loaded. How many beers have you had, kid?" Dean asked Colleen. She threw a breadstick at him.

"Can we talk?" Kell asked Rachel. "*Really* talk? We can go wherever you want. My place. The trailer. Your car. It's all on your terms."

"My car's broken down in the back, so let's do this the easy way. Let's go upstairs and ask Calamine what to do."

"That sounds very risky."

"If we don't like her advice, we can pretend we don't understand her."

"Works for your mom," Dean quipped, earning a smack from Deanna. He just patted her butt and smiled.

Taking Rachel's hand, Kell led her outside and around back, the air so cold now. As they climbed the outside stairs, she was a bit wobbly.

"You okay?"

"I had a double shot back there."

Kell paused on the step below her. "Oh. I don't want you to think I might take advantage of you."

"Kell?"

"Hmm?"

She leaned down for a kiss, bending into him, the wind picking up, a few flakes starting. It was the coldest hot kiss she'd ever had.

Without another word, they went inside, the cozy living room so inviting, and before he kicked the door shut, she was in his arms, kissing him again.

"My beard," he murmured between kisses. "Sorry."

"What beard? You shaved it off."

"I meant this." He rubbed his stubble. "It's going to chafe."

She laughed. "Of all the reasons for chafe marks, this one is the best. My face can handle it."

"I wasn't talking about your face."

Her low chuckle stopped as he kissed her again, the feel of his mouth on hers making her pulse quicken as his words sank in. Getting naked felt liberating, the time she'd been in town leading up to this moment as his hand moved to her breast, thumb teasing her nipple.

"I've wanted this for so long," he confessed, eyes burning with desire. "Wanted you since D.C. I'm sorry I've never been clear enough to say that. It's my fault."

"It's mine, too," she said, happy to talk freely, even as heat coursed through her, concentrated between her legs. As her fingertips found any patch of bare skin on him, she felt a tantalizing thrill of what was to come, anticipation as delightful as the promise of sex. Oh, how she wanted him.

Needed him.

Had him.

Finally, finally she really did.

And he had her right back.

"But it's more mine," he said, stroking her shoulder, kissing one cheek, then the other, his words heavy with meaning. "I can't ask you to sleep with me without asking you to forgive me."

"Forgive? What do I need to forgive?"

"That I didn't believe you."

"Done. Long ago, I forgave you."

"When?"

"The part of me that's wanted you for years, I guess. I came here afraid to see you, but desperate to see you, too. And when you rescued me on that logging road, I felt like fate had intervened. This project was never about the chocolate company. It was about you. Always you, Kell."

"You're my always, too. Let me love you right, Rachel. Let me right all the wrongs. Let me listen and be present. Let me make love to you. You deserve all my attention, all my love, all my... everything. I want to be your *everything*."

Suddenly, she was off the ground, feet mid-air, as Kell carried her into his bedroom, kissing her as he laid her out on top of the thick comforter, Calamine making a hasty retreat out of the room. Kell kicked the door behind her, then stood and watched Rachel, coming in for a kiss.

"I just want you, Kell," she whispered before his mouth took hers, his body spreading over her, the heaviness of him mingling with the heat of her desire. Soft and pliable, the comforter beneath her made her smile, his woodsmoke scent filling her with content.

Not longing.

Grounding.

She was his. He was hers. All the uncertainty was gone.

Finally.

"You're so big," she murmured as he unbuttoned his shirt, pulling it over his shoulders, chest and arms bare now.

"You like big?"

"I love big."

"That happens when you climb as many trees as I do. And you – oh, Rachel. You're perfection." His fingers moved to the hem of her shirt, tugging gently until it was up over her head, flung aside by his controlled movements, her silky bra stroked by his hands. "I love your body. Love what you do to me when I look at you. When I listen to you find a solution to a problem. When you appreciate a great cup of coffee. When you find a way to make something better. But most of all?" he said, moving his hand behind her to unclasp her bra, freeing her breasts. "I love looking down at you like this, with your chocolate hair spread like ribbons on my bed, your gorgeous naked body all mine, in my bed. In my apartment. In my town. All mine. You're all mine now, exactly the way I want you."

"I want to be yours," she whispered as he pressed his body against her, her hands on his ass, his fingers in her hair, cupping her jaw. "It's all I've wanted, all these years."

"Let's give us both what we want. We deserve it."

The look on Kell's face told her he needed her. Wanted her. That everything he said was true, and the steady hold he had on her as he kissed her again, mouth slanting over hers, tongue parting the seam of her lips told her this was real.

No more *almost*.

No more close enough.

No more maybe.

From here on out, every moment with Kell Luview would be certain. Known.

Complete.

"I love you," he whispered against her ear as her hand took the liberty of exploring all the big muscles along his backside, the thick thighs pressing into her so strong, so intense. "I don't care if it's too much to say it."

They took a few breaths together, staring into each other's eyes, each breath deepening the moment. "Never too much," she said.

"Give in, Rachel. Let go. Give yourself the freedom to be with me, without achievement, without worrying about the rules the outside world forces on us. I'm so in your debt."

"My debt?"

"You came here on a mission, and you turned your trip into an act of grace. The town loves you, yes, but you love it back.

And I'm grateful to you for seeing all the good here and wanting to save it."

"Oh, Kell."

"Let me worship you. It's all I've ever wanted."

"How can I say no?"

Those strong hands found the waistband of her pants, opening the button, unzipping, then Kell took one hand and slid it under her ass, lifting her up so she could shimmy her pants down over her hips. The smooth sensation of cold air striking her legs made her gasp, enhanced by his sure touch.

Her own eager hands found his button, his zipper, his waist and thighs, the thickening path of hair from his navel on down a source of mystery she was about to uncover.

Ah. He went commando.

"You're overdressed," he whispered as he hovered over her, on his knees, watching as she pulled her panties down, soon joining him in a state of equal vulnerability.

Being naked with Kell felt like being real for the very first time.

A shiver took over, Kell pulling the comforter up so they could crawl under, his long, powerful body cocooning her. The man was a furnace, hair along his legs, arms, and chest, and he smelled like woodsmoke.

Pine.

Citrus.

And love.

"If love had a scent, it would be you," she murmured in his ear, boldly sliding her flattened palm down his chest, over his rock-hard belly, finding something else rock hard.

He inhaled sharply. "That feels so good."

"Let's make you feel better," she said as she lifted the covers and crawled down his body, his hand on her ass, caressing.

"Do you have any idea how often I've dreamed of being naked in bed with you?" he said, voice a bit muffled by the covers. His words made her smile as she gripped his shaft, stroking once as he groaned.

"If it's as often as I have, then yes."

Her mouth found his tip. He groaned again.

"We have so much catching up to do."

"Mmm," was all she could say, mouth full, his fingers in her hair, gripping as he made low sounds of pleasure.

"Your mouth," he rasped. "Such a divine instrument for torture."

She paused. "You mean now, or when I talk to you?"

Laughter made his abs curl in, the thick, dark hair across them dancing in the gray shadows. He moved one hand from her hair down her shoulder.

"I do not know what to do with you, Rachel."

"How about you let me do this?" As she moved her mouth back, he stretched slightly, her free hand on his thigh, marveling at the sheer power in his body.

Then suddenly, she had all the power for a few minutes.

A cold shock of air made her stop as he lifted the comforter and pulled her to him, kissing her deeply, his hands cupping her breasts.

"Not that. I want to stretch this out. Your mouth is extraordinary. What's that thing you do with your tongue?"

Twisting out of his arms, she dove back under the covers and did the thing.

"That?" she asked.

"You're killing me."

"I hope not, because I want you very much alive for a very long time."

"How about I show you what I can do with *my* tongue," he countered, moving her quickly, as if she weighed nothing. Suddenly, she was on her back, head on the pillows, and his mouth kissed a trail down her chest, taking careful breaks on her breasts, his tongue turning her nipples to tiny buds.

As he made his way down her navel, over her belly, she grinned at the ceiling.

Finally.

Every fevered dream, every what if, every wish, each fantasy was coming to life.

And it was better than she ever imagined.

His hands parted her legs and the first kiss was sweet. So sweet. Tender and light, his scratchy face was the last thing she noticed as he gave her pleasure, her hips riding up to meet what he offered. The surreal quickly became real, hot and seductive, as the man she'd wanted for so long was finally in bed with her, being wicked and wild.

His hands rode up over her belly to stroke her breasts as she felt the growing wave inside her.

"How is this?" he murmured against her inner thigh.

"Perfect."

"I want you to tell me, Rachel. Tell me what feels good."

"Not only is your mouth perfect, so are you."

"Let me 'perfect' you a few times, then," he whispered as Rachel laughed, then gasped, settling into moans that made her core clench, her legs ride up, and she let go over and over and...

So many times she lost count.

"I have a fantasy," he said as he crawled back up from under the sheets, Rachel reaching for his hair on his forehead, the heady musk of sex rising up into the cool air outside the comforter. Kell pulled her into his arms and gave her a cocky look.

"Do tell."

"I want to have Naked Nordic Noir nights with you."

"That's not what I thought you were going to say." She frowned. "You want to watch murder mysteries... now?"

"Not now. A different night. But I want snacks, drinks, a good mystery set in the Arctic, and a naked Rachel under a blanket next to me."

"You have a naked Rachel in bed under a blanket right now."

The sensual way his hand moved between her thighs made her inhale sharply. "I most certainly do."

Their kiss was long and slow, Rachel losing herself in the sheer vastness of emotion as they made out, entwining their bodies in each other as if trying to lose where one began and the other ended. Heat formed under the covers as they slid down, the cave their bodies made one that made her feel safe, secluded, inside a haven for two.

"I've missed you," he said earnestly between kisses, Rachel under him, the impulse to join with him so strong. As if he read her mind, he sat up slightly, finding a condom in the nightstand drawer, taking care of the safeguard without her asking.

With him, like this, she felt whole. Complete. And as she widened her legs, guiding him in, she smiled into his moonlit eyes, feeling so much love between them.

As Kell made love to her, she whispered softly, "Can we just talk?"

"You want me to stop?"

"No. I just wanted to say that and know that we already did."

He jolted, then chuckled, kissing her full on the mouth again as he slowly drove home.

"I can say a lot with my body, Rachel."

Gasping, she felt that in every way possible. "I will enjoy becoming fluent in your body language."

"Do you know how special you are?" he rasped as his tempo quickened, his hand moving between them, touching her exactly where she needed the extra sensation. How did he know? She wanted to ask but words escaped her, until soon he was breathing hard, their rhythm matched to a fine point, the world tipping out of focus, her only connection to reality through his touch.

"I love you," he whispered as they came together, in sync and in love.

"Me, too," she said. "Oh, so much."

Collapsing on her, his chin pressed on her shoulder, hot breath making the curve of her neck nice and warm, but soon he rolled off, pulling her close.

Curled up in his arms, she traced a finger along his nose, following the lines of his face, enjoying unfettered access. Timeless and with all the space they wanted, she could do this.

Just enjoy him.

"I should have done this a long time ago," he whispered against her hair.

"Slept with me?"

"No," he rasped, kissing her finger. "Believed in you. Unconditionally."

Cally jumped onto the bed and curled up at their feet, a long sigh coming out of the cat, as if she were aggrieved and her bed was finally fit for feline occupation. Nestled in Kell's arms, Rachel laughed, Kell joining her, until he kissed her again.

And again.

And again, until Rachel felt that he'd loved her right, all along.

Chapter Nineteen

KELL

This was the second time he'd woken up with her in his bed, and he liked it.

A guy could get used to this kind of luxury.

In fact, he liked it so much, he was going to ask her to stay for a third night. And a fourth. How about twenty thousand more? That sounded good. Twenty-two thousand, if they were lucky and lived well.

She was so soft and smelled so good, a mix of light perfume, chocolate, and sex. All Kell wanted to do was chill under the sheets with her, the brush of cotton against their bodies and the warm cocoon of the down comforter a world apart from everything else.

She smiled in her sleep and he had to kiss those lips.

"Mmmm," she said, kissing him back. "I ache all over."

"That means I did my job."

"You're very good at your job."

"That is the kind of success worth pursuing. Intensively. Consistently, and with as much practice as possible," he murmured as his hand roamed along the curve of her ribs, her hip, her ass.

"Again?" she whispered, her eyes flaring, her smile turning deeper.

"I do love you." The words, so soft, so impulsive, poured out of him as his thumb stroked her lower lip, her wide eyes beautiful in the morning light. Saying it a thousand times would never be enough to convey how he felt.

"I know."

"It's crazy. You've been here a week, and I'm using the L word. And not the kind that ends with -oser."

"I wouldn't be in your bed if you did that!"

"My romantic skills are a bit rusty here, Rachel."

"Not if you're telling me you love me so much."

"Too soon?"

The look between them deepened even more, Rachel's eyes starting to glitter with tears. Were they happy tears? Sad ones? He couldn't tell.

"Look," he said, fingertips lightly tracing her skin, "I wasted five years not believing you. It wasn't you I didn't believe, though. It was me. I didn't believe *me*. That's why it hurt so much. The whole mess back then was a giant failure on my part. I should have seen that I was being used. Not by you. Never by you. But I was a twenty-three-year-old guy from Maine who–what? Was going to be slick and sophisticated and never make a mistake? Seems silly when I say it that way, but yes, I was that naïve. I was naïve about my own naïveté, and then I made it worse by blaming you for something you never did, all to protect my pride."

Her nose wrinkled as she nodded. "Sounds accurate."

"And you were right. Leaving felt easier in the moment, but boy, did it set me up for heartbreak down the road."

"Oh, Kell."

"When I am with you, the world makes sense. It has color, vibrant and real. Your mind is a playground I enjoy playing in, and no woman can keep me so centered. You see all the versions of me and value them. Everyone else in my life knows one. You know them all, and you accept them all."

"I don't really know all your versions," she said with a lush kiss. "I look forward to knowing them, though. We have a long journey ahead of us."

"Do we?" The question was painful but it had to be asked.

"What do you mean?" She pulled back. He could see her closing off and he wanted to take the question back, ask it differently, but he couldn't.

"We have a big problem. I'm not leaving here, and you live in L.A."

"So?"

"You'd never stay in Luview."

"What makes you say that?"

"There's nothing for you here. Your career prospects are less than zero. You could be a director back in L.A."

"I just got fired, Kell. Or I'm about to."

"You can find another job there easily. Markstone's can't prove anything."

"I could be a director here."

"Where?"

"Tom's asking for a meeting to talk about the development job."

"Director of business development for Luview, Maine, isn't exactly comparable. Half your job will be dealing with people complaining about moose patties in the paid parking lots. You'll enforce the red, white, and pink zoning requirements. Any new businesses you try to bring in will be fought tooth and nail by people like..."

"You."

He grunted.

"No, not me. Not anymore. I trust you."

"Really?"

"I do. Fully. One hundred percent. With all my heart." He kissed her hand, then pressed it to his bare chest, right over the spot where four chambers beat for her. Every damn one of them. "You would make great decisions for the town. It's just... this isn't L.A."

"Thank goodness."

"It would be an enormous change for you."

"That's the point. When you love someone, you let yourself change. I wouldn't be changing *for* you, Kell. I would be changing *with* you. I love you, too."

No kiss ever felt as good as this one, and each kiss they shared felt better than the last.

A little gasp came from her. "What time is it?"

He looked at the clock behind her. "Ten past ten."

"Oh, no!" Rachel jumped up and began throwing on her clothes. "I have to go!"

"Go... do what?"

"Check out of Kenny's trailer! It's February 13! He has it booked for someone else and checkout is at eleven!"

"I'll help you," he said. "And I'm sure if you're a little late, it's no big deal. That little trailer takes hardly any time to clean and turn over."

"I still feel responsible. I don't want to make it hard on Kenny."

"That's another reason why I love you. You're so responsible."

"And my flight!"

He went cold. "Flight?"

"I–I rebooked it, last night, when I thought *this–*" she waved her hands between their half-naked bodies, "–this would never happen. I thought we were done. So I rebooked my flight home. I'm supposed to drive down to Boston today, spend the night, and take an early flight out tomorrow. You'd be amazed how many empty seats there are on Valentine's Day."

"Cancel it."

"What?"

He reached for her hand and pulled her back to the bed, her pants pulled up but unbuttoned, her shirt on backward, the tag brushing her chin.

"Cancel it."

"I can't! I have to..."

"Have to what?"

"I have to, well... technically, I guess there's nothing back home that I *have* to do. I just..."

"You just have to stay. Here, with me. Eventually, we'll go back to L.A. And if you decide L.A. is where you really want to be, we'll figure something out."

"I would never ask you to leave your home, Kell."

"And I would never ask you to give up any part of your life that's important to you."

"Can we talk about this on the drive to Kenny's? It's freaking me out that we're so late!"

He fumbled around on his nightstand and found his phone, typing something short.

"I texted him. By the time we're dressed, he'll answer. Not

that I want to get dressed..." He kissed her, then stroked the tag at her chin. "Your shirt is on backward."

"Ack!"

Lifting her arms, she made it clear she needed him to help strip it off her, her breasts right in front of him.

Did they really have to leave? How much could he pay Kenny to give them more time?

Kenny's reply buzzed: *Sorry, cuz. Need it empty by eleven.*

With a sigh, and tremendous restraint, he helped her twist the shirt around and they got dressed. Rachel grabbed her bag while Kell made them a pot of coffee.

"We don't have time!"

"I'm not drinking that crap Kenny has. We're fine."

A two-cup pot was fast, and soon they were all headed down the stairs, the three of them piling into his truck, Calamine jumping in Rachel's lap.

"Oof! How much does she weigh?"

"Close to forty pounds."

"That's a medium sized dog!"

At the word *dog*, Cally shot Rachel an evil look.

"*Shhh.* We don't use the D word around her."

Rachel giggled, drinking her coffee, her face bright and happy.

The way he wanted to see her for the rest of his life.

"I do have to go back to L.A.," she said softly, sadly. "I can't hide here forever."

"Of course. You don't have to rebook. I mean, I *want* you to rebook and stay longer. But I know you need to go back eventually."

"Sooner than eventually. I think the best I can do is through the fifteenth."

"I want you here tomorrow. With me. All mine."

"Won't you be busy, running all over, helping people?"

He reached over and squeezed her hand. "No. Tomorrow is all about you, if you'll let me make it about you."

"About us."

"Yes. Us."

"I've never had a date on Valentine's Day," she confessed. "I haven't had a real boyfriend since college. It's just a non-holiday for me."

"WHAT?" He pretended to have a heart attack, pressing his palm against his ribs. "That's heresy here."

"Not having a sweetheart on Valentine's Day?"

"No. That's fine. Calling it a non-holiday, though..."

"I'd better not say that on a hot mic."

"Especially if you're seriously considering applying to be director of business development."

"Good point. That would be career suicide. I'm kind of an expert on that, though."

"Thank you for doing that."

"You're thanking me for tanking my career?"

"I meant, thank you for tipping Mom off. You put yourself in jeopardy to do that."

"You make it sound like I parachuted into a minefield in enemy territory."

"Don't diminish it. You could have said nothing and let Markstone's go forward. It would have ruined our family's dream, Luke's dream. And Lucinda would have felt like her legacy was destroyed."

"I couldn't let that happen."

"Which is why I love you. You're a good person. And I should have seen it all along. I *did* see it," he corrected himself. "I just couldn't reconcile what I saw with my own eyes with..."

Letting his voice drop off, he sighed. "You know."

"I do. And I could have acted better, too."

"Oh, no, Rachel. This is all on me."

"It's not. You know it's not." She patted his knee. "We're grown ups. Nothing is ever all one person's fault. As long as we stay curious and open, though, we'll be fine."

Kenny's front porch was covered in Valentine's Day decorations, red hearts everywhere, silver foil adding shine.

"Ten thirty," Kell said. "Plenty of time."

"I just have to stuff my clothes into my luggage. Grab some food I bought. Or do I leave it? What's the protocol here?"

"You're coming back to my place. Do whatever you want with it. Just leave his crappy coffee."

"No argument there."

Within five minutes, she'd shoved all her stuff into her bags, and Kell hauled them out to his truck. Calamine had fixated on the trailer hitch, climbing up on it, smelling it intently. Must have Randy's scent all over it.

"What else do you need to do?" he asked, returning to the trailer.

"This." Rachel held up her phone. Miraculously, bars appeared.

She pressed the Mom link in her contacts and set the phone to Speaker mode.

"Rachel! Dad told me all about your legal problem at work, and how you asked him for help. You made his month! I haven't seen him this happy since he clinched that TikTok deal for–"

"Mom?"

"Yes?"

"We're on Speaker. I'm here with Kell."

"Kell? Deanna's hot son?"

"Hot son?" he mouthed. Rachel shrugged.

"I'm in love with a lumberjack in Maine and I'm going to try to get a job here and stay," she said in a rush, the words making him grab her in a huge hug. He didn't want to let go.

Her words were met with silence.

"I think the call dropped. My mom is never silent," she whispered.

"Honey!" her mom gushed. "This would make a perfect Hallmark movie! Let me get a script consultant. I can play the role of the plucky mother. Oooo! If you play yourself, we can be just like Andie McDowell and her daughter in that *Maid* series! Margaret Qualley! We could be Andie and Margaret and my career would skyrocket and yours could be launched! Think of the publicity!"

Kell felt nothing but horror.

"I'm not an actress, Mom," Rachel replied, in a tone that said they'd had this conversation hundreds of times before.

"No, but you could be! You were so good as the lead in *Lysistrata* at drama camp when you were nine."

"It scarred me for life."

"Oh, please. No one *likes* performing in the Greek dramas. It's like eating grapefruit. You do it because it's good for you, not because it's enjoyable."

"I meant the topic. *Lysistrata* is about a group of women

who deny their husbands sex. A nine-year-old playing Helen of Troy was... questionable judgment at best."

"Let's not dwell on the past, Rachel. You said your hot lumberjack is there?"

"Hi, Mrs. Hart. Or Ms. Starman?" Kell said into the phone, earning a sharp intake of air followed by giggles.

"PORTIA! Goodness, Kell, call me *Portia*. If my daughter is going to give up L.A. for the boonies, you must be something special. Didn't we meet when I was filming *Love You Springs Eternal*?"

"Yes. Once. I was the bearded guy in flannel," he said with a deadpan expression that made Rachel whoop with laughter.

"Sorry. I don't remember you. So many bearded guys in flannel in Maine. You're like the state flower."

Rachel caressed his beardless face and giggled.

"Look, Mom, I'm checking out of my trailer."

"TRAILER? Is there already a movie you didn't tell me about?"

"Not that kind of trailer. A camping trailer."

More stunned silence. "You went... camping? In the Arctic?"

Kell rolled his eyes. Wow. Apple didn't fall far from the tree. It hit him that he'd need to turn up the heat in his apartment with Rachel staying.

Though they were pretty good at making their own heat...

"I'm checking out of my hotel," Rachel said, trying to use language her mother understood. "Just wanted to tell you the good news."

"This is great! Way more interesting than all that science and space crap we have to listen to from Tim. I love that you're out in the world doing interesting and romantic things, honey! You go, girl!"

"Love you, Mom."

"Love you too, Rachel. Remember: Confidence. Always–"

"Confidence," she said, joining in with Portia.

As the call ended, Rachel laughed in surprise. "That was easier than I thought."

"So much of life is, huh?"

As she opened her mouth to reply, the trailer shifted to the right, a sudden jerk. Through the door's window, Kell saw Calamine scoot across the yard and under the truck.

Rhythmic shaking began, exactly like an earthquake. Rachel wasn't kidding.

"*Noooooooo*," she groaned.

"What the hell?"

"RANDY!" they shouted.

"Must be his way of saying goodbye," Kell said, laughing his ass off as Rachel grabbed the edge of the top bunk and stabilized her legs.

"I thought Kenny cleaned off the pheromones?"

"HEY!" Kell called in the general direction of the trailer hitch. "GO AWAY! If anyone's going to make this trailer rock, it's me!"

She smiled at him. "Oh, really?"

A quick look at the clock showed they had seventeen minutes.

Calamine let out a yowl from beneath Kell's truck, a ferocious sound followed by a hiss.

Randy stopped, a *whuff* of impatience all they heard before the crunch of snow told them he was in retreat.

"Go Cally," Kell said under his breath, before he walked over to Rachel and kissed her, hand sliding up under her jacket, sweater, and shirt. Her squeal when his cold fingers rested between her warm shoulder blades gave him ample chance to tongue her teeth and deepen the kiss.

"Yes, really. We have seventeen minutes before we have to officially vacate the trailer."

"Seventeen minutes?"

"You're packed up. We can do it in fifteen."

"Says the man who assured me the other day that he needs hours."

"No, no, no," he murmured as his hands went to the button of her jeans. "I said I *wanted* hours. But fifteen minutes for a quickie in a new place – that's a challenge."

"I love challenges."

"So do I. I have to, to be with you."

"You really need to work on your sweet-talking game, dude, if you want to score."

"Think of it as an exorcism. We'll keep Satan the Squirrel and Randy the Lovesick Moose away. My testosterone will permeate the trailer."

"Kell?"

"Mmm?"

"Are you seriously trying to compete with a brain-injured moose?"

He just blinked a few times before lunging at her.

"Yes."

"Then shut up and show me how you win."

Epilogue — September

"Thanksgiving is coming up," Rachel said, eyes attached to the calendar on her laptop screen, wondering how it was suddenly mid-September and a turning point in their relationship was about to hit them:

The first major holiday together.

Love You, Maine, had plenty of festivals, craft shows, parades and fairs, but she and Kell had gotten together in February. She'd interviewed for the director of business development and planning job in March, and broken her lease in L.A. in April, moving to Maine that month, when Tom's acceptance letter had arrived – accompanied by an invitation to have dinner with him and his wife, June, in their backyard.

"A cookout! Nice, warm weather is just in time for it," he'd said as she'd gawked at the thermometer on his deck.

Thirty-nine degrees turned out to be nice and balmy in April. For Maine.

Easter had been spent with Kell's family, Independence Day, too. While her parents had met Kell when he'd flown out to L.A. to help her move, it was time for her family to get a little holiday attention.

Which also meant disappointing Deanna.

"Thanksgiving?" Kell called out from the bathroom, where steam rose in great clouds, pouring out as he cracked the door. Unlike Rachel, who showered before work, Kell always performed the ritual at the end of his workday. Made sense, he said, if he was going to spend all day sweaty anyhow.

Kell's evening showers were part of the new ritual in her life.

Just like living with him.

Moving in to his apartment had been a temporary arrangement, but as weeks stretched into a month, they'd both decided they were ready for the commitment. Living with him had been a surprisingly smooth affair, and while the pressure was on to become engaged and eventually marry, for now she and Kell were happy.

More than happy.

"Yes, *Thanksgiving*. You know. The holiday where all the turkeys run scared, Macy's puts on a parade, and college football gets watched by people who never otherwise look at it?"

"I know what it is. What about it?"

"Whose family are we spending it with?"

Kell came out of the bathroom, dark hair soaked, his beard nice and full again, though he'd kept his hair short. The combination was ideal from Rachel's perspective. It gave him a rugged, sophisticated quality that made her want to rip her clothes off and ride him like a cowgirl at a moment's notice.

Which was just fine by him.

Dressed only in a towel, loose around his hips, he was still quite damp as he stared at her, broad chest glistening in the warm lamp's glow.

"Why are you asking about Thanksgiving?"

"Because if we're going to L.A.," she said, suddenly nervous, "we need plane tickets."

"Oh! That. Yeah. Sure."

"Sure... what?"

"Sure, we'll go to L.A. for Thanksgiving." He walked across the room, kissed her cheek, and disappeared into the bedroom. Calamine left the bedroom the second he walked in, jumping up on the back of the couch behind Rachel's head, purring against her cheek.

"You just want me to feed you again," Rachel groused, gently pushing Cally away. The cat glared at her, walked over to the food dish on the floor in the kitchen, and began making little noises of displeasure.

Surprised by Kell's no-argument answer, she set her laptop on the coffee table and found him in the bedroom, naked and staring at his closet offerings. The view of his muscled, bare ass from behind set off a flurry of butterflies in her stomach, and a flame of heat that flickered between her legs.

Ah, this man.

"What are you doing?"

"Deciding what to wear."

"Wear?"

"We're going out tonight. Remember?"

Rachel jolted. "We are?"

"That new movie. The romantic comedy at the cinema. Parts of it were filmed here and down in Saco. You know."

"That's *tomorrow* night, Kell. And it's a big production. You need your suit. A nice haircut and a beard trim. The state's film commission will be there."

"Tomorrow? Does that mean we get to stay in tonight?" The leer in his voice made her warm up even more, the urge to be naked and wrapped in his arms so great she went for it, reaching one hand around him to grab his ass, the other going around his shoulders, their mouths tangled in a kiss that made her melt.

"Mmmm, this is better than any movie," he whispered against her lips.

"Thanksgiving?" she asked. "L.A.?"

"I already said yes."

Lifting her in his arms, his bare chest felt so fun beneath her fingers, Rachel falling onto him as he stretched on his back on the bed.

"No fight? Won't your mom be sad we're not here?"

"You're really killing the mood," he complained.

"Can we just talk?" she said, Kell chuckling at her words, the saying a familiar one they joked about often. It had become short-hand, an inside joke, the meaning fluid.

"Are you trying to argue that we should stay here for Thanks-giving?' he questioned. "Because that's not happening."

"I'm shocked! What does that mean?"

A painful look covered his face, Rachel instantly alarmed that she'd misstepped somehow. Kell sat up and took her hands in his, sadness replacing lust so fast it gave her hormonal whiplash.

"Honey. Amber died on Thanksgiving."

"I know. It's a tender time. Your family must want to all be together. I want to honor that, but I wanted to talk about this because my mom and dad want us out in California, too."

"I said yes so easily because Luke refuses to celebrate Thanksgiving. Last year it was... interesting."

"Interesting?"

"He was in mourning. Harriet was a clingy little sprite. Mom went and bought all the trimmings for a big family dinner, but two days before, Luke declared he refused to celebrate Thanksgiving, and he and Harriet weren't coming."

"Oh!"

"He said he'd get together with close family only, but he wouldn't ever do anything traditional. No turkey. No mashed potatoes. No stuffing. No green beans." Kell frowned. "I'm salivating just thinking about it."

"He was worried about the food?"

"Not just the food. No watching college football. No Macy's parade. Nothing that we'd ever done on Thanksgiving was tolerable for him."

"What did you do? Your poor mom, with all that food!"

"That was fine. Mom and Dad have freezers. Colleen came up with the solution. Mountain Dragon."

"The Asian fusion place?"

"Yes. And we watched old summer camp movies."

"Family movies?"

"No. Hollywood movies. You know. Meatballs. Camp Beverly Hills. Friday the Thirteenth."

"You watched *horror films* on Thanksgiving?"

"Only once Harriet was asleep."

Rachel held back the fact that her mother had a speaking part in the sixth or seventh movie in that series. She couldn't remember which. Now was not the time to talk about Portia getting "candy appled" by a knife into the top of her head as she screamed, "*No, Jason, no!*"

"And Luke was fine with all that?" she inquired.

"Luke wasn't fine with *anything*. Luke was a wreck. An understandable wreck. It was the one-year anniversary, but we were at least together. He announced that he would never, ever celebrate a traditional turkey day again, and that everyone should just make other plans for the next year."

Lightbulbs went off in Rachel's mind. "I see."

"So – Thanksgiving can be your family's holiday forever."

"Seriously? Because it's my dad's favorite one."

"Stan's a turkey guy?"

"It's the one meal a year where my mother goes off her diet."

Kell's laugh made his broad chest shake on the bed, abs textured and tight as she came back to the reality of a very naked, very hot man under her as she straddled him.

When they'd first met here in Maine seven months ago, she'd been forced to straddle him in a very different way.

This time was not much better.

"I'm so sorry for Luke. What are Deanna and Dean doing?"

"Remember how they're talking about Germany? Visiting Dennis?"

"Right! So soon?"

"Dennis can't pin down his leave just yet, but they're hoping. And Mom has a cousin who works for an airline, so they're trying to get a deal."

"Germany for Thanksgiving sounds amazing."

"They deserve a fun, big trip like that."

"I deserve something fun and big, too," she murmured as she reached down and stroked him. "I'm so excited we'll go home for the holiday."

"I'm excited by what you're doing to me."

"Let's be excited together, Kell."

:)

Thank you so much for reading *Love You Right*, from *New York Times* bestselling author Julia Kent. Keep reading for a sneak peek from *Love You Again*, featuring Kell's brother, Luke Luview, and the woman Luke shared his first kiss with in high school, Kylie Hood.

When chance brings them together as Kylie's trapped in a metal charity donation bin and Luke comes to her rescue, second chances bring more than either of them expect.

Keep flipping the page to read their first chapter!

LOVE YOU AGAIN
Sneak Peek

Chapter One

Kylie

It was the last time she ever had to deal with him.

At least, that's what she told herself.

"What am I doing?" she muttered. White puffs of condensation punctuated her words, the ice-cold night crisp and clear. Returning to western Maine after years of living in Indiana and New York had been a stark reminder of what *real* cold was like.

No snow tonight, at least, which made this easier.

Kylie could use a little *easier* in her life.

The black plastic trash bags mocked her, all six piled up in a mess in her hatchback. Her ex-boyfriend, Perry, had spent the last three months avoiding all her demands to come get his stuff, and it was finally time to act.

Being dumped in August by the guy she'd been in love with for seven years, and lived with for three, had been bad enough. Worse had been the way he'd done it: by phone.

From Thailand.

What was supposed to be a two-month work trip for him had turned into a meet cute that Kylie would find unbearably adorable if it had been anyone but her boyfriend. The call from Thailand had been unexpected, unbelievable, and life-altering.

"I–I know it sounds crazy, Ky, but Systina and I are–well,

we're soulmates. Real ones. I can't explain it any more than that. Sometimes fate comes along and hits you like a lightning bolt, and this is one of those times. I have clarity now about who I am and how the rest of my life needs to be, and I'm so sorry. I really am."

Perry had sounded more excited dumping her than he ever had when he'd claimed to love her.

The call had lasted 7 minutes, 13 seconds.

Her phone said so.

Six years ended in 7 minutes, 13 seconds.

Poof.

Never once had Perry uttered the words *break up*. He just blathered on about soulmates, and Systina, and how she was Swedish royalty with a Nepalese father, and that they'd met at a youth hostel jazz performance, and how Kylie needed to help him close his bank accounts in the U.S., ship his various and sundry personal items to him in Thailand, and basically become his executive assistant, wrapping up his life with her in a neat little bow so he could go out into the big, wide world with his true lightning-bolt soulmate and leave her.

The sad part? Kylie had done it. Most of it, anyway.

Until the rage kicked in.

On autopilot, she'd felt a deep sense of ethical responsibility to not lash out and be unreasonable. To show she was a more evolved adult than Perry. For three months, she had collected his vital records from his desk and couriered them to him in Thailand. She'd shipped items to his sister in California, no small feat from their tiny town in Maine. Jo at the post office in Fixby Hills gave her sad, puppy dog eyes every time Kylie came in with yet another box or thick, padded envelope to ship.

And the gossip mill got another half hour of filler for the day.

Sometime in late October, though, she snapped out of it. She bagged up the rest of Perry's crap and called him and his sister with a single message:

"Come get the rest of your stuff. You have one month. Then I'm donating it to charity."

No reply from either.

Here it was, exactly one month and one day since that message. As a courtesy, she'd sent one final warning yesterday.

No reply.

Exorcising Perry from her physical life was a much-needed rite, one she'd prefer to perform with a sage stick, wine, and her sister, Wendy, but this was a decent substitute on Thanksgiving. Tossing a hatchback's worth of his junk into a charity donation bin would be a great way to lose fifty pounds or so.

She patted her thighs.

Who was she kidding? After this, she'd go back to her apartment, eat the rest of the pumpkin pie she'd had for Thanksgiving dinner, cry, then watch *Elf*.

And laugh.

The thought made her smile as she reached for the first bag, an overstuffed monstrosity that puffed when she grabbed it, the scent of Perry's aftershave wafting up. Three months ago, she'd have sobbed, but now?

Now, she just saw red.

Deke's Service Station and Breakfast Diner was deserted but it would be bustling early with the five a.m. construction crowd, guys coming in for a fill-up, pack of ciggies, and some coffee from the counter. Maybe a nice fresh donut, or a packaged bear claw pastry. Maybe a full breakfast if they had time, eggs and hash browns or pancakes.

This time of night, though, it was creepily quiet, the new moon shining down like it was trying to protect her.

From what? Humiliation?

Too late.

Clutching the first big bag, she reached up for the donation bin's handle, a two-foot-wide bar that you pulled down to reveal an opening that the bags could be tossed into. It reminded her of returning library books, though she hated having that pleasant experience tainted by Perry and his whole "finding himself" experience in Thailand.

Oh, sure. He found himself, all right.

Found himself inside Systina the Wundersoulmate. Perry had never been an introspective guy, so she knew *exactly* what part of him he found "deep" inside Systina.

"Cathartic," she whispered. "This is going to be so catharitic."

As Kylie stood, holding the bar with one hand, the bag in the other, she pondered a moment. She wedged her left elbow into the pull-down door to hold it open. Then she heaved the bag up to the door, hands on the broad side of it, and shoved.

Hard.

"FREE!" she called out. "I'm FREE OF YOU, PERRY!"

Except she pushed with a little too much force, a little too much gusto. Her car keys and phone apparently decided they, too, would be free.

In abject horror, Kylie watched them fall into the steel container and tumble five feet down, swallowed by the dark, empty space. Her breath formed a white billow of anxiety as she screamed one word.

Like FREE, it started with the letter F.

Chapter Two

Luke

It was just a coat.

At least, that's what he told himself.

"You sure about this?" his sister, Colleen, asked yet again, her question making him grind his teeth. Thanksgiving dinner had been anything but traditional, the cartons of Chinese takeout still on the table. No multi-generational gathering. No sprawling extended family. No football.

No turkey, no pumpkin pie, no mashed potatoes, no green bean casserole. No cranberry anything.

And especially no heart-shaped cakes.

His late wife, Amber, had died on Thanksgiving day two years ago, and anything that reminded him of the holiday made his stomach turn.

General Tso's chicken and stir-fried rice, though, didn't.

Plus, it was his six-year-old daughter's favorite.

"Yes. Quit asking. You trying to undermine me?" he grunted at his sis, trying but failing to terminate the topic.

"I'm not." Colleen gave him a sad smile. The two of them looked alike, just like their dad. Blond, blue eyes, dimpled cheeks, and ears they could wiggle without moving another muscle. Not that Colleen did that anymore, but she could when they were kids.

Their brothers, Dennis and Kell, looked like their mom. Dark hair, deep gray eyes with corners that turned down, laugh lines pushed up by apple cheeks when they smiled.

But Luke got the same-shaped eyes as his mom. Ah, family. A big genetic roll of the dice.

"Good. I've made up my mind. That bag haunts me."

"I think you're right. Two years, Luke."

"I know." He shrugged into his jacket, peeking out the window. Cold, clear, and even better, no snow. That would make this easier.

He needed easy.

"And you've wanted to do this for so long."

"Yep."

"And you really don't want to talk about it."

"Nope."

"DADDDDEEEEE!" Harriet launched herself into his arms, her face smeared with orange sauce. "I want to go with you!"

"Can't, honey."

"You have to work? Have to go catch bad guys again?"

Harriet had learned recently in school what police officers do, and had connected the dots.

"Sometimes I catch bad guys, but I do a lot of other work, honey. Most of what I do is help good people."

"How do you know if they're good or bad?" she asked.

Colleen caught his eye and gave a nonverbal cue that asked that same question.

"They have a secret tattoo on the back of their neck that tells you," he said, pulling on one of his daughter's dark braids.

"They do?" Harriet immediately touched the back of hers. "Where is mine?"

Luke bent down and kissed that spot. "There. I just put one on you."

"A good one, right?"

"The good one was already there, sweetie."

"You were born with it!" Colleen chimed in, beginning to clean up their ever-so-fancy holiday meal. Oatmeal butterscotch cookies waited for dessert, but Luke's stomach was having none of that.

He had a job to do before he could come home and enjoy anything.

And the job didn't involve bad guys.

If only.

"How long will you be gone? Aunt Colleen says we're watching that funny movie with the big green man."

"*Elf*?"

"Yeah! The one we watched last week."

"You already saw it?"

"I want maple syrup on my s'getti next time, Daddy."

"Oh, you definitely already watched it." He bent down and planted a kiss on the top of her dark, curly head, the dark hair soft and wispy, but so much like Amber's. His own wavy blond hair, clipped close from a haircut two days ago, didn't show at all in his only child.

Harriet was one hundred percent her mother's daughter. Every day, it was like looking at a miniature Amber.

Which was a mixed blessing. The pain and the beauty mixed together–some days more pain, some days more beauty–made him feel oh, so human.

"Hate to say it, Luke, but I've got to be at work in ninety minutes. That enough time?" Colleen called out from the kitchen, the sound of efficient movement punctuating her words. His big sister had always been embedded in their lives, but even more so since Amber's passing. She practically lived with him and Harriet.

Actually *had* for two months after his wife's sudden death. All the way through that first horrific Christmas. His younger brother, Kell, and parents took plenty of shifts, too, but Colleen had stepped right in, taking over.

"More than enough time."

"You sure you–" Colleen bit her lips, clipping her own words. Already in scrubs for her nursing shift at the local emergency room, she held a crochet hook and a half-finished afghan square, a blend of the standard red, white, and pink that permeated everything in Luview, Maine. For the last few weeks, she'd been trying to teach Harriet.

Emphasis on *try*.

Harriet was more interested in baking than fiber arts.

He cut his sister a glare at the truncated question. It was sharper than he intended, but he couldn't help himself. Rolling his shoulders, he softened the look, then sighed.

"I am. It's–I know it's irrational."

"Feelings usually are."

He made a disgruntled noise in the back of his throat, the kind he used to wrangle drunks at Bilbee's Tavern after closing, when they refused to call for a ride and badgered poor Edina at the bar to give them their keys.

Or a ride.

And not the kind you take in a car.

"That sound doesn't work on me," Colleen said with a snort.

Dang.

"Works fine on Spud."

"Spud is a seventy-eight year old Vietnam vet in love with a bottle."

"Your point?"

"You need different techniques when you're helping *good* people." She smacked his arm and he couldn't help but laugh. Being a small-town police officer meant creating lots of emotional walls to do the most basic elements of his job.

Being a daddy to a sweet, loving little girl who wanted nothing more than her mommy every waking moment meant those walls had to come up and down in ways that were dizzying.

Shifting from one emotional state to another took a level of effort that drained him.

Earlier today, they'd visited Amber's grave, Harriet's tears harder to manage than his own. When she'd asked Luke whether she could ever be good enough to get Mommy to come back, he'd damn near lost his mind. How do you answer that?

You don't. He just held her and told her how much her mother loved her.

Driving around the center of his hometown, the touristy Luview, Maine–aka Love You, Maine, the town where every day is Valentine's Day–had been an exercise in restraint. The last thing he needed was to be love bombed by romantic love when all he felt was the absence of it.

Living in a heart-shaped world was nearly impossible when your own heart had been ripped out by a cruel twist of fate.

Rituals completed, they'd come home, watched TV with Colleen, and ordered takeout. His sister wouldn't leave them on this day; his brother Kell was in L.A. with his girlfriend, Rachel, and their older brother was stationed in Germany, a FaceTime away, with Mom and Dad. They'd decided to visit

Dennis when cheap plane tickets became available earlier in the year.

They'd been his rock two years ago, always there whenever he needed them.

And he'd needed them, all right.

Everyone knew Luke didn't want to celebrate Thanksgiving anyhow, so it was better this way.

"The only good people I'm going to meet on this errand I'm about to run are stray dogs and squirrels," he announced as he reached for the small bag, working hard not to look at it. Amber's special red poncho, the rest of her outfit, and the clothes he'd been wearing the day she died were inside.

He was going to donate them. Wanted to burn them, but it felt wrong somehow. Donation made more sense. Let someone in the world benefit.

Pain was easier to bear if it had a function. A purpose.

The plan was simple: drive half an hour away to an old gas station in Fixby Hills, where no one would see him. The donation bin there was for some charity that would take the items down to Manchester, New Hampshire.

He'd never see the coat again.

Which was the entire point of this strange exercise.

"Don't use your grumpy sound on the animals," Colleen teased.

He harrumphed loudly.

They shared a laugh.

And then Luke walked out to his personal vehicle, a black Jeep parked next to his pink police car, and marveled at the clear night, his breath a silent white message that rose up and disappeared into the ether, as if it didn't quite make it to heaven.

"Amber," he murmured before climbing in. "I'm doing the best I can. But this is so, so hard."

He climbed in. Started the engine. Pressed his lips together.

And backed out of his driveway, determined.

Determined to unstick himself from this place where he couldn't move forward.

He was stuck. Stuck by grief. Stuck by circumstance.

And it was time to set part of him free.

Chapter Three

Kylie

That didn't happen.
   That did not happen.
   This wasn't real.
   This couldn't be happening.
The words looped through her mind, but no matter how intently she thought them, reality didn't change.

Standing on tiptoe, Kylie pulled the handle down again and peered into the bin, eyes straining. The bright moon behind her caught the glint of metal from the carabiner clip of her keychain, and a little sliver of her phone's glass face. The screen was still on, the glow of her open Candy Crush app mocking her, the light just enough to illuminate her keychain.

On top of black plastic trash bags, a good five feet down and a million miles away, her keys and phone smiled up at her as if to say, *"How you doing?"*

"I CANNOT BELIEVE THIS!!" she screamed, letting the door slam shut with a thud that echoed in the dark night. Something in the woods, about twenty feet away, skittered.

She froze in place, body tingling with fear.

Taking stock of her surroundings, she gathered her coat tight around her, pulling her long, loose hair out from its confines at the neckline around the hood. She was shivering as much from fear as cold, heart racing so fast it surely made her blood boil enough to shake off the chill. The sound of her breath in her ears was a kind of torture. The truth was sinking in second by second, her eyes going wide, the cold making her corneas sting, her ears ring, and her feet go numb.

Not from the temperature, either.

"I'm stuck," she whispered, breath warming her nose, which instantly chilled again when she inhaled. "Stuck! What was I thinking?" she groaned, running through the last few minutes in her mind. Holding the keys and phone in her hand was second nature. It was how she made sure she didn't lock them in the car.

And she hadn't.

Looking at the country road, she listened for the sound of a passing car. None had come by in the ten minutes she'd been here. That had been the point, right?

It was late on Thanksgiving evening. No one was driving

anywhere. People were beached whales, eating their third piece of homemade pumpkin pie in a state of extreme self-loathing. Drive somewhere? Not in a food coma.

Privacy. She'd wanted *privacy*.

"Well, I've got plenty of privacy," she muttered, starting to pace. "I'm all alone. Just what I wanted, huh? Thanks, Perry!"

Think, think, think.

How could she get herself out of this?

She took a few steps back from the bin and found herself next to the driver's side door. With a trembling hand, she lifted the car door handle. It opened.

Whew! She could climb in and stay warm, which she did.

And promptly realized there was no way to use the heater.

Her sister had chided her for years for not having an emergency kit in her car, so now she had one. It was for broken car parts, flat tires, getting stuck in snowstorms.

Not for being stupid. If some company made a kit for that, they'd earn billions.

"THIS IS ALL PERRY'S FAULT!" Kylie shouted, banging the steering wheel, the tears hitting her fast and ugly. It was true. If he hadn't been such a jerk, if he hadn't dumped her for a woman whose name was a freaking poetry format spelled wrong, if he had figured out how to get his stuff, if he'd just been a decent human being and loved her back, she wouldn't have accidentally thrown her car keys and phone into a donation drop bin and been stranded in the cold on Thanksgiving night in the middle of nowhere.

This was *definitely* Perry's fault.

But even he couldn't save her.

Not that the rat bastard would. The guy wouldn't even bother to rescue his old concert t-shirts, much less his ex-girlfriend.

Heart thumping like a djembe drum in expert hands, she took deep breaths, working hard to calm herself. "You're safe," she lied into the night, hoping the words would reach a piece of her she couldn't easily access. "You have a car. No one can get you."

Locking the doors was easy, even without keys. She was at a service station with a breakfast diner attached. It would open in nine or ten hours.

Her shoulders relaxed a centimeter. She was safe.

It might be a cold night, but she wouldn't be mauled by a bear.

The thought made her laugh, then start to cry, the seconds ticking by in that unique way loneliness marks time. For the next five minutes, she cried.

And cried.

And cried so hard, it was as if her tear ducts thought that if they worked hard enough, she could conjure her car keys and phone.

Alas, she wasn't capable of that kind of magic.

"If fairies are real, now's the time to show yourself," she said aloud to no one, everyone, opening her swollen eyes slowly in case, well...

You never know, right?

Cold silence and the scent of her own humid breath against the shock of cold was all she got.

She was stuck.

Really stuck.

Her sister, Wendy, was back at their apartment, finishing her packing. On Saturday, Wendy was all wrapped up with Maine. She'd moved in with Kylie after Perry dumped her and stayed longer than the planned month, but her paperwork had finally come through. She was going to work as an au pair for a wealthy family in the South of France.

"Paris at Christmas," was all she muttered these days, starry-eyed. "You should become an au pair, too, Kylie!"

Wendy was eight years younger, fresh out of community college and ready to travel.

But Kylie wanted roots, not wings.

"Ha," she huffed into the night. "I want to set down roots somewhere? Guess I just did. I am sooooo stuck."

Cold seeped into the tips of her toes the way only a frigid night in northern New England really can. Born and raised here, she'd left at fifteen, when The Divorce happened.

And yes, she thought of it with capitals. Their parents had split in the most angry, bitter way possible, her mom announcing the day after their last day at summer camp the August before her sophomore year of high school that they were moving.

To Indiana.

When she'd met Perry seven years ago, in their final year of college, it had been fate. Or so she'd thought. Because Perry's family ran a chain of successful ski resorts, and one of them was 45 minutes away from where she'd grown up, in Luview, Maine. The place where love wasn't just a feeling.

It was an industry.

Luview, Maine–cutely pronounced Love You–turned love into a vacation destination, and romance into an income stream. While that sounded cynical, it was true. Founded in the late 19th century by Abram and Adelaide Luview, a couple who went for a swim in the local hot springs and fell in love, over time the legend spread. By the early 21st century, there was no part of Love You, Maine that didn't involve hearts, love, or the colors red, white, and pink.

Including the pink police cars. Fire engines were already red.

Love You Coffee had heart-shaped mugs and nothing they served was round or square. If you wanted a bagel, it was a heart. Cupcake? A heart.

Plates? Take a wild guess.

Almost every restaurant was tied into the theme, and so was every flower shop, antique store, movie theater, and more. Home of the world's largest romance novel bookstore, Love You, Maine, was a place to find love, fall in love, or fall in love again.

And it was Kylie's hometown.

Perry's family, though... they didn't buy into any of it. His family's company, Nordicbeth Resorts, which ran a number of ski areas, was a behemoth in northern New England. Tiny Love You was just an afterthought to a corporation like that.

Last year, they'd hired her to manage children's programming at one of their resorts. Perry hated the idea of moving up here. He loved life in New York City, where they'd gone to college, but a hefty promotion for him and a full-time, onsite job working with kids for her was a perfect step forward in their life together.

Until Systina the Ubershag crossed Perry's path.

Six months ago, they'd moved here. Busy with life and work that first month, she hadn't bothered to go to her old hometown. Then Perry went on his trip to Thailand.

And never came back.

Too humiliated to do anything but work or stay home, she'd lived in a rut until three weeks ago.

When she was downsized.

Yeah, *downsized*.

Except a few weeks after being let go because her position had been elminated, she was somehow transferred to her replacement.

Which meant she'd essentially been fired.

Perry never did like loose ends.

And speaking of those...

Turning around, she grabbed one of the bags from the back of the hatchback and hauled it forward, doing the same with the other four until she was surrounded by Perry's old crap.

It kept her warm. His clothes were more affectionate and loving than he ever was.

The thought made her cry harder, the plastic warming as she breathed against it, until condensation chilled her cheek.

She couldn't see the time because she had no phone and couldn't turn on the car.

And her feet were starting to get so cold, soon she wouldn't feel them.

Headlights flashed in her rearview mirror, forcing her to shove the bags off her and open the door, her body tumbling out like a pretzel on its side, one hand pressed to the ground so she didn't land on her knee. Scrambling to her feet, she slammed the car door shut and ran to the road, waving wildly.

"HELP! STOP! HELP!" she screamed, but the car was already gone, turning right onto another road so far away, she couldn't see it from here.

Shivering, she jogged back to her car and reached for the handle.

It didn't budge.

Rattling it hard, she willed it to open.

And then she saw that one of the bags had rolled against the door's locking mechanism. The weight of Perry's unclaimed crap must have pressed the lock button. His battery toothbrush poked through the plastic trash bag, spinning away.

Mocking her.

"AHHHHHHHHHHHHHHHHHH!" she screamed, primal and feral, horrified and outright livid. Adrenaline rushed through her, warming her body through sheer will and fury alone, but that wouldn't last long.

And late November in the mountains of Maine meant she had to find warmth.

The wall of glass surrounding the office at Deke's Service Station and Breakfast Diner looked vulnerable. Scanning the ground, she found some cinder blocks dotting the snow-covered ground on either side of the donation box.

One throw and the glass would shatter. The building had to be warmer than out here. Plus, she'd set off an alarm and the police would come.

And then she'd be rescued.

Or... booked and charged with a crime, her mug shot all over the local news, Perry's parents aghast, her arrest permanently on her record, baning her from ever working with children again.

Wait. No. Bad plan.

Bad, bad plan.

Bending down, she looked under the car. It would shield her from the wind, but nothing ese. And a determined animal could gnaw on her leg easily.

The road itself wasn't an option. The nearest house was easily a few miles away, which meant walking on a snow-covered road in late November in Maine, in the dark. Either a band of coyotes would get her, or a plow truck would clip her before she'd reach civilization.

Hmm. What about a friendly coyote? A loner. They were warm, right? Maybe she could befriend one and snuggle with it under the car.

Good grief. Now she'd really lost it.

She had no choice.

Turning slowly, she eyed the donation box. Of average height and maybe slightly-above-average weight, she could do it.

"I have to climb in," she choked out, her only witnesses a few squirrels in the woods.

At least, she *hoped* those were squirrels she heard.

Fisher cats were mean little buggers. Foxes weren't fun, either, and a pack of coyotes or wolves could even kill if they wanted to.

She was unarmed, unprotected, and increasingly unhinged.

Think, think, think, she told herself, staring at the lever for the steel bin. It was chest height on her. When she'd pulled into the parking lot, she'd parked near the donation box but not right in front of it, so she had to find a way to get herself up about two feet, balance her body, and climb in.

Climb in.

Hysterical laughter poured out of her, the sound wobbly as she shivered, her ribs tightening as her muscles contracted and tried to keep her warm.

"Ew. What if there's an animal in there?" she said aloud, because why not talk to herself at this point?

She was a stupid crazy lady who threw her keys and phone in a charity bin.

Might as well talk to herself.

"I'll climb in, find my keys and phone, stack the stuff inside in a big pile, climb up it, and wiggle back out. That's the plan, Kylie."

Eyeing the box, she wondered if she was too short to climb out. What if there wasn't as much stuff in there as she'd thought? What if the door worked in a weird way and you could get in but couldn't get out? Strategy demanded that she think these things through, even as her calves turned into slabs of frozen meat worthy of display at the local butcher shop.

Fate wasn't handing her any real choices, was it?

Over by the gas station's air pump, she spotted more concrete cinder blocks, a few broken but four or five intact. By the time she stacked four cinder blocks in a pile that was frighteningly unstable but sturdy enough to do the job, her fingers were bright red. She knew she'd have burning pain later as they warmed, but she'd left her gloves at home, a terrible decision that brought a heaping dose of shame for a woman born and raised in New England.

Standing on top of the pile, she grabbed the handle, pulled down, and stared into the abyss.

The abyss looked back.

"Hello?" she called into the space, as if a troll lurked inside, waiting to ask her the password.

Nothing replied.

Ears perked, she listened for scuffling noises that might indicate feral inhabitants.

Again, nothing.

A sliver of moonlight shone from behind her, illuminating the curve of the carabiner clip on her keychain. She knew her phone must be nearby, hidden among a few small boxes, loose clothing of all description, loads of white kitchen-size trash bags, some re-used department store bags, overstuffed black utility bags, and what looked like a very broken plastic tricycle.

Her nose was cold, but not so cold that it was numb to the odor.

Oh, man.

Kylie had lived in New York City. She had wandered down back alleys after nightclub trips where she had some instant regrets and some that lasted for days, but nothing compared to the smell in there.

It smelled like her own foolishness.

"There has to be another way," she murmured, but deep in her heart, she knew there wasn't.

Wendy was back at the apartment, half an hour away, sitting on a beanbag chair, triple-checking her flight from Manchester to New York City to Paris and working hard to bring her checked bag down to the 23 kilogram weight limit. How many scarves did she really need?

A new round of frigid shivering made Kylie envy all those scarves, which she would put to good use if she had them.

Suddenly, the yowls of a pack of fighting dogs cut through the relative quiet of the woods behind the gas station. Yipping and howling, the noise assumed a condensed quality, like someone took twenty dogs and crammed them into five.

Some of them sounded like they were in pain.

And close.

Too close.

"Coyotes?" she gasped, looking up at the sky as if chastising God. "Really? This isn't bad enough?"

The dog sounds died down, then ratcheted up again, louder.

Closer.

Standing on tiptoes, she faltered, palm scraping against a metal edge, hard enough to nearly pierce her skin. She wobbled because she couldn't feel her toes. They were *that* cold. If she didn't do something soon, she wouldn't even have the choice to climb in the bin.

Better do it now, while she could.

Just like that, she went from one choice to none.

Cold metal cut into her ribs as she leaned in and assessed the situation, the delicate balance of the levered door making her see the folly of her balance. If she went in face down, head first, and the door closed on her, she could cut herself off at the knees. When it was pulled down, the metal door formed a shelf, wide enough for three large trash bags. Turning around carefully, she used her hands to boost herself up so that she was sitting on the door, legs dangling in front of her. Then she pulled her legs up and curled herself like a kid hiding in a kitchen cabinet during hide-and-seek.

How would she tip herself in?

Unable to look inside, she had to rely on memory. She tried to imagine soft bags of clothing donations in there, ready to break her fall, soft and welcoming, like a mother's arms should be.

"AAAAOOOoooooooooo!" howled the pack, scaring her so abruptly that she pitched to the left, her shoulder pushing hard, and down she went. The loud clang of the door slamming shut was buried by pure panic as she tipped in, falling and landing in a *whuff!* of stale dryer sheets, faint mildew, moth balls, and something rotten.

It was pitch dark.

Hip screaming from the fall, she closed her eyes and took a couple of shallow breaths, rot assaulting her senses. Aside from the hip, she'd banged up her right shoulder, and a stinging sensation ran along the small of her back, where she's scratched against something.

Good thing she'd gotten that tetanus booster two years ago.

But she was in, and she was warmer, and her hand brushed against something that jingled.

"KEYS!" she shouted, pawing for them, wishing her hand had touched her phone first. That, unlike her key ring, had a flashlight. Fingertips brushing against metal that clinked, she grabbed the keys and–

Huh.

Not keys.

"HANDCUFFS?" she gasped, feeling in the dark, something feather-like making her drop the handcuffs instantly. They clinked against something. Instinct made her search, and thank goodness, because she found her phone.

Lumbering up on her knees, phone clutched in her hand, she swiped up, then hit the flashlight icon.

"LIGHT!" Her breath was a hot, humid cluster of air that made her feel warmer.

But illuminating the inside of this metal box didn't help matters much.

It was as scary and stinky as she'd worried. Her landing had ripped open black and white trash bags, the half-broken, smelly donations a testament to the carelessness of the average person.

Because they didn't care. Not one bit.

"Wendy, please answer," she whispered as she went to her contacts, hit the name Wendy, and–

Call failed.

"What?"

She tried again.

Call failed.

And that's when she saw the two most feared words on the planet:

No and *Signal.*

Right there, in the upper corner of her phone where the cell data bars belonged.

"No *signal?*" she screamed. "NO SIGNAL???"

Holding the phone up, she knee-walked to one corner of the bin.

No Signal.

The next corner–

No Signal.

The third?

Same.

The fourth was an exercise in futility, but she was a masochist and tried anyhow, the two words mocking her.

Standing on tiptoes, she managed to push the hinged door open a couple of inches. Maybe, if she held the phone up high, she could–

No.

Just... no signal.

Slumping to the center of the box, she muttered one profanity after another, until she sounded like a chicken.

"I had a signal in the car!" Looking at the wall, her high

school physics raced through her mind. Was the metal blocking the signal? Had she accidentally put herself in a Faraday cage?

That wouldn't be a problem when she got outside. Just had to find her keys, climb back out, and she'd be fine.

The keys weren't hard to locate once she had the flashlight, and as she clutched both in her hands, she swore she'd never let them go, ever, again.

Superglue would be used if needed.

Climbing up a mound of bags, she reached for the top edge of the metal door.

Too short.

Panic hit hard as she looked around, the evidence clear. Eight plastic bags, one of them full of Perry's belongings, two small cardboard boxes, and three brown paper bags stuffed with plastic stuff were it.

And the donation bin was eight feet high.

Of all the luck to climb in when the bin was relatively empty.

Piling everything into the tallest tower possible, she reached on tippy toe, barely able to push the door open an inch. It was easier on the outside because there was a handle to pull down.

Losing her footing, she felt backwards, shoulder slamming into the cold, hard metal side, her head narrowly escaping a bang.

In the distance, the coyotes howled again, perhaps fueled by her noises, or maybe just mating once more.

Joining in their screams, Kylie howled, too.

But the sound just echoed back on her.

She was stuck.

And it was entirely her fault.

Chapter Four

Luke

Deke's Service Station was rusting from the inside out.

Not the cars parked all around, though, half of them waiting for repair, the other half just waiting.

Maybe for a meteor to hit.

The place was a little bit of everything up here in the mountains: gas station, grocery store, coffee shop, auto repair, and in a pinch, Deke could officiate at a wedding and notarize a mortgage refi.

Small town life meant being a Jack of All Trades.

Luke was a police officer, occasionally worked security for big events in Manchester, was on staff at the summer camp before it closed two years ago, and acted as a ref for soccer tournaments in a pinch. A fourteen-week bartending course in college gave him that skill, too, and after EMT certification, he'd even gotten his phlebotomist's certificate to help with Red Cross blood banks.

He could do everything but cheat death.

Give him enough time, and he might succeed.

But not soon enough for his late wife.

The bag next to him on the front seat of his car held exactly sixteen articles of clothing: two pairs of socks, two pairs of underwear, two shirts, two pairs of pants, two pairs of shoes, one standard-issue red leather Luview police officer's jacket, and a big, red, fleece-lined rain poncho. Amber had worn that poncho for years, loving to go on long walks in the rain, one of the many quirks he'd adored about her.

Until it, and a gentle old man having a heart attack at the worst possible moment ever, had led to her death.

All sixteen articles of clothing had been on Luke's or Amber's body the day he'd found her.

By accident.

Training Jude DiPalma that day had meant driving him around the county, pointing out the basics, the new cop as green as a freshly cut maple tree. Twenty-one then and unable to grow a mustache, Jude needed to be cut, chopped, stacked, and seasoned before he could be unleashed on the citizens of Cambridge County, Maine.

And Jude got one hell of a first-day crisis.

In the form of Luke's dead wife.

The shock of red laying in a ditch was bad enough, freakishly beautiful against the fresh white snow, but some piece of Luke knew, before his mind could even form the thought, that it was Amber. Thanksgiving Day had been a rainy one, and the car smashed into the tree next to her let off a terrible sound, like a dying loon, as the horn malfunctioned.

The sound was so loud, it cut through time.

"Just feel it," he muttered aloud in the present. The words

were forced and halting but he said them anyhow, just like he trudged through whatever life threw his way. It was who he was, steady, reliable, and unflinchingly grounded in reality.

Until reality cracked in two.

The grief specialist he and Harriet saw for months after the accident told him that experiencing emotions in the moment was how to get through the mourning, stressing that then-four-year-old Harriet would be confused.

"Children are masters at feeling emotions in the present. They haven't learned to tamp them down yet. Let her express what she needs to and just be there with her. It's enough to hold her. You don't have to have all the answers. Your presence and love is the answer," Maura Kirkendaal had stressed. She was still a constant in their lives, though he'd left counseling a year ago.

Harriet really was a pro at processing her emotions.

Luke? Not so much.

A white puff of air filled the space between him and the steering wheel, and he realized he'd sighed. How long had he been sitting here, mind and memory in the past? Shoving his hands into gloves, he opened the rear door, grabbed the white plastic bag, and made his way to the front of the bin.

Determined, focused, and grim: That was Luke Luview these days. A bad match for a town that existed to make people feel good about love.

Living in Love You, Maine–heck, *being* a Luview–was never harder than when you had a broken heart.

Time to let go of some of the pain.

"AAAAAAooooooooo," called out a band of coyotes in the distance, making Luke jolt. His personal weapon was at home. He didn't carry it in the glove compartment or on his body when he was off duty, but as the coyote population grew in the area, maybe he should.

A few feet from the donation bin's front, he looked at the lever to pull down, squeezing the bag slightly. A whiff of Amber's perfume caught his nose, so faint he almost imagined it.

A skitter inside the box made him frown.

Damn animals. They got in those bins all the time. He felt sorry for the poor sap who emptied these metal boxes, carting all the goods to the warehouse in Manchester where they cleaned and sorted, getting it all ready for the second-hand retail stores.

Just do this, he thought, swallowing hard as the coyotes mated in the distance. The sound was violent and creepy, but for whatever reason, it felt fitting.

Throwing the tangible reminders of that terrible day into the donation box felt dangerous, too.

"I love you, Amber," he murmured. "But I have to let you go. Have to let that day go. Harriet needs a daddy who isn't tied down by grief. Just because I'm doing this doesn't mean I love you any less, though."

Tears pricked his eyes. "Why is this so hard? Because it's hard," he said with a huff. "That's what you would say if you were here. You'd hug me and comfort me and tell me feelings are meant to be felt or they'd be called something else. You'd have all the right words. I don't have any. I just have a big hole in my life, Amber. And you're never going to fill it. Colleen says I can't feel guilty for moving on. I don't. But I sure do feel weird."

And then he reached for the handle, pulled it down, and threw the bag in while calling out, "I love you."

To his utter shock, she replied from the darkness of the box, "I'm in here!"

Read the rest of *Love You Again* right now, to find out all about Luke and Kylie's journey together in Love You, Maine, and return to the town where love isn't just a feeling... it's a way of life. <3

About the Author

New York Times and *USA Today* bestselling author Julia Kent writes romantic comedy with an edge. Since 2013, she has sold more than 2 million books, with 4 New York Times bestsellers and more than 21 appearances on the USA Today bestseller list. Her books have been translated into French, Italian, and German, with more titles releasing in the future.

From billionaires to BBWs to new adult rock stars, Julia finds a sensual, goofy joy in every contemporary romance she writes. Unlike Shannon from *Shopping for a Billionaire*, she did not meet her husband after dropping her phone in a men's room toilet (and he isn't a billionaire in a rom com).

She lives in New England with her husband and children in a household where everyone but Julia lacks the gene to change empty toilet paper rolls.

Join her newsletter at http://www.jkentauthor.com

Also by Julia Kent

Shopping for a Billionaire: The Collection (Parts 1-5 in one bundle, 500 pages!)

- Shopping for a Billionaire 1
- Shopping for a Billionaire 2
- Shopping for a Billionaire 3
- Shopping for a Billionaire 4
- Christmas Shopping for a Billionaire

Shopping for a Billionaire's Fiancée

Shopping for a CEO

Shopping for a Billionaire's Wife

Shopping for a CEO's Fiancée

Shopping for an Heir

Shopping for a Billionaire's Honeymoon

Shopping for a CEO's Wife

Shopping for a Billionaire's Baby

Shopping for a CEO's Honeymoon

Shopping for a Baby's First Christmas

Shopping for a CEO's Baby

Shopping for a Yankee Swap

Shopping for a Turkey

Shopping for a Highlander

Little Miss Perfect

Fluffy

Perky

Feisty

Hasty

In Your Dreams
Her Billionaires
It's Complicated
Completely Complicated
It's Always Complicated
Eternally Complicated

Random Acts of Crazy
Random Acts of Trust
Random Acts of Fantasy
Random Acts of Hope
Randomly Acts of Yes
Random Acts of Love
Random Acts of LA
Random Acts of Christmas
Random Acts of Vegas
Random Acts of New Year
Random Acts of Baby

Maliciously Obedient
Suspiciously Obedient
Deliciously Obedient
Christmasly Obedient

Our Options Have Changed (with Elisa Reed)
Thank You For Holding (with Elisa Reed)